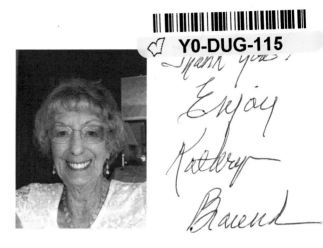

Also by Kathryn Braund

The Uncommon Breeds

The First Ten Weeks

The Second Ten Weeks

The Complete Portuguese Water Dog

Devoted To Dogs

The New Complete Portuguese Water Dog

The Joyous Havanese

Rosa and The Prince

To My Sons

Patrick C Fournier

Gary L. Fournier

and also to

Penny and Terry Braund

Copyright 2009 Kathryn Braund All Rights Reserved
Library of Congress Control Number: 2009910624
ISBN: 978-0-9720585-4-4 Paperback

This is a work of fiction. Names, characters, places and incidents either are the product of the author's imagination or are used fictitiously, and any resemblance to any actual persons, living or dead, events, or locales is entirely coincidental.

Printed in the United States of America
by
PrintingCenterUSA.com
117 9th Street North, Great Falls, MT 59401
406-761-1555 or 1-800-995-1555

Publication Date: October 2009
To order additional copies of this Book, contact
kbraund@bresnan.net
Kathryn Braund Publications
P.O. Box 3044, Great Falls, MT 59403
www.kathrynbraund.com
www.joyoushavanese.com
www.ourhavanese.com
or
PrintingCenterUSA
Amazon.com
S&E Fulfillment & Distribution
or Your Fine Book Store

Acknowledgements

I wish to thank
Margaret Dominy
for the exciting cover she has designed.
and thank you,
Ernestine Ferguson
for your assistance
in getting this book ready for printing
and
Craig Barber CEO
The Printing Center
who has always
been right there when I needed help.

Chapter One

M arvin Alicorn was 62 years of age.
　　He was handsome too. Not handsome like those middle-aged men who posed for Playboy magazine advertisements in striped tees and tight jeans with what Marv called "goofy smiles" on their supercilious faces; Marv was rough-hewn. He didn't care about wearing ties or sport shirts or tees or jeans in popular styles. After all, he was Montana born, raised, and quite content to be just the way he was, thank you. "I can still pull down a 14 hour day fixing fences, because I have plenty of hard muscle," he liked to say. "Give those guys a 25 lb water bottle to pick up and they'd fall over trying."

　　Marv was a man people looked at, even when in work clothes because everything Marv wore took on style the moment it landed on him; simple, sleek and just right. He walked straight, stood straight, moved gracefully and if a body had charisma, his six foot two tall body with no paunch certainly did. He exuded confidence and everybody paid attention to him even when his large, almond-shaped, piercing, mountain-blue colored eyes were narrowed in anger. "Your eyes are as blue as a cloudless sky in Montana in July," his daughter, Melissa, would laughingly tell him as she ruffled his very short cut sandy hair that had streaks of white running through it. "In the sunlight," she would tease," your hair looks like the color of a cut hay field with slivers of snow jutting through the short stubble. Why don't you ever let it grow, Dad?" He would shake his perfectly oval head contentedly, instead of answering as she massaged his back; to rub him just right she nudged him forward slightly in his huge chair. Those magnetic blue eyes smiling thankfully for the rubdown didn't see too well without glasses any more, and he hated glasses like he hated those plastic cups one stuck in one's eyes, so he usually squinted when whatever he was looking at, blurred. His nose was the one oddity on his well-tanned face, wide at its opening and unevenly tilted upwards from a long-ago broken nose. Nevertheless, it appeared to sit on his face expressly to highlight his high cheekbones.

Right now, he was sitting on the edge of Annabelle Stone's bed; the sheets and blanket tumbled from their lovemaking. He was pulling on his boots. His seductive lips, which lay half-hidden under a full and graying mustache, moved. As he spoke, he lifted his eyes up to the dark-haired, slim and attractive fifty-year old woman standing before him, dressed in a tan business suit, its straight skirt just a smidgen above her nice-looking knees; the woman who a half hour ago was skin-tight against his naked body. She was listening to him, but shaking her pretty head negatively as he spoke.

"I'm disappointed in you, my dear friend," Marvin said to her in his soft, husky voice, the huskiness partially covering his extreme annoyance. "We've meant so much to each other. I can't understand your packing up and leaving Mission."

"It's because of you that I am, you fool," Annabelle replied evenly, as if she didn't care (and she did). "I don't want to live like this any more."

"We've shared a great deal these last years," he continued,

convinced her stated leaving was another of her recent ploys to get him to commit himself, "and now you tell me you decided to chuck it all and move to California."

"Marv," Annabelle said, exasperated at his failure to believe her, "we've shared a bed, many happy weekends. Not enough for me any more, Marv." She turned away. It was difficult looking at this man she loved with all her heart, really saying goodbye.

"Ah, come on, Annabelle. We've traveled to conventions together; you're welcome at the ranch any time. The kids love you. We go hunting together, fishing."

"Please, Marv. I don't want to hear any more. As I told you last night, I've loved you all these years. But I don't want to be left in the outfield anymore."

"Left in the outfield? What in the hell does that mean?" He slammed his boot on the floor for emphasis.

"I'm tired of being the other woman in your life when your wife has been dead for years. Your children know we are lovers, so do our friends, yet when I'm at your home, you're so stiff - almost discourteous to me - as if you were apologizing to your dead wife Teresa for having me there. Your children feel the diffidence with which you treat me. They, like me, become unsettled. I'm weary of it."

"Annabelle," he pleaded. Damn it, he didn't want Annabelle to go away. He needed her. She was like icing on his cake. He couldn't eat one without the other.

"You come to me, Marv, when you need me. You want your ego pumped up. 'I'm blue,' you say to yourself. 'I'll go see Annabelle. She'll fix me up.'"

"Annabelle, it's not been like that."

She looked him full in his wonderful face. He was staring hard at her with his magnetic eyes. She turned away from them afraid they would make her change her mind, so she was silent for a long moment simply because it was difficult for her to continue. Then she asked softly, sadly, "How has it been?"

He was speechless, but only for a moment.

"You are the most beautiful, sweetest woman I know."

"Oh, stop it, Marv. You can't let go, that's what's the matter. As long as I've known you, you've been mooning for your dead wife. I've finally come to the realization that there is no use in my thinking you'll change — that I'll ever be what she was to you. Remember when I asked you to marry me last month? Remember what you answered? 'Not now, Annabelle. Maybe in a couple of years.' Well, I am not waiting any longer. I've had enough. I'm out of this."

Annabelle turned away from him, and then swung back, her eyes flashing.

"That's final, too." Annabelle's thick, dark, shoulder length hair smoothed in an easy and becoming pageboy style swept over half her face she turned so quickly. Her dark brown eyes glistened with tears, but her voice was staunch.

"It's done, Marv. It's over with. I told you that last night. It was our final night together. My bags are packed. They are not sitting empty by my dressing table. I'm not pretending. I've got my plane ticket, and I'm going away. It's goodbye Mission, Montana. Hello, Temecula, California."

He retorted quickly, "What really shocks me is the fact you did all this behind my back. God damn it. You never told me."

For a moment she ignored what he said, then she shrugged her shoulders emptily and after a long sigh, she answered simply, "I had to."

Moving to the doorway, purse in hand, half praying he'd jump up and pull her back, she faced him again. With a choked laugh, the words came out. "If I had told you, would you have listened to me? No. You would have laughed at me, secure in your power over me."

In consternation, boot in hand, he blew out his breath, puffing his cheeks, wondering how to answer.

She changed the subject. "You asked me for advice about Janice last night. I told you then and I tell you again, let her go. She's grown up. You're so damn stubborn you want to keep her hanging onto your pant legs like she's a young girl. Well, she isn't. She's a young woman who has to build her own life. You need to stop pulling the strings."

Without waiting for an answer, she said sadly, "Goodbye, Marv. Close the front door after you, please. I'm going to be late for breakfast if I don't leave now."

With that, Annabelle Stone, Marv Alicorn's paramour of fourteen years, slammed the bedroom door behind her.

Marv sat motionless, his hands on a boot, frowning. He listened to her footsteps as she went down the hallway. He heard their sound as she went through the living room and out the front door. She slammed that door too. He flinched.

He pulled on the second boot.

"Damn you!" he spat out, his heart racing in anger. He got up off the bed, kicked at a suitcase sitting next to her dressing table and laughed when it toppled a suitcase next to it.

"Damn you!" he said again, this time vehemently. He went

to the closet, yanked his jacket off its hanger, put it on, then turned and grimaced as he looked around the room.

"You'll miss me, you bitch." His face tightened from the pain of her rejection.

Suddenly, he cried out. "Annabelle, why are you doing this to me? I need you. Dammit. Janice is going to leave me; I need you, Annabelle. Dammit." He kicked at the toppled suitcases again. One of them crashed into the dressing table and knocked down the lamp that had sat on it. Its glass shade broke.

"Who the hell cares," he muttered, hardly looking at the disarray he had created. He slammed the bedroom door behind him, started for the front door and then turned back. Pulling out his key chain he searched for the key that opened Annabelle's front door. When he found it and removed it from the chain, he returned to the bedroom and threw it on her pillow.

"Take your god damn key, you bitch," he muttered, his voice harsh and resentful, and then he moaned bitterly, his voice swollen with distress, "Damnit, Annabelle, what a hell of a time to leave me!"

He slammed the door behind him and went out into the dawn looking like the stricken man he was.

Mission, Montana, was a small town serving ranchers over a wide rural area. Worn out houses stretched north, south, east and west on gravel roads behind the five-block Main Street. Mission was not big enough to boast two malls, but it had them. They were what would be called mini-malls or string malls if in a big city. Sprawling beside one another on Main Street between Forest Glen Boulevard (yes, called a

Boulevard) and Green Apple Way, the one closest to Green Apple Way, East mall, shouted its birth age of decades past to anyone who looked. Its unwashed and old brick fronts, faded wood sidings and signs that had worn out their printed letters cried out for repairs, but there was never enough given. There were five stores in the East mall and seven in the West mall, the latter closest to Forest Glen Way. Each mall had stores the other did not, although two dress shops and two grocery stores vied with one another for customers. The West mall grocery belonged to a chain, it was kept lit, even when the doors closed for the day, while the East Mall grocery was strictly hometown and going broke. West mall had a tire shop, East an auto parts store. The crafts store at the West mall drew the most customers, ranch wives who wiled away the long summer evenings when the cattle grazed on higher ground making photo albums, stone necklace and earring creations; they lay dried wild flowers on frames and placed them all on consignment in Stone's Gift Shop.

Annabelle Stone's gift shop (Stone's Gifts) sat at the far end of the West mall. Her counters were covered with fancy towels, aprons (most inscribed with painted or hand-sewn Montana sayings which were eagerly grabbed up by tourists), trinkets, and all sorts of jewelry from $4.99 sets of cheap but fun fashionable earrings to sets that had a top price of $199.00. Stone's Gift Shop did the bulk of its business with the summer traffic traveling from Great Falls to the Canadian border and vice versa. It sat closest to the road right at the foot of the hill townspeople called Blue Hill. A restaurant and gas station stood at the top of Blue Hill, both edifices painted a garish blue, so people driving along the freeway could see them from a distance. And they did. Because freeways in Montana were full of long, lonely miles, the Blue Hill restaurant and gas station enjoyed plenty of paying traffic. If drivers did not want to go up the hill, they could get off the exit road and fifty feet south stop at a motel with once-upon-a-time quality linked cabins (fifteen) with a busy two-year old restaurant and bar on one side.

Marv glanced over at Annabelle's shop as he spun around the corner of Green Apple Way onto Main Street, his car's streaking turn flinging gravel onto fall-tired, yellowing lawns. The white night lights of Stone's Gift Shop were still on, covering the dying darkness with muted light. Her shop's parking stalls were empty. She's probably down at the restaurant at the east mall, he thought. Well, I'll not go there to find her. Let her go to California. Good riddance. He swore but his throat caught and he clamped his teeth together.

He tore down the rest of Main Street at 50 miles an hour. He was out of town on the freeway west when he heard the siren behind him. He pulled over, slamming his hands angrily on the steering wheel.

Joe Chobin, the sheriff, strode up to his car.

"Good morning," said Joe, as Marv flicked the window switch to open it. "Something wrong, Marv?"

"No."

"You drive like you have bad news."

"Everything is okay." Marv's voice held resentment of the query.

Joe looked at his friend for a moment, studying his lean, tense face. The wrinkles Marv did have, thought Joe, appeared in this early morning light to have furrowed deep into his cheeks. Even so, Marv surely is a handsome man, thought Joe, in that instant of looking. Straight, tight mouth, straight, wide-set winter blue eyes, white and sandy colored eyebrows that hung quizzically from his wide forehead, along with a nose which should have been straight, but instead lifted in a slight curve — a ski-jump nose.

"Want a ticket, Marv?"

"If you must, Joe. My mind got cluttered."

"I'm going to give you a warning, not a ticket. If your mind gets cluttered again, stop and rest. You went sizzling through town."

"I guess I did." Resentfully.

"Don't let there be a next time. Somebody crossing the street, they could have been killed."

"Yes."

Marv was certainly upset about something, thought Joe, standing with his belly resting on Marv's car door. Marv's face was frozen in a tense smile. But he has strength, thought Joe, not only from his wiry, lean body, but also from someplace inside, and that was the trouble now. He's at odds with himself, whatever happened, and he won't let himself give in to it. Was it something one of the two girls did or Andrew?

"How are the kids? Okay?"

"Yes." Marv's answer was short, clipped.

"Andrew still away at school?"

"Yes."

"In Spokane, right?"

"Right."

"That Janice. She surely is a beautiful young girl. You did

all right in the gene department, Marv."

Marv didn't answer. He frowned and pushed his lips together tightly. He didn't like that kind of a reference.

"Say hello to the kids. Don't forget Melissa."

"Yes."

"Take it easy."

"I will."

Marv waited impatiently until Joe went back to his car and flicked off the flashing lights. He drove on, carefully now, even glancing at the speedometer every once in a while. His fingers gripped the wheel tensely.

Marv Alicorn's ranch — Windy Hills Double Bar M — half lay in a long, low valley twenty miles northwest of Mission. In the distance the cattle land reached up like giant steps, topping multiple hills and stopping just in front of the mountains. The far distance heaved with breaks, reaching up and up. One could see the green of the far-away pines. But then, bareness took over, for few trees lived in the highest distance, not in this part of Montana; wind ruled here.

Once off the freeway, his mood sullen, he braked his car to a quick stop in front of the gate to his ranch. Marv glanced up unseeing at the pockets of planted and well-cared-for birch and ash protecting his sprawling two-story ranch house. He didn't even greet, as he usually did, the majestic ancient cottonwoods with trunks as wide as an outdoor privy that hugged two sides of the barns just beyond the gate. A small creek nearby, fall dry right now, fed them. His every thought festered from Annabelle's deception.

Getting out of his car, he opened the gate, moved the car, closed the gate, got back in the car, and drove up to the garage attached to the house. His hand reached up to the garage opener control on the visor. Holding his hand there for a moment thinking, his tongue worrying his lower lip, he finally took his hand away, shut off the motor, parked the car in front of the garage, and got out.

The sky was gaining color now, not much, very slowly. Storm grey, fast moving clouds would keep the land in low light awhile longer.

He headed straight towards the second barn past two of his beloved cottonwoods. He knew Coll, his favorite horse, would be waiting for him. Marv tended to Coll each morning after breakfast, a ritual not to be denied. He was late this morning. "Damn her." He could not shake what he called Annabelle's sneaky desertion from his mind.

He stopped short at the entrance hearing an unfamiliar voice from inside. He didn't like what it was saying. He moved noiselessly inside and what he saw made him wince.

A cowboy was kissing his daughter Janice. It was a deep, passionate throat kiss. The cowboy's hands had already reached down her back to her buttocks. Marv could tell it was an action his daughter was familiar with because as the cowboy's hands fondled and pulled at her buttocks, she folded herself into his body. Marv, standing in shock, knew that in a moment the cowboy was ready to fling her down on the ground.

"God damn," he said, his voice low, menacing, his words anticipating the next action. "Get off my daughter."

His daughter, Janice, and the cowboy froze. Quickly they withdrew their lips from each other. The cowboy's hands left her body. Both straightened. They turned and faced him.

"What in the hell do you think you're doing?" It wasn't wrath in Marv's voice, it was hate and shock. He walked up to the cowboy and hit him full in the face.

The tall, dark-haired, common looking cowboy reeled from the impact.   Blood from a broken nose vein began running into his mouth, but he stood his ground silently with a look of repressed anger in his face.

Janice, Marv's beautiful daughter, screamed.

"Get out of here, you son of a bitch," said Marv.

"Daddy, don't!" Janice screamed again, for without thinking, Marv was swinging his left hand at her. He caught himself and stopped short of her mouth. The cowboy had come forward at his gesture, but stopped when Marv did.

"Go up to the house," Marv told his daughter quietly after a long stark moment. The look in his eyes sent her stomach churning. "I'll finish here."

"Leave him alone, Daddy. He didn't do anything to you."

"Get going . . . now!" Marv's voice, like his face, was coated with ice.

"Daddy, Daddy, please . . . don't hit him again," Janice begged, her chest heaving with fear, her mouth agape, her lovely face dead white.

"No. I won't hit him again." Marv's eyes were slits. "But I don't want you here while I speak to him. Leave."

"Yes, father."

The beautiful girl, her long, straight, corn-colored hair streaming down her back, turned away and walked out of the barn. Marv watched her silently. She moved like a mountain lion in heat, in a smooth, proud glide. As he watched her, his mind whirled for what had occurred, he suddenly realized, had been as much her fault as that of the hired hand. Any man would be a fool not to want to make love with her when all that was needed was an invitation. Evidently, this one had seized upon opportunity. Even now, although she was in obvious distress over her father catching her kissing a ranch hand, she still moved with an enticing dare in her step. It seemed she said with each movement, "Look at me. Come for me. I am here but you will have to catch me."

He shook his head. How unobservant he had been. He hadn't been aware of his beloved daughter's sexuality before, or of her vulnerability.

He turned to the ranch hand, his face inscrutable. There was something about this cowhand he didn't like. He stared at him hard. Dark, long messy hair, a day's growth on his face, big boned body, tall, heavily-muscled with his blue denim shirt and blue jeans looking as if they were ready to jump his body they were so dirty. Sullen black eyes stared at him above an ungroomed, mustached mouth. That's what it is, thought Marv, it's in his eyes. He's got something unwholesome about him, like he's been around in bad places. He can't hide it.

"What's your name?"

"Rob Christianson." The cowboy reached into his jeans pocket for a handkerchief.

"How long have you been working for me?"

"Two weeks."

He was surly too.

"What have you been hired to do?"

Rob held the handkerchief to his nose even though the blood was practically stemmed. "Keep the barns clean. Check cattle."

"Where are you from?"

"Billings."

"Before that?"

"California."

He ran away from something he did in California, thought Marv. He's a misfit.

"Who hired you?"

"Why?"

"I want to know."

"One of your ranch hands. Said you needed help."

"Who is that?"

"Randy."

"And?"

"The Indian hired me."

This ranch hand did not like Indians.

"How long have you been kissing my daughter?"

The cowboy's mouth turned down into a sneer. His eyes narrowed and pulling away the handkerchief from his nostrils, he formed a half-mocking smile on his mouth. "Well," he began, but it was obvious he wasn't going to finish the sentence.

"Never mind. I don't want you to go near her again. Understand?"

"Yeah . . . " The yeah came with a miniscule scornful laugh.

It was obvious he didn't mean it.

"Go find Lamedeer. Tell him where I am." Marv's voice was tough.

"Yeah, sure." The tall, dark-haired cowhand, handkerchief

again covering his nose, turned and strode haughtily out of the barn.

Marv moved to Coll's stall, his body shaking with anger. He ran his hand down the horse's face and neck. Coll opened his mouth and took a gentle hold of Marv's arm with his lips.

"Ah, that was close, Coll." Preoccupied with the scene he had just witnessed, particularly with his daughter's actions, he put his head against the horse's face and moaned, "God, Coll, what a mess this morning is."

Suddenly Coll moved away. Marv felt Lamedeer's arm on his shoulder.

"What's the matter, Marv?" asked his foreman.

Lamedeer, a short, stocky Blackfoot Indian, was ranch manager of Windy Hills Double Bar M. Red Lamedeer was his full Indian name; "Red" because when he was born, he was beef-red in color, and "Lamedeer" because he was born with a clubfoot. Robert Lamar was his Christian name but few knew it other than his childhood Sunday school teachers, public school teachers and others a sundry. He never used it for he preferred his Indian name having intense pride in his Blackfoot heritage.

Marv didn't answer Lamedeer's question. Without moving away from Coll, he asked, "Where's that cowhand I sent after you?"

"He's outside the barn door."

Marv turned. "Fire him."

"Rob? What's he done?"

"Janice!"

"Oh. Anything happen?"

"I don't think so yet, but you better get rid of him. And

fast."

"I'll be shorthanded without him," Lamedeer interrupted. "He's good at the job. I'll send him up into the mountains with Ben after the strays."

"No."

"No?

"Lamedeer, No. Hell no. I don't often overrule you, but this time I do. There's something about him I don't like." He added very slowly, enunciating each word, "Get him out of here."

"Okay, Marv."

"Pay him off now. Watch him. See that he leaves. Fast."

"All right," answered Lamedeer, starting for the barn door. Then he turned, looked at Marv, and said slowly, "You know, Marv, you need to let Janice go."

"Why? So she can pick up with some other common guy?"

Marv walked away from his horse towards Lamedeer and told Lamedeer angrily, "We're not talking about Janice now, Lamedeer."

"I just brought her into the subject, Marv. Aw, come on, lighten up. You've given Janice high ideals. She'll come back to them once she has her fling."

Marv retorted angrily, "I don't believe in my girls having flings."

"Janice is in love with love. You have to understand your daughter, Marv. She has always missed her mother even though she was only five when Teresa died. She continually reaches out to find affection. She craves affection like you crave just one more acre of land."

"I don't have to listen to this."

"Yes, you do. It's about time you listen. Let her go to New York, that's where she wants to go. The excitement of being in the big city will eliminate this cowboy from her mind."

"And what will happen if she falls in love with the wrong man there?" Marv cried.

"Janice has goodness honed into her," insisted Lamedeer. "She will return to her ideals. Give her time."

"How?"

"Release her. Janice is not cut out to be a farm girl, not like Melissa. She wants to become a model, and she should make it. She is certainly beautiful enough. Also, she has plenty of your drive to get her to the top in whatever she wants to do. You can still hope some rich young man there becomes her prince."

"And if not?"

"Pray for her. And love her. That is all you can do. You can't keep her here much longer. She has to test her wings. Give her enough money so she can at least fling if she has to, first class. Whatever you do, Marv," Lamedeer added, "friend to friend, you've got to get her away from the confining atmosphere of the ranch. Janice has grown up on a hard working, driving ranch with rough men all around her, and that is all she has known. If you want to move her into new territory, you've got to accustom her first to the habitat."

"Melissa is not like that."

"Melissa is not Janice. They had different childhoods. Melissa never missed what she did not really know while Janice has always cried inside her heart for her mother, like Andrew - like you. They picked that up from you."

Marv swung his head sharply, questioning Lamedeer's

statement.

"Just like you still do for Teresa," added Lamedeer, emphasizing each word.

Marv kept his head immobile but his eyes narrowed in indignation, and he felt his stomach wrench with an old pain. He shook his head angrily at Lamedeer's retort. "This has been a hell of a morning and to top it off I get a lecture from you. You pay off that cowhand. Watch him and see he leaves. Fast. You hear me?"

"Yes, Marv." Lamedeer smiled inside. He could easily see from his boss's arrogant stance, that he had listened to what he had to say about Janice.

"I'm going on up to the house. I'll have Merry pack me a couple of sandwiches and hot coffee. I want to check a couple of fences and visit Teresa."

"Marv, there's a storm coming in this afternoon."

"Hell, I don't care, it's been a messy morning and your lecture topped it!"

Lamedeer laughed. "Wait for me. As soon as I get the girls off safely to town, we'll go together."

"No. I want to be by myself."

Lamedeer shrugged his shoulders. It was useless to argue with Marv.

"Well, you better bundle. The wind's coming up, and it'll be from the north."

Chapter Two

A half hour later when Marv rode away from the ranch house on Coll, his big, ten-year-old Roan, he had dressed for bad weather. Under his checked flannel shirt and jeans, he wore long underwear, both tops and bottom in grey wool. "Longies just the color of your eyes when you are angry, Dad," Melissa had giggled the first time she saw him wearing them as he sauntered along the upstairs hallway. Covering his shirt was his favorite leather jacket, and over two pairs of knee length socks, he wore high leather laced boots. He also carried his 38 Ruger pistol, 11 shells in the gun clip. The cartridge case on his belt held another 15.

In his saddlebag lay a steel thermos of hot coffee (reboiled from last night's pot), and two sandwiches thick with beef and butter on dark bread. His pocketknife was fastened to his jeans belt with the scabbard. He also carried a tarp and blanket.

He was prepared for vagrancies in weather or accident from horse or terrain. He was not prepared for tragedy.

The October morning, once the sun pushed aside the clouds, was glorious. He had just passed the last barn when the clouds disappeared and the sun's rays swallowed up the daybreak tints. Now the clean blue of the big Montana sky outlined the humps of the mountains ahead of him with the cloudless sky spilling over the trees and valleys and meadows, touching the melting snow with day shadows here and there. Marv, on his big Roan, rode slowly through the long, narrow canyon, moving along winter deer trails and summer cow paths.

When he reached the top of the draw he halted, for the snow that had fallen a week earlier was deeper than he had thought it would be; ice crusts clung onto some of the stubble in the fields. He dismounted to rest.

Despite the chill, damn, it was good to be out in the air with the morning wind on his face, even though, as the wind grew in strength, it pushed through the spaces in his clothing. Not that it mattered what the wind did to his rough skin. Annabelle never complained, and only she, along with his daughters, put their hands upon his brow and caressed his cheeks.

"I like your skin just the way it is," his daughter Melissa had told him only last week, as he sat fully stretched in his big chair in the living room watching the evening news on TV. She had come up behind him, gathered her hands over his forehead, rubbing it.

"I'm smoothing out the weather creases, Dad. Now, don't frown and put them back. Anyway, why don't you wear your hat outside? Your little thin spot is sunburned."

The little 'thin spot' was a bald patch an inch wide and an inch thick on the crown of his head, the only mar in a thick head of faded sandy, grey-streaked hair, and although his daughter liked to smooth the wrinkles on his brow, he didn't believe there was any smoothing of the facial wrinkles that seemed to multiply by the dozens each year.

He hated to look in the mirror because of these lines. "Handsome furrows they are, Dad," both his girls told him time and again. "We wouldn't have you look another way. You're the Marlboro man to outdo all Marlboro ad men, the handsomest sun-furrowed ranch owner this side of heaven."

He didn't feel like the Marlboro man right now. His mind criss-crossed with thoughts of each of his three children. How different they were. His beloved Janice, so like in looks of Teresa, his dead wife, so beautiful with her corn-colored hair, her dark grey but deeply burnished, glowing eyes - the long legs, the small but full young breasts, the trim narrow waist – the sultry, confident way of walking that demanded everyone's eyes gather in her perfect young body; the low yet beguiling voice that turned even the unacquainted into devotees. How could he ever let her go away? He needed her home to protect her knowing she was vulnerable to events around her; she listened and agreed with anyone who told her one thing but acted another. Naivety! Despite her latest obsession wanting to go to New York City, she continually overextended her allowance with new clothes, new cosmetics, then pleaded successfully for more even though she lifted no finger to chores or togetherness with the rest of her family; instead, spent hours listening to horrible loud and uncontrollable music and purchasing tons of DVDs, CDs and movies to watch on the flat-screen TV in her bedroom. Despite her pouty attitude when asked to contribute to family discussions and her forever unhappiness with the secluded home life she lived since she graduated from high school, and her ever-growing distaste for ranch life, he adored her. She could wear him down to gift her with anything her selfish heart desired. But she kept him annoyingly distracted with her incessant, "Please let me go to New York." He did not feel she could be trusted to take care of herself if far away from home.

Melissa was her older sister's opposite from the color of her hair (which was darkening to brown and which she kept shortened to the bottom of her ears), to her tall, late developing skinny body to her attitude. If only Janice had the joy inherent in Melissa's every word and every step. Ah, what an absolute delight Janice would be then. Melissa grew up a tomboy, and he wondered if she would ever change. She appeared to have no interest in boys as Janice did. In school, she was a gymnastic delight; excelled in basketball, softball, track, any sport that demanded close teamwork. On the ranch she helped birth cattle, rode as hard as a man when gathering strays, each year dug and worked a small garden, forbade anyone else from mowing with the yard tractor, helped mend fences, liked people and overlooked the temper outbursts of both her younger brother and older sister with common-sense compassion. She adored him and never beseeched him for favors as Janice did nor acted woebegone as Janice ("I have nothing to do") when the fickle Montana winter weather imprisoned them inside. She had little thought to what clothes she wore, jeans and blouses and high-necked sweaters became her favorite garb as she grew out of her early teens. Clean they must be but ragged, okay. She read voraciously not seemingly caring what the subject was, digesting everything, which made it pleasant to talk to her, although historical themes attracted her most.

Andrew was a puzzle. As a little boy he was a holy terror, full of temper tantrums, a "go-away and leave me alone" disposition when he did not get his small-boy way, and Marv had never had a clue to Andrew's private thoughts although he really wasn't interested. In fact, he was glad that Merry and Lamedeer took the boy in hand. He wondered sometimes if the more children he had, the less he liked them when they were small. But then, if it had not been for Andrew, Teresa would not have died, and she did painfully, in his birthing. It took a year or more after the squirming, screaming boy baby settled down to a routine that Marv even cared to be near him. He was glad now that Andrew was away at a technical college. Marv had little use for modern technology; he was impatient when one of his computers or whatever they were had problems. He couldn't understand when they paid so much money for these technological wonders that they could ever have down time. He was glad both Lamedeer and Gustav were in charge of the ranch's electronic contraptions and knew the programs necessary to run them. It also bothered him that he could never interest Andrew in the ranch or the ever-necessary duties it imposed on its inhabitants. The kid even kept away from the ranch's computer duties, and he became more sullen as he grew older, until Marv's fervent wish was that the boy go away. Only Melissa, his boy in girl's clothes, cared and missed her brother.

Standing on the edge of a high meadow, ready to remount, he realized he didn't have the zip he thought he had when he and Coll had started out. All of a sudden he was tired. Bone tired. "God damn," he swore. He no longer had any inclination to inspect any fence post line, besides he certainly could no longer think of any valid reason for wanting to revisit Teresa's grave, even though he had an intense longing for the type of communication that spending time at Teresa's grave heretofore seemed to give him. Until this moment visiting Teresa's grave gave him solace. It did not seem possible now. He'd been fooling himself knowing damn well the bones in the grave he was going to could not give it to him. She was dead.

Oh God, his dear wife whom he loved so much was dead, had been dead for years and he never had let her go, not until this moment. He had kept her lying in her grave in a godforsaken windy, cold pasture miles from the house so he could talk to her, cry to her, and beg her to come back. And now Annabelle had left him because he was ever mooning for a dead wife and he loved Annabelle. He knew he did, even though he kept denying it.

"You walk around without any feeling. Until you let her go you'll never be comfortable in anything you do," Annabelle had told him. Annabelle was right, of course.

He felt his age. He took a couple of deep breaths, letting the air out slowly in an effort to give new life to his suddenly exhausted body, which felt so damn tired he was wishing he was home in his plasticized log living room, resting in his big comfortable chair, his left arm hanging over its side, rubbing his daughter's dog and snacking on a sandwich Merry had made for him. God knows this was a time of his life when he should be able to relax, put up his feet when he wanted to in a warm, cozy, snug house instead of acting like a fool, traipsing over the rugged terrain checking fence posts and visiting a gravesite. He said to himself once again, "Oh, Teresa, why did I let you choose this desolate place to sleep?"

He put his foot in the stirrups. "Come on, Coll," he grunted stubbornly, determined to complete this foolish outing. His horse moved to allow him to mount the instant he pulled back the reins, and he climbed back onto his horse slowly, his breath moving through his body in short jabs. He shook his head almost afraid, definitely puzzled, because his breathing never acted like that before.

"Come on, Coll," he said again, his voice cracking with weariness. They moved around the edge of the high pasture, the guard line of trees absorbing the blunt edges of a rising, cold north wind.

He felt an urge to hurry now. He wanted to get to the gravesite and sit down on the imported Italian marble seat facing her grave. He needed to rest. Since Coll was walking in snow, he knew the stone would be decked with snow. Of course. And after he swept off the snow, the seat would be wet, cold and chilling. Not a good seat for a man to sit on, for sure, he said aloud, causing Coll to lift his ears. But who the hell cared. He needed to rest, talk to Teresa, look at the grave one last time, then eat his sandwiches, and go home. Right now he almost felt like turning back, he was so damn, damn tired, yet he was too far along on his idle errand to do so.

Foolish trip, he said to himself, feeling the wind bite his face. He squinted his eyes against the sun, pulled his hat down over his forehead, and with his head humped down into his collar, he and Coll rode on until they reached the top of the draw where his wife's body was buried.

He almost walked Coll into the fence around the head stone. The week-old snow had been pushed by the wind up over the south fence and hung itself like a stretched out sink over the edge, dripping water from an elongated spout whenever the sun softened it and forming icicles when the sun hid.

"Good God, Teresa," Marv exclaimed in a shaky voice, feeling himself completely drained once he had made a path with his saddle shovel. He opened the gate and hoisted the snow over the fence. "Some day soon I'm moving your grave back to civilization. I could have talked to you right at home as well as trekking all the way up here. You're dead. If anyone other than Lamedeer knew, they'd say I was 'tetched in the head.'

"Since he's an Indian, he believes your spirit is here. God, if it was," and he looked around at the expanse of wild desert-like land, "it'd be frozen by now. I must have been mad to say 'yes' to your wish to be buried here. The only thing you liked about this place were the wild flowers that bloomed in the spring and the view of the mountains. Yeah, it's a great view, Teresa, but you can't see anything when the snow is swirling. And it is awful lonely. You never liked being alone, remember, Teresa? I had to come to tell you that Janice wants to leave home. She's been saying for over two months, 'Dad, I want to go to New York. I don't like ranching and I don't want to live way out here. I never will.' That's what she has been telling me. She is so beautiful, Teresa, I worry about her. Lamedeer says I have to let her go. That's the real reason I came here, Teresa, so if your spirit is here, please send it with her. I don't want to lose her as I lost you."

He sat down hard on the bench, wet and cold though it was. Suddenly, he winced. A rock fell on his head.

Impossible. He arched his neck to look up. There was nothing above him but sky. Then his arms began to tingle. He tried to lift one arm to his head, which was throbbing with a sudden, fierce headache. Whoosh! Another rock! Not a rock! It's inside me, he realized.   Without warning, pain began coursing through his body. From where, he didn't know. The pain inside him was making him dizzy, and his left arm locked in mid-air, numb. Something was pounding hard inside his temple, also inside his chest. God, he hurt. All he could think of was that he knew rocks weren't falling on his head or on his body, the pain came from inside. The shuddering pain was shooting up to his head from his chest, and it was affecting his mind. His thoughts were falling apart. Oh God, I am having a stroke. I'm having a heart attack. Oh God damn. Oh, please, God, I don't want to die.

Suddenly the pain was all encompassing. Unbelievable pain. He tried to put his hand on his chest. He couldn't feel it move, and the pain was everywhere. Even when he tried to call for help, the only sounds that came out were croaks. He tried to shake the pain from his head and in the shaking he fell to the ground, unconscious.

Chapter Three

Lamedeer had been a boyhood playmate of Marv Alicorn even though they had spent only one brief summer together. However, in that brief time Marv learned about land and animals from the Indian boy. After Marv graduated from the University of Montana and took possession of his inheritance — Windy Hills — he tracked down Lamedeer, who was then working as a ranch hand in Arizona and persuaded him to come back to Montana to help run his ranch.

Lamedeer never regretted the decision to work for the tall, slim, sandy-haired white man.

From the beginning, Marv treated him like a full partner. When Lamedeer married, Marv gifted him with choice acreage alongside the blacktop road close to his own ranch house so Lamedeer could build his home.

When Lamedeer's first wife was killed in a car accident, a scant two years after Marv's own wife died, Marv begged him to take on a new wife to help mother his three children. Marv never raised an eyebrow when Lamedeer returned from Browning with two women ('wives,' he said). One was Merry, older sister to his first wife. She, Lamedeer told Marv, would serve as housemother and cook while Swallowmaid, a comely twenty-five year old, would be his bed mistress.

Without a word, Marv had his ranch hands cut and cure and deliver to Lamedeer's cabin enough lumber so Lamedeer could add an extra room. In Lamedeer's next paycheck he found a bonus - enough money to purchase all other necessary material for the new room. While Lamedeer was adding the extra room, Marv sent Merry to a school in Seattle, Washington, where she learned to sew and cook the way Marv liked food to taste, at the same time he sent Swallow to a girl's finishing school in Billings to learn social graces.

Merry returned an excellent cook and seamstress; Swallow became a spirited, graceful companion to his children, although she never gave Lamedeer what he desired most, children. The absence of a son who could carry on his name deeply saddened Lamedeer. Nevertheless, he refused to take on another wife, as Marv once drunkenly suggested.

"I love Swallow," the Indian teetotaler said stoically. "And it must be written with the gods that they don't want any more Lamedeers brought into the world."

That was one of the rare times Marv heard Lamedeer refer to his affliction, his clubfoot, which was never taken care of when he was a little boy. Lamedeer ignored his disability just as he ignored calamity. But he did have arthritis in his affected foot that caused him pain; his heel was turned in so far that his left leg was shorter than his right, and he walked with a decided limp. Outsiders were often amazed when they learned of his clubfoot because he hid it well with his usual stoic determination as well as training his right leg and foot to do everything his left could not; also clothes covered his disfigurement.

On this particular morning, shortly after Marv rode off to visit Teresa's grave, Lamedeer was on his way to the house.

He had paid off the cowboy Rob, yet it was difficult to hold his tongue after Rob commented, "Yeah, I knew he'd fire me. Tough shit. I can work anyplace. Nice bitch, though."

He kept silent, but gritted his teeth in anger as he followed Rob to the bunkhouse to get his clothes and gear, load them into his decaying 1991 Subaru, and speed nosily away from the ranch.

Melissa's dog, Lincoln, was in the vegetable patch. Lamedeer saw him because the dog was jumping about snapping at grasshoppers. Melissa was on her knees picking garden squash.

Lamedeer shook his head in bemused wonderment. Marv Alicorn's two daughters had always been unlikely sisters.

Taller than Janice, although two years younger, Melissa's hair wasn't colored a gorgeous corn color, hers was almost brown. Neither did she wear her hair long down to her waist, as Janice did, she wore it short. "Easier to care for," she answered breezily, whenever she was chided about her boyish haircuts. "The wind whips a nice hairdo apart. I don't want to be bothered."

And unlike her sister, Melissa did not wear makeup. Heavily freckled, like her twenty-month younger brother Andrew, she joked that her face already looked like she wore beige foundation. She also did not realize that her face, although different in structure than her sister's, was going to be lovely when fully formed. As yet, no lines of tragedy or ecstasy marked the edges of her brow, her eyes, or swept down the outline of her slightly aquiline nose, across her petal-thin lips or edged her long and softly chiseled chin. Her eighteen-year-old face was clothed with innocence.

"Did any of the vegetables survive after last night's low temperature?" Lamedeer asked as he drew near.

"I had them covered, Lamedeer. I'm picking the last and they look good." She held up a well-bodied, particularly succulent looking yellow squash she was about to place in her basket.

"That's nice," complimented Lamedeer. He began laughing, watching Lincoln jumping about nosily snapping his jaws together, hoping to snare a grasshopper in his mouth and swallow it. "I see you still have grasshoppers."

"Oh, they are dying." She laughed too, looking up at her dog. "Is father nearly ready?"

"He already left for the high pasture."

"He left without me?" Melissa sat up immediately, incredulous.

"Your father wants you to go to Mission with Janice."

"He knew I wouldn't. I told him yesterday I wouldn't go with her." Her hazel eyes filled with anger.

"I do not know about your quarrel," Lamedeer answered quietly. "I do know that before he left this morning he told me you were to go with her." Lamedeer accented the word 'her.'

"Well, I won't," retorted Melissa. "I refuse to go with Janice into town again. All she wants to do is shop. I hate shopping. Lamedeer," and Melissa lowered her voice beseechingly, "please don't tell me I have to go into Mission with Janice."

"Melissa, your father ordered."

Melissa pursed her lips and stared at Lamedeer stubbornly. He watched her set the half full basket of vegetables down on the ground.

"See that Merry takes these to the house," she told him tartly, jumping up and pointing to the basket; then ran to the fence, swinging herself over the low varmint-proofed wire stretched around the garden patch and started towards the barn. Lincoln, her dog, leapt the fence right behind her.

"Miss Melissa," Lamedeer called after her, ignoring the basket of vegetables, "your father has forbidden you to go anywhere without backup. You know that."

"Then why did he?" she yelled back, unabashed. She ran on.

Marv had an ironclad rule. No one was allowed to leave the proximity of the ranch house — whether walking, riding or driving — alone. "Accidents happen to those who travel by themselves," he said. One of his ranch hands many years ago had fallen to his death climbing after a stray along one of the hill walls. Since that tragedy, those who lived or worked on Windy Hills Double Bar M obeyed Marv's rule or lost their bed and board. The rule extended to his daughters and son when they became old enough to drive cars. "Nothing is going to happen to my children on a lonely Montana highway," he insisted. He backed up his rule.

The big house, immediate grounds and valley pastures were within limits. While Janice, his oldest daughter, had little interest in what lay beyond the house and driveway, Melissa and Andrew wandered happily over the in-limit acreage to their hearts' content, Melissa often going with only her dog as companion, because as Andrew grew older, he preferred to be inside playing games on his computer.

Melissa had a halter on Atlas, the paint, and was climbing

onto his back, bare of saddle, when Lamedeer reached the barn.

"Your father expressly told me to tell you to remain here," he said to her as severely as he could.

"I don't care what he told you," Melissa answered tartly, yet not without respect. Lamedeer was the man who had taught her the ways of the wild and was the man she loved next to her father. "He promised I could go with him. That's why I am wearing these heavy clothes.

"Anyway, Lamedeer," she added, tears welling in her eyes, "he hasn't been well. He was sick with flu all last week. You know it and yet you let him go off alone. What if something should happen to him? He should have backup too."

She put her spurs to the horse's flanks and shot past Lamedeer, calling back airily, "You're a shadow in my light, Lamedeer, and I can't hear a thing you're saying."

Immediately guilt struck at her tone, so she pulled up and shouted back to him, "I'm sorry to talk back to you. But I've got Lincoln to guard me. Father has no one. He went off by himself. You can follow me if you like," she added brightly, hating to disobey, but determined to do so. "I'm just taking my usual handicap."

With a merry laugh, she touched her horse's flanks again and sped away with Lincoln following on the run.

Lamedeer's face was benignly inscrutable as he watched Melissa gallop off. He knew full well that even if he followed her now he could not overtake her; the Paint of Melissa's was the fastest horse on the ranch even though Fleet, his horse, was named for speed. Anyway, before he could ride after her

he had to take care of Janice. He hurried to the ranch house.
Janice was, as he suspected she would be, dressed for town.
She was sitting staring out the west window in the living
room. He knew by the way she inclined her head she was
upset. She had seen Marv leave, and she surely saw Rob
leave and now watched Melissa gallop out of the yard. She
turned as Lamedeer entered the living room.

He spoke first. "Your sister is not going with you. Merry
and Gustav will go to town with you. You will be in their
care."

"Merry and Gustav!" exclaimed Janice, getting up from
the couch, her eyes flashing. Even in anger, this twenty-year-
old was breathtakingly beautiful. Pencil slim, yet voluptuous,
her beauty dressed up everything she wore. She had changed
from the jeans her father found her in with the ranch hand.
She now wore black pants and a black jacket, the black
relieved by a white blouse and white gloves. Black showed
off her long golden hair, which lay enclosed securely on her
neck in a simple, elegant bun. Her deep violet eyes, velvet
white skin, and the way she cocked her head when she spoke,
so reminded Lamedeer of how her dead mother had looked
when Marv had married her; however, there was yet no
evidence that Janice had inherited her mother's sweet
disposition, for while she possessed the same quality of
elegance, she acted like a vixen. A heartbroken man who saw
only the radiance of his lost wife in his eldest daughter's
loveliness had spoiled her. Still, there was grace in her,
thought Lamedeer. She had been well brought up despite her
father's indulgence. Her problem was she was handmaiden to
her own beauty, sometimes flaunting it and sometimes hiding

from it.

Lamedeer faced the lovely girl in front of him. "Your father is going to allow you to go to New York. I think you already know that. So humor him."

"But Lamedeer . . ." she began, closing her mouth when he put up his hand in caution. A confrontation with Janice never went well, so he did not want her answering him; with her temper she might blurt out that she was in love with the ranch hand he had just paid off. At that moment, Merry, his cook wife, entered. Thank the Gods, he muttered to himself.

Immaculate, dressed in a plain, but well-fitting black suit, which she had made herself, it hid the bulge around the long-disappeared girlish waist of her short, square, stocky body. Her plumpness was testimony to her appetite as her name was to her round, happy face. Merry took Janice's arm and led her from the rustic living room and out the main door, turning to smile at Lamedeer.

Lamedeer let out a sigh of relief and moved to the long bank of windows facing the driveway watching Gustav, Marv's mechanic and part-time driver, who stood beside the four-wheel drive SUV sitting in the driveway. As soon as Gustav saw the two women, he snuffed out his cigarette under a foot, picked up the stub, and opened the door for Merry. Janice had moved around to the passenger's side in the front. She obviously did not want to ride in back.

Chapter Four

A stride her Paint, Atlas, riding to meet up with her father, Melissa's whole expression displayed delight. She was galloping through the valley of her father's ranch with Lincoln, her Dalmatian dog, running at her side. Rejoicing in the flawless, if slightly chilly autumn morning, she was on her way to the high pasture.

It was late enough in the morning so that the sun stretched itself out over the whole valley. As a matter of fact, it was heating the valley so cozily that before she had ridden a mile from the north side of the ranch barns, Melissa loosened the snaps of her denim field jacket, allowing the chest flaps to blow apart. The speed at which she and Atlas made their way lifted her short hair with the wind swinging strands this way and that. She began to sweat as she drove her horse west across the open valley towards the long draw and the rambling hills beyond.

She passed the great silver poplars on the north side and moved into autumn tree color that took her breath away. The color stood in front of her, sat on all sides of her, and followed her; scarlet belonging to the scattered clumps of maple (some that her mother had planted before she was born), yellow of the cottonwood, lemon of the aspen and birch, red of the oaks and dogwoods, oranges of bitterroot, huckle and choke-berries, along with the grays, silvers, browns and blues of thickets of sage and briar and tattered grass and faded stalks of wildflowers. The riot of fall color was simply glorious.

Several times during her gallop over the valley floor Melissa closed her eyes and prayed that the autumn-colored leaves would cling on the branches in the exact color they were forever. In the bright sunshine, with a gathering breeze flowing down from the mountains, the mixed colors were outlined distinctly against the browns of the valley and the blue-grey and white mountains; if they were alive they would be celebrating their colors against the dark green pines and yews standing like sentinels guarding the whole of the horizon - the panorama took her breath away.

Once, from a rip-roaring gallop, she snapped Atlas to an abrupt halt. "I simply have to feast on all this beauty," she cried aloud, letting the reins slip through her fingers.

The huge Paint's head went down immediately to taste grasses while Lincoln collapsed wearily upon the ground allowing his haunches to fall where they may. His tongue fell out of his mouth, and his long white tail ceased its wagging. He perked an eye and ear upward and grinned delightedly when his mistress began singing "Oh, what a beautiful morning . . ." Then he settled back and shut his eyes. Melissa gazed on her dog lovingly. She loved looking at his handsome fifty-five lbs, remembering the day she first saw him and he came home with her. He was one of seven Dalmatian puppies in the big cage at the Humane Society's old, worn kennels in Great Falls. None of the seven were awake when her eyes opened wide in amazement, and she cried out delightedly at seeing their adorable little black and white spotted bodies all gathered together for warmth in a corner on the cold, cement floor. She immediately halted and placed her hands against the bars of the kennel to stare at them. Instantaneously, the seven puppies woke up, each one cocking its little head at her and then abruptly and quickly dashing on little long, long skinny legs to the bars to whine and utter little barks, begging to be touched and begging to be let out. Melissa cried out in anguish that these six week old baby dogs, so she had been told, had been found inside a plastic bag in a closed Dumpster, almost dead, yet still had no mother to care for them. How could the attendants in the shelter do it, when they were always so busy? "Oh, Lamedeer," she cried out, who had been looking at a sheepdog type on the other side of the aisle. He turned back to Melissa and told her that her Dad did not want her to get a puppy that young because it would take too much care.

"Oh, we have to," Melissa had replied. "I love Dalmatians. The AKC Dog Book says they are gentlemen's dogs. And look, Lamedeer, look at that little guy – the one who is limping. Look at his spotting. Isn't he gorgeous."

"You cannot take home a sick puppy, Melissa, or one with a bent leg. Your Dad wouldn't want that."

"Well, I want him. And here he comes." Twelve-year-old Melissa immediately lay down in the aisle on the cement floor sliding her hand through the bars to reach the lame puppy, who appeared just as anxious to touch her as she was to touch him. Lamedeer watched helplessly as the two made contact, although that particular contact was difficult to see since the six other puppies were also making contact with Melissa's hands.

That was how Lincoln (named for the town in which the Dumpster had sat) went to live at the Alicorn's ranch. He grew up, housetrained and obedience-mannered by his young mistress, Melissa, and he followed her everywhere. Although Marv would have preferred that the short coated white and black spotted four-legged companion of Melissa stay outside in a doghouse in the daytime, he could not say no to Melissa's pleas, even though Lincoln left humongous strands of short hair all over the house every day of the year. "This is the goldarn awful worst shedding breed of any breed I ever knew," he complained, as his hands continually swept off tiny white and black hairs from his pants or off his living room chair when Lincoln laid on it when Marv wasn't around to chase him off. Lincoln liked that chair as much as Marv did. However, Lincoln was soon sitting on Marv's lap whenever Marv sat down on their shared chair because Marv was a sucker for loving dogs and Lincoln obviously knew it.

Like now, the second his mistress thought of grabbing the halter again, six year old Lincoln was on his feet, pulling his tongue securely inside his mouth, ready to run with his tail, like a long, white banner, swinging to and fro in the field-scented air.

When Melissa shouted, "Up, up and away, Atlas!" Lincoln swept into place alongside the horse, striking his feet on the ground in cadence with the horse's hoofs. He positioned himself squarely in the deepest shadow of the moving stallion, determinedly maintaining a full shade alignment between the sun and himself.

They began moving out of the valley's bottom into the draw, Melissa slowing Atlas to a trot. Boulders appeared on the well-worn cow path, and so did small patches of snow. Several times she reined Atlas to a halt, and turned to search for movement in the valley behind her.

"Wish you were here, Andrew," she muttered pensively, thinking of her brother, leaning back and taking in a deep breath. "This is just the kind of day you like for tracking. But I suppose when you finish that schooling about computers, you'll go away to work in some lab in a big city. That's a pity, Andrew. You could stay home with me and have fun. Ah well, to each his own. Both you and Janice want to do other things; obviously, the ranch is not in your hearts as it is in mine. It's the only place I want to be."

The slower pace she was taking allowed her to chatter at Lincoln. As she rode and talked, her short coffee-colored hair tip-tipped in tune with the motion of the horse's movement. The dog, naturally, did not understand what she was saying, but he listened to the sounds of her voice, and whenever he recognized a lilting tone, he tilted his ears straight up, wagged his tail as fast as he could as if she said something he should agree with, and cocked his big head contentedly to one side. Even so, he was not distracted from his watch. An inordinately protective dog of his mistress, he was not concerned with the scent or appearances of opossum, ground squirrels or even coyotes - he knew they would crouch motionless where they were until danger had passed. Temporary intrusion upon their territory was common. However, he was always ready to protect against treacherous predators, like bobcats, brown bears, and rattlers. He never wanted to be surprised. So, although his tail wagged to and fro merrily, and his feet moved in unison with the horse's hoofs, all his muscles were flexed with readiness as he maintained a sharp and wary eye, ear and nose upon the path.

Atlas, skittish except when Melissa sat upon his back, was in high fettle. As was daily habit, he had been fed and groomed at dawn, then tethered in his stall in the big barn while his mistress performed early morning garden chores. Accustomed to hard riding over rough ground, often in bad weather, he, as the girl and dog, each in their fashion, was enjoying the perfect autumn morning.

Melissa's backward glances were not without purpose. Just before she disappeared into the slope forest, she saw what she had been searching for, two moving specks. She knew the specks to be two horses carrying two men and that they were moving toward her, leaving the distant ranch yard.

She laughed gaily and called into the wind, "Come on, come on, Lamedeer, and catch up with me." She knew full well he could not because she was riding Atlas, the fastest horse on the ranch.

"Lincoln," she shouted to the dog as they reached the alleys of the tall hills trying to drown out the noise of the wind, which had suddenly decided to blow fiercely from the north and chill them: "Lincoln!" She was urging him to return to her side faster. "That's a boy," she said, as he came bounding up to her. "Were you looking for Dad? Come on, we'll find him together." She made a clucking sound, dug her heels into Atlas's flanks and sped across the fall-decked pasture with its wilted carpet of short straw. Specks and edgings of snow turned into several inches. She was surprised at its depth. She was surprised too that the wind had picked up so violently, and that it was turning bitter cold; the wind howled and whistled through the gorge, blowing in from the north; a storm was headed their way, for sure. She stopped, buttoned her jacket, put on her wool cap and gloves, and then followed the line of trees up the remainder of the snow-decked hills to the high pasture. Two hard minutes and she, Lincoln running beside her, came to the old line shed and paddocks that stood above the southeastern hollow. She saw where Coll, her father's horse, had made a new path through crusted snow. She could find her father easily once she reached the high ground for her mother's gravesite lay just above the rise.

Coll was standing in the shadows. He was not tethered, his back faced the yelling wind, and his head was pulled down with his ears plastered against it. He turned an oblique eye towards her as she approached at top speed and pulled up short. As she dismounted, uneasiness tightened in her chest. Why was her father's horse standing alone in the middle of the flat pastureland bearing the onslaught of the widening, cold wind? Coll pawed the ground once with his right hoof and then pulled his body away, galloping off. Lincoln backed up, started barking and in full voice followed Coll. They flew towards the gravesite. Melissa turned Atlas around following at a gallop.

Coll stopped beside the gravesite fence. Lincoln bounded over it, landing in a deep mound of snow. His bark grew nosier. Melissa dismounted quickly and saw what he was looking at on the ground.

"Oh, my God, father," she wailed, seeing him lying at the foot of the cement bench. She ran to him, went down on her knees, grasping for his head, while Lincoln pushed against her and began licking her face.

"Oh, Father . . . Lincoln, cut it out . . . father!"

Marv lay, half twisted on his right side, his right arm flung over his head, his fingers still clutched in trying to grasp at the dirt and snow beneath him. His mouth, when she was able to partly turn his head, was half full of dirt and twigs as if he had been trying to bite the earth because of pain. His left arm lay in a straight line and his knees were drawn up high against his chest. There was a large cut on the front of his head, high on the forehead. He must have hit the cement bench when he fell, thought Melissa, and looking up at it, saw he had, the blood there had coagulated on the bench. There was a second fierce cut on his right arm. Blood had seeped through his underclothes and jacket, but it too appeared to have been stemmed. Thank God.

She felt for his heart. It was beating. He was not dead. But he was cold. Hurriedly, she took off her jacket, covered him, then reached up to Coll standing outside the fence, slid off the blanket and covered him with that also. She ran her hands under the blanket and rubbed his hands, his legs, his body, and his face — talking to him all the while, trying to awaken him. Finally she fell silent.

I must do something, she said to herself. I must get up, lift him on my horse in some way and take him to the doctor. No, I can't. I can't move him.

"Oh God," she cried aloud, "help me."

She realized she had to stay with him until Lamedeer arrived. And there was no point in trying to see if the men were coming this way. The view from where her father lay did not encompass the hill or trees below them.

She got up and ran to Coll. She led him to the path down the hill. "Go home," she said, taking his halter, leading him forward for a few steps, and then yanking it forward. "Go home." But the horse did not obey. He moved forward a few steps to release the tug of the halter and then turned and went back to the gravesite, waiting for his master to rise.

Desperately she turned to Lincoln.

"I've never asked you to do something like this," she said, apprehensively, "but I'll try. I hope you'll listen. Go," she commanded firmly, pushing her hand against his muzzle and pointing down the trail. "Go, Lincoln. Get HELP. Go!"

The dog cocked his head and looked at her.

"Go," she repeated, almost crying. "Dad will die if we don't get help. Go get Lamedeer." Something clicked. As she took a step forward, so did Lincoln. But when she stopped, he stopped and looked at her in confusion. She took another step forward.

"Go, go!" she repeated. "Go get Lamedeer. Hurry home."

Lincoln sat down. He cocked his head again, obviously puzzled.

"Oh, never mind, you don't understand."

She tried once more. This time as she commanded, she pushed him down the trail. He resisted the push and sat down again.

"Please, Lincoln," she almost laughed, he looked at her so funny, wanting to please her, yet not knowing how. She tried one more time. This time he moved forward a step as she commanded. She praised him. His face lit up.

Again! He took several more steps forward.

"Good dog. Go home," she began saying over and over, accenting the word 'home.' She ran after him as he moved and pushed him forward. Unfortunately, when she turned to climb back up the hill, he came back too but his tail didn't wag. While he did not know what she wanted him to do, he knew he wasn't doing the right thing by returning to her.

"I can't keep doing this," she finally said aloud. "I have to stay with father." She looked down at her dog one more time, her eyes blinking with tears.

She screamed, "GO HOME!", and pointed down the trail.

Lincoln moved a few steps down the trail, then turned and looked at her. He sat again. She smiled. "Yes, yes, go on home. Good dog," she said eagerly. He went on.

"Good." She pushed her arm in front of her. "Go home. Get Lamedeer. GO."

The dog disappeared.

Melissa ran back to her father. His eyes were open. He was looking at her as she bent down.

"Oh, father," she cried in gratitude. "You are okay."

"Yes," he mumbled, the words slurring, "I think I fell."

"Yes."

"How long have you been here?" he asked, his words still pushing themselves together mushily. He tried to rise, falling back as he tried, his skin instantly turning grey.

"Wait," begged Melissa. "I've got blankets around you. You were cold. You are cold. Don't try to get up."

"Yes, I am cold."

"I don't want you to move yet. I want to know you are really okay first."

"I'm not sure."

"Dizzy?"

"Yes."

"Do you feel weak?"

"Yes."

"Then lie still. We need to get your circulation moving before you try to get up."

He mumbled.

She reached out to rub him.

"I'm okay now, dear daughter. God, I'm glad you came to get me."

"You went alone," she admonished gently, fearful again. His words sounded choked; his color ashen.

"Yes."

"Are you going to be all right?" Anxiously.

"I'm shaky. My left arm is numb. But I'm okay. Help me up."

"I don't know if I should."

"Please." His facial muscles twitched. He was trying to smile. Her heart stopped in fear.

"Are you certain you can sit up?"

"Yes."

She helped him steady himself and with her arm around him, attempted to lift him to a sitting position. It was not possible. His voice caught, and his lips were turning blue.

She tucked the blanket around him again, then looked hard at him.

"I don't think I had better move you. I'm not going to try to sit you. You look like you are nauseous."

I am. But I need to get off this cold ground."

"Okay. Give me a minute."

He was breathless. "As long as you want."

After a few minutes without movement, he said, "That's better. I believe I can function now. God, I don't know what hit me."

"Don't talk, Dad. Grab my arms. I'll sit you if at all possible. I'm only thankful I'm here. Lamedeer is on his way."

"Did he tell you he was coming after me?"

"No, but I looked back as I was leaving the valley and saw two men on horses. I know one of the horses was Fleet."

Lamedeer and the ranch hand reached Melissa several minutes later before she could get her father into a sitting position. Lincoln was ahead of them and ran to his mistress, dropping at her feet, panting hard.

Both men dismounted quickly. Lamedeer gathered Melissa in his arms. He saw she was shaking. She told him how she found her father.

"Good girl," he said, releasing her and rushing to Marv.

"Thank goodness for Melissa, Marv. You could have died out here."

Lamedeer didn't wait for an answer but went back over the wall to his horse and returned with a brown, wool army blanket. He pulled it around the other blanket still half wrapped around Marv. Melissa took back her jacket gratefully.

"You're white as a ghost, Marv. You are going to Mission to the doctor immediately."

He turned to Melissa and helped her onto her horse. "I wish you'd ride with a saddle," he said, shaking his head. "It would have been a help now."

"I'm sorry." She straightened herself on Atlas as if she was chained to the horse.

Lamedeer patted her hand. "We can't stay here any longer,

Melissa," he said quietly, looking at her stricken face, and squeezing her hands with tender regard. "The wind is bringing in a storm and we must get back to the ranch."

"What are we going to do?"

"You go ahead; call 911. Get an ambulance out here. I don't like the way Marv looks. They can drive it along the south pasture. It's good and dry, although rutty, I admit. I'll try to carry your father on my horse. Randy will lead Coll. If you are fast, we'll probably meet half way. Hurry, Melissa. And call Doctor Witt. Tell him what you know."

Melissa nodded, looked down at Lincoln, who sat beside Atlas panting but patiently waiting. She rode off.

The two men gently and gradually lifted Marv onto Lamedeer's horse. They gathered the blankets tightly around him.

Lamedeer mounted in back of him and told Randy to tie them together with a rope.

"This is the only way I can secure you, Marv, in case you have another blackout," Lamedeer said.

Marv, his face ashen, his breath coming quick and hard, nodded.

"Follow me closely," Lamedeer told Randy. "If I'm in trouble, get up here quickly."

Randy nodded.

The two began the descent and the long ride through the valley back to the ranch house.

Chapter Five

Andrew Alicorn's hair was so red, wherever he went people stopped to stare at it. The first thought that came into their minds was that it was dyed. However, if one observed the heavily freckled face that lay under the bright blood-red, rumpled head of hair, the observer realized it was not dyed.

Andrew himself belied his rough and tumble headpiece. At seventeen years of age, he was long and skinny and he couldn't seem to program his body to respond rhythmically. Like his wandering thoughts, his feet moved erratically. He fell over them.

Andrew was often contentious. It showed in his deep-set, dark blue eyes. They were usually lit up like sparks of war against one thing or another. He became irritable shortly after he woke up in the morning and remained irritable during much of the day. Sometimes in the evenings when he had a place to go to, he'd plant a half smile on his young, impressionable face, offer friendly words and loud laughs to those he was with. But when the time came to put his tall, lean body to sleep after an hour's physical workout, he went to bed with his mind unsettled, unhappy. He didn't know why. Some people called him shy; if he was, it held him so steadfast in its grip that it did not allow him to inquire within himself why he acted the way he did.

"Stop being so pouty," his sister Melissa would tell him when he stomped away from a situation that upset him.

"Laugh with me. You have such a neat laugh, Andy. Your whole face lights up, just like Dad's. Please laugh with me."

Somehow he couldn't. Oh, he enjoyed the rides with her over the longest valley of their ranch - the valley closest to the barns - and he would give her lessons on how to track the animals that used this valley as a crossing place to either the hills on the west or to the Marias River on the east. "This is a footprint of that big buck I saw yesterday," he'd say, jumping off his horse and leaning down on the track, examining it. "I can't tell that," Melissa would exclaim as she knelt beside him. He'd smile that warming smile of his and explain how he knew from the almost imperceptible depressions.

With his two sisters, especially with Melissa, he was confident, but get him to where people were, although he did not stutter his mental set was as if he did.

And he held grudges. He held a big one against his father for not allowing him to go to the Senior Prom at Mission High. Andrew had invited Jesse Cain, a very pretty senior, who was just as shy as he was, to be his date. When she had said yes, he whooped and hollered so much around the ranch about taking this pretty senior to the prom that the ranch hands began to tease him, and they gave him suggestions on how to act, not all of them being helpful or nice. Two days before the prom, he took one of his father's cars out of the garage (while his father was away) to practice opening and closing the door for his date. While backing it up in the field alongside the second barn, he ran over a lamb, which was running away from a marauding coyote the ranch hands were chasing. In the running over, he damaged the right rear door of the car, not very badly, but the lamb's head had dented the door frame and her struggling toe marks had scraped the side of the door. To compound the happening, he then denied he had caused the accident. His father, discovering the damage to the car and hearing Andrew's denial, took away his son's car rights for two weeks. Marv Alicorn didn't care if his son couldn't go to the prom. Responsibility to duty came first and mistakes because of lack of judgment had to be punished, lying was not to be tolerated.

Heartsick, distraught, Andrew begged his sister Janice to call his prom date and tell her he was ill with the flu. She did, but Jesse learned the truth and soon the whole school knew with the bullies calling him, "Lamb killer."

It was after the prom disaster that he began shutting himself in his room retreating into his computer whenever he could, and using the work he was doing on it to excuse himself from family activities. Contentiousness and loneliness became a part of him.

Upon graduation from high school (he was an honor student), he asked to go to a college far away from home. His purpose was to get away from his father, whom he now openly detested. Marv Alicorn, after repeated frustrating attempts to make Andrew over into what he thought his son should act and think like, agreed readily. "Two years away from home might be a good thing," he said to Lamedeer. "He's too rebellious for me to handle right now."

Subconsciously and sometimes consciously, Andrew continually wished to hell his mother hadn't died when he was born. Because she had, he reasoned nobody really liked him, a feeling that had begun when he was a little boy. What he mostly remembered about those years was that his father

ignored him while forever oozing sweet talk to his two older
sisters. His father's foreman, Lamedeer, understood. He
knew Andrew resented the enviable attentions his sisters
received, and Lamedeer did his best to pay attention to
Andrew but Andrew never really liked sitting on Lamedeer's
lap being read to. All the time he grew up, he prayed his
father would treat him like he was supposed to be treated, the
young man of the house, instead of a boy who caused his
mother's death; who fell over his own two feet, which
unfortunate happenings always drew a laugh. He hated
hearing his father say, "God damn it, don't be so clumsy." He
hated being told not to cry.

"Where the hell did you get that red hair? Your mother's
was black as coal and I'm brown-haired. We must have a
redheaded nigger in the woodpile someplace. It's curly too,
just like a nigger's."

He wondered who niggers were until on a visit to the
town, Mission, with his two sisters and father, they passed a
black man loading grain onto a truck.

"What in the hell is that nigger doing in Montana?" he
heard his father, who was not always tolerant, say. That's
how he knew the dark-skinned man was a black American,
not an Indian, like Lamedeer.

At this particular moment, Andrew was not discontent nor
was he angry. He was half lying in a tub of warm water. As
the tub was filling, he had thrown in two packets of bubble
bath powder; they were still at the height of bubbling and
Andrew felt mighty comfortable. Melissa, his sister, knowing
he liked bubble baths, had sent him a case of bubble bath
packets, and he kept the box locked in the bottom drawer of

his bureau in the dorm room. No need for others to snitch them.

The door opened. It seemed the door was always opening and closing when he was taking a bath. The third floor dormitory bathroom held not a single toilet, it held three of them plus a wide mirror over three sinks, along with this very big old-fashioned tub with the four claw feet, in which he was relaxing.

"I'm going to stink up the place," the intruder said annoyingly, smirking at Andrew as he moved towards the stall closest to the bathtub.

"Why can't you use the bathroom on the second floor?"

"I like to emit unpleasant odors near you."

"Yeah, damn you, you do this every time I take a bath."

"You look like a gay sitting in that tub. Are you?"

"Why, you bastard . . ."

"You got that wrong. My mother and father were married when I was conceived. I doubt yours were."

Andrew pulled the stopper out of the tub to empty it. He rose to his feet, furious. The water in the tub began to gurgle and the bubbles began to dissipate.

"Get out of here before I throw you out," he said vehemently.

"Oh, look at the sissy with the bubbles on his prick," Andrew's tormentor teased, laughing, Then he ran to the door, opened it and yelled down the hall.

"Hey, guys, come here and look at the sissy redhead."

Within seconds, before Andrew had a chance to grab his towel, which lay on a stool beside the tub, three other dorm occupants entered the bathroom. Two unzipped the flies on their jeans and began urinating into the bathtub.

"Gee, we're sorry you got out," taunted one. "You could have had yellow bubbles."

The four tormentors joined in a raucous laugh.

Andrew, still naked, stared at them, his blood boiling. They were making fun of him like his father did. He, with A grades at the Spokane Technical College, wanted to flail out at them and then run away and cry; instead, he stood dead still, unflinching, remembering what Lamedeer told him he must do. "Be stoic. Don't ever let anybody see you care when someone is mean to you. Get even by outsmarting them."

So he drew in a deep breath and poised himself and calmly pulled his towel around his body pretending to be indifferent to the boys watching him, sneering at him. Slowly, deliberately, he rubbed himself until he was completely dry. The four watched him silently. No one said a word, but the silence was ominous.

Since the huge beach towel was the only clothing item he had taken into the bathroom, he gathered it around his body nonchalantly, smiling benignly at the boys whose silence was taunting him for a comeback. He left the bathroom, yelling back in a carefree manner, "Well, now that you are stinking up the bathroom, you can all go do your homework. Maybe if you study hard none of you will fail our next programming class test." The programming class was the toughest class this term.

He slammed the dorm room door behind him.

He ran to his section of the room, yanked the curtain around the area that sheltered his bed, chest of drawers and desk from those of his two roommates and dressed quickly.

He had already laid out a fresh pair of socks, shorts, jeans and a sweatshirt. He pulled them on hurriedly. Tossing the wet towel on the floor beside his bed, he picked up his wallet and keys from the top of the chest, pushed in the lock that protected the four drawers, pulled back the curtains, went out into the big room, grabbed his jacket off the coat rack, opened the door quickly and dashed down the hall and the two flights of stairs to the outside.

He turned west, starting off on a run. He was headed for the bar-restaurant, Shingles and Eaves, five blocks away. It was a restaurant other students did not frequent. That's why he liked it. He didn't want any of those damn fools following him.

The sign, "Shingles and Eaves," lit up the near evening sky. It was not a large sign; however, the lettering was orange and green and every fifteen seconds orange lights flashed, then dimmed, green lights flashed, then dimmed. The sign did its job of luring passersby to look at it, and Andrew could see the sign flashing when he was still four blocks away. The bar-restaurant sat on the main floor of a three-story flat with two large windows facing the street.

Andrew entered breathless and moved quietly towards the bar at the back of the restaurant. It was good to be inside. Late autumn winds were never comfortable winds, wherever one lived, and he was cold. He hadn't really dried thoroughly after his bath, and the wind had pushed its chilling tendrils right through the threads of his sweatshirt, coiling itself all around his bare skin.

"Brrrr," he groaned, taking a seat in a booth close to the darkest end of the bar. Maybe I'll see that pretty girl again tonight, he said to himself, as he wrapped one long leg around the other.

"Hello."

The smooth, sultry voice was right behind him.

Unlocking his legs, he spun around on the bench quickly, startled. It was she, the pretty girl.

"Where did you come from?" he asked, surprised. She was sure pretty, he thought, although kind of on a lower level than he had been brought up to think of girls. He knew she dyed her hair blond, it was so even in color. He could tell that even in this dim light because it curled around her small face beguilingly, accenting her dark eyes and almost swollen, bright, full, red lipsticked mouth.

"I've been looking for you ever since you were here last." She smiled.

Ah, what a smile. It spread up at the corners and seemed to light up her whole slender small face. It told you it liked you. He grinned back.

"I've been busy at school," he said awkwardly, as if that would tell her he was too young for her to be talking to him.

"I guess you have." She smiled again, crinkling her nose at him. "You are from Montana, and you know how to travel over rough terrain like Indians do."

"Yeah." He couldn't help it. He burst out in a large free laugh, leaning backwards, relaxing, and remembering the evening they had spent talking together in one of the small booths next to the bar.

"You're funny," he said, when he had stopped laughing.

"I have a friend who wants to meet you."

"Oh?"

The bartender was standing, waiting.

"Your ID?" he asked Andrew, putting out his hand.

Andrew was embarrassed. "I . . . ah, I only want a coke."

"Yeah, sure," nodded the bartender, moving away to get the soft drink, "but you'll have to drink it sitting at the booth."

"If you can wait a few minutes," smiled the pretty girl ignoring the bartender, "I'll go get my friend."

"Do you have to?" asked Andrew, summoning his up-front courage. "I'd rather talk to you alone."

She looked at him, thinking. Then her mouth curved slightly, as if she had a secret he was not to know about and she lowered her eyes. He noticed how long her lashes were.

She said softly, "No, I guess I don't have to."

He sighed happily. He had done that one okay. He summoned more courage.

"Would you like a drink? Or ," and he grinned at her again, "are you old enough?"

"Yes, I am old enough, and yes, I'd love to have a drink with you." She came to his side and sat on the bench next to him. "And we don't need to get my friend who wants to meet you. I'd like to hear more stories about Montana and how you can track animals by paw marks which most people can hardly see." She moved closer to him and put her bare arm through his.

Andrew didn't move. He didn't dare move. He didn't know what to think; she was treating him as if he was somebody.

The bartender returned with Andrew's coke.

"The young man, Stan," the pretty girl said, "is buying me

a drink. I'll have scotch on the rocks. Oh, tell Mike," and she winked twice with her right eye, the one Andrew could not see, "that I am busy. You know."

The bartender nodded and moved away to the far end of the bar, but before he fixed her drink, he picked up the phone, and then looking back at Andrew and the blond girl, he dialed and spoke briefly into it.

"Who's Mike?"

"An employee of someone I work for."

"Oh." They were both silent.

"I never did know your name," said Andrew.

"It's a plain name, Betty," she said.

"My name is Andrew."

"Yes. You told me that the last time you were here. And you are from Montana. Wow! That is dream country. We're so close to it. Yet, I've never been there." Her arm squeezed his.

He felt a surge of blood flood through his body. Yes, he was younger than Betty, but obviously she liked him. Wow, he thought, guess I'm not so bad at all.

"You have quite a head of hair, Andrew," Betty said, her voice sliding sweetly over his name. "Do you have brothers and sisters, and if so, do all of them have red hair?"

"I have two sisters. One is kinda blond and the other has very beautiful blond hair."

"Your mother? Your father?"

"My father has brown hair. Well, it's kinda sandy-colored with grey now. And my mother...she had dark hair." His voice veiled. "She died when I was born."

"Oh, I'm so sorry."

Both were quiet for a moment. Then she said brightly, "She would have loved you."

"My father doesn't."

"Why not?" she exclaimed.

"I guess because my mother died."

"How sad. Well now, he's going to love the grown-up Andrew."

He looked at her as if he couldn't believe what he heard. His chest almost swelled. She was sitting so close to him he thought he could feel her heart beat.

"Well," and she smiled at him seductively, "would you like to go to Canada this weekend with me?"

"Huh?" He couldn't believe his ears. "What did you say?"

Betty laughed. She answered evenly, enjoiningly, moving her face close to his. "I have to go to Canada this weekend. I wonder if you had time to go with me. I'd like to have some company."

"You don't know me," he exclaimed.

"What I see I like." She smiled again.

"Well," he began.

"That is, of course," she continued hurriedly, putting all her charm into her husky voice, "if you don't have any classes. You could skip the ones on Monday and Tuesday."

Andrew was silent. His heart was now beating wildly.

Betty rubbed her face against his shoulder.

"I've thought so much about you since you were here last, and well, you look so strong and capable." She moved slightly away, and then faced him fully, her lips inches from his. "I don't like to travel by myself," she added.

"Well, yeah," stammered Andrew. He fell silent.

Her eyes fluttered. "I'm waiting for an answer."

"Well, yeah, I guess I could skip classes. But . . . well, where are you going to go to in Canada? What do you have to go there for?"

"I thought we could drive to Calgary."

"Calgary? Do you realize what a long trip that would be? We're in Spokane. We're not near Calgary. Calgary is a long way north and east. You couldn't get there in four days and back again without spending most of your time driving."

"With both me and you driving . . .?" She interrupted herself. "You do drive, don't you Andrew?"

"Of course. I started driving tractors when I was six. On our ranch, you know."

"Yes?"

"I got my license this past summer. I'm a good driver."

"I bet you are." Her voice was sultry again.

"Why do you want to go to Calgary?"

"Well, you won't say anything to anybody if I tell you, will you, Andrew?"

"Noo. . ." He wasn't sure.

"It will be a secret?"

"Yes," unsurely.

"I have an uncle in Calgary . . . now, we don't have to go to Calgary to meet him. I'll call him and we can meet him in Lethbridge. That's south of Calgary . . . near the Montana border. You know where Lethbridge is, don't you?"

"Of course. It's not too far from our ranch. I've been to Lethbridge lots of times."

"It's about 90 miles from the Montana border."

"Right. But why do you have to meet your uncle?"

"He has some jewelry he wants to get across the border without paying the high tariffs. I promised him I'd come and get it and take it across."

"And how will you sneak the jewelry across the border?"

"That's where you come in, Andrew."

"Oh?" His heart sank. She was trying to use him.

"You know all about border crossings. That's what you told me the last time we talked." Her cheek brushed his. Suddenly she turned abruptly to a sound she heard behind the booth. There was a chunky man standing behind her. Turning back to Andrew, checking to see if he had noticed the man and he had not, he looked deep in conflicted thought, she shook her head side to side as if smoothing her hair in place but meaning no. The man moved silently away, sitting down at a booth next to them.

"Yeah. I know the border crossings",
Andrew finally said, testily very upset.

"Particularly the one at Sweetgrass, south of Lethbridge, right?"

"Yeah." He was becoming irritable. His lips meshed together into a frown and he started to rise.

Her arms reached out to him, pulling him back down and she said softly, insistently, "You could sneak them across the border for me."

Andrew's mouth opened in shock and dismay.

"Couldn't you?" She pulled him closer and rubbed her cheek against his.

"That's why you've been nice to me," he said angrily. He half pushed her away from him. "You're trying to use me." He stood up, moving quickly to slide past her body.

She pulled him back with her arms.

"No," she said. "I fell for you the last time you were in here, Andrew. I'm crazy about you, don't you see? I know I'm being bold, but I thought maybe we could get together, and then when my uncle called me, well . . . ,"She stopped, watching the expression on his face, and then began again, brightly, "You don't have to go with me. I'll go by myself." Her lips began trembling. "You can come see me when you don't have classes." She hung her head.

Oh God, thought Andrew, this girl really likes me and if we go to Canada together, she's going to sleep with me. He stopped thinking of what she wanted him to do.

"Where will we stay while we're there?" he asked Betty, his mind already conjuring what would happen when their bodies locked together tightly.

"We could leave about six tomorrow morning," she answered softly, so as not to disrupt the smooth flow of their conversation, "and if we drive hard we can sleep in Lethbridge tomorrow night. I know just the place." Her voice caressed the word 'place.'

"My Mom and Dad used to stay there," she added brightly. "You see I am from Canada. You and I will have a real good time."

"Oh." Andrew was nonplussed. He did not know how to answer. All he could think about was this pretty, warm girl who liked him was sitting next to him and asking him to go away with her.

He looked at her carefully. She sure was pretty. Her nose was a little bit upturned, but not too much, and her eyes, large oval and dark brown, sparkled and kept their gaze directly on him when she spoke. Her manner was nice too. She seemed so sincere. Still, he'd better learn more. Just then, she leaned forward and kissed him right on his lips. He shoved out a startled breath and felt a shiver surge through his body and a slow exciting hardening of his penis. So he sat motionless for a moment, silently, his mind churning, his nerves tingling. He simply could not think logically.

"Don't you want another coke?" she asked, sighing. "Oh, that was so nice." She meant the kiss. She hung her head shyly and lowered her eyes.

"Yes, it was nice."

"Another coke?"

"Yes."

"Come. There's a better booth back in the corner. I'd like another kiss. If you don't mind, that is." Her lips parted in a small, embarrassed grin. "That first one was so good," she said, getting up, taking his hand and pulling him towards a darkened booth.

"No, I don't mind," he said. He felt his penis beginning to push against the zipper of his pants.

They passed the short, chunky man who was sitting, half leaning against the wall in the booth next to them. Andrew did not notice him; Betty did. The man pursed his fingers together in an 'okay' mode and smiled.

Boy, she is really something, Andrew thought, as they sidled along the bench of the booth and he felt one of her legs climb over his.

He put his hand on her leg. It was bare. He kissed her.

"Wow, Betty," he mumbled. He kissed her again.

Chapter Six

J anice slid into the front seat of the car gracefully although her body was tense with anger. With a grim face, she stared straight front at nothing, turning only to glare at Gustav as he shut the car door. It was difficult for her to think she was so upset, she was furious with her father for sending her to the house and for firing Rob, which she was certain he did as soon as she was out of sight. So what if she was kissing him and he was kissing her! She liked being kissed. She was twenty years old and every romance she had had since she had entered high school had been nipped in the bud. Trips away, clothes galore, a horse, a cat, all manner of gifts, none of which took the place of affection! It was as if she was never old enough to decide whom she wanted to make friends with, to kiss, to make love to.

Ah, if her father only knew. Well, no matter, she would see Rob tonight at their usual meeting place and find out for sure if her father fired him, even though she was certain without inquiring that her father had. It was his pattern. And she was infatuated with Rob. She knew she became infatuated easily, that was a problem of hers, but she loved to flirt and always got in over her head. She'd marry Rob and that would make her father angry. Well, he deserved it, never allowing her to do anything, to go anyplace without a chaperone, to be anything all by herself; she had to be Daddy's little girl! Huh! She always had to be his 'dear dear daughter,' so like your mother. Mother was dead.

Oh, she was furious. All she wanted to do was to get away once and for all and if she had any money, she would.

"Is it Mission?" Gustav asked, breaking into her thoughts as he pulled out of the driveway, peering over at her hesitatingly, aware she was in an ugly mood.

`'"Mission, Gustav. Stop at the Mission Inn restaurant. I'd like a cup of coffee and a doughnut."

"You just drank three cups at the house," Merry said. "You've been drinking too much coffee lately, Janice. Is something wrong?"

"No, dear Merry," she answered, spitting out the words, "of course nothing is the matter. My world has fallen apart, that's all. Anyway, I am hungry for a doughnut, and the Mission Inn has wonderful doughnuts."

"We'll stop there," said Gustav, hoping her mood would take a different direction, "as long as we can join you."

"Of course you can join me," Janice laughed. "I'm really bribing you. If you fill up with doughnuts and coffee, you won't mind my asking you to take me to Great Falls. I want to shop at an expensive dress shop."

"Halls Dress Store in Mission is expensive," said Merry.

"Yes, Merry, but Mrs. Hall does most of her shopping in Great Falls and ups the prices. I want to go to the Gown Shop on Central; their buyer goes to New York and Los Angeles for new styles. Anyway, I want to see a variety, not just two or three different styles."

"Okay, Janice," laughed Gustav. "We consider ourselves bribed. Even before we have doughnuts. Your beautiful smile bribes us every time."

"Oh, Gustav, I'm not smiling and you know it," she said, sighing deeply. "I'm so upset."

Oh, oh, he thought, she's back on the bad mood track.

"I see that, Janice. What's wrong today?"

"Today?" She spat the word at him.

"I'm sorry, Janice, but . . . "

"Oh, I know why you use the word 'but' . . . I'm like this often." She sighed again. "I'm nothing, Gustav." She almost shouted the word. "Nothing. I can't do anything. I can't be myself, ever. I'm nothing, Merry," she repeated, turning her head to include the Indian woman who was sitting in the back seat frowning, head and shoulders hunched forward, so she could hear everything said between Gustav and Janice. Merry was upset because Janice was upset; she loved her very much.

"Father had Rob fired this morning."

"That cowboy Lamedeer hired two weeks ago?"

"Yes. He was nice; he was some one to talk to and most of all he listened to me. He thought what I had to say was important, not just words to shove away. Anyway, I think I am falling in love with him, and then father had to do that. That is why I'm furious because he had no right - Rob did his job, and what we wanted to do together was none of Father's business."

"Oh, Janice," exclaimed Merry, her voice on edge. "You can't be infatuated with that ranch hand."

"Why not?" Janice suddenly burst into tears. "Rob was fun. He was my comfort ever since Lamedeer hired him. Merry, Father never gives me a chance and he never lets me do anything. Why do you think I always want to go shopping? I'll never wear all the clothes in my closet even though I dress up in them, show myself to my rag doll, Oscar, and undress again. Damn, I'm grown up. Why doesn't father let me go?" Janice kept crying.

Merry leaned forward and put her arms on the back of Janice's seat. "He is going to let you go, Janice. Lamedeer told me he agreed to let you go to New York."

"Hah! When!"

"As soon as you want to leave. Lamedeer told me that this morning. He had a talk with your father."

"Yes, Merry. My father will sit down and tell me yes, and then have an excuse to keep me here. You know full well he didn't let me go anyplace this past summer." She lowered her voice in imitation of her father. "'We are having two guests from Denmark, and you're to show them Montana.' Yes, and how did I show them Montana? With Gustav driving and you as chaperone, Merry. No, if we wanted to go dancing, NO if we wanted to spend the weekend at a spa. It was always NO to whatever took me away from him or you as my chaperone overnight. You always had to be at my side." Janice's voice was tremulous with her anger until she fell silent. When she finished complaining, neither Gustav nor Merry said anything so the only sounds were moving car sounds.

Janice looked back at Merry, who sat stricken. "I'm sorry, Merry. I know how good you are, and how you wish things were different for me, but nobody understands. I'm grown up. Father doesn't want me to have a life, and I'm really nothing to him but a look alike of a memory."

"Janice . . ." interrupted Merry.

"Oh, Merry, please don't sympathize with him. Yes, he is

a sweet man. Yes, he is a handsome man. Yes, he is a good-hearted man. Yes, he loves his family. Hah! He's a hard taskmaster, just look at Annabelle; she's been in love with father for years. He uses her but he won't let her go, and he's mean to her and he's like that with me. All he thinks about is how much I look like my mother, and he won't let me go. Now he finds me kissing Rob and he fires him. Oh, he's awful."

Gustav and Merry swung their heads.

"That cowboy, Rob . . . Janice," said Merry, "he's not much good except for being a cowboy, Janice."

"How do you know?"

"I know just by looking at the way he acts."

"Well, he's good to me, and he's exciting. He's like father in some ways because he wants what he wants and he won't let go."

"Oh Janice!" interrupted Merry softly. Then she added quickly, leaning forward in her seat and touching Gustav's shoulder. "Slow down. Stop, Gustav. I want Janice here in the back seat with me. She needs my arms around her." She leaned towards Janice who was now, her head tilted forward, crying silently into her hands.

"Thank goodness, there's nobody in front or behind, we've got a lonely freeway," mused Gustav as he slowed and moved the car onto the shoulder. "Not like those big city freeways, for sure," he muttered, "your comforting would have been back to front, if it were."

The car stopped. Merry's hands were already on the doorknob. She swung it open. Barely had the car halted, she deftly pulled the front door open while Janice was undoing her seat belt. She maneuvered Janice into the back seat quickly.

"Here now, my sweet girl, lean your head against my shoulders and cry. You haven't cried for a long time, have you dear?"

"No." Janice answered in a soft, wavering voice.

"Go ahead, Gustav," said Merry. "We're okay now."

"To Mission? Or back home?"

"To Mission." Janice spoke up, her voice suddenly clear and clean. "I still want that doughnut." Her eyes were not quite dry.

"Why not Blue Hill?"

"No. The motel." Janice turned to Merry. "I'm okay now, Merry. Thank you. I just get out of sorts at times. Father makes me so upset."

"Janice, my dear," soothed Merry. "It's all right. And don't forget, you are going to New York soon. That ought to make you very happy."

Janice was silent.

"Would you like me to go with you?"

Janice rolled her eyes, one still with a tear hanging from the bottom lid, lifted her head and laughed. "Oh Merry, how sweet, but no, of course not. I want this adventure to be all my own."

"Good," laughed Merry back at her. "So you're not in love with that dumb cowboy anymore." It was a statement, not a question.

"Oh, he's nice, so nice," sighed Miranda.

"If you thought you were, how awful that would have been for you," said Merry. "You'd soon be really drowning in sorrow. You, who hate ranch life, married to a cowpoke. You'd be dragging yourself down - going from ranch to ranch, living from hand to mouth, bringing up children who would never know a bedroom they could call their own for more than a few months; you'd be absolutely miserable, beautiful Janice, throwing your life away like that - all for a fleeting, passionate love affair."

Janice looked surprised. "I never thought of it like that."

"No, so naive you are. I had better go with you to New York. If I don't, you'll probably fall for the first man who smiles at you."

"No, I wouldn't," Janice answered. "It's not attention I want, Merry. I just want everybody to know it's me they are looking at. Most of all I want Father to know it's me he's looking at. I don't want to be a memory of my mother who's dead. My father is always saying he loves me, but he doesn't even know who I am. He knows who Melissa and Andrew are, but not me. I'm a porcelain doll who resembles some one else, and it's like I sit on a shelf unless he wants to show me off to someone. Then he takes me off the shelf and says, 'Look, doesn't she resemble her mother?'"

"Janice, if I didn't know you so well and love you so well, I would say you were spoiled. Your imagination goes wild. Your father is not like that. Don't portray him to be such a difficult man. You know he's always attentive to whatever you want even though he's protective of you. I don't know if there is anything you wanted he hasn't given you."

"So you think, Merry," said Janice, annoyed. "I know better. I'll be so glad to go to New York and learn how to be myself, not what Father pretends I am like."

Merry frowned and shook her head sadly.

"I am sorry to have argued with you, Janice, it is not my place, but I am anxious about you at times."

Janice shook her head defiantly. "Look how you are! Here I am twenty years old and everybody - everybody - treats me like a baby."

They both fell silent. Janice freed herself of Merry's arms and stared out the window at the brown prairie landscape.

Janice was such a complex girl, thought Merry, so difficult to be with at times, yet so sweet and beguiling, one could not help but love her, and love Janice, Merry did. Her beauty seemed to stand in the way of everything she wanted to do. That's why Marv, Lamedeer, she (Merry) and the whole ranch family were so careful with her. She sat quietly, remembering the first time Janice got into man trouble. Merry's cousin, Martha, had telephoned her on a school holiday afternoon, several years past.

"Do you know where Marv's oldest girl, Janice, is right now?" her cousin had asked her.

"Yes, Martha. She's in Great Falls shopping for a dress for the Junior Prom."

"Humph," had answered her cousin.

"Gustav drove four girls from school down there. Why? Is something wrong?"

"You better do some checking, Merry."

"What has happened to Janice?" Merry's voice had become shrill with anxiety.

"Well, when I saw her just a few minutes ago she wasn't shopping with any girls, instead, she was sitting in a booth at the Royal Casino, very lovey dovey with an older man."

"How do you know this?"

"I saw them. Remember, I deliver wrapped sandwiches from the deli" (where she worked) "every afternoon to Royal. Janice didn't see me when I walked by her."

"How do you know it was Janice?"

"How could anybody forget her after they laid eyes on her?"

There had been more to the discovery, and Merry realized her cousin was telling the truth. When Janice returned home with Gustav that afternoon, empty handed, with no packages, Merry was able to question her. She asked if she had not liked any of the dresses she and the other three girls had tried on. "No, none," Janice had answered tersely, adding, "I have to go to town again tomorrow and look some more."

"And I'll chaperone you this time," said Merry easily. "I can always tell what looks best on you."

"No," Janice had answered irritably. "I'm going again with my friend Susie with Gustav driving. I don't need you to chaperone me." She had then hurried away quickly towards the stairs to go to her room, tossing back the words, "Thanks just the same, Merry." Merry, of course, found a way to accompany Janice and Gustav the next day, much to Janice's chagrin.

The "older man" soon surfaced as Janice's history teacher. Their tête-à-têtes were revealed when Janice's after school volunteering was found out to be a front for their romantic meetings. Gustav had been the discoverer along with the school's principal, so Janice spent the next two weeks at home, allegedly suffering from a bad case of flu. A substitute history teacher appeared and finished out the term since the original one resigned due to "pressing family matters."

There were other secretive romances; Lamedeer, Merry, Swallow and Gustav nipped most in the bud. Marv was never told of Janice's alleged indiscretions. And Merry suffered for her beautiful young charge who was headstrong, unpredictable, and obviously full of hormonal desires. Merry thought she understood the reasons for Janice's rebellion. It seemed Janice had to reach out and grab affection from strangers in order to get even with her family for taking away her mother; that concept was not a nice one to attach to Janice, yet Merry knew Janice harbored resentment along with a deep lonely grief for a missing mother.

Gustav was slowing the car. "Stop your muttering," he said good naturedly, turning his head towards the silent back. "We're here."

"Oh darn," said Janice, suddenly light of voice, "we're at the motel and my crying on your shoulder, Merry, has loosened my hair bun."

"Undo it. We love your hair down, hanging naturally."

"Let me get my comb out of my purse. It's on the front seat." Gustav parked in a stall in front of the motel and waited until Merry had retrieved Janice's purse from the front seat and helped rearrange her hair.

Chapter Seven

J ohn Territoni stood quietly in the corner of the horse shed, waiting. He could feel his heart pounding in anticipation. Within the hour he was going to kill a redheaded young drug courier. He was eagerly looking forward to the killing of the unsuspecting courier — that is, if the young man showed up, if he hadn't been apprehended by custom agents. John hadn't killed anyone for some time.

It was a cold, dark October night, fog raw. Even though fur-lined gloves covered John's hands, he had to squeeze and unsqueeze his long, slim fingers every few minutes to keep circulation moving.

His body was warm. He had layered his clothes well. On the outside, he wore a lined, western great coat with hood. It covered his Eddie Bauer wool shirt that covered a wool undershirt. His New York styled jeans covered long johns. Warm though his body was, even though he wore two pair of heavy wool socks under his boots, he had to wiggle his toes periodically. His feet, like his fingers, went numb if he didn't keep them moving.

John was a tall man. He stood six foot three in stocking feet. His hair was dark, his face swarthy. An aquiline nose was molded onto an unlined, deeply tanned face that, though thirty-five years of age, still held a trace of childhood. It was the kind of boyish face that enchanted women. His trim, narrow, black mustache hung over full pouting lips. He had grown the mustache fifteen years earlier, just after he had turned twenty. He grew it because a man at a party told him it appeared his lower jaw jutted over his upper jaw.

"Like undershot?" he had asked the man, his mouth twitching angrily. He did not like being criticized.

"Let's look at your teeth."

"I have an even bite," he had snarled.

"Ah. So you have. That's why, then. You ought to grow a mustache."

"Why?"

"You'd look better in profile."

"Thanks," John had said roughly, sizing up the lanky towhead, dressed in black slacks, a white tee-shirt with two filled pockets on the left side, white tennis shoes on his feet, and with a smooth face with hardly a trace of a five-o'clock shadow; a young busybody who had dared criticize his appearance. He strode away haughtily to the bar where his bodyguard was waiting.

"Mike," he said to the older man, who sat with one well-muscled and tattooed arm resting on the bar and the other lifting a shot glass to his mouth. His Adams apple moved up and down with each swallow of liquor.

"Yeah, John, what is it?"

"See that goon - the skinny towhead over by the punchbowl?"

"Yeah." John's bodyguard, short, dumpy, his squat figure belying a hard-knit, heavily muscled body under the blue-black pin-striped suit he wore, was at least fifteen years older than John. He quickly scanned the banquet room. His eyes stopped when he located the young man who was lifting a glass to his mouth.

"Follow him home. I want to pay him a visit."

"Yeah?" Mike's eyebrows raised, a frown appearing on his forehead.

"Yeah. He deserves it."

"What's he done, John?"

"He insulted me."

"He doesn't look very menacing."

"Well," and John smiled, his wide lips showing an even line of orthodontist-groomed teeth, "I haven't had any fun for awhile. I'm bored."

Mike shook his head slowly. "I'll follow him home, John. I'll tell you where he lives. But Christ, man, someday you're going to get into trouble doing this."

John shrugged his handsome shoulders.

The police found the young man several days later in his tiny one-room apartment. His body had begun to stink and a neighbor had called the police. Nothing was out of place, but the kitchenette counter held several empty hypodermic needles and blood from a sloppy castration that spilled all over his lower body. It filled his right hand too because those fingers held several cut-off pieces placed there. His gruesome murder was never solved.

This night, fifteen years later, John Territoni smiled as he thought about that dead young man. He planned to execute his courier the same way. There would be those shining moments when the courier would look in horror at John realizing what John had done to him and that he was going to die. What John did and how his victim reacted was what gave him his incredible sexual high.

It reminded him of the look his mother gave him when she

realized the deaths of her beloved cats were because her son killed them by injecting each of the six, over a period of several years, with poison. It was the look she gave him when she came out of the bathroom wearing a see-through chiffon robe over her naked body and found her lover dead on the floor in her bedroom, his cut-off penis stuck in his hand with John still standing over the bloody body with a needle and a large wire bloody fence-cutter in his hands.

"Dead as a doornail," laughed John's father heartily, when he arrived home a quarter of an hour later. He patted his 16-year-old son on his shoulders.

Although he patted his tall, dark haired son, who stood with a self-satisfied snarl hanging on his lips, he turned a different face, one of almost fearful shock, to his two bodyguards who stood behind him, one finally retching and then running to the bathroom, his hands full of his regurgitated stomach contents.

That was the last time John saw his mother. She still had the look of horror on her face when his father's goons pulled her out of the bedroom and down the stairs, still in the chiffon robe, still naked underneath.

"Don't trust my son," John's father, Joseph, told his gang members at their next meeting. "I love him but I don't trust him. He has a gruesome side to him, and I think he's getting his sex from cutting off penises. He's always been a dirty-minded kid, vengeful and arrogant and I've never been able to tame him. Those characteristics don't belong in our world, at least not in the body business we're in. I'm warning you, don't ever let him lead, or he will eventually take you down with him. I'm aware of his goddamn sadistic faults, that's why I'm going to give him a bodyguard full time from now on.

John's father was the head of a lucrative sex-slave organization, its headquarters in New York City. The trade extended throughout Asia, Europe and Africa, not only in the United States. His various employees who lived in big cities lured young runaways into prostitution, first with dinner dates, then with feigned affection, stylish clothes and money. They also enjoyed snatching pretty high school girls right off the bus stops while they were waiting for buses and from automobiles in shopping mall parking lots into which they were placing packages. These girls were raped, drugged and put to work, many of them flown overseas to the Philippines or China or Europe. The men who grabbed these innocent young girls, some of them only 12 or 13 years old, were bold, dirty men, eager-at-the-ready accomplices. Most of the girls appeared in well-publicized, missing girl reports long after they had been spirited out of the country on the organization's jets to work in their "destination country's" prostitution houses, so they were never found.

One of the jobs John's father gave to him was to introduce girls to prostitution through the use of drugged drinks and beatings, then when thought necessary, needles. After John got through with their bodies, the battered and cowed girls who learned how to please the best went next to his father, who was addicted to fetishism, before they were sent overseas to other fetishists.

The organization owned many hidden companies. One of these was an obscure film company called Novelette Films. Its main studio was located on the fifth floor of a seedy, six story printing company (also owned by the gang) in New York City's midtown west side.

The girls used in the films were, of course, innocents being introduced to the multi-billion dollar sex trade by acting in pornographic movies, Novelette Films was always well in the black with its sought after films featuring all kinds of sexual activity with young girls. To justify its respectability, once in a while the company made a C western (could there be such a thing?). Looking for sites for a new western was supposed to be the reason John had flown to Montana. The only reason this despicable hoodlum was allowed to meet with two ranchers was that he could cunningly charm the seat off of anyone's pants and he had a bodyguard with him who was always ready to prevent John from showing his ugly side. Each of the ranchers was hoping sites on his particular ranch would be chosen for this western. They did not suspect Novelette Films was a porn film company; few people did for the company hid its sexual charged films well.

John stood shivering in the horse shed, his mind wandering back and forth with memories, at the same time squeezing his fingers and wiggling his toes to keep the cold from numbing them. He waited patiently for the young redheaded courier he had chosen to carry the heroin across the border, the one he was going to kill. Mike, his bodyguard of fifteen years, only knew John was picking up drugs and paying out some money. He had no idea John decided to kill the messenger. Mike was waiting for him in a car 200 yards away off the highway, hidden by a good growth of fur trees.

John clicked the light switch on his watch to see the time, 2:10 a.m. The courier was now twenty minutes late. Another five minutes passed. He heard footsteps, light and measured footsteps on rough frozen ground. Smiling, he slowly removed his left glove, dropped it on the ground beside his left foot and ran his fingers over the outside of the leather case he carried on a belt over his greatcoat. He smiled again. The needles inside were poised for action. He bent down to look at his new heavy wire fence cutters that he had bought in Spokane on their scheduled stop and sneaked past Mike by hiding them in the inside pocket of his greatcoat; touching them brought a big grin on his face in anticipation of what he was going to do. Lastly he picked up the thermos, it too was ready. Just then he heard the sound of a hand softly touching the sidewall of the horse shed.

His welcoming cough was barely audible.

"That you, John?"

"Yes."

"Andrew here."

He grinned, intent on what lay ahead. He whispered back in a thin, emotion choked voice, "You are late."

The form came into view. Not that he could see it very well, but he knew it by heart from the interview several nights earlier. He had watched Mike question the young man from the transom in the room next to where they talked. The form was of a lanky, skinny young man in his teens, red headed, blue eyed, with a heavily freckled face.

"How come you're late?"

"Those border patrol agents are pretty hip. They kept touring up and down the ranch road I crossed. Thank God they didn't have dogs with them. I lay holed up in a tree until they gave up."

"Good for you. Thirsty?"

"Yeah. Like to see my money first though."

"Of course. I have it here in this little satchel." His key ring flashlight blinked onto the ground where the satchel lay. "And your back pack?"

"On my back, man," laughed the courier. "And it's heavy. Your friends put some BC Bud in with the other stuff." His young voice turned gruff. "I've been really lied to. This wasn't a diamond bust. These are drugs I am carrying."

"But you had a real good time before you got the stuff, right?"

Andrew blushed.

John didn't wait for an answer. "So you really didn't mind doing this. We'll get your back pack off in a minute," he said.

"First, your drink."

John pointed the light from the tiny flash onto the ground along the back of the wood wall where the thermos lay. "Here, it's a drink of water. It's all I have with me. After me, I need some too."

John turned off the light, opened the thermos and lifted it to his lips, although he did not drink, he gurgled noisily as if he was drinking. The GHB he had slipped into the water was odorless, colorless too, as if that mattered in the dark. The amount he put into the drink would cause fairly quick incapacity.

"Here." He handed the thermos to Andrew. Turning on the light again, he watched smiling as the redheaded boy leaned backward as if swallowing several long drinks from the thermos. John smiled and his eyes glistened in anticipation of what he was going to do. "Here's your money," he said, catching his breath, grinning ear to ear, his heart pounding, his prick hardening because he knew that when he killed this god-damned courier and cut off his prick he would experience a full and absolutely magnificent, heady sexual explosion. His body could hardly wait.

After Andrew slowly capped the thermos and handed it back to him. John bent down, picked up the satchel as if to hand it to Andrew, but before he could straighten up, he found himself down on the ground, felled by a terrific blow on his head. Along with the blow, which dizzied him so completely that he could not get up immediately, he felt his hands being jerked behind his back and tied with a thick rope. "I need your help, I can't knot it well enough," a woman's voice was saying. Indeed, John was pulling against the rope, jerking his hands away from the rope but another sudden blow, this time to his groin made him pull up his legs in anguish. And again! John screamed. The fucking redheaded courier was kicking his penis.

"Whoops," he heard in a sympathetic tone. "You must be tired. Here, I've got something for you to fix that." Hands pulled open his mouth and liquid poured from the thermos down his throat. Although John coughed and sputtered, none of it came back up.

"You'll wake you up in a while," he heard the redhead say. "Don't get too cold. You don't want to freeze to death." A second or two later, he felt his hands being pulled sideways with the rope tightening hard over them, but that was all he felt, his eyes were closing because his body was relaxing as the GHB solution he had put in the thermos of water to drug the courier raced through his own bloodstream. His handsome face struck with horror as his eyelids shut down.

"Ha ha ha ha," Before he passed out he heard laughing, not from just one voice, but two and one of them from a woman.

When he woke up, it was still dark and a rifle was poking him in his side.

The voice above him was tough, but not a cop's voice.

"Who are you?" it asked. "You are on my property and obviously up to no good, or you wouldn't be tied up. What in the hell are you doing on my ranch and who tied you up?"

"Well . . " began John slowly, his mouth so dry he could hardly speak, "I came here to meet someone and he attacked me. He tied me up and stole the money I brought to buy his gun." He was shivering from the cold so badly his voice came out in bits and pieces.

"Why did you meet here?"

"We were talking at the restaurant some miles back, and the man suggested we stop at the first turn off. Everything on the road is fenced. This is the first place that looked like a good turn off. Sheltered and out of the way, you know."

"You didn't know this man before you talked to him at the restaurant."

"No. I am from New York and just passing through. Can you untie me now?" John maneuvered himself to a sitting position by pushing his two numbed legs together and jamming them against the ground for traction - God, his penis hurt - and he used his tied hands to push forward.

The man standing above him backed off a foot before he asked, "Do you have a gun?"

"No. You are not very trusting, are you?" John asked that question as nice as he could, even though he was growing angrier by the second.

"You just told me you parked your car here, but I don't see one."

"Oh. They stole that too." John groaned. "How will I ever get back on the road?"

"Where are you going?"

"I am meeting two ranchers in Great Falls in the morning. I am a movie producer and I am looking over their sites for some of our shots, plus scenery."

He had convinced the farmer because the heavy-set, balding man then knelt down beside him and taking out a pocketknife from his heavy work pants, slit the rope.

"Thank you," said John civilly, wondering what he was going to do about this farmer; he did not want him to know his real business here or even that he was here. In an instant, he decided he was going to do what he came to do, kill. This would be a fun killing. Standing up, shaking his hands to remove their chilled tingling, he quickly planned the steps he would take to end this stupid farmer's life. First, he felt for his leather case on his hips. It was there. He knew the needles inside were ready. Then he measured the distance between him and the farmer. The stupid farmer was standing too trusting close to him.

This was going to be easy.

"You know," he began, but on the words, 'you know,' his right arm hit the farmer who was still holding his rifle in his hand. The rifle tumbled over several times and hit the ground, so did the farmer. John knew how to hit. In a split second, he opened his leather case, grabbed a needle and with the needle poised in his left hand he hit the farmer, who had gotten up and was lunging at him, full on his face. He heard the needle break as it hit bone. Instinctively, the farmer recoiled. John moved forward quickly and shoved the farmer back onto the ground. Grabbing a second needle, he sunk the point into the farmer's cheek just below the bone. The farmer's voice was loud with fury as John deftly reached into his leather case again.

He grabbed a third needle, hit the farmer on his nose with his free hand and jumped on top of the farmer, ripping the buttons off his heavy jacket, tearing the sleeve of his heavy shirt and shoving the needle into his arm. The farmer tried in vain to push him away.

"That's okay, friend," chuckled John softly. "You're done for now. I just injected you with poison. You're dead, man." John then punched him in the face. The punch wasn't hard enough to knock him out but it sure shut him up. He laughed gleefully, got off the farmer's chest, leaped to his feet again and grabbed the brand new fence cutter. In an instant, the farmer's sounds were too loud even for this desolate place. John pulled a white rag out of a pocket and stuffed it in the farmer's mouth.

After a great while, exhausted but wonderfully ecstatic from his wild orgasm, he pulled out another white rag from his greatcoat, wiped two needles, laid them on the farmer's chest, smoothed the ground with his broom, feeling for the broken part of the third needle, couldn't find it, shrugged his shoulders, smoothed the ground again after placing the pieces he had cut off in his castration in the farmer's outstretched dead hand, picked up his belongings — yeah, this backpack is sure heavy, he smirked to himself — and started to leave.

"Damn, I forgot the fence cutter," he muttered and returned to pick it up. It was bloody but he had to carry it off. He jammed it, with the telltale blood of the farmer on it, in his large inside pocket where it had been hidden before.

The road lay less than 50 feet away. At its edge, he pulled out slippers from his greatcoat back pocket, pulled off his boots, replaced them with the slippers and with the boots encumbering his already loaded arms moved across the road. The car sat another 100 feet up the road. Mike was sitting tensely at the wheel.

"All okay," said John. "Once I'm in, get going. Nice and easy now."

"Yeah," answered Mike.

The car moved. Mike turned on the headlights a half mile down the road. John was busy shredding his boots with a knife.

"Where's the cylinder?" he asked, the car traveling smoothly down the highway within the speed limit.

"On the floor right in back of my seat."

"Okay."

Quickly, stealing a glance at Mike who was busy watching the road, he pulled the wire cutters out of his coat and quickly stuffed it inside the cylinder. Then within a few more minutes, the shredded boots, even the soles, were also shoved inside the long round cylinder. John called to Mike to open the glove compartment and give him the package tape. When it was in hand, he wrapped the end of the cylinder tightly, tearing the tape when he had secured the package.

"Mail this in Billings."

"Right."

"Whew," sighed John finally, settling wearily back in his seat.

"How did it go? You were there a long time. Was he late?"

"Yeah." John decided not to tell Mike right now that the redheaded courier had outsmarted him. He was so filled with venom on how he had been deceived; he didn't even want to talk about it. Anyway, if Mike knew, he wouldn't let him do the actual killing of the fucking bastard and the woman. "Fun with a capital F," laughed John, ending it with a false giggle. "Except . . ."

"Except what?"

"I had to kill a farmer."

"You son of a bitch. Tell me."

"Later. It's all right. I obscured my tracks. He must have seen us a couple of days ago. He didn't know about the courier. He got there too late," and John laughed again.

"Hell. Your father will be furious."

"Hell! It was necessary. Absolutely necessary." His voice rose.

There was silence.

"We'll be in Mission in five minutes."

"Right." John rolled down the window and hung the thermos upside down to empty it, then he remembered it was empty.

He undid the backpack. "They gave him some marijuana too, buds," he said, as he removed a half dozen cellophane packets and stuffed them in one of his Eddie Bauer shirt pockets. He was leaving his bloody greatcoat for Mike to get rid of. "So it's heavy. Be careful when you leave me. I don't think there's any problem at this point."

"Oh, I'll be careful, John. You be careful. You shouldn't be staying here."

"I can't leave now."

"I know."

"Let me off at the far end of the motel." As John spoke, he was removing his slippers, replacing them with heavy-soled shoes. "And put these slippers and the leather pouch in that other cylinder. Send them off, too."

"Yeah. It's all arranged, John. We'll be at the motel in a minute. See the lights?"

"Yeah. Just slow down, Mike. Don't stop. No need making my exit obvious. Right here, Mike. I'm getting out."

Mike slowed the car. John jumped out, carrying nothing but what he had in his pockets.

He stood on the edge of the highway and watched the car disappear. He walked slowly to the motel, his mind reeling with ideas on how to find and then how to kill the fucking redheaded courier along with whoever was with him. Suddenly he stopped dead. He swore. He knew who the female with the redhead was. It was that prick-sucking cunt from the bar, the skinny blond his boss moved up from the street to serve Shingles and Eaves customers. The cunt he taught. Oh, he knew how to kill her.

He went on; saw no one, met no one. If he had, the fog would have obscured him just as it obscured the lights of the motel and the night around him. He felt for the key to his room long before he reached the long row of linked cabins. Making out the outline of his black jeep, he moved silently to the door closest to it and with his hand on the knob quietly slid the key in the lock. He opened the door; it was black inside.

"Good," he said to himself, knowing a chair was by the door because he had carefully placed it there himself earlier in the evening. He sat on it and silently took off his shoes and his two pair of socks, then stood up and shed his shirt, his wool undershirt, socks and pants on the chair. When naked, he went to the dresser beside the bed, picked up the traveling alarm clock that sat there, took it in hand and moved to the bathroom, again silently. He shut the door behind him; turned on the light, reset the clock from 4 a.m. back to 1 a.m. He reset his watch to the same time. He ran the water for a shower. He left the shower when his body was hot with no trace of the cold that had pervaded it earlier, put on his wristwatch and took the small clock back to the dresser. Then he moved to the bed, smiling as he did.

He thought to himself, I gave her enough. As he got into the bed, he said, "Come on, baby. Let's at it one more time." He shook the body of the woman that lay there.

There was no answer.

He shook her again.

"Ah. . . ," the naked woman in the bed opened her eyes sleepily.

He shook her again, gently.

"Ah, no. I'm so tired." Her voice was muffled with sleep.

"Hey baby. I paid for this. Spread those legs."

"What time is it?" she murmured.

"I think it's one o'clock. Let me look. Yeah. See?" He shoved his hand with the watch on it in front of her face and lit the dial.

"Yeah, I see," she sighed sleepily, testily. "If you have to."

"Yeah. I want another piece. I want it active too. Got to get my money's worth, you know. Then we can both go back to sleep. Here, have a cough drop," he added, reaching to the little table beside the bed, taking up a pill and shoving it into her mouth. "Your breath smells funny."

"Ugh, that cough drop tastes funny."

"That's why it's called a cough drop."

The pill was covered with enough sedative to knock her out in about ten minutes. He had decided he wanted to ride her without much participation. She wasn't a great piece but held his alibi.

She fell asleep in the middle of the woo. He climbed off her, got up and took another shower. This time he wanted to remove the sweat of both their bodies. Then he reset the watch and the alarm clock to the correct time, opened his suitcase, which earlier he had placed under the chair, took out a white shirt, blue silk tie, socks and a tan jacket with matching colored slacks, shoved everything he had worn to the horse shed inside the suitcase, dressed, shaved, sat in the chair by the door and dozed. He awoke about 7 a.m., checked that everything he had brought into the motel room was in the suitcase and closed the door behind him.

Once in his jeep, which sat directly outside the motel room door, he took three of the cocaine packets, which he had removed from his shirt earlier, out of his jacket pocket and carefully shoved them one at a time into the spines of several books he carried with him. He started the jeep and moved it down to the other end of the motel in front of the door of the restaurant. He plunked fifty cents into the newspaper carrier (just outside the door), and when he pulled the cover open, removed a newspaper and placed three packets of cocaine into a side plastic pocket in the carrier.

He entered the restaurant. He sat down in a booth next to the doorway where he could observe the newspaper carrier whenever it was approached.

"Good morning, Annie," he said in his smooth, suave voice as the stout, grey-haired, wrinkle-faced waitress approached with a cup, saucer and a pot of hot coffee.

"Have a good sleep, John?" She winked at him, knowing full well who had shared the room with him. It was her niece.

"You betcha," he grinned. "Maybe that's why I need my coffee nice and strong this morning. Energy, you know!"

They both smiled.

Chapter Eight

John Territoni sat at a table with two other men in the Mission Motel restaurant when Janice, Merry and Gustav walked in. He was seated so he could face the door, waiting for the bartender to pick up the three white envelopes of cocaine from the paper box. John wished he would hurry and do so. He did not dare leave until that was done. Although his eyes were on the door, he was also explaining to the two ranchers he had invited to breakfast that his New York film company (he lied, it was not his company), Novelette Pictures, wanted to shoot high prairie scenes on one or both of their ranches. Their next film, he explained, was to be a western. The film's opening would feature the heroine and hero riding over high Montana prairies with the backdrop of mountains beautifying the scene. Other shots throughout the screenplay would feature flat winter landscapes with only the top stubble of worn grasses rising above the snow, perhaps a horse shed and a ranch house. While the three were discussing different terrains, John's mind kept going back to the horse shed and the stupid kids who tricked him. He was anxious to get on the phone (he never carried a cell phone, hated them) so his bosses could locate the two stupid kids. They could not have gone far and would not live very long when found.

"This is my last cup of coffee," John said with forced casualness, raising the cup to his mouth with tired hands (it had been a hell of a night), when he saw the restaurant door opening. He immediately glanced beyond the door to the paper box. He's not here yet. Damn, he said wordlessly; he wanted to get the morning's work done with, inspecting both ranches for exact places of camera shots and allow the ranchers to draw up crude maps of the proposed areas while he drove back to Spokane. He was determined to go back to Spokane. No way was he going to leave the area and fly home until he found those suckers. They'd go back there. And his New York bosses could fucking wait for his report.

Suddenly his coffee cup landed back on the saucer with a loud bang. John's body, for a split second, froze. With a rush of blood gushing through his head, he found he could hardly swallow the sips of coffee that had, a moment earlier, started down his throat. He coughed up several drops of the hot liquid, his eyes fixed on Janice entering the restaurant. He drank in the perfect triangle of eyes and mouth sitting on high cheekbones on a perfectly porcelain skin, almost feeling the softness of her skin from where he sat. He then focused on the most exquisite, large, azure eyes he had ever seen, which were now looking right at him, startled by his coughing. Yearning eyes they were, exquisitely veiled, yet with a beckoning, taunting expression, incongruous in one so young. The hair on her head was a golden yellow, he knew she had to be a natural blond; no dye could cause the strands to shimmer with such colorful high and low lights. It hung seductively straight down to her waist with a few deliberately cut tendrils whispering beguilingly around her high smooth temples. God, she was beautiful. The morning light coming in from outside as she stood in the doorway settled in her hair, glorifying it with tiny, moving flashes of sunlight. And her cheeks! High though they were, there was an innocent, arresting, childlike fullness about them, which he had never seen on any woman's face before and he had observed many lovely young faces. The only mar was her full, sensuous, but hard-set mouth. It had a set to it that was tantalizingly defiant of the innocence above. One wanted to take her face in one's hands, pull it to one, and kiss it until those glorious eyes filled with rapturous tears. She was breathtaking. He really didn't have to go down the long, slim lines of the rest of her form. He knew it to be perfect, succulent, and ripe for fucking.

The two ranchers noted John's look of amazement.

"That's Janice Alicorn," one of them said, the other smiling and murmuring his appreciation.

As for Janice, she was oblivious to the stares and comments from others who noticed her entrance (she was used to being looked at). She was staring back at the man who was staring at her. In him she saw Rob, the ranch hand in his dark, strong and forceful face; in him she saw both her father, in his controlled, unstained strength, and her brother, Andrew, in the hint of repressed sullenness. She felt shivers run up and down her spine. She sensed his arrogance, she sensed his desire for her. He was looking at her like the three she had had affairs with, her high school teacher, a boy in the senior class when she was a sophomore, and the sociology college instructor (oh, she still ached for him). John's piercing eyes sent blood surging through her body. She would not have looked away if Merry hadn't spoken, taken her by the hand and led her to a booth against the window.

"Is she a model?" asked John of the heavy-set, balding

rancher, Henry Knutson, who was sitting to the left of him.

"Nah. She goes to the University, I think. Marv keeps pretty close tabs on that one."

"She's not going this year," the younger rancher added. He was short and square, with brown-cropped hair, wearing a summer-type, short-sleeved, striped shirt. He pushed back his chair. Like John, he was anxious to leave the restaurant and be about the business at hand, they had done their talking.

"Can she ride a horse?" asked John. Not that it mattered.

"Yes," they both answered, the heavy one with a snicker. "All those Alicorns can ride. And ride well. They were born in saddles."

"I've got to meet her," said John in his strong, deep voice. "If she can act, what a leading lady she will be in this movie." Not that it mattered.

"Come, Mr. Territoni, I'll introduce you," said the young rancher, Jed Nordstrom, by name. He got up, pushing back his chair nosily.

John rose too, wiping his mouth clean with his napkin. Aloud, he said, "Damn, my father is going to love her." Realizing he had voiced his thoughts with the ranchers looking at him questionably, he amended quickly, "My director will love her."

As the three made their way to the booth where Janice, Gustav and Merry now sat, he asked, "Who are the others?"

"Chaperones," answered Jed.

"Marv doesn't allow anyone to get close to Janice," smiled Henry Knutson, the other rancher, "and I don't blame him."

They had reached the booth. Janice had kept her eyes focused on John as they approached, not realizing the waitress was waiting for her order.

Merry answered for Janice, frowning at the girl's intense stare at John.

"Coffee and a doughnut for the young lady. Janice, what kind of doughnut?"

"Oh." Janice smiled foolishly, taking her eyes off John and almost blushing as she faced the waitress. "I want," she began sweetly, her voice deliberately low and husky, for she knew this man was watching and listening, "two plain cake doughnuts. No frostings. I need cream for my coffee," she added, turning away from the waitress and looking down at the table as she picked up her napkin, knowing full well John Territoni's eyes were upon her, watching every move.

The waitress left the table. Jed spoke.

"Janice Alicorn, how nice to see you out. And you both," he nodded courteously at Merry and Gustav.

Janice, with her head lowered, smiled sweetly, her eyes focusing on Jed. "Father's been wondering why you haven't been around to see us."

"Just busy, Janice," Jed said. Jed had always been interested in Janice, but without encouragement from either her or her father, Marv, his visits to Windy Hills became few and far between.

"I'd like to introduce you to Mr. Territoni. You know Henry Knutson. John, this is Janice Alicorn, Merry Landis and Gustav. . ., I don't know your last name, Gustav."

"It's Smith."

"Smith? Gustav Smith? Interesting name combination," said Jed, laughing.

"I am glad to meet you," said John, shaking hands with

both, and then stretching his arm across the table to Janice.

"Good morning, Miss Alicorn," he said graciously.

"Good morning to you," she answered, barely glancing at him, deliberately keeping her eyes down while extending her right hand.

John nodded again at Merry and Gustav. He continued pleasantly, "I had to meet you, Miss Alicorn. I know many people like to meet you for you are a beautiful young lady."

At those words Janice looked up, her lovely eyes shining directly into John's. She quickly lowered them again but her sexual import was apparent. "Thank you," she said quietly, a chill sweeping through her because of the intense manner he had looking at her. He had undressed her with his eyes.

"I want to meet you for that reason and also for a different reason," said John, reaching into his jacket pocket and taking out a business card. "I am a producer of motion pictures." That statement got the immediate attention of Janice, Merry and Gustav. They listened intently. "We are presently conducting screen tests of several young ladies with acting potential. I am wondering if you would be interested in having a screen test. Ah!" he added, as a side note, "do you or have you ever acted in a play, on radio or television?"

John liked to see reactions when he asked his questions. It made him feel important. He noted the chaperones glancing at each other with a quick look of surprise before studying his card. Janice looked at the card first then up at him, answering his sexual gaze, a self-conscious smile sliding across her face.

Hah, thought John, staring back at her, she is not innocent in love. Those are bedroom eyes as my father would say.

John liked initiating virgins to sex. He enjoyed the pain he inflicted on them as they learned the intricacies of lovemaking. But no matter how many lovers this young girl had had, he had plenty to teach her. Just looking at her made him horny. His father would love her when he passed her on to him. He sighed. I'll have to be careful, her chaperones know me, as do these two ranchers, and her family will undoubtedly keep tabs on her, still, I've taken girls away from protective families before, and I've always been successful before I passed them on.

He smiled at Janice, blandly now, for the woman sitting with her was staring at him with a frown and narrowed lids. He turned to her, sensing she was getting ready to speak.

"Where will the screen tests be held?" she asked. "In Hollywood?"

"Novelette Studios are in New York," he answered as smoothly as he could. "This young lady's test will be accomplished in New York City. Janice Alicorn?" He turned back to the girl. "Is that correct?"

"Yes," both Merry and Janice answered.

"I've never heard of Novelette Studios," said Janice, speaking up.

"We produce many short features, sometimes a mystery, love story or western. We're about to begin a western with some scenes to be on these gentlemen's ranches." He turned and nodded to each rancher. "That is why I am here. However, seeing you, young lady, such a beautiful girl as you out here in Montana. . .."

"Montana is a state with lots of attractive people," Janice interrupted haughtily

John laughed. "Of course. And you, Janice Alicorn," he bowed his head slightly, his eyes boring into hers, his voice smooth and tempting, "are surely the loveliest of all."

"Thank you," answered Janice, her voice barely above a whisper, and her face in a full blush. She recovered quickly, looking again at his card and then back at him, a teasing smile crossing her lips as she said his name, "Mister Territoni, thank you."

Merry did not like the looks or the exchange between the two nor did she like this man. He looked more like a criminal than a producer despite his fancy clothes and good looks. "When would you want Miss Alicorn to be in New York and will you be sending her a round trip ticket? I would accompany Miss Alicorn." Her voice had a hostile edge to it.

"Merry!" warned Janice.

"Of course we will send a round-trip ticket for Miss Alicorn," John answered suavely, enunciating each word. "And she will stay at one of the finest New York hotels while she is there," he added, again disturbingly smooth-voiced. "The readings and screen test usually take about five days."

Merry was well aware of his underlying hostility to her. She looked up questioningly at both Jed and Henry, ranchers she knew. Jed shrugged his shoulders, but Henry raised his eyebrows in a "maybe you are right' mode.

Just then, the restaurant door opened. Glancing quickly that way, John saw the bartender open the newspaper box as another man walked into the restaurant. He turned and looked at Janice again, saying, "We must leave. We are examining scenic areas on both Mr. Nordstrom's and Mr. Knutson's ranches. My plane for New York departs early this afternoon.

If you would kindly jot down your name and address on this card," and he took another one from his jacket pocket, "and phone number, I'll have my secretary call you. Better yet, you call my office early next week. We'll set up an appointment for you, Miss Alicorn." He turned to go and then stopped.

"Oh," he added, sizing her up once more with his piercing black eyes as she sat in the center of the booth in her black outfit with the neck of her white blouse offsetting the black's severe line and making him want to rip the line of buttons down the center of her blouse and grab at her breasts. This young girl, her yellow hair streaming down her back, was ripe for plucking. He smiled at her. "Do you ride horses?"

"Of course, Mr. Territoni," she answered.

"Good," he said. "Perhaps we have a part for you in this coming western. Good day." He pulled himself away, bowing his head slightly at Janice, Merry and Gustav.

"Come, gentlemen," he said. "We have much to do. And I don't want to miss my plane."

Chapter Nine

J anice watched the restaurant door close on John Territoni and the two ranchers.

"Oh, Merry," she exclaimed, her eyes dancing. "I'm going to have a screen test. In New York! Oh! Isn't that exciting."

With a side-glance Merry answered suspiciously, "We shall see. He doesn't look very savory to me, my child, for all his important airs."

Merry's tone was lost on Janice. Her euphoria was such she could not think of anything but her own excitement. "He looked wonderful to me, Merry."

"We'll let your father decide."

"How can he decide when Mr. Territoni won't even be here? Don't be silly, Merry," Janice said, anger rising. "This is my chance to go to New York. And no one is going to take this opportunity away from me." She flung the words at Merry and Gustav, moving to get up. "Let's go, Merry, Gustav," she said, visually disturbed, without noting if they had or had not eaten their doughnuts or drunk their coffee, which they had not. "I have shopping to do." She spoke haughtily.

"We are going to finish our doughnuts first, Miss Janice," countered Merry. "You may sit there and dream your dreams while we do so."

In silence, Janice pursed her lips and slid back to where she had been sitting. She too, drank her coffee, and then waited for Merry and Gustav to finish theirs. When they had finished, as one they left the booth. Janice opened her purse and took out a five-dollar bill, placing it on the table for a tip.

"I think that instead of shopping I want to go home and tell Melissa what happened."

"She went after your father. They won't be home until early afternoon," said Gustav.

Well then, I'm going to call Gerdie," Gerdie being a school friend.

"If you wish," said Gustav, as they reached the car.

"No. I changed my mind, Gustav," she said giddily. "Let's go to Great Falls. I want to shop. I'm going to New York." She almost sang her words, "and I want to buy a beautiful suit and dress to wear."

Merry looked at her and said flatly, halfway to herself, "Hmmmmmmmmp!"

It was early afternoon when they returned to Windy Hills. Janice's packages contained several new dresses and a suit, "just right for New York City," she told Merry when she had tried them on.

Only Swallow was at home. She came running out to meet them in the driveway dressed in her usual daily attire, a white blouse accentuating her pretty face, a big blue sweater, jeans and well-worn boots.

"Something horrible has happened," she said breathlessly. "Your father is in the hospital, Janice. He had a stroke or heart attack or something awful out at the grave. Melissa and Lamedeer found him. And an ambulance went through here – twice, once going to get him and then again, coming back. He's in the Great Falls hospital."

"Is he okay?"

Swallow made a long face. "I don't know."

"Turn the car around, Gustav. We're going to Dad," said Janice, as stoic as she could be, stifling an urge to cry. "Oh God, let him be okay," she added, her face pale, as Gustav turned the car around and headed to Great Falls.

Dr. Witt came into the waiting room shortly before midnight. The four, Janice, Melissa, Merry and Lamedeer (Gustav had returned to the ranch) worn from waiting and hungry – none had eaten - rose from their chairs immediately.

"Marv had a close one. Good thing you got him here when you did. We put a heart monitor on him; it went down to two beats a minute, that was pretty close. We need your permission to implant a pacemaker."

"Good God," exclaimed Lamedeer, "Never knew there was anything wrong with Marv's heart."

"He's always so active," said Melissa, tears beginning to flow. "He's never complained of anything, least of all being tired."

"I can't believe it," said Janice. "Thank God, he is going to be all right."

Merry shook her head in distress.

Dr. Witt waited patiently for his answer. At last, from the upset silence of the group, Janice spoke. "Of course you have our permission, Dr. Witt."

"Good. We'll keep him here a day or two while we do tests because he also has a slight concussion. His cat-scan showed a little blood in the frontal lobe in his brain."

"That was from the fall at the gravesite," exclaimed Melissa.

Dr. Witt nodded. "When he gets home, he'll need bed rest

for about a week. After that, if tests are okay and there is no reason they won't be," Dr. Witt added hastily, seeing the look of consternation on their anxious faces, "Marv should be just fine, although he'll have to cut down on some of his more strenuous activities."

None of the four spoke.

"I suggest all of you go home and get some sleep. He's resting well and you can see him in the morning."

"You are sure my Dad is going to be okay?" asked Janice.

"Absolutely certain," Dr. Witt answered.

They nodded and thanked the doctor, then moved down the corridor silently, each absorbed in their own thoughts wondering what Marv's newfound disability would mean.

Melissa spoke up before they reached the car. "I want to stop at Annabelle's house. She needs to be told."

"Why?" asked Janice. "You can tell her tomorrow."

"She means a great deal to father. She should know now."

"We're all so tired, Melissa. I want to go home and go to bed. Can't you call her from home?" Janice asked petulantly.

"We'll stop so you can tell Annabelle what happened," interrupted Lamedeer, in a conciliatory tone. "Won't take a minute, it's on our way."

They rode in silence the half hour it took to drive to Mission where Annabelle lived. Lamedeer turned off the freeway, past the night-darkened mini-malls and turned into a narrow two lane paved road which ran in back of one of the malls and dead-ended after a three-block subdivision. Annabelle's house stood in the middle of the second block. Her house looked exactly like the house at the far end of the street. Built by the same contractor, it was built with an identical sloping roof over the identical shape of the white-painted stucco outside walls, the identical horizontal molding over the large front window and door. It was a small two-bedroom ranch styled house in a sub-division of almost other identical ranch-styled houses.

No lights were on inside Annabelle's house. The short, paved walk was dark; Melissa found her way along it because it was walled in on both sides by a well-tended grass lawn and she could see the outline of the grass. She sprang up the three steps to the porch and rang the bell. After a pause, she rang it again. A light inside and outside (on the porch) lit simultaneously. But the door did not open. A voice from inside, asked, "Who is it?"

"Melissa Alicorn. Is Annabelle there?"

The turning of a lock sounded and the door flew open. Molly Anderson, Annabelle's 'Stone Gifts' partner, stood in the bright porch light. A short, stocky, nicely faced woman of about forty years of age, she wore a long blue flannel robe over pajamas of which only multi-colored hems showed under the bottom of the robe. Her permanent waved, curly, dark-brown hair was a little wild, strands sticking up here and there since she had been sleeping when Melissa rang the bell. Molly's eyes were wide and frightened at this late hour awakening.

"What happened, Melissa? Something wrong?"

"It's my father. He's in the hospital. Where is Annabelle? He's okay, or will be," she amended, seeing the stricken look on Molly's usually cheery face. "It's something with his heart. They have to put in a pacemaker, so he'll be okay." Her voice quivered with distress.

"Thank God," said Molly, not certain if she could be glad. The pacemaker obviously did not reassure Melissa that her father would get well. Molly reached out her arms. Melissa fell into them, not crying but visually upset.

"Thank you, Molly," she said, her voice muffled as her face lay tight against Molly's shoulder. "We're so upset."

"Of course." Molly patted Melissa on the back, comforting her, and then blurted, not knowing how else to say it, "Annabelle is leaving for California tomorrow. She went on down to Great Falls today to finish some business. She's leaving on a flight at six in the morning."

"California?" Melissa broke away from her arms, startled. "Whatever for?"

"Ah, that's a long story. She's at the Heritage Inn. You can reach her there. She'll want to know what happened to Marv. Do you want to come in and call her from here?"

For Annabelle to go away without telling either Janice or her, stunned Melissa. She could not think clearly. "I . . . I don't know." Then shaking her head and sighing bewilderingly, she said, "Thank you, Molly. I'll call her as soon as we get home."

"You're welcome to use the phone here."

"I know. Thank you, Molly. Say a prayer for my Dad, please."

"Of course." She put out her arms again and hugged Melissa warmly.

"I'll call Annabelle as soon as I get home. The Heritage Inn, right?"

"Right."

Of the three waiting in the car, only Janice had been able

to tell it was Molly, not Annabelle, at the door. "Was Annabelle sleeping?" she asked, her face inscrutable in the dim light, her voice shaky. She had been weeping.

"No. She's in Great Falls. I'm going to call her as soon as I get home."

"Oh, sis, you always have to tell Annabelle everything that happens right away."

"Yes, Janice, I do," answered Melissa firmly, putting on her seat belt and settling in her seat as Lamedeer drove down the highway.

"I suppose with Dad sick," complained Janice, "now I won't be able to go to New York to have my screen test."

No one answered her but Melissa uttered a small groan and rolled her eyes in frustration.

After a moment, Janice said in a low voice, "I'm sorry, sis. I didn't mean that. It's just that . . . " She did not finish, she knew Melissa understood.

Melissa put her hand over her sister's hand to comfort her. "I'm sure Dad's going to be just fine. I'm certain you can go to New York," and she took a firmer hold of Janice's hand, squeezing it gently.

As they neared the ranch, on a long, smooth stretch of the highway, two cars sped by. One was the county Sheriff's car. His sirens made their ears ring. They watched, puzzled, as he braked his car and moved to the shoulder in front of them. It sat there, lights blazing, sirens blaring. The other sped on.

"He wants me to stop," said Lamedeer, slowing and moving to the shoulder, parking behind the Sheriff's car.

"Good God, what now?" exclaimed Janice.

Lamedeer was out of the car quickly.

"What in the world is the matter?" he asked the Sheriff as they approached one another.

"Is Marv with you?" Joe Chobin asked.

"Marv's in the hospital," said Lamedeer. He explained briefly what had happened, relieved the pullover wasn't about Marv. "What in the world is it with you? Anything on fire? What is it, Joe? You wouldn't be stopping us if it didn't pertain to the Alicorns."

"Once we are on your property, I'll tell you," answered Joe grimly. "No, it is not about an Alicorn: it's definitely not about Marv, no."

That was not the kind of answer Lamedeer wanted, but Joe had already turned around to get back in his car. So Lamedeer shrugged his shoulders helplessly, tensely running over in his mind whom it could be about – it certainly had something to do with the Alicorn family – and Lamedeer suffered a prolonged twinge of fear. He got back in the car, moved silently behind the driver's seat, started the engine and answered his passengers' anxious questions with a lame, "I don't know yet. The sheriff said he would tell us when we got back to the ranch." Ahead, Joe Chobin turned off the sirens and lights and proceeded to the ranch.

The other car was already parked in the long driveway, close to the house, its lights shining, with the driver waiting for them to appear. Swallow, who had been sitting by the living room windows, impatiently waiting, jumped up and went to the switch to turn on the driveway lights, flooding the near yards and trees with bright light. Lamedeer pulled into the garage, and the four exited the car quickly and apprehensively hurried into the house.

Swallow, pretty, but who always wore too much makeup, particularly mascara (a heavy black) and under eye liner (again heavy black), was still dressed in her day clothes except now she had slippers on her feet instead of boots. She hurried to her husband's side, who was standing in the doorway waiting for the Sheriff. She feared the worst about Marv since two cars parking in the driveway could only portend bad news. Lamedeer answered her as he had the others in the car, "Marv is going to be just fine," he said, "but something has happened to someone we know and Joe Chobin wanted us all together to hear it. It's not about Marv, though," he added, observing Swallow's distress with both her hands flying to her face as he spoke. She moved back into the house to help the girls take off their jackets.

Marv Alicorn's living room was immense. It almost swallowed up the main floor of the two-story ranch house. A red cloth covered the dining room table, which stood to the left on the south side of the room in front of a long window and close to the door leading to the kitchen. Eight chairs, the seats covered in a homey red flowered chintz, were gathered haphazardly around it as if all the occupants had just left the table and had not yet placed the chairs back where they belonged. A huge woven basket filled with apples and oranges sat in the middle of the table. To the table's left, a large empty space was decorated with a tan and red patterned carpet. A game table with several stools hugged another long window facing east, an unfinished jigsaw puzzle spread on the table. In the corner, facing into the room, sat two large easy chairs, each in brown, a table and lamp between them. Taking up the center of the north wall was a huge stone fireplace with two deep-seating brown leather couches stretched on either side of it. The handsome stones making up the fireplace came from a quarry in eastern Washington. Centered at the end of the couches facing the fireplace was Marv's large easy chair with a table and lamp on either side. Both tables were piled high with magazines, some opened, some still in their plastic covers. The living room was large, homey and well lived in.

The three ladies shed their jackets; Swallow quickly hung them on the cherry wood hall tree at the entryway and moved with them to the couches. The two girls anxiously sat down with Merry between them, gathering their hands in hers. Swallow sat on the other couch.

"I hope it isn't something about Andrew," whispered Melissa to Merry, her face contorted with anxiety, as they watched Lamedeer and the Sheriff enter the house.

"The Sheriff said it wasn't about one of the family," Merry reminded her.

"I am sorry to have to tell you this," said Joe, standing in front of Marv's chair. "But I have bad news about one of your neighbors." A tall, lean young man, not in any uniform but dressed in a dark brown suit with a matching color tie, who drove the second car, had entered and stood unnoticed by the front door.

"How does this concern us, if not about Dad?" Melissa asked, grabbing her sister's hand for support.

Lamedeer and Merry were quiet, waiting.

"It's George Culbertson." Joe said. "I know your family was close to his."

Melissa, jumping up, was the first to find her voice. "Was

he in an accident?" she asked, her eyes wide, fear sweeping through her body. The whole family knew George Culbertson. He and his wife, Carol, often shared dinner with them at either their or the Alicorn's house, and Marv was George's fishing buddy.

"No. We found his body at the edge of his ranch. Dead." Cynthia Culbertson has already identified her husband's body. He has been murdered."

"George Culbertson? Why, he's a friend of everyone." Lamedeer had sprung up from the edge of the sofa where Swallow sat, stunned.

"Yes," answered the Sheriff grimly, unconsciously pulling at his lower lip with his teeth, a habit that was exposed when he was upset. "That's why I'm sorry to have to tell you this, he was meaningful to me too." He swiped at his nose, closed his eyes to quell any emotion, opened them and bit his lip again. "I came here to ask when anyone of you saw George last. And when you did, how did he act?"

"I saw him last week," Lamedeer said. "We were both after strays. He was fine. Just tired from being so busy."

For more than a half hour, Sheriff Chobin questioned them informally, each one in turn, in the kitchen away from the rest of the family. The young man, who had been standing at the door, introduced himself as Peter Green and was taking notes. Melissa rushed into the kitchen, halting Sheriff Chobin's interview with Merry.

"Janice and I must call Annabelle Stone. She is leaving for California in the morning and we have to get in touch with her now. Please put us last."

"Make your call," agreed Sheriff Chobin kindly.

The girls rushed up the stairs and hurried down the hall into Melissa's bedroom. Melissa located the phone book on the bottom shelf of her bookcase. "She's at the Heritage Inn in Great Falls. You dial, Janice, when I call out the numbers, please."

Within moments, Annabelle was on the phone. Janice told her about her father and where he was, then Melissa told her about George Culbertson's murder. They did not need to beg her to cancel her flight and be with them in the morning when they went back to the hospital. She agreed readily

Hanging up the phone, Melissa turned a pleased face to her sister. "She's going to be here at 9:30 in the morning, Janice."

"Good," answered her sister. "I know how much you love Annabelle, and I'm sorry for what I said at her house earlier. It's just that Dad getting a heart attack is so awful when the morning started out so wonderful, now it's all smithereens. I was so excited about getting a screen test. Damn." Then, lowering her head so she didn't have to look at her sister, she murmured, "I have to tell you something."

"What?"

"I was supposed to meet Rob Christianson tonight."

"Janice, last night is over with. It is now almost 2 a.m. in the morning. How could you think of him with all this happening?

"I know. But that won't matter to Rob. He'll wait for me at our meeting place."

"Oh, come on, Janice, stop it. You are so darn romantic. That ranch hand doesn't really care. I'm sure he is infatuated with you. But waiting until two a.m.? Besides, he can't mean anything to you now, can he?"

Janice looked at her sister full in the face and shook her head. "I don't care about him any longer. All I care about is going to New York and getting my screen test. But he's out there somewhere, waiting for me."

"Go tell Lamedeer to send him away."

"I can't. He wouldn't believe Lamedeer."

"Oh, Janice," Melissa was exasperated. "Sometimes I think I'm the wiser of the two of us even though I'm the youngest. You want to believe everyone is in love with you or you want to be in love with everyone." She rose from the chair by the phone. "Go tell Lamedeer to send that Bob, or whatever his name is, away. Tell him never to come back." Her voice rose. "If you don't, I will."

"Help me with this, Melissa. You can do things like this so much better than I."

"Good gosh, Janice, what will happen to you when you go to New York?"

The sisters looked at each other. Then Janice spoke with a small apologetic laugh in her voice. "I'll have Oscar with me."

"Oscar! Ye Gads, Janice."

"Oscar comforts me."

"Oscar! A rag doll."

"I still go to sleep with him every night."

"Well, you can't do that forever. Whomever you marry will throw Oscar away."

The thought made them both laugh.

"Yes, I know," giggled Janice. Then she tossed her corn colored hair and said sadly, "Oh, what are we doing laughing? Dad's in the hospital, Mr. Culbertson has been murdered and I'm acting like a fool. I'm sorry. Yes, let's go downstairs and I'll try to act like an adult, and yes, please, ask Lamedeer to send Rob away." She moved into Melissa's arms. They put their heads on each other's shoulders, hugging. "To think we were worried about Dad, because I know he's going to be okay, Dr. Witt wouldn't have said so if Dad was very ill."

Downstairs, Melissa took Lamedeer aside and told him what was needed about Rob and where to find him. Although he shook his head displeased, without glancing back at Janice, who was sitting in the middle of the couch watching, he put on his jacket and went out the front door. He was back within five minutes, extended his fingers forward in a "I did it for you" action directed at Janice, and then slumped into a chair, lowering his head, immersed in his own thoughts. The others, like Lamedeer, sat on couches or chairs, each tense, sending covert glances at the others, then turning reluctantly away, not wanting to converse. They remained quiet and self-absorbed waiting for their turn to be interviewed by Sheriff Chobin.

Finally, it was over. Everyone had been questioned. Joe Chobin came out of the kitchen, the young man with him. "I see how tired you all are," Joe said. "It's after 2 a.m. and I am sorry I had to interject right now. I'm also sorry Marv is ill. I saw him myself just this morning; he was stressed. Are you sure none of you know what was bothering him?" He was repeating what he had asked each in private.

They all shook their heads no.

"He had the flu last week, and I don't think he was quite

over it," offered Melissa.

"It was more than that," answered the Sheriff, saying his goodbyes. Lamedeer accompanied the two men outside, and in the driveway he asked the Sheriff how George Culbertson was killed. The Sheriff shook his head. "I can't tell you that now, Lamedeer, but it was the most gruesome death I've ever witnessed. It had to be someone who knew George and had a grudge against him. That's why all the questions. One more question, Lamedeer. Did you ever see George Culbertson take drugs or know if he took them?"

"No. He wouldn't take drugs. Not George Culbertson."

"Well, it appears he probably OD' on them."

When Lamedeer returned to the house, Melissa asked, "Did he tell you how he was killed?"

"No," answered Lamedeer frowning, he was not going to upset the family by relating anything the Sheriff told him, besides, he could not erase the thought of drugs from his mind; it was impossible for George Culbertson to take drugs, except of course there had to be a reason why he was murdered. As far as Lamedeer knew, and that would include Marv, George was not an addict – the denial kept pushing every other thought out of his mind – certainly he had no enemies, everyone in this spread-out community was a friend. He was highly respected.

I think we better call Andrew." Melissa said, breaking into his thoughts.

Lamedeer suggested Melissa look at the clock. Nothing could be accomplished at 2 o'clock in the morning; she could call Andrew in the morning but now she needed to get to bed. "Your sister is already upstairs and rightfully so. Everybody is worn out and we'll all have a busy day tomorrow."

Calling Andrew at 8:00 a.m. Spokane time, 9:00 a.m. Montana time, elicited no answer on his cell phone. Melissa next called the college's line to the men's dormitory. The girl who answered, after checking the student traffic binder, told her Andrew had not signed out or in the past three days. Try the school office, she suggested. After attempting to reach Andrew on his cell once more she talked to the college's switchboard operator who immediately turned Melissa's call over to a supervisor; he told her Andrew had not shown up for his Monday classes and on the customary dorm check, his bed had not slept in for three nights. "He's not here today, either, and we'd like to know where he is. Missing classes is never a good option."

When Melissa hung up, she rushed out to the barns where Lamedeer was supervising a new and totally inexperienced teen-age employee cleaning the stalls.

Finding Lamedeer in Fleet's stall, examining one of his hoofs, she said, "Andrew's not at school."

"Well, he's obviously playing hooky, nothing to worry about."

"He does not answer his cell phone, Lamedeer."

"That's no crime either, Melissa," he said to her gently, opening the stall door and brushing straw off his hands.

"He hasn't been at school for three days. That's what they told me."

"Well, we'll just have to wait for him to get back." Lamedeer put his arms around her shoulders. "Did you leave a message about your father?"

"No."

"I suggest you do that, then get ready. We're taking off for the hospital at ten.."

There was no need to open the door for Annabelle. She drove up to the house promptly at 9:30, rushed into the living room, stopped by the fireplace to remove her gloves and warm her hands, then looked at the two girls before going over to Melissa, who sat hunched at the far end of one of the couches. Janice, who sat beside her sister, moved over allowing Annabelle to sit down between them.

"Tell me, dear," said Annabelle to Melissa. "Everything."

Melissa did. When she had finished, including the offer of a screen test for Janice and how worried she was that Andrew was not at school, Annabelle said quietly, "We're going now. Get your coats on, girls. I am anxious to see Marv." The four left, leaving Merry and Swallow behind.

Chapter Ten

Andrew and Betty ran away from the horse shed as fast as they could, arriving breathless at Betty's car which she had parked on one of Culbertson's gravel ranch roads. As they reached the car, both panting hard, Andrew put his arms around Betty, who practically fell into them from exhaustion. He said gently, stammering between breaths, "It's okay, Betty, we're here now, and you were right, he was going to drug me. I realized that when he pretended to drink out of that thermos."

"He is the most evil man I ever knew," Betty answered, pushing strands of hair away from her face. "Let's get in the car quickly. He might wake up and undo his hands."

"I don't think so, but yeah, let's get out of here." Andrew held the small satchel tight against his chest, eager to open it once he was in the car.

Betty, still panting, felt in her coat's side pocket for her keys, thankful the pocket was deep. It would have been awful if the keys had fallen out while they were running to the car. She unlocked the driver's door, pushed down the switch so Andrew could get in the passenger's side, and in another moment she had swung the car around leaving the ranch and turning to go back the way they came. Andrew opened the satchel, lifting out a rubber-banded packet inside. He could see well enough to observe the dollar bill that lay on top of a several dozen strips of newspaper, cut the same size as the dollar bill. He cried out, "He cheated us. There is no money here, Betty. I brought all that stuff to him for nothing."

"Are you sure there is nothing more in that satchel?"

He lifted up the satchel and turned it upside down so Betty could see it.

"It's empty. And now I am a criminal for carrying drugs. God, what did I do?"

He put his head in his hands, and then suddenly jerked his hands away and touched Betty's hand gently on the wheel. "But it brought me you," he amended, moving closer to her so he could kiss her cheek, "and you are not going to do any of that stuff anymore."

"No, but I have less than twenty dollars in my purse. Jonah (her boss at Shingles and Eves) was careful not to give me too much to spend so I'd have to come right back."

"You're not going back ever, not to that life," Andrew said fiercely. "We are going away together and in February when I am eighteen, we are getting married." Before she could answer he looked out at the darkness and asked quickly, "Which way are we headed?"

"Going back to Spokane."

"Good grief, Betty, they'll catch up with us. You better turn around. We need to head to North Dakota or someplace like that."

"I have a friend we can stay with in Spokane. Jonah won't find us there."

"What about this guy John, who I took the drugs to."

"He's going back to New York."

"Yeah, but he has friends. That dope isn't all for him."

"I promise you Andy, we'll be safe in Spokane."

Andrew leaned back in the seat hoping she was right. He

thought back to the beginning of the weekend when he had hopped in her car and away they went, she in blue jeans, a heavy brown jacket over a yellow blouse, and he in a plain cream tee with one side pocket, jeans and a tan jacket he bundled up in a corner of his seat. He was excited to be going with her but her manner had been difficult to understand, answering coldly to the nice things he talked about until they stopped for lunch just over the border. Then she began talking to him, a rush of words coming out of her pretty little mouth. The first thing she said to him was that she couldn't do this to him, he was too nice, and she told him he was going to carry drugs over the border, not jewelry. He was going to be a drug courier. He was silent after that and finally he said in a heavy voice that he wanted to get out of the car as soon as possible. He wondered how he was going to get back to Spokane, but he did not want to be a drug carrier. She drove on a few miles further stopping at a rest stop and parking at the far end under some trees. As he moved to get out and retrieve his suitcase, she suddenly began crying. She bawled so hard he got back into the car to help her stop; he put his arms around her as a friend would, patting her on the back gently, and every once in a while taking a hand away to brush his unruly hair out of his eyes. Finally she stopped crying. She looked up at him, with that awful dyed yellow hair and her pretty little face bloated and streaked with undried tears, and she began blurting out all the things that had happened to her. When she had finished, he said in a shocked and brother-like voice, for he could never imagine things like that went on in the world, "Okay, I'm not leaving you. I'll help you do this, but you're never going back to what you were doing."

She told him it all began when she was thirteen and on her way home from school, sitting on a bench, waiting for the transfer bus to take her home. Another girl Annie sat beside her. Suddenly a big black limousine slammed to a sudden stop right in front of them and two men jumped out; one grabbed her while the other man grabbed Annie. They were so quick that both girls were shocked into silence and then before either recovered enough to scream, the men shoved cloths into their mouths and they were lifted, squirming and hitting out with their arms and legs, and literally thrown into the black limousine. There were two other men inside who grabbed them, pulled up the sleeves of their jackets and shoved needles into their arms. Whatever was injected made Betty dizzy and within seconds she threw up her breakfast and lunch all over the man's lap (the one who had his arms clamped tight around her body); she lost consciousness, waking up to find herself lying naked on a bed in a dark room. She lay there terrified, finally calling out in a pleading whisper, Annie. If Annie was there she did not answer. In fact, Betty never saw Annie again.

For hours, she could not even make out a sound, the world had stopped making any kind of noise and nobody came into the room. She got up to look for her clothes but there was nothing in the room but the bed and a sink with a used towel hanging from a rack alongside the sink. Shaking with cold, she even looked under the bed hoping to find a blanket, anything to cover her nakedness and make her warmer. But there was nothing so she lay back on the mattress that was covered with only one sheet. She wanted to cry out but was too terrified to do so, instead she drew her arms and legs close to her body in a fetal-like position and lay on top of the sheet shivering and sobbing.

Suddenly there was noise. She heard voices, doors opening and closing, yelling, a couple of screams (could that be Annie?) and the door to the room in which she lay opened wide, and two male forms entered.

They came right to her bed, one using a flashlight, shining it all over her. The other pulled her legs and arms away from her body and with his hands began examining her private parts. She tried to get away, but he hit her hard in the face. She couldn't tell Andrew any more details then; she just sobbed and kept crying that they raped her. When they stopped, three other men came in and raped her again and again and again. She hated everything they did to her, she told Andrew and fought them every chance she had. Some of the men who raped her in the next two weeks, and there must have been fifty – mostly middle-aged men who liked her to struggle, so they could they beat her when she did. One day five men held her down, making her do whatever they told her to do; it was unspeakable. One of the men told her that if she didn't decide to be cooperative and enjoy what was happening, her pimps were going to put her on drugs to control her. Drugs don't fail us, he said, because in a few days you'll do anything to get more. So she began to cooperate. I was brainwashed, she told Andrew. Anyway, after she had been a prostitute for five years, one of the women who came in for sex, liked Betty kissing her breasts so much, she told the owner, Jonah, of Shingles and Eaves she would pay a bonus if they put Betty in the bar to serve special customers like her. Jonah also considered Betty 'special,' and she serviced him regularly. Soon she became so trusted that he sent her on several drug jobs as a courier. "That is why I went after you, Andrew, to turn you into a drug courier.

"But I didn't think John was going to drug you, although I hated him. I hated him because one time when he came to Spokane and saw me in the bar, he asked for me and was so sadistic, even putting handcuffs on my arms and legs and beating me with a whip, that I was afraid for my life. Now I just never want to go back. Neither did the two boys I helped make into drug couriers affect me the way you do. I only know I don't want to do any of this any more, and you are too nice to do this too." She burst into fresh sobs.

"And you won't do any of this any more, you poor girl," Andrew said, again sounding like a loving brother; tears were streaming down his cheeks too. After a while when both had settled themselves, he patted the passenger seat, saying, "Let's go on and finish this job. I won't even touch you tonight."

And he did not. Betty would not let him. "I'm going to die of HIV," she said, "and I would infect you. I was going to allow you, but you are too nice and the life I live is horrible." So he held her in his arms and fell in love with Betty. She taught him things to do "with a clean girl," since he had never lain with a woman. Betty was older than he by five years, and wasn't as pretty outside the dark bar as he thought she would be, but was honest, nice, and had had a miserable life. She had told him the slave ring bosses had brought her to Spokane from Seattle a year after she was kidnapped – she was only fourteen then – and she and two other girls were kept locked in a room servicing men with just curtains between the three beds and they had to allow at least ten men to rape them every day. They were never paid. Only the pimps were, and they beat them if they were so inclined. Neither was there any way she could find out if her parents still lived in Seattle. She never found their names in the phone book.

They drove on. Andrew dozed but woke up when the noise of a busy Spokane freeway startled him awake. "Gosh," he murmured sleepily, "I didn't mean for you to do all the driving. Where are we, anyway?"

"We are getting close to Marian's house; just about five more minutes."

"Marian is your friend's name, I take it."

"Yes. She told me that anytime I wanted to get away I could hide in her house."

Something about what Betty said bothered Andrew. "And how did you meet her? What makes you think her place is secure for us?" he asked.

"She's the lady who gave Jonah a bonus so I could be treated well.

"Good gosh, Betty, she's not going to hide you, not if I go with you." Andrew got the weirdest knot in his stomach. He intuitively knew that this was the wrong place to go.

"Oh, she's fine, she won't tell anybody," but Betty turned her eyes off the road a moment, with them widening in doubt. Perhaps Andy was right.

"Can't we go someplace else?"

"I'm almost out of gas and we are just about at her house."

"How come you were there before?" Betty didn't tell him why; she did not answer him, yet his doubts suddenly spread through her body. It was too late. They were only a block away from Miriam Sandowsky's house.

When Miriam Sandowsky opened the door and saw Betty, she smiled eagerly; when she saw the redheaded boy with her, her smile went away. She listened to Betty explain that she and the boy had to go away and that they hoped to borrow money from Miriam. Miriam, in a faded, not too clean housedress, questioned both at length, her fat face like her large hanging breasts and fat body silently quivering with anger after she heard all the details of their unpleasant adventures. Betty told her most of the story with Andrew sitting silently, anxiety spread over his expression. She excused herself to get her purse and give them a check. But she closed the bedroom door behind her, and called Jonah at Shingles & Eaves to complain that the bonus she continually gave him for Betty's favors was now all in vein. She was very angry. Jonah told her he would send someone to pick up Betty and her friend immediately, and to hold them there without telling them she called him.

Andrew's whole body was in knots while Betty and Marian chatted. He wanted to believe that Betty knew what she was doing, but he couldn't; neither could he suggest they leave since neither had any money. He was a scared seventeen-year-old boy. He asked twice, very politely about the check, but Marian waved her hand at him, smiling a false smile, saying "In a few minutes."

When the doorbell rang, Andrew jumped up in fright. He was correct in doing so because the moment the door was opened, three men rushed in with guns in their hands telling the three to get on the floor face down. Not one of the three did, so one of the men shot Andrew in his right chest. He would have aimed for his heart, but Jonah had told the three to bring both the girl and boy back.

Andrew fell back from the force of the bullet, Betty screamed and Marian cried out, her eyes bolting with fear, "I am the one who called. Don't shoot me."

The men did not say anything but dove after Betty, grabbing her and knocking her out with their fists before her screams could alarm the whole neighborhood. Andrew jumped back on his feet, blood oozing from his chest where the bullet had hit, a large surge of adrenalin aiding him as he lunged at one of the men, but the man laughed as he shoved Andrew back on the floor. Andrew got up again as two of the men carried Betty out of the house. He hit the remaining man with his fist as hard as he could and the man dropped, his gun flying out of his hands. Andrew picked it up, almost falling over with dizziness, pointed it at the man, then backed up and ran out of the living room, down the hall, into the kitchen, out the back door - blood spotting the ground behind him - through a fenceless yard, and out onto a street and kept running and running until he fell over, as if dead.

The men did not dare search for him; the gunshot and noise that had ensued brought neighbors to doorways looking up and down the street. Instead, the men pulled away in their car, taking Betty back to Shingles and Eaves.

John Territoni had just arrived, talked to Jonah, heard about Betty and the redhead and told Jonah he wanted the girl alone in the room upstairs where they kept runaways until their destination placements in prostitution were set up. Once there, he undressed completely, keeping an eye on Betty, who lay almost comatose on the floor, hands tied behind her back, suffering from the blows she had received, watching him in terror. He then brutally jerked her up off the floor and tortured her sexually until she died. Leaving the room with her blood covering his hands, he hurried into the shower room and stood under the water cleansing himself. That done, he went back for his clothes, his brain still tingling by the tremendous elation he had torturing Betty and went downstairs to tell Jonah to dump her body.

John then left to go to a motel intending to grab a plane the next morning for LaGuardia Airport in New York. He left behind men who vomited at what they saw he had done to Betty.

"God fucking damn," Jonah said. "I thought his bodyguard was with him all the time. I'm sure going to call his father about him."

"I wouldn't if I were you," said one of the men. "He might come back for you. That man is damn fucking crazy."

Chapter Eleven

M elissa was beside herself. She could not reach Andrew on either his cell or the school's phone. So she called her friend, Ginnie, in Missoula and told her she was thinking of driving over to see her. She knew she would be taking advantage of Marv's iron-clad rule which did not allow her to travel alone, but she had to go to Spokane to find Andrew and she wanted to go by herself.

She told the family – Janice, Merry, Swallow and Lamedeer – at breakfast the next morning she was thinking of visiting Ginnie while Dad was in the hospital, because when he came home she did not want to leave his side. Ginnie had called her, she lied, and asked her to visit.

"We'll talk about it when we come back from the hospital this morning," Merry said, who assumed control over the girls' activities.

"Well, I don't think I should go with you this morning," Melissa said, smiling apologetically, "I want to clean out the garden patch while the weather is still decent. I'll go see Dad tonight or tomorrow if he's not coming home then."

Her reason for remaining home was a good one, so the others left for Great Falls without her. As soon as their car passed out of the gate, Melissa ran up the stairs to her bedroom, grabbed her small suitcase, took money out of her private stash in her locked file (Melissa held all her treasured mementos and letters in a two drawer file), ran downstairs and into the kitchen to pack some food for Lincoln, and was on her way to Spokane. She did not take the time to stop and see her friend Ginnie in Missoula. She drove the two-year old white and black Subaru station wagon with Lincoln sprawled comfortably on the middle back seat as fast as she dared arriving in Spokane five hours later.

Back home when the others returned from visiting Marv at the hospital, Janice found the note Melissa left on her bed; she immediately attempted to contact Melissa on her cell phone, but then located it on her sister's desk, still connected to its battery charger. No one could find Lincoln. They were upset and angry, but there was little they could do although Lamedeer immediately called Andrew's school, talking to several administrators, asking them to look out for a visit from Melissa and to keep her there until she could talk to him. He then told the others that if she did not call home by evening, he would contact Sheriff Joe Chobin and ask him to have the Spokane police look for her.

Melissa entered the frat house where Andrew lived and made her way nervously up the stairs to the third floor, room 302. She knew the number by heart. "It's a nemeses room," Andrew had told her often, both in voice and on e-mail. "Every time I enter it, I get into a fight with one of my roommates."

The door was closed. She knocked.

"Hey, come on in," she heard.

She entered hesitatingly, knowing she did not belong in the building. The front door had been unlocked and no one had appeared in either the hallway or on the stairwell to stop her.

There was one boy in the room. He was lying on his bed wearing a tee shirt emblazoned with 'Seattle Mariners' and a pair of wild-colored under-shorts on his long, skinny form.

"Hey, what are you doing here? Who are you?" he half shouted. Melissa lowered her eyes, so as not to look at him in his underwear.

"I'm Andrew's sister," she said quietly.

"Oh. Yeah, Andrew." There was a pause. She knew he was pulling on jeans.

"You know you're not supposed to be here."

"Yes. No one saw me come in."

"Yeah. I gather that."

There was an embarrassing pause.

"Is this where Andrew sleeps?" she asked timidly, looking around her, her gaze settling on the alcove closest to the door.

"Yeah." He leaped off the bed and came to stand next to her. "We told the principal everything we knew about where he could be and that was nothing," he laughed, offering the words in an insolent voice.

"I'm sure you did. I just wanted to hear it too. Something has happened to my brother and I want to find him."

"Yeah. I guess you do."

"Does he ever talk about me?"

"Naw. Well, that picture of you on his desk. I recognized you from the picture."

"Where do you think he is?"

He shrugged his flat shoulders and pushed his lower jaw out in a 'I don't know' manner. "He isn't very sociable."

"Andrew is shy."

"Is that what you call it? He could be high on drugs. That's probably why he didn't want to be friends with anybody else."

"My brother doesn't do drugs." She was emphatic.

"How do you know what your brother does or doesn't do?"

Melissa ignored his question. Frustrated, she said, "You don't like him, do you?"

"Well, if you want to know the truth, no - none of us like him."

"Why not?"

"He isn't sociable. Well, he …," he did not finish. "Hey, I'm sorry that you don't know where he is."

"What do you know about what he was doing the last time you saw him?"

The boy shrugged his shoulders again. "Nothing much. Your brother keeps to himself. We don't care. He's smart, yeah, too smart. Well, I guess I can't say that."

"Hey, I'm sorry," he called after Melissa, who suddenly with tears streaming down her face, was hurrying out of the room.

What a deadhead, what a stupid conversation that was, she thought, as she sped down the stairs, almost running into two boys on the second landing and a maintenance man on the first. All three stared after her as if they couldn't believe she was in the building. The maintenance man turned to say something to her, but she slid swiftly by him completing her descent.

No wonder Andrew hated that place. Obnoxious roommate. Dreary furniture in a dark, musty, smelling building. Now, what was she to do? While she didn't learn anything from that miserable boy, it was probably stupid of her to have run away just because she didn't want to listen to him. She had no other place to go. She hurried across the street to where she had parked her car with her dog, Lincoln, inside.

She had taken Andrew's picture with her. She'd go to the neighborhood restaurants and show it to the waitresses. Somebody would know him. Who could forget her beloved brother's red hair and bright smile?

Her car was parked just beyond a corner newspaper and magazine stand. As she reached it and turned the key to unlock the door on the passenger side, a man's voice behind her called out, "Are you Andrew's sister?"

She spun around.

The voice belonged to an old, white-haired, just about too plump paraplegic dressed all in black, sitting in a wheelchair. She almost fell into him as she turned, he had drawn his chair so close to her.

"Yes, I am."

"Where is Andrew?"

She almost screamed, "I don't know." Instead, she asked in a questing voice, "How do you know Andrew?"

"He's my buddy. Where is he? Is he sick?"

"I don't know." The words came out in a deep sigh. "I don't know," she repeated forlornly, shaking her head. "He's not sick. He has just disappeared."

The man's blue-grey eyes took on a happier shape even though he looked at her questionably.

"Well, maybe he's catching up on his homework, huh?"

"No. I . . . I don't know who you are. Please tell me how

you know Andrew. And how you know about me, for that matter?"

The old man raised his thick, white eyebrows and studied her fully before he answered.

"I saw these Montana plates on your car and the Dalmatian in the driver's seat. Nice looking dog, incidentally." Melissa acknowledged his compliment with a nod. "Andrew told me lots about his family, especially about you and your dog."

"Ah," she said, in a loving tone, holding back a sob.

"We got to be buddies when he first came over here to buy a computer magazine. I run this stand," and the old man swung his head around slowly, his arthritis making him halt midway with a grimace of pain spreading over his face, checking to see if he had any customers. "At first he felt sorry for me because I am what I am." He paused to look down at his body. "But he got to like me and I certainly got to like him. What a kid and what a smile. What a great hunk of red hair." The old man laughed. "We talked computers, family and girls. The last is something he needed. He always seemed awful lonely. I don't know why, everybody should like him. He's a good kid and smart as anything."

"What is your name?" she asked.

"Ben."

"Ben, let me get my dog out of the car. Then let's find a place to talk."

"Sure." He backed up so she could open the car door. He watched as she leashed Lincoln. When the dog was standing at her side with the car door closed, he motioned her to follow him to the back of the 12-foot long stand. He wheeled himself through a narrow passageway, Melissa following.

Stopping next to a cash register, he motioned her to sit. "Sit in this chair, I save it for guests, like for Andrew. Your brother has sat in it a lot. Before we talk, do you need to take your dog for a walk? There's an empty lot on the next street."

"No. He had a great run in the fields just before we got to Spokane."

"Well, then," said Ben, "except for interruptions from customers, and there aren't many this time of day, I'm listening."

It was a difficult moment for Melissa. She motioned with her hand for Lincoln to lie down beside her chair in the narrow aisle, looked up and down the street and let her eyes linger at the tops of the three rows of magazines in the long racks in front of where she was sitting. Finally, tears welling in her eyes, looking directly into Ben's eyes, she said, "Nobody has seen or heard from him for five days. He didn't go to classes, he didn't tell anyone where he was going. He's just disappeared. My brother would let me know if he was sick or had to go someplace. That is why I know something happened to him."

"I'm sorry. Do you have any idea where he might have gone these last five days?" Ben reached out his hand and took one of hers in his. He watched her sob quietly.

" He only comes . . . came home on breaks or holidays. And he likes school."

Ben shut his eyes, thinking. Melissa watched him as he sat, biting his lips and shaking his head. When at last he opened his eyes, they formed narrow slits. His whole face closed together in a cascade of worried wrinkles.

"Was there a girl he was interested in that you knew of?"

he asked.

"No. Should there be?"

"Well, I don't know. He could have gone away with a girl last weekend."

"Andrew went away with a girl?"

"Well, he could have. I usually see him on weekends, but I wasn't here last weekend. I was sick so I don't know if he came by or went away. A friend of my nephew from Yakima took care of my stand. My nephew's friend doesn't speak English too well. Oh, he converses okay - and he's honest with money - he's from Mexico – but if Andrew came by to see me, he probably just shook his shoulders saying no that he didn't know where I was. I'll have to call my nephew and ask him to find out."

"Where would Andrew and this girl go?"

"To Canada."

"Are you sure? Not Montana?"

"No, I am not sure. Maybe they were going to go there too."

"Who was the girl, Ben? Andrew never told me about having a girl friend."

"I think it was a spur of the moment date. He came by and told me there was a waitress who wanted him to drive her to Lethbridge. He was excited about it. He asked me if he should go. I told him yes, he needed to go out with a girl, and taking a weekend and going to Lethbridge with one was just the ticket. I figured he'd come back a man. So I encouraged him, not that he needed my encouragement. He would have gone if I had said, 'Hell no.'"

"Did you meet this girl? This waitress?"

"No, but I bet she works at Shingles and Eaves, down that street." He pointed. "About four or five blocks. Andrew likes going there. It was not a hangout for the college kids, that's why he goes there."

"Why isn't Andrew liked?"

"Oh, I think he's a born loner. He likes what he does without any interference; his mind is always on single-track come hell or high water. He is so engrossed in what he is doing or what he wants to do, he doesn't have time for anybody or anything else. On top of that he is awkward - guess you'd call it shy, and that's the kind bullies like to pick on. Even if some of these kids aren't bullies, all groups have to have someone to pick on - tear apart, if you will. That's human nature. Andrew fit the bill. His red hair makes him a great come on too."

"My dear poor Andrew. I love my brother so much."

"Of course you do. Dear Miss . . . you know, I don't remember your name."

"Melissa."

"Well, Melissa, keep your chin up. I know you're going to find him. If he and the girl went to Canada, they're probably having a real good time."

Melissa blushed, embarrassed.

"Ben," she began slowly, "I'm all mixed up. And I'm very impatient sitting here talking to you. I do want to know all about what my brother does at school, and you seem a wealth of information. Of course, I haven't contacted his teachers yet. The one roommate I talked to, and I did not like him, was noncommittal. Right now, I want to know all about Andrew's girlfriend, and I guess I think I'll go try to find her if I can. Is there anything more you can tell me about her and Andrew? I realize you didn't meet her, but did Andrew describe her to you? I've got to find her. I think she's an important clue to what happened to my brother."

Ben shook his head several times as Melissa's words came tumbling out faster and faster. "I don't know anything more about the girl, even her name; all Andrew told me was that she was blond and pretty. I'm sure she is older than he. He only spoke about her twice, rather shyly too. He said she was friendly and seemed to like him. The second time he spoke about her, he asked my opinion if he should go away with her for a few days. That's all I can remember. Since he liked to go to Shingles and Eaves, I bet that is where he met her, most likely it is where she works. You might inquire about her there. It is five blocks from here. I've never been there but you might be careful going that way, the neighborhood deteriorates and I've heard they do drugs down in that area. But you have a car and a dog." Ben looked down at Lincoln who had his head in Melissa's lap, watching his mistress intently. "Just don't hang around that area at night. That restaurant has a bar in it and I'd imagine any man would like to pick you up - you are a beautiful young girl."

"Oh, Ben," said Melissa, blushing, "thank you. And I'll do as you say. I'd like to come back and tell you if I found her or found somebody who knows her and what he or she has to say."

"My roommate picks me up in a hour," said Ben, consulting his wristwatch. "We don't do much business late afternoons and evenings, so I close at 4:30. Will you still be here tomorrow?"

"Yes. I hope to see Andrew's teachers if I don't find Andrew."

"I open at 6 a.m. I make coffee here too." Smiling, Ben motioned towards the small table beside his chair, which held a cash register, paper, a coffee maker and cups. "That is, if you drink it, you're kinda young for coffee."

"I'm not too young for coffee," countered Melissa, grinning. "I just don't like it. I'll be back to see you tomorrow morning. Thanks Ben for your great help. I'm so glad to have met you."

"Likewise," the old man said.

He watched her as she and her dog went to her car. Before she opened the door she turned and called back to him, "Down which of these streets?"

He motioned the way. She nodded, opened the door for Lincoln who leapt into the front passenger seat. She then went around to the driver's side and drove away.

Chapter Twelve

M elissa drove slowly down the street towards the garish, on-off Shingles and Eaves sign. Goose bumps from nervousness swarmed through her as she neared the restaurant. She parked her car in an empty space across the street - two cars down from the restaurant. She checked her purse to be certain Andrew's picture was easy to reach for, it was. She patted Lincoln on his head, rolled the front window down one quarter even though it was cold - he had to have air - she locked the car, crossed the street and entered the restaurant.

She almost sat down in the second booth nearest the entrance. Then she noticed a brunette girl moving about in the back at the end of a bar. She said to the waitress who was approaching, "Can one eat back there?"

"Yep."

"Thank you." She headed towards the back, found a booth and sat down. She watched the brunette as she came forward to wait on her. Pretty she was but cheap looking, her lipstick too red. The green uniform she wore did not favor her. It was too tight around her breast and hips and the skirt could hardly be called a skirt. Her movement was fluid, sensual, as if she wanted everyone to know the flesh that was on her was in all the right places. The uniform on the waitress in front was loose; this one was molded on a come-hither body. It did not appear attractive.

"Would you like coffee?" asked the brunette, as she offered Melissa a menu.

"No, thank you. I will have a glass of water though." She ordered without saying anything further. This brunette was obviously not the girl Andrew may have gone away with, but she could know her.

When she brought Melissa her food and asked if she wanted dessert, Melissa answered quickly, "No thank you. But wait. I'd like to ask you something." She reached into her purse where Andrew's picture lay in a plastic sleeve and pulled it out.

"Do you know Andrew?" she asked, handing the picture to the waitress..

She watched the waitress' face closely as she asked the question. Even in this dim light she saw her face blanch. Her answer did not match her reaction.

"No."

She was lying.

"Do you know of any other waitress here that did?"

"No."

"Does a little blond waitress work here?"

"I doubt it. I never saw her."

"This is my brother's picture. You would know him if you saw him. I understand he often eats in here."

"I never saw him."

Melissa persisted, even though the waitress was turning away.

"You could not forget him. He has bright red hair."

"Sorry. Would you like your check?"

"Yes." The waitress was definitely lying. In fact, she acted almost frightened. She had to be aware of something about the girl Andrew might have gone away with. Melissa watched her disappear through a door at the back end of the bar. She kept her eyes on the door, very nervous now. She had the feeling the waitress had gone to tell someone about her queries before making out her dinner check.

She was not wrong. When the door opened her eyes widened. A man was staring at her. He was tall, dark and good-looking. But he was staring at her with the most malevolent look she had ever imagined possible and his face disappeared almost as quickly and quietly as it had appeared. Melissa began to shake. He frightened her. Five whole minutes later the waitress opened the same door, went to a cashier station at the bar, made out a check, and brought it over to the booth. Melissa examined it with shaking hands. She wanted to get out of the restaurant quickly. She reached into her wallet for money without looking up (she knew the girl was standing stiffly, as nervous as she was, waiting for the check to be paid). The intensity of feeling between them was electric though not a word was spoken. Melissa put money on the table to cover the check plus two extra dollars for a tip. The waitress took it without saying anything and moved briskly away. As Melissa left the booth, she took a last glance at the waitress who was now standing behind the bar pretending not to notice her.

"Oh, you know the girl and my brother," Melissa thought to herself, but I can't ask you about him. I'm afraid. You told that man I was sitting here, and he came to look at me as if he wanted to embed my face in his mind. I've got to find somebody to tell about that man. But first I have to get out of here. She felt in her jacket pocket for her car keys as she hurried to the exit noting darkness had descended. It was night now. The garish Singles and Eaves sign made light where it radiated but it was still night. She hurried across the street to her car, moving quickly to the driver's door. As she did, she heard the restaurant door open and close. She turned the key in the lock, heard footsteps cross the street. She opened the door with trembling fingers, slid into the driver's seat and locked the door quickly. Lincoln greeted her with a wet tongue on her cheek. She turned on the ignition and the lights, backed up and drove away. Somewhere in back of her another car had its lights turned on. As she drove down the street she realized she was headed in the wrong direction. These strange streets did not have houses with driveways that she could use to turn around in, there were only apartment buildings stuck one against the other. She drove forward two blocks, still seeing the lights from the car moving in back of her.

At the second intersection, she was able to make a quick about turn. She sighed in relief. She was now headed back towards first, the restaurant, and five blocks ahead of it, the paper stand. The car behind her turned when she did. Was it the one whose lights came on with the driver the one who left the bar moments after she did? She was sure it was, if so, she was being followed.

Oh God, Lincoln! I'm glad you are with me. Why didn't I remember to take my cell phone with me? I could call the police. How come I told Dad when he asked that I didn't need to always carry a cell phone? I need it now. Or at least I think I do. Guess I'm silly. There is the news stand, closed of course. I make a left turn here. About three blocks ahead there are businesses, which surely are still open. They will have lights on. It is only just past five o'clock yet it is dark, winter dark. I wonder if a police station is close by. I don't know a thing about Spokane. Oh, that car turned too, it IS following me. That man had such a malevolent look in his eyes. There's a gas station ahead on my side of the boulevard and they'll have a phone. If I pass it and keep on driving, in another few blocks I'll meet the freeway entrance; if I go on the freeway and that car is following me, I'll shortly be in the country and alone. If I go past the freeway entrance I don't know what is ahead. I won't know where to turn or anything so I have to stop at this station. I pray they will help me.

She pulled in. She stopped right in front of the office door. Windows lined the whole front. A young man, twenty or so, looked up from the desk inside. She jumped out of the car, ran inside, and said breathlessly, "I need to call 911."

"What's the matter? He leaped out of his chair.

"I'm being followed."

"By whom?" He looked, no cars presently sat in the pump lanes.

"They're there. Please let me phone."

"Sure. Here." He pointed to the phone on the far side of the desk.

She dialed.

"911."

"Please send police. I am being followed."

"Where are you? Who are you?"

"Where am I?" she asked the boy. She turned, but he had gone out the door because a car had driven up to one of the pumps.

She panicked, and then with her mind racing, she said quickly, "I'm at a gas station about five blocks south of the Compute University on Straight Boulevard, I think. Please hurry. I see the men getting out of their car and coming to get me."

"What is your name?"

"I am Melissa Alicorn. Please hurry. They'll kill me."

"What is your address?"

"Please. They are coming in here."

"Who are they?"

"Two men from the bar."

"You met them in a bar?"

"No."

"Are you drinking?"

"No. Please help me." Her voice was desperate.

"There is a squad car one block away. He is turning on his siren now. If you are fooling or drunk, you'll have a ticket."

She heard the siren. So did the two men about to open the office door. And they stopped short. A police car came into view, sirens blasting, lights blaring and as it pulled into the station, the men turned, moved cautiously to their car and as the police officers got out of the car, they slowly drove away.

Melissa dropped the telephone receiver, leaving it dangling in the air off the desk and rushed out the door, yelling to the young attendant, who was standing, puzzled, in the doorway. "Get their license number." Simultaneously, two police officers approached the office and confronted Melissa.

"Are you the young lady who called 911?"

"Yes, I am. Get that car's license number."

The attendant spoke up, addressing the policemen. "I have most of it."

"Good," said one. "Let's write it down." The attendant and one officer went into the office.

"You were in a bar talking to these men?" asked the other policeman.

"No, no, no." Melissa haltingly explained why she went to the restaurant bar. The policeman listened intently, excused himself, went into the office and spoke to his partner. He then went out to the squad car, returning after a few minutes with both officers checking Melissa's ID. Then one spoke.

"Young lady, your name is Melissa Alicorn and a private agent who knows you is in our station right now. We're going to take you to him."

Within minutes, with Lincoln heeling at her side, she was greeting a tall young man in civilian clothes in the Spokane station, He looked familiar. He quickly explained he was at their home when Sheriff Chobin told them of George Culbertson's murder. He told her his name was Peter Morgan and that he used to be a detective working out of this station. He led her to a desk in a large room where several policemen sat at other desks working. She slowly outlined her visit with the schoolmate, with Ben and the brunette waitress.

Peter marveled at Melissa's composure as she recounted the events. She spoke confidently, clearly and dispassionately, even at his startled reactions or when he asked her to repeat certain impressions. He questioned her several times about the man who appeared in the doorway.

"Describe him again," he asked, after making notes in a

binder.

"He was very tall, at least I think so. I only saw his face. But from what I can remember, he stood just a little below the top doorframe. His hair was dark and he wore a mustache. He also had the most evil eyes I ever saw." She shuddered.

Peter was quiet for a long while. Then he said quietly, "You have done a fine job with your sleuthing, although you should not have done any of it. You put yourself needlessly in a dangerous situation. You should not have come to Spokane," he scolded.

"I had to."

He continued, "I had no idea your brother was missing from school. Did you call the hospitals? Spokane has at least six where he could be. Your brother might have been in an accident."

"I was going to call after I left the school, but I met Ben and then I went to the restaurant bar and all that happened."

"Now that you are here, tell me all about your brother. Do you have a picture of him with you?" Melissa pulled Andrew's photo out of her purse and described Andrew to him.

Peter rose and said, "I am going to call your home and tell them where you are; then I will call the hospitals. After that, I'll see you to a motel for the night."

Suddenly Melissa's composure crumbled. "Oh no," she cried out, her face turning ashen. "Please no. I can't go to a motel alone. They'll find me and kill me. You don't know how that man looked at me."

Peter, surprised she was so frightened, sat down again;

almost wanting to take her in his arms to comfort her, she was so forlorn. He had been attracted to her the first time he saw her as she sat on the couch with her sister. And his heart had taken an unexpected leap when she strode into this station with her dog heeling close beside her. However, they were sitting at a desk in the station with several policemen working at other desks. One had looked up as Melissa cried out. Peter did reach out to take one of her hands in his.

"Those men!" she exclaimed. "And the way the man who opened the door looked at me . . . " She closed her eyes as if to erase the memory of his malignant stare. "I won't go to a motel. I'll sit here until daylight. I'll be safe here."

"No, Melissa," Peter told her gently. "You cannot stay here. I'll see you to a safe house."

"With you?"

He grinned. He enjoyed her remark. "Now that would be nice."

She blushed.

"Let me check on what is available. You'll stay in Spokane until either your father or Lamedeer arrive to take you home."

"Are you going back to Montana?"

He shook his head no. "I grew up here," Peter said, "though my purpose here this weekend is not to see friends. I am on another mission."

"Well, I can drive home by myself in the morning."

"Daylight will not stop these men from trying to find you. You would be foolish to travel on the highway alone, and once you are home you should not go any place without a guardian. If these men mean to do you harm, they can harm you there as well as here. I work in narcotics and am   not traveling right now. I've been checking several possible leads about George Culbertson. I have confidence your father or Lamedeer can get you home safely. We'll also alert both Idaho and Montana Sheriffs to keep a watch on you as you travel. Now excuse me, Melissa. I'm going to call your home, the hospitals, and then check on a safe house. I forgot your father is in the hospital, but, Janice, your sister is home and is it . . . Lamedeer?" she nodded, "is there." He patted her hand, rose, and asked, "Would you like a soda or a cup of hot tea while you are waiting?"

She shook her head.

"I will not be long." Seeing her misery, he leaned down and said very gently, "I must make arrangements to ensure your safety."

She sat quietly while he was gone, thinking about him. It was good to think about him instead of how the day had been. How nice he was and how good looking. She loved his large brown eyes (wonderful eyes) and his clean-shaven face. He had such a handsome face, even with that awful scar running down one side of his cheek. And he had a mustache - much like her Dad's - he had a gentler voice than her Dad and his street clothes showed off his body to be strong and taut, also his big black boots told her he had big feet. Well, of course, she laughed to herself, he looks so good because he works out to keep fit; scary job, working with criminals. But I still do not really know what he does.

While she was waiting, a policeman came to her and asked for the picture of her brother plus a verbal description. After she told him, he took the photo of Andrew over to a copy machine, made several copies and brought her back the photo. Then Peter was again beside her, a box of Kleenex in his hands. She took several tissues and wiped her eyes.

Silently, he led her and Lincoln outside to her car. Behind it was a patrol car, a policeman as driver. Peter asked for her car keys, opened the passenger side for her and took the driver's seat. "We have a patrol car checking on us as we drive," he told her. "If we are being followed, they will alert us. Now stop shivering. I'm not going to let anything happen to you."

They rode in silence for 15 minutes. Twice the patrolman in the other car talked to Peter on his phone to report all was well. At last they stopped on a street with snow-covered lawns. Peter led Melissa and Lincoln (on leash) up a short walk to a well groomed, two-story home. They were greeted by two women police officers.

"She'll be fine with us; so will this nice dog," one said, as they escorted Melissa inside and bade Peter goodnight.

"I'll park Melissa's car down the street and we'll hold there for awhile. Thanks, ladies."

There were no recriminations when, late the next morning, Peter brought Annabelle, Janice and Lamedeer to the house. No one mentioned the fact that Melissa had disobeyed Marv's rule about driving away from the ranch without a companion. Janice hugged her sister and told her how wonderful she was. Annabelle gave her kisses and Lamedeer smiled approval.

"You are riding with Lamedeer," Annabelle told Melissa. "If anything should arouse his interest, he's a good detective. And Janice and I will be right behind you - all the way."

"Take care," Peter said to Melissa, patting Lincoln on the head as they got back into her car. "And remember what I told you. From now on do not leave the ranch alone."

Glad Peter was concerned, Melissa told him thanks.

The two cars began traveling. There were no incidents to be concerned about. An Idaho Sheriff's car stopped them just inside the city limits of Wallace, a small Idaho town. They ate lunch there while the Sheriff sat in his car observing east bound traffic. A Sheriff's car preceded them out of Missoula, on Highway 200, finally waving them ahead. It was snowing lightly at first, then heavily as they neared Rogers Pass on the divide. The trip, usually five hours from Spokane to the ranch, took seven. They passed no one; no one passed them. They were grateful to drive into the ranch garages without incident. Lincoln leaped out of Melissa's car, his tail wagging. He sloughed through the snow on his own adventure as the others went into the house.

Chapter Thirteen

T hey had not been home for two hours when Peter called. They had located Andrew in one of the Spokane hospitals. He was weak and puny, but the doctor Janice spoke to told her Andrew could fly on a regular airline to Great Falls and be transferred to Benefis Hospital for further treatment. He had been shot in his right chest and had lost over half his blood when a man and wife out on an evening walk found him. They thought he was dying and he almost did, Peter told them. But he'll be okay, though complete recovery will take several months.

The family was esthetic. Both Melissa and Janice cried with joy. Arrangements were quickly made for Andrew's transport. Andrew would be taken by ambulance to the airport in Spokane, placed on the plane with a nurse attending him, picked up in Great Falls by ambulance and taken to Benefis.

In the morning, even Swallow went with the others to see Andrew. They did not do much talking; he was so pale even his freckles seemed to have disappeared under his paleness and, of course, he was extremely weak. They did as much kissing and hugging as allowed, and then left him to take Marv home. Two days later George Culbertson's Memorial Service was held – his body had been autopsied before it was cremated, but services were delayed until the autopsy reports had come back and Marv could attend. The blow of his heart attack and the loss of his friend – and to murder - the pain sat naked on his face with sunken cheeks and vacant eyes as he and his two daughters entered the chapel. He didn't shuffle, but he walked haltingly, grimly, his eyes straight ahead staring at nothing. It was as if he was oblivious to his surroundings. Everyone got out of his way so as not to be in his way. He didn't speak to any of his friends. He was alone.

The chapel was packed with mourners. Ranchers from across Montana were there with their families. Mourners overflowed out the door, standing in winter jackets and coats, buttoned or zipped tight up around their necks, protecting them from the bitter wind. They stood shivering, their shoes and boots icily colliding with the cold October ground.

Marv halted in surprise at the profusion of flowers. Melissa said, "The flowers aren't for Mr. Culbertson. He's dead. They are for all of us, to placate us. I don't like that. I wish he could have known how he was to be honored by his friends."

Marv's eyes softened momentarily. He took Melissa's hand and squeezed it.

When the service was over, and after he had spoken to George's widow, Carol Culbertson, he said to Lamedeer, "We enjoyed our times together, but there is nothing I can do to mitigate the guilt I have for the way I often ignored George."

Melissa saw Peter Morgan standing alongside Sheriff Chobin and two county policemen as they left the chapel, but they did not speak to anyone. It was obvious they were there watching people.

"I've got that damn headache again," Marv moaned as he

got into the car. He also slammed into the house on their return and went straight to his bedroom, remaining there the next several days, telling anyone who knocked on his door to get the hell away. He did take broth when Merry brought it to him but nothing else.

Melissa and Janice took turns (accompanied by either Lamedeer or Gustav) going to the hospital to see Andrew. He could now walk slowly up and down the hospital corridors accompanied by nurses' aides. He also received physical therapy several times a day, but he did not speak to any one. Dr. Witt told them something had shocked Andrew so greatly that he could not cope with what happened. He was suffering temporary amnesia. He was being given anti-depression tablets but it would take several weeks before any beneficial effects could take over. "When we try to talk to him," Dr. Witt said, "he just stares at us. This amnesia will pass, don't worry," he told the sisters whose faces had crumpled with bewilderment and distress. "We have to be patient. We have a psychiatrist attending him."

When home, the girls sat together by the fireplace in the living room, both miserable because the two men in the family were ill and there was little they could do to help. On the third day Melissa called Annabelle.

"Please come see us," she begged. "Maybe you can do something with Dad and help us pray for Andrew."

When Annabelle arrived, the girls had tea ready. Merry set cookies and small cakes on the library table and after the three had hugged and kissed and spoke of their sadness, Annabelle beckoned both of them to sit beside her on the long couch. "Before I leave today, I'll see your father. But I will not tell him what I am telling you two now."

"You're not thinking of going away again, are you?" Melissa asked.

"Yes. Nothing has changed, dear Melissa. I am leaving."

"Oh, please don't," both Melissa and Janice begged.

"Sssssh. Let me finish, dear girls, so you will understand. My business here is good in the summer but is practically non-existent during the winter months. Oh, I make enough to sneak by and it would be okay for a retired couple with an income or for someone like Molly. But I have at least twenty years of work life ahead of me. I have to make more money than I am making now.

"I believe I have an excellent opportunity to do this in a little town in southern California, Temecula. The town is situated halfway between Riverside and San Diego. It's right on the edge of the desert. It's warm. Tourists visit that area twelve months of the year. Temecula has enough historical value to entice tourists to exit the freeway and pause to eat and shop. They make wonderful wine there too.

"There's a nice gift shop for sale. I've already rented it with an option to buy. I'll still be making trips to New York to stock it, adding Mexico City on my itinerary."

Annabelle stopped, noting the glum, worried looks on both girls.

"I have to do this." Firmly.

"But Dad loves you," insisted Janice.

"That he may. But I am not satisfied with our relationship. And I need to make more money than I am now. I have to put something away for retirement. I don't like scrimping the way I must now.

"I shall miss you with all my heart, but we all have lives to live and sometimes we have to go different ways. Each new way is a new adventure and we must go into it smiling.

"As for you two - Janice, you go to New York. If your screen test turns out well, and it should, you'll begin a new career. Don't let anything or anyone stand in your way, least of all your father. Call that producer, set a departure date and leave. You are almost twenty-one years of age. You need to start living your own life. We'll all worry about you; you are so impressionable, but you have been brought up well. Although," and she laughed softly, "you have been over protected. You have been, you know," she added as she noted a look of consternation settle on Janice's beautiful face. "Go with one plan in front of you. Don't deviate from it. You must discipline yourself, Janice, to succeed.

"I know," and she smiled tenderly, reaching out her hand, "that I am giving you advice. Perhaps I shouldn't be, but please, take it to heart. I love you so much. I'm going to send you my phone number in Temecula. I want you to promise to call me day or night with any problem you encounter, big or small. If you are lonely, tired, happy, please let me share with you. I love you, Janice. Please do that."

"I will."

"Good. Melissa, you will take good care of your father and brother. I know how happy you are that Andrew is home. You, of anybody, can help him get over whatever horrible thing he experienced. You've also got Merry, Swallow and Lamedeer to help you. It is obvious you love this ranch. It will prosper with you. And you'll have my phone number too. I don't want to be forgotten. A big part of my life and heart will always be here. Oh, and don't allow your father to go on a rampage about George Culbertson or Andrew. The police and the FBI — I understand they have been called in —they will find Culbertson's killer.

"We're all so wrought up with these bad adventures, but we do have to go on. Think of the wonderful times ahead of you. Don't allow your mind to dwell on what you have just been through.

"Well," Annabelle added, hugging each of them in turn, "I'm off. Wish me happiness, my dear, sweet girls. And let's not say goodbye. I want you both to come visit me. No, no, sit still. I'm going up to see your father just like it's a normal day."

She moved up the stairs looking back at them, not sitting together, but huddled together, as if they were one. She smiled down at them lovingly, shaking her head, her eyes brimming with sadness. Then, with eyes wet, she walked on to Marv's bedroom.

She knocked on the door.

"I don't need anything. Let me rest." She laughed. She had heard him loud and clear.

Her answer was to herself. "I'm not about to, Marv."

She opened the door and went in. He lay in his king-size poster bed, a silent, unmoving long form filling its length. One thin pillow was under his head and one fat pillow lay over his head keeping out the light from the western skies, which was pushing sunlight through the panes of the large picture window opposite the bed.

"Hi Marv," she said sweetly, "do you want me to close the blinds?"

"No!"

His bellowing voice made her laugh.

She approached the bed, pulling up the straight-backed, plaid-cushioned chair, so that she could sit close beside him.

"Ah, it's you. It's my Annabelle." His voice softened.

"Yes, it's I, my dear Marv," she answered, as she sat down and took hold of the hand he held out. His eyes were still closed.

"And how is your head?"

"It hurts like hell."

"What did they give you for pain?"

"Aspirin, God damn it. Nothing else."

"You had bleeding there."

"Yes, I know. You'd think they'd have something better to give me."

She ignored his complaint.

'Merry says you won't eat."

"Damn it, it hurts to eat."

Silence.

"It hurts to talk too."

"You have to eat something. Or at least drink water and broth."

"In good time I will."

"Marv. . ."

"Shut up, Annabelle. Just hold my hand."

"Okay, Marv."

After a while he spoke again.

"I miss you when you're not here, Annabelle."

She did not answer.

"Why don't you come every day?"

"I've been busy, Marv."

"Unbusy yourself. Come sit by me until I get better."

She did not answer.

"You hear me, Annabelle?" He opened his eyes, pushing away the pillow. "You look very pretty today, Annabelle," he added, his eyes caressing her body as they went over her form.

"Thank you, Marv."

"Yes, you are lovely. I need to stop talking now. My head pains. I can't have another aspirin for an hour. Will you give it to me then?" he pleaded.

"I have to go now, Marv," she said.

"You are always leaving. Well, be back tomorrow. And be prepared to stay awhile. I need you, Annabelle."

"Yes, Marv," she whispered, rising and kissing him on the tip of his nose gently. "You rest well tonight, Marv."

"Ummmmm," he answered.

She closed the door behind her.

Chapter Fourteen

Annabelle's plane landed in Ontario, California, two hours late because her connecting flight in Seattle was late; it had flown around storms in both northern California and Washington. So she looked down on clouds and snow-covered terrain most of the flight; however, in the last half hour the sky became bright and clear and the ground below looked warm. It was because Ontario was warm.

She had purchased a used car on an earlier trip, and the young man from the car agency who was delivering it to her at the airport was testy.

"The plane's two hours late," he grumbled as he handed her the keys.

"Yes," she answered. She pulled an extra twenty dollars from her purse and handed it to him.

"It's a nice sedan," he said, mollified, "full of gas. It gets good mileage - about 25 to a gallon."

"Thank you again," she told him. He walked away. She didn't know how he was getting back to the dealership but she didn't care; he had stood watching, not assisting, as she had lifted her two heavy bags into the car's hatchback.

She knew the way, straight down I-15 past Riverside, Corona, Lake Elsinore, Wildomar and turn left off the freeway at the Temecula sign of Greene Street.

She stopped at a small grocery store, bought staples and a cake from a list she had prepared, and then drove to the furnished house she had rented for three months. It sat in an attractive twenty-year-old subdivision with mature trees and shrubs decorating each lawn of the one and two story ranch style homes.

"Even in late fall," she mused, as she parked her car in the driveway and walked across the lawn to the front door, "grass is green. How nice."

She unlocked the door and entered a pleasant living room with Venetian blinds covering the wide front windows. She found the drawstring on the left side of the flowered-cloth-covered couch that sat in front of the windows and opened the blinds. Old dust danced in the sunlight that flooded the room. It was late afternoon, a pretty sunlit afternoon. She turned on a light switch. The living room lit up from a chandelier hanging dead center as if a table belonged below it but no table was there.

"Good," she said, "the lights work." She immediately turned off the switch and carried two large bags of groceries and her purse to the kitchen. The kitchen was small, too small for her liking. It did possess a bay window with a lovely shelf on which she could place pots of plants or knick-knacks. And the window looked out on a long and wide cemented patio. Beyond the patio were trees (she did not know what kind they were). Trees grew tall in California, she mused, they didn't wither from lack of moisture, and shallow roots didn't tear out of the ground and die from the constant wind as trees did in Montana, these sheltered the patio with lovely colored leaves of many shapes. Beautiful trees, whatever kind they were. Grass took up all other extra space. It was an attractive back yard.

She busied herself, lining two cupboard shelves with paper

after cutting them to shape with a scissors she had purchased along with her groceries. She then placed the few cans and a loaf of bread on them. Taking out two slices of bread, she spread them with peanut butter and jelly, remarking as she did, "What a staple this is!" She sat down at a small table in a family-type room off the kitchen and began eating the sandwich with a glass of milk. All of a sudden her eyes misted, and her throat constricted.

"Damn, why do I have to think about you!" she muttered. She got up, took her plate with its half-eaten sandwich and glass back to the kitchen, and set them on the counter.

Oh, Marv, she wailed, it's over, Marv. I know I did the right thing, she said to herself, attempting to bolster her feelings, but closing her eyes and wishing she were in Montana close to Marv. "I did do the right thing!" she answered herself. Straighten up and fly right, Annabelle, she muttered, trying to push the past away.

Quickly, moving her thoughts on what she had to do, she lugged the two heavy suitcases, each one in turn, through the house and into the master bedroom.

Sighing with weariness, she went back to the kitchen and looked out at the yard one more time. "Beautiful," she said aloud. "It's beautiful here. Be happy. That's what you want to be." She moved to the laundry closet in the long hallway, took towels to the master bathroom, undressed, showered and went to bed.

Tired as she was, sleep was evasive a good part of the night. The bed was comfortable but she wasn't. Finally, at five in the morning, still dark, she fell asleep. She woke up at 7:15, leaped out of bed, went to the bathroom, dressed quickly, and then hurried to the kitchen, turning on the light.

She screamed. The counter was black. "Oh, my God," she exclaimed, recoiling. "What in the world are those?"

They were tiny black ants, millions of them, covering the counter and the walls next to the sink. They were everywhere she looked, on the stove, on the pretty shelf above the sink under the window and she felt them on her feet. They almost covered the floor too. She began jumping up and down trying to shake them off her slippers. She ran from the kitchen into the family room turning on that light switch. They weren't in there. They weren't in the living room either. She next ran into her bedroom; it was ant free also.

"Good God," she kept exclaiming. "How awful. What to do? I don't want to go back in there."

But back into the kitchen she had to go. She carried a pail she found in the garage, filling it with hot water from a sink in the garage. She dumped it on the counter. While hundreds of tiny ants went sliding off the counter into the sink and down the drain in the splashes of hot water, millions remained on the counter and walls and floor. She grimaced when she noted that her cake box and half eaten peanut butter sandwich were thick with them.

"Damn," she exploded, "and here I am without a phone." Her house telephone would not be connected for four more days. This was Monday morning and the telephone company appointment was for the coming Friday.

Making sure she carried no ants on her clothes, she got her purse and car keys, left the house and drove to the small grocery store where she had shopped the afternoon before. A lady of Mexican descent was behind the cash register.

Annabelle explained what was going on in her kitchen.

"Ah, those are Argentine ants," chuckled the storekeeper. "They are horrible, aren't they? If you leave anything on the counters, particularly meat or sweets, they come swarming into the house in huge armies. Ah, they are horrible."

"I need to call an exterminator," Annabelle said. "You have a telephone here and a phone book I can use?"

"Yes. The phone booth is at the back. Here, call my brother. He exterminates these ants." She was writing down a telephone number on a slip of paper as she spoke.

The exterminator was at her house within the hour. She followed him to the kitchen, but only watched from the doorway. He took out several insecticide filled rags from a large sack, wiped the walls and counters, then shoved the rags into a large plastic bag.

"These ants are dead. You don't have to worry about them anymore," he said, looking back at her, grinning. He then took a screwdriver and opened the light switch on the wall.

"What in the world are you doing?" she asked.

"These little guys make their nests in the walls of these houses. It's cool, safe and moist. They travel along the wires so we put poison where their nests are. You don't have to worry about breathing ant poison powder in your lungs."

She watched him as he took a long tube, evidently filled with ant poison, and inserted it into the open conduit. She watched as he opened several more light switches to insert poison; another in the kitchen and one in the family room.

"They'll all be dead by evening," he told her when he had finished. "Just try to put everything away after this. Whatever you leave on the counter or stove is fair game to these ants.

Even crumbs. And keep the garbage cans outside by the front yard gate. A good dousing of the garbage cans every week with ant spray will hold them at bay. Call me when you need me again."

She paid him and he left.

She shook her head thinking no wonder I like the north country. Not many bugs, and definitely none at this time of year. She shook her head again telling herself to shut up. You are here, it's nice and warm, there's no wind, so be happy.

She worked the rest of the day studying the inventory sheets of the store she was going to lease, rereading the contract and browsing through a dozen catalogs. It was not a very productive day, but it was one filled with necessary chores. She returned to the kitchen several times, twice rescrubbed the walls, the counters, the surfaces of the stove, refrigerator and microwave. Each time she found an ant she shuddered. She remembered that when she was a little girl she had wanted a glassed ant nest she saw in a hobby shop. I don't know why, she now thought, because I hate those insects.

The next few days were busy ones. She sat in her car in front of the shop she was about to lease and watched traffic. She stood in the shop and spoke to prospective buyers about merchandise they were interested in. She ate lunch with the owner sitting at a table in the shop and after lunch going over the contract and inventory lists. She visited a lawyer, showing him the papers the shop owner had prepared. and asked him to represent her in the closure of this transaction. She then went shopping for spring clothes which she could now wear in October, the daytime weather being so mild.

And she ate at Mexican restaurants - loving the food.

Thursday evening as she sat on the back patio of her house browsing through a women's magazine, she startled when the doorbell chimed. It was the first time she had heard it She looked down at the white blouse and the pale green summer skirt she wore, knew she was dressed appropriately for visitors (probably neighbors) and got up to answer the doorbell.

Her heart flip-flopped. She took a deep breath.

Marv stood in the doorway. His hair was a little longer than he liked it to be, his face pale, but his eyes and lips were smiling.

"So I had to come all the way down here to get you to come back home."

"Marv!"

"Yes, it's me, Marv. What do you have to say for yourself, leaving me almost dead and taking off."

"Marv . . ."

"Never mind. Don't answer. Just give me a kiss."

Without waiting for an answer, he grabbed her, lifted her off her feet, put his arms tightly around her and kissed her. She grew numb with the emotions coursing through her. All she could think of was that it was delicious to be kissed by Marv again, his tongue moving inside her mouth, spreading desire throughout her body. It was a good minute before he let her go.

"Come on," he said, the second he allowed her out of his arms. "I have a car and a driver here. We're going for a ride."

"Where?"

"None of your business. Get your purse and your personal

papers so somebody doesn't steal them. Get your lipstick case and come on. Turn off the stove if you have anything on it. Lock the house."

"Where are we going?"

"You'll find out when we get there."

She did as she was told because she was too intoxicated emotionally to do otherwise. She shook with relief and excitement that Marv was here.

Marv waited impatiently by the front door. When she reappeared, purse in hand, her eyes still wide with disbelief (was he really here?), he took hold of her arm gently and led her to a waiting limousine.

"Where are we going, Marv?"

"Out to dinner."

"Oh." Her voice almost sounded disappointed. And then you will leave, she thought.

"You are a very bad Annabelle," he said, once they were seated in the car and he had his arms around her.

"Oh, Marv. I'm glad you are here but you shouldn't be here."

"Shut up, Annabelle. I don't feel too swift yet. So be quiet and let me hold you."

She looked at him, wanting to take his face, pull it down to hers and kiss it.

"Your heart is pounding pretty hard," he said.

"Yes, Marv. How long are you here for?"

"Don't talk right now. I'm not going to answer you."

"I need to know."

"You don't want me to leave, do you?"

"No, but you will, so I want to know when."

"You'll find out."

She broke out of his arms and moved over to the window.

Marv laughed as hard as he could. "Come back here, my Annabelle. Get back in my arms." He pulled her back, putting his arm tightly around her. "There," he said tenderly, kissing her cheek, "that's where you belong. Now shut up and be quiet."

Annabelle rolled her eyes at him, but said nothing. She sat, almost stiffly in his arms for a moment, then relaxed.

"That's better," he said, kissing her on the top of her head.

They rode in silence.

"We're at the Ontario airport!" she suddenly exclaimed.

"Yes. We are going to meet Janice and Melissa."

"We are?"

"We have to fly to meet them."

"Marv! Where, for goodness sakes?"

"I'm not telling." He burst into laugher again.

When he had stopped laughing, he said simply, "You'll find out, but first we have to get on this plane."

"What plane? Where are you going?"

"You mean 'where are we going?' It's a secret, Annabelle. You'll find out when you get there."

"You're not taking me back to Montana."

"No. I said we were going to meet Janice and Melissa. Now be quiet, Annabelle. Let the events fall as they may." He laughed again.

"What about Andrew?, she asked, "You haven't told me how he is."

"He's home but he hasn't spoken yet."

"Oh, Marv," her face was grave.

"Melissa is doing a great job caring for him. He's walking all over the ranch with her. And I have a lot of remedial time to make up to him, my dear son."

The limousine had parked in front of a hangar.

"Come, you have to get out and get on this plane."

She couldn't believe she was, but she was obeying Marv and being very quiet while the small jet took off. She didn't even ask who was paying an exorbitant fee for the charter of the plane and pilot.

"I now live in Temecula," she said at last, weakly.

He did not answer.

"Well," he finally said, "I'll have to tell you. Janice and Melissa are in Las Vegas enjoying some gambling . . . "

"Marv!"

"They are enjoying the sights; they needed to get away. We three needed to get away."

"I grant you that. Why didn't they come down here for dinner?"

"They wanted to go to Las Vegas. So we are meeting them there for dinner."

"Oh."

"We'll be there in 30 more minutes. I'm going to hold you in my arms the whole 30 minutes."

"Marv."

"Come here, you silly woman. Put your head on my shoulder."

She did, joyfully, tears flowing down her cheeks.

When they had landed and debarked, another limousine was waiting. But neither Janice nor Melissa was there. Marv explained he did not want them to drive out to the airport.

"We're going to meet them in a few minutes."

"I don't believe this is happening," said Annabelle.

"It happens in the best of families."

His voice changed. He became very serious. "Tell me, Annabelle, do you love me?" He looked her fully in the face, staring at her, his lips apart in a small smile. "No, don't answer, my Annabelle. I don't need an answer. I know you love me."

"Yes, I do love you, Marv, but . . .. "

"The word but is not in our English language today, Annabelle. Ah, here we are."

She looked out of the window. The limousine had parked in front of a white stucco building. It was a small chapel.

Standing in the doorway were Janice and Melissa each holding a huge bouquet of red roses in their arms.

Annabelle stared out the window of the limousine. Her mouth went slack, her face white, her eyes wide and staring. She tried to say something, to ask a question, but nothing came out of her mouth.

Marv turned her to him, took her by the shoulders and spoke to her in a voice, low and husky with emotion. "We are going to get married, Annabelle. That is why you are here. I want you to be my wife. I love you with all my heart and soul. I know you love me. If you wish, I'll ask you to marry me." Before she could say anything he took one hand away from her shoulder and reaching down to a pocket on his slacks, he took out a small box.

"There's a ring in here for you," he said, quietly opening the box. "Here it is, my love, our engagement ring. Will you marry me, Annabelle?"

Tears were streaming down Annabelle's cheeks. "Oh, Marv. I love you. I love you."

"I know you do, dearest. Yes or no, please."

"Yes."

"Let me place this ring on your finger."

She held out her hand.

"There," he said, grinning through misty eyes. "We're engaged, but only for a few minutes. Now we're going to get married. And I have another ring for you."

Suddenly his head went back and he laughed. Uproariously. It was a wonderful laugh, tumbling from his lips and filled with glorious joy. "I'm so happy," he said. "And hey, that was a pretty good surprise game we played, huh?"

Speechless, Annabelle could hardly nod her head. "Oh, Marv, you are so wonderful. . ."

"And so are you. Come on, the girls are waiting."

The chauffeur opened the door. Janice and Melissa rushed to greet them and the four stood hugging.

They went into the chapel where bouquets of flowers filled the small room.

"These flowers are for you, my dearest," Marv said to Annabelle. "I didn't want a big wedding but I wanted to please you with flowers."

In a few minutes the service was over and the four hugged and kissed again.

"Now, Mrs. Alicorn," said Marv, as they got into the limousine, their arms filled with bouquets, "we are going to have our wedding dinner. The girls will then catch a plane for Great Falls, and you and I have a hotel suite awaiting us.

When our honeymoon is over, we'll fly back to your Temecula and make plans for the rest of our lives."

"It's very simple," Marv explained to Annabelle later driving to the hotel where he had rented a suite. They had just watched the plane carrying Miranda and Melissa lift off for Great Falls.

"We shall let lawyers handle everything. I've already talked to Jim, our lawyer in Great Falls. He doesn't know what you've done or signed, but he'll undo and unsign everything necessary."

"I hired a lawyer yesterday, one who practices in Escondido."

"Where is that?"

"That's a city south of Temecula, on the way to San Diego."

"Well, in the morning you give me his telephone number; I'll have Jim call him. We are going to stay here a few days and I want you to pick up a new wardrobe at the stores while I nap. I'm not all well yet, Annabelle, and need to rest several times each day. And now that I am married, in order to truly enjoy my honeymoon with my beautiful bride," and Marv grinned, "I require my naps.

"If you can't get out of the house you rented for three months, that's okay," he continued. "The landlord will make out like a bandit with a couple of months rent in his pocket. We'll stop there in a couple of days and pick up the things you took there."

"I bought a car, Marv."

"Oh? Did you pay cash? If so, we'll take it back to the dealership; they can sell it all over again."

"No. I purchased it on time."

"Well, we'll pay it off and take it back to the dealership. Is it new? What is it?"

"It's a '96 Ford sedan."

"Well, we don't want it. Do you want it?"

"No."

"I'm going to buy you a new car when we get home. I'll have the lawyers take care of that too. You know, you are not going to have to work twenty more years."

"The girls told you."

"Of course. And if something happens to me in the next twenty years, you'll have plenty to live on for the rest of your life except the ranch goes to Andrew and the girls. Now, I'll take care of all the details when you are out shopping tomorrow. Right now we are approaching the hotel we're staying at, and we're going to play. We'll do whatever you want to do and go where you want to go for the next few days. It's our honeymoon. It ends Tuesday because we have to be home for Janice. She leaves for New York for her screen test Wednesday morning and I want to have a serious talk with her."

The limousine parked in front of the hotel. They were immediately ushered into the lobby and to a beautiful suite on the top floor.

Annabelle looked about her as the door closed behind them. She examined the contents of the tables in each room of the three-room suite. Bouquets of flowers decorated each table. Several tables held platters of crackers and cheese, others of wine with two iced glasses and on another sat a miniature cake with a toy bride and groom standing on the top of it. In the bedroom on the satin-bedspread lay two large packages decorated with ribbons of every color of the rainbow.

Marv followed Annabelle as she inspected each room and oohed and aahed at the decorations, taking her hand as they entered the bedroom.

"Those are gifts for you," he said simply.

She didn't answer, just smiled at him, her mouth quivering, and went over to the bed and slowly opened her presents. The first held a beautiful violet-colored chiffon nightgown and robe.

"The color matches your eyes," he said.

"You are spoiling me."

"I intend to spoil you completely."

She opened the second. It was a makeup case, filled with lipsticks and powders and creams of every sort. Marv watched her marvel at the contents. "The only things that aren't in there are shampoos and other bathroom stuff," he said. "The hotel supplies those. Do you like your presents?"

She could not answer. She rose and came to him. She lifted her chin and kissed him.

"I'd like you to undress in front of me," he said. "I'd like to see what my wife looks like."

She blushed. "You've seen me naked before, Marv."

"Yes, but not with your new rings on. Please. .," he said.

She stood for a moment quietly in front of him and then began taking off her clothes. As she shed her blouse, he came up to her and took her head in his hands, kissing her hard, his tongue searching deep inside her mouth until she shuddered with desire. As she took off her brassiere, he went around to the back of her kissing her shoulders, turning her when her brassiere lay on the thick blue carpet and kissing both of her breasts. Then he stood back.

"Go on," he murmured huskily.

She shed her green skirt. He came forward again, putting his arms around her, lowering them slowly to her hips caressing her buttocks as he pulled down her panties. "Ah," he said, again huskily, his breath quick. "You are so lovely, my wife. Wait for me, dearest."

He shed his clothes, letting them fall as he took them off. He looked at her, quietly standing naked in the position in which he had left her and took her to bed. He kissed her forehead, her eyes, her nose, her cheeks, her lips, her ears; his mouth went down her body, to her breasts, her stomach, her thighs. She waited as his mouth traveled up her body again. He climbed up upon her and their passion did not subside. In an instant they were one again, unable to leave the other until both were awash with the pure joy of their togetherness. As they lay content, holding each other closely, he whispered over and over, "I love you, my dearest Annabelle."

Suddenly he was asleep. She lay awake a long time watching him as he slept, sighing, smiling, reliving over and over the wonders of the day.

"We are married," she said to herself, unbelieving, then looking at her rings. "Ah, oh Marv," she whispered, looking at him beside her.

"I love you, Marv."

And she too fell asleep, lying back against the pillows, her mouth in a wide smile.

Chapter Fifteen

T hey flew back to Great Falls the next Tuesday. On the flight, Annabelle told Marv about the Argentine ants.

"How long have they been in California?" he guffawed.

"I guess a very long time. They are all over southern California, I understand," replied Annabelle.

"You don't have to worry your beautiful self about ants when you get home again," Marv assured her, kissing her on the cheek. "You will have to get out your 22 next Spring and help get rid of some of those Richardson ground squirrels though. They are as destructive as those Argentine ants of yours, only in a bigger way. And Melissa has decided to become an environmentalist as far as gophers go. I told her wait until Atlas falls in one of their holes, and she'll change her mind.

"There is one thing I'm going to ask you not to do," he added soberly. "I know how you like to go traipsing about, and Melissa won't always be tagging along. Do not go near the old line shed, particularly in the hollow below it."

"Is that where you dynamited that snake den two years ago?"

"Yes. Well, they're back. Snakes are creatures of habit just like all animals. And they've established their winter den - same place! Gustav almost ran into it this fall, taking a short cut to the line cabin. He said there were dozens - all kinds, of course - and that the mama rattlers had plenty of new babies. You know how dangerous the venom is of newborn rattlers."

"Ugh," shivered Annabelle.

" I do like a few snakes around," mused Marv. "They certainly control our mice and gophers and they don't bother us because we respect their hissing bluffs. But you stay away from there, hear me?"

"Are you going to dynamite the den again come spring?"

"Yes, this time we're going to have to get rid of the rocks and logs down there and keep those weeds down. My only fear is if we do that they'll establish a new den closer to the barns. After all, we've got plenty of varmints around there.

"Changing the subject," he said mischievously, putting his hand over hers, which lay on her lap, "do you realize if you had not listened to me and taken your personal papers along with you the night we went to Las Vegas, we'd be living in sin? Wonder what that would be like?"

"Oh, Marv," Annabelle answered, giggling, her eyes dancing merrily, "you are feeling ever so much better to tease like that."

Annabelle," he responded seriously.. "I should be the happiest man alive having you." He leaned over, pulled her face towards his and kissed her hard. He settled back in his seat and said somberly, "and I will be once we get Andrew out of this funk or psychosis or whatever it is. My neglect of him when he needed me is my pain. I have a lot to make up to him, and I know you'll help me learn how. Thank God for you and your love. You are making this terrible time livable."

Lamedeer and Melissa picked them up at the airport in Great Falls.

"Where's Janice?" Marv asked immediately.

"Janice and Merry left early this morning for New York."

"They did?"

"Yes."

"They weren't supposed to leave until tomorrow morning." Marv was more than annoyed, he was furious.

"The Territoni office called and said they wanted her at the beginning of the week. She needed to practice or something for the test."

"Oh. Well, I guess so. Have you heard from them yet?"

"No, they are still in flight."

"Of course."

"When is Janice coming back?" asked Annabelle.

"As soon as she has her screen test." Marv was emphatic.

When they opened the door of the ranch house, the library table in the living room was piled high with presents and flowers. "Melissa and Janice told the world," Lamedeer said, before the newly-weds could ask. "And the Great Falls Tribune wants to do a story."

"Annabelle, please send the paper something. I don't want a story at this time," said Marv, annoyed.

She nodded her head and went forward to receive hugs from Swallow, who was waiting by the door to the kitchen.

"You have hot soup for lunch awaiting you," said Swallow. "And the ranch hands want to come in and offer congratulations."

"Send them in," smiled Marv.

It was a busy hour before Annabelle, Marv, Melissa and Lamedeer sat down to eat lunch.

Before they had finished, Peter Morgan arrived. Lamedeer left the table and waited in the living room with Peter until Marv was ready to receive him.

"Hello, young man." Marv directed him to one of the two couches that sat on each side of the long, stone fireplace. Marv sat down on the other one. Lamedeer turned to leave.

"Stay here," said Marv. "You're in on this investigation as much as I." Lamedeer nodded and silently pulled up to the fireplace a hard-backed chair from the library table that sat dead center in the great log-walled living room.

"Congratulations on your marriage, Mr. Alicorn."

"Thank you. I am a happy man to be married to such a wonderful woman."

"I gather you are feeling better now. You had a rough episode, Mr. Alicorn. I'll bet this community is glad you have something to be happy about."

Marv examined Peter as he settled himself in the couch. Peter looked lean and hard-muscled. He had a good head of brown hair, cut short, thick brown brows and a small mustache sat above his lips along with a wide-set jaw. A fight with a knife-wielding criminal had left a deep scar running from his left ear to the center of his left cheek, which gave him a roguish look.

"I'm physically fine now, " answered Marv. "Took me a bit to recover from that episode, however, I'm going to begin an exercise program with some necessary pressure from my doctor, Lamedeer and my wife." Marv smiled and turned his head slightly, acknowledging his friend and foreman. "But it will take some time for me to be over the tragedy of losing my friend, George, particularly in the way he was killed. I'm opting to see that justice is done. I won't rest until then. So I want to be a part of this investigation in every way I can." He leaned forward in his chair. "Now tell me how the investigation is proceeding. And what exactly is your part in it? I'm not sure what you do."

"I was a detective with the Spokane police department for five years. I decided to work with a private non-profit agency concerned with narcotics and child slavery. A local police department cannot be everywhere and I wanted to be everywhere. I now have an opportunity to work in Great Falls with the police force. The whole country is exploding in child sexual molestation, and I feel I can do better staying here solving some of these tragic cases. I guess you could say I am weary of going across the country and finding the same thing happening wherever I go. However, an FBI man will be assigned to the Culbertson case this coming week; he'll be in charge."

"I see. What have you learned since you were last here?"

"Quite a bit, Mr. Alicorn."

"Marv, please. We're in this together for the short or long haul. Whatever. I don't like false formality. I'm going to call you Peter. That's your name, isn't it? Peter Morgan?"

Peter nodded. "We found a broken needle on the site where George Culbertson was killed. It is in the lab now. It was obvious Culbertson had come on to the scene as an innocent and surprised your son and the murderer."

"My son? What do you mean, my son?"

"Hold on please. We know Culbertson was not a drug addict, although he OD'd. This was a nasty murder - Marv, Lamedeer."

`'"God damn, I know that," interjected Marv passionately. "What about my son? How does he fit into this?"

"We do not know," Peter continued, " why your son was

there, but he was."

"My son Andrew was there?" Marv exploded, incredulous.

Peter raised his hand. "Let me finish please. We assume he was part of the drug meet, a courier perhaps. That and why, we have not yet determined. The evidence points to wrongdoing on his part because he was there. This may be why he is suffering a neurosis now. Whatever went on, it has certainly affected him."

Marv shook his head vehemently. "I can't believe it. My son is a good boy. He doesn't do drugs. He doesn't need money. He excels in his studies."

"That may all be true, Marv. However, we look at facts. On the plus side, we did not find any money or drugs in his room at school, nor on his person. The toxicology report done at the hospital showed no drugs in his system. But so far in the investigation he appears guilty of a criminal act, which is part and parcel of why we are investigating your son thoroughly. We examined the shoes he was wearing when he was found wounded, and fresh soil from Culbertson's ranch matched the fresh soil found on his shoes."

Marv interjected quickly. "He could have picked that up at an earlier time when he was visiting George."

"The soils and dates match."

Marv stared intently at Peter for a long time. Then he said slowly, "Yes, Andrew did do something wrong apparently. But why? We need to find out why."

"How is your son doing?" asked Peter.

"He isn't talking yet and he doesn't seem to have much contact with what is going on. A physiatrist is working with him and so is his sister Melissa. His physiatrist told me he is improving. I can't tell any difference in him yet."

"That's because he suffers from severe emotional distress. Besides, that bullet hit him so hard he almost died from the shock to his heart, as well as to the extensive loss of blood. How is he doing here at home?"

"He is still very weak."

Peter put the comments of Andrew aside and continued explaining what was going on. "Perhaps you are not aware, Marv, but we have gone over just about every car that stopped at both Blue Hill and the Mission Motel that night. On those we examined, we found no traces of soil from the murder site. We have conducted interviews, both in person and by phone, with each individual staying at those motels that night. We went over the cars rented at the Great Falls airport. So we are fairly certain the car used to get to and from the site was driven away as soon as Culbertson was murdered. We also know from ground disturbances at the site, that the ground was brushed clean by the murderer, we traced broom marks. Some heavy object had been placed on the ground and moved several times. We also know the border guards at Sweetgrass were after somebody that night. They were after someone who knew how to slip through, who knew how to cover his tracks; who knew the area. That had to be your son, Marv."

"How can you be sure?"

"Events. Two detectives are tracing his disappearance from the computer college. No report is in yet, but it will prove productive, I know.

"One interesting fact is this, a producer, a John Territoni, stayed at the Mission Motel the night of the murders. And we know he slept with a woman there. We want to know why he stayed at a small motel in Mission when he could have reserved a room in Great Falls until his meeting with Jed Nordstrom and Henry Knutson the next morning. We also know John Territoni is not a reputable producer."

"He isn't?" Marv was clearly jolted.

"He is the son of Joseph Territoni, a well-known eastern racketeer who owns a pornographic movie company."

"Good God," Marv exploded, jumping to his feet, his face flooding. "Janice flew to New York today. She is doing a screen test with him. His production company is Novelette Pictures."

An astonished Peter sat temporarily speechless, his eyes narrowing. He heard what Marv said, but he still queried, "She what?"

"Janice, my daughter and Merry, Lamedeer's wife, flew to New York to meet with Mr. Territoni."

"I suggest, Marv," said Peter intently, shaking his head, his frown deepening, "you get in touch with them immediately. Forestall this screen test. Where are they staying?"

"At a hotel of Mr. Territoni's choosing. It's the Mount Royal."

"Call them now, Marv. Instruct them not to leave that hotel with Mr. Territoni."

"God damn it," Marv swore, moving quickly to the library table. "I have always been protective of my daughter, Janice. She is very beautiful and impulsive. This time with everything that was happening, I did not investigate thoroughly. Damn it, I didn't listen when Merry told me she did not like this man."

Peter was not interested in an apology. "I'd make that call now," he said abruptly.

Marv picked up a tray, and unlike his normal cool, deliberate manner, frantically sorted through the cards that lay on it, his breath exploding with relief as he found the one he was looking for. He picked up the phone, dialed the long distance number of the Mount Royal. He spoke to the clerk who told him Miss Alicorn had not yet checked in. He left a message for her or Merry to call home immediately on an urgent manner.

"I'm going to help," interjected Peter. "We are already conducting an investigation of the Territoni family." Peter did not tell Marv and Lamedeer that the investigation included sex trade allegations. "I'll contact our liaison in New York right now. Excuse me. I'll be back in a few minutes." He went out of the house to his car.

"Lamedeer," said Marv anxiously, "Annabelle and I are flying to New York. Get us on the next flight out." Lamedeer swung to the phone. Marv bit his lip, thinking, and motioned a 'no' with his hand. "No, not Annabelle and I, it might be dangerous for her. She stays here with Melissa and Andrew. You and I are going to New York, the next flight. And before we leave, get your foreman in here."

As Lamedeer picked up the phone book, Marv added, "Do this from your house. We don't want that young man to know that we are going to New York. He'd try to stop us for sure. And by the way, put your best suit on. We're not getting on that plane looking like hicks from Montana."

Chapter Sixteen

The flight from Great Falls to New York City was five hours long. However, it was necessary to change planes in Minneapolis, and this particular wait was for four hours (very tiring). Merry was so unnerved by the bumpy flight from Great Falls that she was too upset to eat or window shop so she and Janice settled themselves in the comfortable waiting area until their connecting flight was called. Janice would have liked to stroll by the enticing shops but she did not complain. She remained with Merry.

"Your tummy's upset because you were scared," Janice offered consolingly.

"I didn't know airplanes would be so frightening," Merry shot back, her expression agape.

"Oh, Merry, ours was a rather smooth flight, and look, it only took a couple of hours to fly to Minneapolis. It would have taken us a day and a half to drive here."

"But I don't want or ever wanted to be in Minneapolis," retorted Merry.

They both laughed, Merry half-heartedly, Janice in high spirits. She sat most of the time with her lovely legs (she was wearing very tight fitting dress slacks) flung out in front of her with her right arm hanging lazily on the arm of Merry's chair. She mused, eyes half closed, allowing the fancied images of a brilliant movie career dance about in her mind.

"I'm going to be a star, I just know it, Merry," she said. But Janice's joyful outbursts annoyed Merry, and she closed her ears, returning to dozing and worrying about the next and last leg of the flight.

Janice's exuberance was unrestrained. She sighed; she laughed; she got up and stretched; she sat down again, her mind all the while bursting with movie star fantasies.

Her attitude did not change when at last they boarded the plane to New York. She did wish the clouds that seemed to cover the whole sky underneath them would vanish so she could look at the earth. She did have to comfort Merry who became highly distressed when the plane hit turbulence and remained in turbulence a good part of the flight. Janice's attentions were of no help. Merry was terrified of every slight movement the plane made as it bumped its way through the cloudy skies.

"We're landing, Merry," said Janice, as the plane moved down the runway at La Guardia airport. Although relieved to hear they were finally back on ground, Merry's eyes remained tightly shut (she had kept them closed in fear most of the flight) until the plane stopped and people began pulling their luggage down from the overhead racks.

"How am I ever going to get back to Montana?" she queried of no one but herself, as they exited the jet.

Janice hearing her, said gently, "I'll make certain you are safe." She patted Merry's shoulder.

"Mount Royal," Janice told the cab driver, when at last they left the baggage area and had rolled their suitcases outside.

"Why wasn't somebody here to meet us?" queried Merry annoyed.

"I was told by Mr. Territoni's secretary to take a cab to the

Mount Royal. A studio driver will pick us up at 10 a.m. tomorrow."

"That is not good," Merry whispered in the back seat of the cab. "He," and her finger pointed at the driver in the front seat, "could take us someplace else."

"He'll take us to the hotel, Merry. And we'll be okay."

They were.

There was no doorman at the Mount Royal, it being a third-class hotel in midtown Manhattan. The cab driver carried their baggage into the lobby and directed them to the long mahogany veneered counter.

"We have Miss Alicorn listed as a single," said the desk clerk, after looking up the reservation.

"Hmmmmmmmmph," and Merry pursed her lips. "She has not arrived as a single," she pointed out tersely.

"Our double rooms are booked up," answered the clerk, running his fingers down the reservation sheet. "We can send a cot to the room. The only bed in the room right now is queen sized. Is that acceptable or would you like a cot set up?"

"Yes, a cot please," answered Janice.

"I'll have it sent up. Mr. Territoni has the room reserved for you for a full week's stay," he went on, his smirky smile turning to admiration, as he looked her up and down.

Janice blushed. "Thank you," she said haughtily, picking up the key from the brightly polished counter. She looked around her. The lobby was neither large nor ornate, nor was it expensively decorated. The plaid woven carpet was faded and worn. She felt deflated. She had envisioned a large and ornately decorated lobby, this hotel lived in an old building, and although dressed up in a shabby sort of way, nevertheless old. Perhaps it was close to the studios, she thought, as they followed the middle-aged bellboy in his wrinkled black trousers and black jacket. It was not the kind of bellboy Janice had expected, one who would be young, sprightly and smiling. This one was old with grey hair and a tired demeanor.

They made their way to the old fashioned elevator with its outdated, grill-faced door. The three were silent as they ascended to the fourth floor. Janice had noted this hotel was only six floors tall and her face showed her disappointment at its lack of grandeur. Merry's showed disgust.

The hallway was long, a worn red carpet led the way to their room at the far end of the corridor.

"I don't like this hotel," Merry said, as they moved down the hall. "It's not new. It's old and it smells."

The bellboy heard her. "Most of the buildings in New York are old," he said, "except for the Trump establishments and our skyscrapers. It's a wonderful Big Apple once you get out and walk in it." His cheerful voice belied his solemn attitude.

"We shall do that tomorrow," Janice said. "Can you tell us of a good restaurant near here to have breakfast in?"

"Sure. Right down the end of the block. Can't miss it. It's called the Market Stop. They have great omelets and if you drink coffee, theirs can't be beat."

"What time do they open?"

"Six."

"Thank you."

"We're here." He showed Janice how to unlock the door

with a small white plastic card. "See the little green light?" he pointed out after he inserted the card into a narrow slot in the door.

"Yes."

"Push the card in, with the hotel name on the left; the green light comes on and the door opens."

"Thank you again." Janice opened her purse and handed him a five-dollar bill.

"You need anything, just call downstairs. Dial eight, it's our extension. Goodnight. And enjoy the beautiful flowers Mr. Territoni sent you. Oh, here comes the cot. I forgot about it." They all had. They turned watching it, the noisy wheels on the carrier telling of its many travels down the corridor. The young man who was wheeling it came into the room and set it up, the bellboy watching that it was done correctly.

As they waited, Janice admired each of the bouquets of cut flowers that decorated the room. Two bouquets of carnations sat in short glass vases on the modern maple colored bureau, another sat on the end table at the left side of the queen size bed, one on each side of the heavily ornamented mirror at the dressing table, one on the writing desk and a dozen pin roses in a tall vase on the right bedside table. She reached out for the cards that hung on the side of each vase on a rose ribbon. On each were printed these words, "To a beautiful new star." Janice gasped in delighted surprise. The bellboy was still in the room and she couldn't resist asking him, "You know Mr. Territoni?"

"Oh, we do a lot of business for him," he commented, nodding at the flowers and then looking at her slyly. He said goodnight and closed the door behind him.

As soon as the bellboy and clerk had left and Merry was opening a suitcase on one of the two luggage stands, Janice excitedly called out the words written on the cards.

Merry was not impressed.

"I do not like that producer," she said tartly. "He is after you."

"Yes, Merry," answered Janice blandly, not wishing to continue a discussion which would have no agreeable ending. Instead, she said, "Shall we go to bed? It's been a long day and at 10 o'clock tomorrow morning when we are going to be picked up to go to the studios, it will be only eight o'clock our time."

"I agree," said Merry, who hung her outfits on the open hooks against the wall of the bathroom while Janice undressed. Janice then reopened her suitcase and took out Oscar, her rag doll. She placed it in bed beside her.

Barely were they in bed when the phone rang. Janice reached over to the bedside table to answer. She recognized the voice to be that of John Territoni.

"You are here," he said. "This is John Territoni."

"Yes," she answered, breathless. "And thank you for the beautiful flowers. And the words on the cards."

"It is my pleasure and it is your fate, lovely Miss Alicorn." There was a pause. Then he asked in a low voice, "If you are not too tired after your long trip, I would like to personally welcome you to New York. I am close by."

"Both Merry and I are already in bed, Mr. Territoni."

"Merry and you? Who is Merry?"

"Merry Lamar is our ranch foreman's wife. She came with me to New York."

There was silence.

In a voice no longer low and husky, John Territoni answered, "I see. Well then, we'll meet tomorrow at the studio. Goodnight." He terminated the call.

"Oh, my gosh," began Janice, as Merry asked her who had called.

"Mr. Territoni," she answered, "And I think he is upset, he didn't know you were here. We did tell the secretary at the studio, didn't we?"

"What did he want?"

"He wanted to see me."

"Tonight?"

"Yes."

"But alone."

"Yes."

"I told you, Janice. That producer is not to be trusted. You are not going to see him alone."

"Oh, Merry, how you imagine." And Janice plunked herself down under the covers angrily, rebelling about being supervised. Oscar's head disappeared also.

Neither slept well.

The clatter of garbage trucks lifting curbside Dumpsters woke them up. The shrill noise of several fire engines rushing by on a neighborhood street bolted them upright. Shouts and blaring music from cruising cars on the street below woke them up.

"What a horrible night that was!" exclaimed Merry, picking up and looking at the alarm clock she had placed on the floor beside the cot. "It's 6:30 a.m. I have slept hardly at all. And there is no use trying to go back to sleep now."

"Let's go for coffee and doughnuts," said Janice, yawning, "before I have to come back and get dressed for the screen test." She gave a kiss to Oscar, positioned him neatly under the covers with his head on a pillow and rose. Merry watched her and muttered under her breath, "such a little girl."

Janice dressed in a crewel-necked white sweater and grey wool skirt, slit from the top of her knee to the bottom of her calf, in the current fashion. Over it she wore the nubbed Canadian coat she had worn on the plane. On the short walk from hotel to restaurant, her delight at being in New York and her "butterfly tummy" excitement about the coming screen test danced in her eyes. They glistened like dewdrops in the cold morning air.

"I'm scared, Merry," she said nervously as they left the restaurant. "Coffee and doughnuts were excellent. But I'm giddy, I'm so excited."

Merry grimaced. She did not like the noise, the screeching of tires, the din of trucks; all normal early morning city bustle and she found Janice's lighthearted exuberance annoying.

"What are those?" she asked anxiously as the two passed by a steaming grill.

"I think that goes down to the subway," exclaimed Janice.

"Ugh." Merry looked at the grill in disgust, almost bumping into someone going the other way.

Janice too almost collided several times with passersby, so intent was she looking up at buildings and watching people. She insisted they walk around the block before heading back to the Mt. Royal. She did not at first realize the distance between the numbered streets was three times the distance between the named streets. They turned back at the corner, passed the restaurant again and headed up Sixth Avenue to the hotel which was sandwiched between two other hotels, each one faded grey in color and old physically. As they approached the entrance to the Mt. Royal, a man came running up to them. He stepped right in front of them, halting them, saying breathlessly, "I beg your pardon. I would like to speak to you for a moment." He addressed Janice, yet nodded to Merry courteously.

"What is it?" asked Janice, shaken by his unusual intrusion, yet taken with his pleasant bearing. He must be at least thirtyt-five, she thought, as she noted the creases across his forehead, around his eyes and mouth. Taller than she was, but only slightly, his slate colored eyes, under thinning short brown hair, crinkled with friendliness as he addressed them. His grey suit and white sweater were expensive. He looked honest, not like a criminal about to molest them.

"You were eating breakfast in the Market Stop."

"Yes." Both she and Merry felt for and looked at their purses, wondering if they had dropped something out of them. "Did we forget something?"

"No." The man chuckled, his hand drawing out two business cards from a high jacket pocket, giving one to Merry and one to Janice as he guided them away from the center of the entrance to the hotel; they were in the way of the heavy early-morning pedestrian traffic.

"My boss, Ms. Stanton," and he nodded at the cards each held, "owns 'Models Plus.' Perhaps you have heard of the agency."

The card meant nothing to Merry. However, the name captured a corner of Janice's memory. She frowned as she tried to remember.

"No. I'm not sure."

"Models Plus is a most prestigious modeling agency." He waited for the look of interest on Janice's face.

She looked surprised but confused. "May I ask your name?" he continued.

"My name is Janice Alicorn. This is Mrs. Merry Lamar."

"Ah, Miss Alicorn. How do you do. How do you do, Mrs. Lamar. Let me introduce myself. My name is Will MacIntosh. I am a photographer employed by Models Plus. I gather you are not from New York."

"No."

"May I ask where you are from?"

"Montana."

"Ah then, that is why you have not heard of Models Plus."

"I seem to have heard the name someplace," countered Janice politely.

"I'll impress you. Models Plus is the most famous modeling agency in the world. Our clients include some of the biggest names in theatre, business, food, drink - you name it."

Janice's eyes widened.

"Ms. Stanton and I - I am her lead photographer, have been looking for a new face for a world-renown drink advertiser. We were discussing a coming photo shoot while drinking coffee at the Market Stop a little earlier and we saw you enter. She immediately asked me to call you to our table when our discussion was over, but by then you had disappeared. I had to come running after you. Ms. Stanton would like you to return to the restaurant because she wants to meet you."

"Oh!" Janice's stomach began whirling those butterflies again. Someone wanted her to be a model. Then she remembered her screen test. She looked at her watch. "I have an appointment at ten o'clock."

"It is only two minutes after eight right now," said Will MacIntosh, checking his watch. "Surely you have a few minutes."

"I must get dressed."

"You look very beautiful in what you are wearing. Come, I will not take no for an answer. Your meeting with Ms. Stanton will be brief, I assure you. One cup of coffee brief, she never wastes time. Then you can return to the hotel. You'll have plenty of time to freshen and redress." He turned to Merry. "Are you willing to come back to the Market Stop for ten minutes, Mrs. Lamar?"

"Yes." Merry had listened and thought a modeling agency job was much preferable to a part in a movie. Anyway, she didn't like that producer, John Territoni. ever since his phone call last night - the idea - calling late at night and wanting to visit her in the hotel room at that time. She knew what he was after. If Janice had been alone she would have said yes to his visiting her, she was so gullible. But that man! He could convince Janice of anything, she bet, once he had control of the situation. Thank God she had accompanied her to New York. She feared what would happen to Janice when she left knowing she had to call Marv and warn him of consequences. Janice may be twenty years old, she thought, shaking her head, but her actions were much too unpredictable. She was still a very little girl mentally, particularly when it came to men and the attentions they gave her.

"And what are you doing in New York?"

"I'm going to have a screen test at 10 a.m."

"Oh? How wonderful. At Gem Studios? Or perhaps RCC?"

"No." Janice gazed at the man walking beside her, her eyes starry. "Novellete Studios," she told him, her smile bright.

"John Territoni?"

"Yes."

Will MacIntosh stopped short. Because he stopped, Janice and Merry had to stop. Some one in back of them complained as he ran into them. "Damn it, look where you are going," they heard as the man strode angrily by.

"Do you know what kind of pictures Territoni produces?"

"He came to Montana to set some scenes on one of the ranches close to us," said Miranda proudly. "He is producing a western."

"Hah!" Will MacIntosh shook his head. "Come," he said, "here we are. Let's go sit down with Ms. Stanton. I need to think about this before I say anything further. I can see you do not know what you are having a screen test for." He led them to a table where a heavy-set but absolutely stunning looking, black haired, middle aged woman sat, lifting a cup to her lips. She placed it back on the table as Will pulled out two chairs for Janice and Merry. "Would you both like coffee?" he asked, standing behind Janice's chair.

"I don't dare drink any more," she said. "My tummy's very nervous as it is."

"Thank you, yes," said Merry.

"Ms. Stanton, I present Janice Alicorn and Mrs. Merry Lamar. Excuse me, I'll be right back."

He strode off to the counter.

When he returned, his boss, Ms. Stanton, was talking. Janice and Merry were listening intently.

He sat down. The three looked at him.

Ms. Stanton spoke. "She's absolutely perfect, Will."

He lowered his eyes and his "yes" went from a high to low tone, as emphatic as it could be. "But," he said, addressing his boss, "did she tell you why she is in New York? What she is about to do?"

"No." The black-haired model agency owner leaned forward and said very sweetly, very softly, "Now you know, Will, I've been holding the floor." She leaned back, laughing. "How could she tell me anything." It wasn't a question. It was a statement intended to stir laugher from Will.

"She is supposed to have a screen test with Territoni."

"Oh, my God, NO!" Mrs. Stanton's huge black eyes, a grey liner highlighting the lids above and the lashes below, seemed to leap out of her head. She sat back and glared at Janice. "You didn't tell me." Her words oozed slowly out of her mouth, disgustingly.

"Patsy, wait," said Will, raising his hand. "She has no idea what he is."

"Oh." Patsy Stanton digested this fact for a moment. "Well," she then exclaimed, "it's about time she knew." She leaned forward again.

"Young lady," she said, "and Merry, whoever you are, John Territoni and his father produce porn films, very unsavory porn films. They pick up young girls, drug them, then shoot sex scenes of them and themselves and other terrible creatures like they are."

"I knew he was bad," Merry said, her lips pursing together tightly, not quite sure what porn films were, except they were bad.

Patsy Stanton ignored Merry. "How did he get hold of you?" she asked Janice whose happy countenance was beginning to unravel.

"He came to Montana to film some scenes for a new picture he was making. He saw me and said he wanted to make a screen test of me." Her voice began to fall apart. "He sent me a round trip ticket and I'm to meet him at his studios at 10 o'clock this morning for my screen test." Her eyes began to mist. "He sent me flowers too, my room is full of them. He paid for my hotel room for a week and is sending someone to pick me up and take me to the studios at 10 a.m." She looked at her watch but couldn't see the dial through her tears. "What am I going to do? I am supposed to have a screen test." Her world had come crashing down and a lake of tears hid her beautiful eyes.

"Good Lord, Will. She's even gorgeous crying. What a shot that would be. We can change the beginning of an ad with that soulful outcry."

"Ms. Stanton," interrupted Merry, getting up to comfort Janice. "I think our thoughts should be on the serious side. I don't want my Janice to go to Mr. Territoni and have that porn screen test. But we are in his hotel room. What are we going to do? And, I might add, who are you to tell us all this? Are you as bad as you say he is and are you lying to us? We are strangers here; we don't know anyone. You," she pointed and looked at Will MacIntosh, "come up to us on the street, give us cards and they may be fake cards, and tell us one thing and then another to try to get us to like you and believe you. But who are we to believe? I, myself, do not like this Mr. Territoni, but maybe he isn't as bad as you are. Huh?"

Merry patted Janice and sat down again, looking lovingly at her beautiful young ward, who now sat white of face, shaken, hapless. "I'm not going to let anything bad happen to her while I am around. I think I will call the police."

Patsy Stanton and Will MacIntosh momentarily lost their voices. They stared at each other.

It was Will who finally spoke. "Good idea," he said, pulling out his cell phone. "I will have the police escort us to Ms. Stanton's offices. You will know then who we are and what we are. After that introduction, we'll deal with your belongings in the hotel and deal with Mr. Territoni. All right?"

He turned to Merry for consent. She nodded. "All right," she said. "You are sure you will call the police, not some imposters."

He smiled. "Of course. I am calling now." He dialed 911.

Chapter Seventeen

Patsy Stanton's "Models Plus" offices were spread over a large section of the 24th floor of the 42nd story Yamosoto Building, three blocks from the Mountain Stop restaurant. The eye-arresting, slim, glass-walled building was best known to the New York City visitors who flocked there as the Aquarium Building. That is because the lobby, which one entered through double swinging doors, contained a forty foot round salt water tropical pool in the center of the exquisite, luminously lighted, soft green toned, smooth tiled floor. The spectacular lobby also boasted of two exquisitely maintained miniature Japanese gardens. Further distinguishing the lobby was a colored sky-blue ceiling descending to walls of soft green with splashes of muted blues and yellows. At the back sat a rectangular glass office manned by a caretaker and a guide. In front of the office were three tables, on top of each lay a large picture encyclopedia of tropical fish along with their descriptions. A decorative bubble-glass cover protected the pool, the cover fitted with forty large port holes (for adults) and smaller ones below these (for children). A visitor could explore the whole of the pool through these port holes and enjoy viewing at leisure the hundreds of brightly colored tropical fish. The pool contained at least two-hundred unusual species, including, of course, the Sea Robin, the Dragon Eel, Walking Fish, Glass Fish, Butterfly Fish, the Kissing Fish, the Common Puffer and the Flying Fish. Waterfalls, long underwater ridges of stone, a miniature reef, tunnels and caves decorated the waterscape and on the bottom lay all varieties of shells along with sundry tropical ocean floor artifacts.

Five elevators lined each sidewall of the lobby; one of which on each side was labeled "private." Patsy Stanton's "Models Plus" boasted a private elevator on the left wall.

A Japanese architect, in honor of his wife, who unfortunately died before it could be finished, had built the Yamasoto Building. The lobby with its pool and two Japanese gardens became her memorial. Mr. Yamasoto died shortly after the pool had been installed, leaving millions for its upkeep in an ever-growing trust. However, the building's new owners had recently installed a "courtesy donation" receptacle at the front of the lobby for those who wished to view the fish. Donation receptacles were also placed at the entrance of each of the Japanese gardens. (Each garden held a stand on which sat a book describing the garden's furnishings and growth patterns of the plants.) Books and artifacts of each exhibit were for sale at an unique gift shop at the back wall.

Two policemen accompanied the richly black-clothed and elegant Ms. Stanton, Will MacIntosh, Janice and Merry. The latter two were wide-eyed as they entered the magnificent lobby and gazed at the scene in front of them. They did not pause long, Ms. Stanton hurried them to her private elevator. Janice kept looking at her watch reminding Will (she did not dare remind the daunting Ms. Stanton) several times of her coming appointment. "Despite what you say," she pleaded quietly to Will, "I want my screen test. I cannot believe Mr. Territoni is like you say he is."

As the elevator door closed behind them, she whispered to him, "It is now 8:30. We can only visit your offices for the longest, 15 minutes."

"Of course," muttered Will, smiling. Patsy Stanton, who had heard Janice, raised her pencil-lined, thin eyebrows in disgust.

Will MacIntosh certainly does have an infectious smile, thought Janice. Yet, despite his cheerfulness there was something different about him, like a sadness that sat deep down in his heart and emerged through his eyes only for fleeting seconds then sank back down out of sight again. And he gestured and walked with such grace, one would think him a dancer.

The elevator door opened. The room before them appeared as spectacular as the lobby. Janice and Merry both gaped. It was an opulent setting, decorated with couches and tables with huge photographs decorating three of the walls. On the fourth wall stretched a tier of windows gazing at the Manhattan sky. An unusually long desk, its high-backed chair inhabited by an attractive secretary, sat about 15 feet back from the elevator. The secretary rounded her desk, came up to Ms. Stanton and spoke to her. She then returned to her desk.

Ms. Stanton turned to the policemen. "You may go back to your duties as soon as you enjoy our morning coffee and rolls." Hardly had they looked at each other deciding, when, with a motion of her hand she called over a young man standing by the secretary's desk. "You have entered my wonderful world of marketing," Ms. Stanton said to the policemen. "While drinking your coffee, also drink in the exquisite photos of our clients' models and the merchandise they sell. Many of these photos were shot by this genius of picture taking, Will MacIntosh. Excuse me; I must get to my office.

"As for you young lady," and she turned to Janice, who was still standing just beyond the elevator door gazing raptly about her, "I am sure that if you keep your appointment with the despicable Territoni, he'll do you no harm today. But that doesn't mean he isn't thinking about it. He first has to get rid of your Mrs. Lamar. I know how he works. So you will not return to his studios after today. I am sure you are much too besotted to lie to him, but I charge you to say absolutely nothing about where you have been or where you are going. I am sending one . . . no, two young men to pick you up after an hour at his sex studios. No one will know they are from here. I don't want his goons haunting us. And neither of you," she pointed a finger at Janice and then waved it in the direction of Merry, "will say a word as to where they are from. You will be mum on that score, understand?" She did not wait for an answer but continued laconically, "You will be escorted to your hotel by these two young men, your baggage brought here, at which time we will discuss a contract for modeling services. Once we have trained you - and you have much to learn, Miss Janice Alicorn - you'll become one of the most famous models in the world. You'd like that, wouldn't you, lovely girl?" Her bright red lips spread into a small smile at the incredulous looks of amazement and astonishment. "In due time, when we no longer require all of your services, you will be free to become a movie star. Contracts and films will clutter your life. First, however, you'll be a model under contract to me."

She turned abruptly and walked away. Several employees rushed to her side, gathered around her, vying for her attention, two with papers in hand, one with a large photo. She glanced at the photo, said something to the worker carrying it, who then hurried into a side office. Suddenly she stopped, turned and called to Will. He ran forward, they conversed, each speaking with a multitude of arm gestures and intermittent glances back at Janice. Then suddenly she was walking again, speaking to a girl at her side. Will returned.

Janice still stood awe struck, Merry wide-eyed.

"It is settled," Will smiled, as he glanced at their expressions. "You two (he nodded to Merry) have ten minutes left to acquaint yourself with Models Plus. Let me introduce you to some of my favorite photos."

He led them slowly around the spacious, salon type office with its incredible photographs. Outstanding beauties of the model world — men as well as women — seduced with picture charisma; their elegance, their smiles, their charm, their every day grace. All poses and postures were designed to win the viewer over to purchase the product the model was espousing in the photo, whether it was a breakfast cereal, a chair, linens, furnishings, automobiles, boats, houses; each photograph was an aggregate of beautiful design befitting its role in superb marketing.

"Oh, they are so wonderful," exclaimed Janice. Merry was speechless.

Will pointed out several of his proudly. "As a matter of fact, I've got a photo shoot at 10:30 this morning. I need to leave you. I should be here when you return." He touched Janice's arm gently, motioning her and Merry to a couch. "Wait here a few moments. The young men who will take you to your hotel and then call for you at Territoni's studio will be here shortly. You can trust your life with them."

He left. Janice looked at her watch impatiently.

Merry said to her in a low voice, "What a lucky girl you are. We come to New York, eat doughnuts in a restaurant, and you are discovered by these good people. Thank God, we don't have to deal with that producer Territoni after today."

Janice didn't answer. She merely gave Merry an angry disputed glance.

Two young men appeared in front of them, coming from the direction Ms. Stanton had disappeared. One was tall and blond, the other short and blond.

"I am David, from Long Island. I am a friend of your cousin," said the tall one, grinning at Janice. "Lucky cousin!" He grinned again.

"I am John, your cousin, from Miami," said the short one. "Come," he continued, extending his hands to Merry and Janice. "We are to take both of you to the Mt. Royal Hotel and then pick you up later at the Territoni studio."

Janice barely had time to change into a dark blue, silk dress with matching fur-lined coat when the phone in their hotel room rang. The clerk announced that a driver from Mr. Territoni's studio was waiting for them in the lobby.

"My hair, how does it look? How do I look?" asked Janice of Merry, who had been waiting quietly on the cot while Janice changed her clothes.

"Just fine."

"I don't feel fine. I am so nervous, I am tingling."

"It will be all right," said Merry. "Just keep your tongue inside your mouth. Don't say anything you do not have to say."

Janice laughed, slightly annoyed. "Oh Merry, you are so silly. Of course I'll be careful. I do think everyone is imaging too much."

"After being in Ms. Stanton's offices, I'll believe anything she says. You better too. "

A middle-aged, stout, balding man, who was conversing with the clerk at the counter, approached them as they excited the elevator. "My name is Mike Johnson," he said. "I am to take you to the Novelette Studios."

"Thank you," said Janice, as she and Merry followed him outside to a black limousine, double-parked. Horns were blaring from cars unable to get by the limousine. Mike opened the passenger door for them and made certain they were seated before he moved unhurriedly to the driver's side. The ride was short. No one spoke.

The building they entered was ugly and the elevator dirty. Janice reached for Merry's hand. She was frightened, no more so than Merry. When the elevator halted, however, and the door opened, they found themselves in a well-groomed office with an elderly lady sitting at a mahogany desk; fresh flowers sat in vases on tables and two couches and four chairs were assembled along one side. Pictures of famous film stars covered the walls.

"Look at those," Janice said to Merry, as if the photos imparted a statement of excellence for this film company.

"Do sit down," said the driver, Mike. "Elsie, tell John we

have arrived."

Within moments a door opened and John Territoni appeared. He loomed taller and more handsome than he had appeared in Montana. He has a wonderful face, thought Janice, and shivers, like the shivers she had experienced when she first saw him in Montana, ran up and down her spine. He smiled at her as he came forward.

"Ah, at last," he said succulently, with powerful appeal in his husky voice, "you are here. You beautiful young lady, my Novelette Studios future star."

He reached out his hand and lifted her out of the chair. She rose giddily.

"I have a script for you to look at and study," he said, boring his black eyes right through hers as if he were undressing her. Pulling them away reluctantly, he turned to Merry.

"You will excuse us. You are Mrs. Lamar, I believe? My receptionist will bring you coffee or a soda if you prefer, while you are waiting."

Merry, scowling, said emphatically, "I will remain with Miss Alicorn while she studies the script."

"Well, of course," John replied smoothly, as if he expected her to say just that. "Miss Alicorn can study the script here. However, when we screen her, the studio is open to cameramen and actors only."

He turned immediately to the secretary and glared at Mike, who could tell John was angry. "Mrs Dawson, come with me to get the script for Miss Alicorn."

Janice sat trembling, Merry sat stiffly, resolutely, each muscle in her body, taut with resolve, while they waited.

The secretary returned with three pages that she handed to Janice. "You have fifteen minutes to study this script," she said. "I will then take you to the studio for the test."

"Thank you," said Janice, embarrassed. She sensed John Territoni was upset. She did not dare speak to Merry.

She moved away from Merry on the couch, lowered her head and read what was on the pages. "I really would rather study this script privately, Merry," she said after a bit, turning to her chaperone. "It's rather difficult to do it sitting here on this couch in the waiting room."

"It doesn't matter, Janice. What matters is that we are together."

"We won't be in fifteen minutes."

"You better study the script," Merry muttered. "Let's get this over with."

They both fell silent.

In fifteen minutes, Janice was led away by the secretary, leaving Merry alone in the waiting room. She was taken to a stage in a small auditorium. On the stage was a backdrop of a barn, with a loft filled with hay. Real hay was scattered on the stage's wooden floor, with several stacks of it piled center stage. A young man, Sam, wearing a plaid shirt, jeans, and cowboy boots sat on one of the stacks. His eyes bored into Janice as she entered the stage. She thought him ugly. John Territoni approached from a corner of the stage where he had been conversing with an old man. The old man followed John and stood beside him when they reached Janice and the secretary. John dismissed the secretary, put his arm around Janice's waist saying, "I'd like to introduce you to my father. You see, Dad, she is all I told you she would be."

"I'm ready for her now," was his answer from the old man, who leered at Janice and leaned forward to touch her hair. She drew back from him.

"We're not ready, Dad. In time. Go sit down, Dad. You can watch." He nodded to the driver of the car, Mike, who was at his side instantly, taking John's father by the arm, and helping him off the stage into the auditorium. When they had disappeared from view John turned to Janice, who appeared confused by their conversation. She did not like the old man.

"Have you read the script?" asked John Territoni.

"Yes. There weren't too many words."

"No. This is an action scene."

"A love scene."

"Yes. I'll show you how it plays." John motioned to a man with a 35 mm camera in his hand while Sam stepped forward.

"You have to have a sob in your voice when you speak," said John.

She nodded and spoke the lines. Sam grabbed her and pulled her to him. The camera clicked.

"No, Sam, not that way. Here, let me show you."

John Territoni motioned for Sam to get out of the way so he could demonstrate what he wanted. "Repeat the words, Janice."

"Oh, John, I don't want you to go away."

"The name is Paul."

Janice blushed.

"Oh, Paul, I don't want you to go away."

John grabbed her and drew her close to him, lifting her off her feet. His hands went around her and he pulled her body tightly against his. She heard the camera clicking.

He did not let go. Janice knew he could feel her trembling. She was strangely affected by his holding her. She liked him holding her. It was as if she was being protected, but then as he kept holding her, it was obvious he was exploring her, not just with his hands, but also with his mind and muscles. He tugged at her buttocks, then pulled quickly away.

"Well," he said in a very low, husky voice, "You are a lovely thing." He moved away.

She blushed again.

"That's what I want, Sam. Grab her, pull her to you and hold her tight. Repeat the words, Janice."

She did. She did not like this leading man fondling her. His hands moved up and down her back roughly when he gathered her to him.

John laughed softly at her discomfort. "Leading ladies get kissed and hugged," he smiled benignly. "You must be prepared for that, Janice."

She nodded, lowering her head. "I didn't know," she stated, "that this screen test would include kissing."

"We have to set the goodbye scene. Go on with the script." His words shot back at her testy and short.

They worked. While they worked the cameraman filmed them. Every sentence she spoke, she had to repeat three or four times. John, who insisted on showing Sam just how she was to be held repeatedly groped her and each time John moved in to hold her, she felt strangely affected by his closeness. Once he kissed her. It was a hard, tongue in mouth kiss, which she did not expect and did not like, and she began shivering, almost in fear. She did not think the script called for those actions.

At the end of fifteen minutes, John said, "That's it for today. We'll shoot this scene at the end of the week." He walked with her to the door leading to the waiting room. "How long is Mrs. Lamar going to stay with you?" he asked casually.

"I don't know." She lied.

"Is she returning to Montana?"

"I . . . I don't know yet."

"Well," he said, "go back to the hotel. We'll have breakfast together, you and I, tomorrow morning before we return to work on the script. I'll call for you at nine a.m. Sam, you are excused tomorrow. I want to help Miss Alicorn on several scenes."

"Yeah," the young man said, leering at Janice again, smiling knowingly at John as if he knew something Janice did not know, then disappearing.

"I'm going to give you several more pages of this script. The scenes you will study are not kissing scenes. You will be working in a ranch kitchen baking bread."

"Oh, that's good."

"I did want to orient you to part of the job of a leading lady. Actors act out what the script says to act out."

"Yes sir."

"I'll have Mike drive you and Mrs. Lamar back to the hotel."

Mike rose from a chair in the corner of the stage. He motioned her to follow him. When they reached the waiting room, the two young blond men from Models Plus were sitting beside Merry on the couch.

"I am Janice's cousin and this is a friend of mine. We'll

take the ladies back to the hotel," said the short blond to a surprised Mike.

Mike glanced over at the secretary who looked back at him as surprised as he was, her eyebrows raised.

"All right then," said Mike. "We'll see you in the morning, Miss Alicorn."

Mike hurried to John who was still on stage.

"John," he began.

John turned. "What is the matter?"

"A cousin and a friend came to pick them up."

"What?"

"I think you should tread very carefully here. She's got too many relatives looking out for her."

"Get rid of them."

"John, that's not going to be easy to do. I believe you ought to let her do the C movie and say goodbye. Better yet, tell her she's not good enough."

"I'll do no such thing. I want that one. She'll be mush in my hands within two weeks. I have a great future for her, starting with my father."

Mike shook his head slowly.

"Mike," said John, looking at him, "I'll take it easy. We've had girls from hovering families do disappearing acts before. We just have to set up this one very carefully. And I'll have plans in shape by the time I pick her up tomorrow."

Chapter Eighteen

M erry entered the hotel first. She shrieked. Lamedeer was standing by the door.

"Lamedeer," she shouted, "that is you, isn't it?" She ran forward and touched him. "Yes, it is, thank the Gods. Where did you come from?"

"We're here to take you home."

"You're in a suit and tie! You look so different. You are handsome, Lamedeer. Oh, Lamedeer, I'm so glad to see you." They hugged.

Marv was already hugging Janice.

"Thank the Gods you are here," repeated Merry. "I do not want to be here any more."

"We do not want you to be here, period."

In moments, the tall blond, whose name was David, was explaining to Marv and Lamedeer what was going on. When he had finished, he suggested the two go immediately upstairs with the women and carry down their luggage. He would remain in the lobby to check them out. "I have money to pay for Territoni's bill. Ms. Stanton wants no recriminations - nothing left undone."

Within the half hour, the four Montanans and their luggage were on the way to the Yamasoto building. David informed Marv he and John would leave them there and take their luggage to Ms. Stanton's home. "She'll put you up for the night, if not at her home, then close by."

Marv and Lamedeer sat down with Patsy Stanton after she

took them on a tour of her offices. Marv thought Patsy as fascinating as the superlative photographs lining the walls of her spacious offices. She was not a tall woman, not fat, not thin, and certainly did not have a great body from what he could see in her loose-fitting black "sheet of a dress," as he liked to call that particular style, yet there was something indefinable about her that made you look at her twice. It had to be the way she carried herself, he thought. She was elegant, all her lines and curves blending into a square. Every step she took gave the onlooker the impression she owned the world. While her face was plain, one did not notice the flat cheeks, the large ears when they separated from her shoulder length, straight, black hair, the middle-age droop of her mouth, the lines around it, and the thin lips under a rosebud painted mouth. It was her eyes that held one; they were large, oval, dark green eyes sparkling with every word she spoke. The best thing Marv liked about her, he thought, was that when she spoke she looked directly at the person she was speaking to, her melodic voice caressing each word.

Marv and Patsy were on first names halfway through the tour with Lamedeer, Merry and Janice trailing. Janice was silent, of mixed emotions. She felt trapped because here she was in New York City having left her father who dominated her, yet he arrived one day after she arrived, conversing with a woman who obviously wanted to dominate her new life. Half of her felt honored, of course, that she was being discovered by a famous modeling agency, but the other half wanted to run away and go back to the Novelette Studios where she could act in a new movie. She had been given the leading lady part, just like that! The producer had told her she had it, true; he may not be the honorable producer she had thought him to be, and true, he affected her the wrong way, like her history teacher had. That part she was afraid of, it could be worrisome. But overall he seemed nice and it was a movie he was producing and she would go back to Montana to shoot scenes of it. Most of all she would become a movie star. Nobody would be dominating her.

"There you could be, young lady, in a different pose, of course, six months from now, working for this world-renowned client." Patsy pointed out a photo to her as they moved along, pulling her out of her reverie. "We'll change the scenery behind you when we repeat this ad. Have to have your glorious hair blowing in the breeze." She moved on to another photo. "See the way this model cocks her head. Ah, ah, you will be like her, breathlessly beautiful, a sought after model."

"How on earth did you find my daughter?" Janice heard her father ask Patsy.

"It was Will who did, my photographer. We were having coffee in a restaurant, they walked in and Will exclaimed, 'Patsy, look at that.' I turned and saw her. Everybody else in the restaurant turned to look at her too, they couldn't help it, she is a beautiful young thing. I knew immediately she belonged in my model line. You should be very proud of her. Where is her mother?"

"Teresa is dead," Marv said quietly. "That's okay, Patsy. She's been dead many years. Janice is almost a spitting image of her."

"My, my," Patsy replied, and then fell silent.

As they moved into her office he again marveled at the

way she walked. Each foot encased in high heels came down as if she was queen of the earth. She was an elegant and obviously highly intelligent lady. Janice seated herself in the middle of a luxuriously deep and comfortable couch; her father moved to be near her on one side, Merry and Lamedeer on the other.

As Patsy explained what was going to happen to Janice over the next three months, Janice sank unhappily deeper into the couch's folds at odds with the forces controlling her life.

"Janice will live in my home for three months while we train her. She will work in a gym with weights and treadmills; she'll swim and exercise in my pool. She'll also learn some basic ballet steps including tricks of the modeling trade: how to stand, walk, sit, cock her head, move her hands, smile, cry — all the nuances of movement which entice, cajole, excite — and sell products. She'll also have acting lessons. My top models do many talking TV commercials.

"Since it will be necessary to maintain her svelte figure, she'll learn what to eat, how to manage and groom her hair, her face, how to choose clothes. She'll room with another aspiring model. At the end of three to five months, she'll begin working. She'll then move out of my home into her own apartment, perhaps doubling up with another model. A mentor will accompany her on her assignments for a month. At the end of her apprenticeship, which could be as long as four or six months, she'll be sent on photo-shoots on her own. She'll begin to make money."

"Sounds great," said Marv beaming, looking at his daughter. "It is what my daughter always wanted to be, a model."

Janice sat silent, expressionless.

"It's an exciting, if different schedule than one you are used to, isn't it?" Patsy asked Janice, her eyes narrowing as she noted her expression. "It's every girl's dream," she continued, "even though the initial period will be grueling. You feel you can tackle this to become a famous model?" she asked, aware of the answer Janice would grudgingly give.

"I'm a bit overwhelmed," said Janice in a small, almost petulant voice.

"Of course you are overwhelmed," Patsy went on, as if the girl had not said anything. "Everything will fall into place," she continued, a smile spreading over her flat face as she looked Janice over carefully. Janice's reaction was no different than other beautiful and family spoiled aspirants, who believed their beauty was enough to land them lush contracts without being called to account.

"I have papers drawn up which outline the loan for her training. Modeling fees will pay this back. The contract defines her employment for two years. Hopefully, she will be so happy she'll stay on with us for a long and profitable career."

Patsy rose, handed one copy of the contract to Janice and another to Marv. "Please read the contract carefully. If you have any questions, jot them down on this tablet," she added, handing each a note pad and pen. "I have an appointment with a client this half hour. When I return, we can agree or disagree. We'll cement the contract with dinner, after which you'll inspect your daughter's training grounds."

When Patsy had gone out of the office and closed the door behind her, Marv said to his daughter, "You don't look as excited as I think you should be."

"Well," she began timidly, gaining courage as she went on, shaking her head in perplexity and dismay, "I came to New York to act in a movie. I'm happy to have been discovered by a modeling agency, but it seems . . . well, it isn't what I came here for. I do have the part as leading lady of the film Novelette Studios is going to produce. Now you take me away from it." She added boldly, though hiding her eyes from her father, "Just like you've taken me away from other things I wanted to do."

Marv searched his daughter's face for a long moment, shock disrupting his composure. Then he spoke. "Janice, you don't know why Lamedeer and I got on that plane to take you home, do you?"

"No."

"The police in Montana informed me that this producer, Mr. Territoni, is a drug dealer. He drugs young girls and then gets them to work in porn films. Is that what you want to become, a prostitute actress?"

"Oh Daddy, I don't believe that."

"No, because you do not want to believe it. But listen to this. If indeed this Territoni is a drug dealer, he could have had something to do with George Culbertson's murder."

"How could he have something to do with that? They didn't know each other."

"He was in Mission that night." He looked at his daughter completely perplexed that she could not, or would not, understand.

Janice shivered. Her mind went back to the moments when John Territoni had kissed her and examined her body as he was explaining the scenes to the actor. She had even liked being kissed by him. She shivered again. "Oh Daddy. Daddy, are you sure?"

"Absolutely dead certain."

"I don't know, Daddy, that seems difficult to believe."

"Believe it."

She turned away from him.

"We were afraid for you, my dear beloved daughter. That's why Lamedeer and I hurried here."

"If he is a drug dealer, why don't they arrest him?"

"They need proof. What they have is circumstantial evidence only. Lamedeer and I are going to confront him tomorrow morning."

"Oh Daddy, don't."

"We'll be careful. We're just going to speak with him. Lamedeer can identify a liar when he sees one, just like he can see the tracks of animals no one else can see."

Janice wanted to be doubtful. She fervently wished they had not interfered. "But Daddy, he just doesn't seem like that. How could Mr. Territoni come to Montana and pretend to film a movie there if he is a drug dealer?"

"Bad people do many things good people do. They criminalize every endeavor they undertake. They know how to get away with what they are doing for a time but this man will not continue to get away with what he is doing. The police are unraveling his past. So, my dear, dear Janice, you had better forget about playing in a movie directed by him and you should thank your lucky stars Ms. Stanton wants to train you to be a model. If she hadn't come into this picture, you'd be going back to Montana with me."

He smiled and hugged her although she remained aloof, stiffening her body as he put his arms around her. "The only reason I am allowing you to remain in New York is because, as little as I know her, I have a hell of a lot of respect for Ms. Stanton and what she can do for your career. You do want to stay here under her tutelage?"

"Yes," begrudgingly.

"Okay. Let's sign these contracts then and get on with it."

Chapter Nineteen

P atsy Stanton lived in a brownstone on the upper East side. It was tall and narrow on the outside, identical to the hundreds of other brownstones. But once you entered the front door, you walked into a magical kingdom. There had been no constraints when the inside had been gutted and remodeled. Patsy liked white and red and aquamarine. White was the rule for walls and ceilings in her home. A white walled hallway led to a white kitchen, of which one wall was a dramatic red. The kitchen led to a huge white pantry that looked perfectly delicious with its shelves and trays and hooks of colorful packaged condiments, food and pots and pans.

Off the kitchen stretched a long, narrow dining area. Modern furniture dominated the area, one wall was aquamarine and spread across the windows were colorful drapes depicting a serene seascape. Beyond the dining room lay another long railroad car type room with fitness its sole design; the furnishings were all exercise related with its dominant feature was a 15 x 8 foot lap pool.

"Swimming is a marvelous exercise," asserted Patsy (who seldom swam), "and this pool is stupendous. It is small; its brand name is *Endless*, because it is. One is forced to swim against the current. We adjust the current, fast or slow." She flicked a wall switch to demonstrate. "A daily swim here builds stamina, it also makes for a good night's sleep." Her melodic laugh filled the room.

There were no stairs in Patsy's house. An escalator carried one up to the second and third floors and back down again. When the motor was shut off, one walked up and down the escalator steps (the motor was usually shut off). An office/library, with one aquamarine wall; Patsy's spacious bedroom, and a small bedroom completed the second story. The third floor held three bedrooms, each with a private bath.

"Here you are, Janice," said Patsy, after dinner had been served and Marv, Lamedeer and Merry had been driven to a nearby hotel. The escalator machinery was silent as she and Janice ascended to the third floor. "Your luggage is already here and so is your roommate, Mary Guttman."

A tall brunette girl lounged on one of the two beds along the sidewall of the long, narrow bedroom.

"Good night, girls. Have a delicious sleep. I shan't see you in the morning. I'm off to the office at 6 a.m. You'll be up by that time, of course, exercising in the gym."

"Hello," said Janice, looking at the long form on the bed nearest the door.

"Hi," answered the form, not looking up, the voice's owner immersed in reading a book.

"Is this my bed?"

"Yeah, I guess so."

"My name is Janice Alicorn."

"Okay, I'll stop reading in a moment. I want to finish this chapter."

Janice stood in the middle of the room, looking at the brunette, waiting.

"There. That was an exciting story." The brunette turned around, leaped out of the bed, and took her long form to where Janice was standing and hugged her.

"I'm Mary," she said brightly. "You are going to be my new roommate, I take it."

"Yes."

"Welcome to our jail."

"Our jail?"

"Well, our time is not our own here."

"Oh?"

"None of it is, well, except for Saturday night." She raised her arms over the top of her head and danced in a circle. "Then we can go and play. But it's difficult to get someone to play with you when you have only one night off."

The brunette stepped back from Janice. "You are really, really pretty. Spectacular pretty!"

"You are beautiful."

"Oh, I know that. Neither of us would be here if we weren't. There are your suitcases. Right in my way. Here is your closet. And my name is Mary. What's yours? I didn't listen when Madame Patsy was telling me."

"Janice Alicorn."

"Do you have a nickname?"

"No." Janice had lifted one of her suitcases onto the bed and was opening it.

"I have. Guffy."

"Really? What does Guffy stand for?"

"It should have been Goofy, but I didn't like that, although everyone says I am. I changed it to Guffy. There isn't anyone around though to call me by my nickname." She giggled merrily.

Janice thought it would be courteous to laugh, so she did.

"What in the hell is that you are taking out of the suitcase?"

"That's Oscar, my doll."

"Good God. What a mangy looking thing. What do you want a doll for?"

"Oh, Oscar has been with me since I was a little girl. He knows all my secrets. He used to carry messages between me, my sister and brother." She lifted Oscar's multi-colored shirt and showed Mary a slit running down its front. "We hid them in here. Now I just like him on my bed." Janice hugged him, then lay his four foot cloth form down, moving the covers, so all but his head was under them.

"We should call you Goofy. Guffy and Goofy, ha ha."

Janice didn't say anything; instead, she busied herself hanging her clothes in the closet on the back wall.

"Where are you from?"

"Montana. My father owns a ranch outside of Mission."

"Ranches have names, don't they? What's yours called?"

"Windy Hills Double Bar M."

"Wow. Is it a big ranch?"

"Big enough."

"I'm from New York. Manhattan, New York. Right here in East River City!" Mary laughed again. "We should make a good pair. I bet you're good at weights and bikes and . . . hey, can you swim?"

"Yes."

"Wait till you get in the swimming pool downstairs. That'll be a blast. God damn. My third father used to say that all the time." She mimicked him. "That'll be a blast, God damn."

"Your third father?"

"Yeah," scornfully. "He's the father that raped me whenever he felt like it."

"Mary!"

They were both sitting on Janice's bed.

"Well, he did. He made me hate men. Oh, sometimes I like what they do," she giggled, "but I like to use them. I'll show them someday we don't need them and that will be a blast, God damn."

Janice studied her roommate. Mary was very tall; she must be at least 5 foot 10 inches. She was also very beautiful from the tip of her brunette head down to her toes in a very willowy way. There wasn't anything that appeared out of place. Her leanness was exquisite; small breasts, small waist, narrow hips, long straight legs - every bone and muscle indented delicately by nature. Mary's refined face emphasized her body form. It was lean and narrow with superlative high cheekbones and wide, dark eyes, deep-set under a narrow brow. Yet for all her delicate beauty she had a puckish look about her, and she oozed with friendliness.

Janice said gently, "I'm sorry you were raped."

"Well, that's long gone, the first time, I mean." She laughed uproariously. "My mother found us after I had begun to like it. She called it my fault and sent me off to boarding school. They got a divorce anyway. I think the only reason he married her was to fuck me, her ten-year-old daughter." She laughed again, this time with a hint of sadness. "But it scared her. She wouldn't let me live with her when she married my fourth father. And that is kinda why I am here. My mother keeps sending me places so I won't bother her. I'm eighteen now, but still ," she paused, pensive. "Of course because I am so beautiful, Patsy couldn't refuse her. Patsy knows my mother. I'll show her when I'll be a famous model and I'll go home and say to her present husband, 'Rape me.' That'll get her going."

"Mary, that would be awful."

"Awful what I am saying, or what they did to me? What's awful, huh?" Tears suddenly welled from her eyes. She got up from the bed and climbed into hers, shedding her purple dress, bra and panties and dropping them on the floor.

"I'm sorry," Janice said, getting up from her bed and turning towards the bathroom. "I didn't mean to upset you."

"Oh, you didn't make me feel badly. I make myself feel badly. I'm going to read for a little while and then I'll turn off my bed light. Would you please turn off the big light when you go to bed?"

"Of course."

"We're going to have fun," Mary called after her. "No, I don't want to read. When you get out of the bathroom, come over to my bed and tell me about Montana. Talking will be better than reading. You don't mind if I sneak a smoke, do you?"

"Sneak a smoke?"

"Patsy's models aren't supposed to smoke. Bad for whatever, she says. But this isn't a regular cigarette. I'll tell you what it is if you promise not to tell anyone. And you can have a puff if you want to."

"I don't want a puff, thank you Mary. I don't care to smoke. What is it if it is not a cigarette?"

"Marijuana."

"That's illegal."

"Yeah. So is rape. I'm just getting even."

"Oh, Mary."

"Oh, Mary yourself."

"I really don't like smoking."

"Then go in the bathroom and close the door. I'll have my few puffs in secret. Relaxes me. Then I'll hear all about Montana."

Janice saw Mary's clothes on the floor and leaned over to pick them up.

"Hey, leave those alone," Mary cried.

"I'm going to hang them up for you."

"No siree. Let the maid do it."

"Maid? Do we have a maid?"

"Of course. I never hang up my own clothes."

"Your dress is so pretty it might get wrinkled."

"I don't care. I wore it once. That's enough."

"You won't wear that pretty dress again?" Janice was incredulous.

"Oh, I might. But don't you dare pick it up."

"How strange." Janice started for the bathroom.

Chapter Twenty

Peter Morgan found Melissa in the barn. She was rubbing down Atlas. Lincoln leaped up from the ground just outside the stall, and was at Peter's side in an instant, his tail straight back, his hackles raised. He emitted a low growl, even though Peter held out his hand for the dog to sniff.

"Who is it?" Melissa called out, leaning backward awkwardly, attempting to see who had entered the barn.

"There you are, Miss Melissa Alicorn," said Peter, as he reached the stall, watching her turn and look at him. Her eyes grew wide with mingled surprise and fear, her mouth open in a questioning mien.

Looking at her, Peter recalled he had been attracted to her both times he had seen her. On his visit with Marv, he had looked at her father and said to himself, "You're going to be my father-in-law some day." He liked the directness of Marv, his clean, strong aura. Melissa possessed the same traits.

First though, he had to find George Culbertson's killer. The murder and the facts, few that there were and the lack of them, consumed him. There was really nothing in the investigation that required him to return to the Alicorn ranch after his visit with Marv. His primary motive today was to see Melissa, although he would not tell her this.

"Good morning, Miss Melissa Alicorn," he smiled in return at her greeting. "I looked for your father at the house. Your maid told me he is not home."

"That maid," she smiled softly, "is Lamedeer's wife,

Swallow. Dad and Lamedeer flew to New York to bring back Janice."

"They what?"

"It's okay." Melissa saw his startled look. "She's fine, in fact they left her there. And they are now on their way home."

Peter was trying to suppress his shock.

"Tell me about it."

"Oh, they did not see the producer." Melissa noted the relaxing of Peter's face muscles. "Janice has been hired by a world-famous modeling agency. And she's living in the owner's home. It's really a very wonderful opportunity for Janice and us. I know she's going to be a famous model." The words gushed out as Melissa put the brushes back into her grooming pail, stood up and faced Peter. Although she was not his height, she was almost as tall. She remembered him from Spokane and his friendliness. "Peter. . . that is your name, isn't it? You were so nice to me in Spokane."

"Peter Morgan," he said. "I'd like you to call me Peter."

"I will."

"When are they due back?"

"Their plane should get in two hours from now, about 10:30 a.m. I'm going to meet them."

"I'd like to meet them. We could go together."

"Annabelle and I will ride with you and we'll pick them up together, or if you'd rather we can meet at the airport."

"Ride with me." Peter smiled. Melissa laughed merrily. "Oh, what fun!" The beginning of a wide smile disappeared as quickly as it had begun. "Even in this non-fun time."

"How is Andrew? And where is he?"

Melissa's face turned solemn. "He's in the house. He doesn't get out of bed or his room much, except to eat, although both Annabelle and I force him to go on walks. He looks around, sometimes like he is frightened, but he never says a word. The psychiatrist is here every other day, and he says Andrew is about ready to come back to life but we haven't seen much change."

"I'm, sorry." He had no intention of telling Melissa about their investigation of Andrew. "I am heading to Spokane this weekend," Peter said, as Melissa closed the gate to the stall and they left the barn. "We have a few leads to check out."

Melissa's "oh" was muffled. "If you don't mind waiting in the living room, I'll just change from my barn clothes." She looked Peter full in the face, tiny, young laugh wrinkles at the sides of her eyes closing into one another as she smiled at him, "and put on my Great Falls clothes. And of course, Annabelle will come with us."

Melissa's 'Great Falls' or city clothes consisted of slim black jeans, accentuating her long, slender legs, and a patterned red and black flannel shirt over which she wore a down-lined, short-waisted black jacket. Her head was bare. In the sunlight her hair glistened with red highlights as the three walked to Peter's car. Annabelle wore a green slack suit; over it a heavy full-length coat to ward off the chill. Lincoln had been left in the house. "Too cold for you to be wandering around outside," Melissa told him as her dog reached up to her on his hind legs to receive her kiss on his forehead before she closed the door.

The plane was on time. Marv and Annabelle greeted each other enthusiastically.

Melissa asked anxiously, "Janice is okay with this Mrs. Stanton?"

"She's just fine," said her father, hugging her and then giving Annabelle a long, tender kiss. "Ms. Stanton is like an angel from heaven. What a wonderful career our Janice has ahead of her."

"Did you see that producer?"

`"No." Marv recited the events of his and Lamedeer's adventure in New York as they walked to Peter's car. Lamedeer followed with the two carry-on suitcases.

"I would have liked to meet up with the son of a bitch," Marv told Peter, "but he was a no-show at the hotel where he had put up Janice and Merry. I believe one of the clerks told him her family came after her. Good thing. We did take a cab and cased the building where his studios are. Patsy (he explained Patsy) had nothing good to say about him. We thought it better not to see him or tip our hand. At this point it is not in our place to pursue him. If he is anyway involved in George's death, I don't want to mess up the work of the FBI." He then changed the subject, adding proudly, "Our mission is accomplished as far as Janice is concerned. She's in extremely competent hands with Patsy, and I'm glad we saw her settled. Quite something, she being discovered, so to speak, in a restaurant. Now, what's going on with the investigation?"

"We are moving ahead," answered Peter cautiously.

"That's not answering my question."

"I'm off to Spokane Friday," Peter said. "I have several solid leads to follow up."

Marv did not answer. He shook his head, his mouth pulled

down. On the way home he kept one arm tightly around Annabelle, happy to hold her. She felt his tension, particularly when she told him about Andrew and the caretaking they were doing each day with him.

Before Marv entered the house he turned to Peter who was standing by his car watching Lincoln greet his mistress with high leaps and bounds. Marv said flatly, "I trust this weekend will bring results."

Peter nodded. "I hope so too, sir," he said.

"If not, I'm going to jump into this. I don't like waiting. That damn producer has got to be involved somehow. Even if he isn't, I'm going to do something to shut him down."

Chapter Twenty-One

Andrew woke up frightened. He was breathless. He had been running and running and running, but he did not know from what or where. Opening his eyes, he saw he was home in his room, but he did not know how he got here. As he started to look about him, he began running and he ran and ran until he had to lie back and close his eyes.

The next time he woke up, his mother was standing in front of him. She didn't look like his mother was supposed to look, but she said she loved him and could be his mother now. She didn't kiss him like Betty kissed him and where was Betty? Suddenly, he saw her. She was being carried away from him and he yelled and screamed at the dark figures that were pulling at her body. He felt people nudging him as he was crying out for Betty. "Betty, Betty stay with me," and they sat him up in his bed and hugged him, but he threw their arms away. So he went back to sleep because he hurt all over and he couldn't get Betty to come back.

Then again, when he woke up, his face was being washed so he sat up and let his sister, yes, he knew it was his sister, finish washing it. He got up when she told him to and went down the stairs with her and Annabelle, Dad's mistress, both holding on to him as they counted the steps for him. "Nine, ten, eleven, we are almost down all the steps, Andrew. Just one more." But he did not answer them. He knew if he started to speak, he would begin running again and he did not want to run any more. Running was scary.

Tonight, when he woke up, he got up, although his chest hurt like hell. He knew he had been hurt and he could hardly move his right arm, lift his shoulder or breathe deeply without being in pain, but he could get up by holding on to the chair beside his bed with his right hand and arm. He was weak but he wanted to go to his computer; there was something he had to find which would tell him something he wanted to know so he could find Betty. He wasn't sure what that was but it was important. So he went over to his desk silently so no one would hear him, sat down and hit the mechanical mouse that lay beside the computer, and typed in Google, then Human Trafficking. He didn't even have to think of the two words he typed, they just flew out of his fingers. But that was all he could type because he began running and running. He couldn't go through this any longer so he called out, "Betty, Melissa." He hoped one of them would answer him.

When he opened his eyes, his family was standing in front of him and he was on the floor, every one was here except Betty. He knew she wasn't part of the family, but he wanted her here. He saw his father, Annabelle, Melissa and Lamedeer, and Swallow, Lamedeer's wife. They were all crying. He was smiling, he was so glad to see them.

" Where's Janice and Merry?" he asked as he lay there, Melissa sitting on the floor holding his head in her lap. His father knelt down on the floor beside him and told him that Janice was in New York and Merry was fixing his breakfast. "And I love you very much," his father said. So Andrew went back to sleep. He felt peaceful.

Later that day, after he woke up again and was taken

downstairs by his father, who held him close (and that felt good); after he ate he sat on a chair in the big living room with his father and the long-faced man with grey hair, a belly that almost wasn't, who was dressed like he worked in the city and had to wear a suit (which he did), a dark brown suit but with no tie who had kept coming to see him when he was so frightened.

Father was sitting next to him, his arm over Andrew's shoulder, and the man asked, "How are you today, Andrew?"

Andrew immediately burst into tears and all the pent-up words and everything that had happened to him after he left the ranch to go to school came tumbling out of his mouth.

Three hours later the two men lifted Andrew, who had fallen asleep, out of the chair and laid him down on one of the couches, covering him with a blanket. They looked at each other, shaking their heads, and talked about all the things Andrew had told them.

"You know," Marv said, after their discussion had worn down, "he is a very brave young man. I am proud of him."

Marv called the FBI man, who came out the next morning with Sheriff Chobin and they listened to Marv and spoke briefly to Andrew. The FBI man said Andrew would not be arrested at the present time, but that he would be back to tape Andrew's story when he was stronger, probably in the coming week.

Chapter Twenty-Two

"Dear Melissa," her sister wrote, sitting at the desk in the third floor bedroom. "I love my new life. It is exhausting but I adore it. I'm learning so much. Here's a typical day at Ms. Patsy's.

"We are awakened at 5:30 a.m. (an ungodly hour). Our morning trainer says getting up at that time will become ingrained in us, that we'll never sleep past 5:30 for the rest of our lives. Ugh! I can't imagine that! Neither can I imagine what time our trainer gets up. She wakes us with a full-face makeup and hairdo just so. She's not young so it's not an instant fix. Oh, our morning trainer's name is Mitzi. She doesn't look like a Mitzi though. She looks and acts more like Dracula (ha ha).

"We get up at 5:30, do five minutes of stretching under her watchful eyes (yes, of course, after we go to the bathroom, brush our teeth and wash our faces). Ms. Patsy even has two toilets in our bathroom. No bathtub though. Two shower stalls, one with pipes that squeak, and two sinks. It took me a week before I got over my modesty.

"My roommate, Mary, doesn't have any modesty. She's kind of wild and very, very rebellious about just anything. Even so, you'd like her, Melissa. She's a lot of fun to be with when she's in a happy mood. Anyway, after our calisthenics - we go down on the escalator in our gym clothes. We walk down. The escalator's motor is usually turned off because

Ms. Patsy says walking up and down steps improves the look of our buns. Into the exercise room we go.

"Mind you, Melissa, I have a completely empty tummy. Not even one cup of coffee to wake me up! Next, the Endless pool; does seventy degrees sound warm, huh! Not in a cold, damp New York winter. The cold seeps through the walls in these old brownstones; it's really damp here not nice and dry like Montana. Anyway, we swim. And Lady Dracula turns the dial and we have to swim harder and harder against the current. I hated this the first two weeks. Now I love it. It's not only Mary and me competing against one another, one of Ms. Patsy's famous models has joined us. She's been gaining weight, so she has to come here three times a week to exercise. She's a gorgeous brunette, name of Maxine. She's the cover model on one of the big mags now on the stands. We swim against each other, ten whole minutes worth. Then Mrs. Dracula lets us float or whatever for five minutes. Out of the pool we climb and I'm beat and I've only been out of bed forty-five minutes. We shower, get on the weight machine and then - guess what! A masseuse comes in and Mary and I lie on warm tables and get massaged all over. That's almost the best part of the day. Wow!

"Then it's breakfast time. The menu is monstrous as well as monotonous. Orange juice, hot oatmeal with a teaspoonful of real maple syrup, one egg (cooked any way we want), and a glass of milk. NO COFFEE! Gee, do I miss coffee. It's only 7:30 a.m. when we finish eating. We go back to our room and dress. Mrs. Dracula is also a makeup artist and we spend another hour - oh, Melissa, I must be boring you. I'm boring myself. Suffice it to say that every minute of every day is chuck full of things to learn and do. Most of it boring, like this letter.

"The best part of each day is when Will, the photographer who discovered me (ahem) picks us up in the afternoon and takes me (and Mary) to his studio, a fantastic loft on East 44th Street. He teaches us to pose - every way imaginable. I'm getting good at it. Will told Ms. Patsy I'm going to be a most sought after model in the country in a couple of years. How about that, Melissa!!!

"I'm tired now and not good at writing long letters. You know that. I think about Andrew quite a lot. Sometimes I feel like I should be home, helping you get him better. I get so sad thinking about him and about the story of Betty who nobody can find.

"I don't think the movie producer, John Territoni, could have had anything to do with George Culbertson's death. If he did, they would have arrested him by now, wouldn't they have? Will says he's bad stuff, but I have met a couple of models that say he's A-1 okay. One of them is going to be the lead in his next picture. She says they are going to shoot a lot of it in Tunis, Africa. I almost wish it were me (I? - me sounds better) going. Yes, I know what you are thinking, I'm mixed up and you're right. Please, please don't tell anyone what I just said, particularly Dad. But sometimes I am disappointed I didn't have a chance at that movie I was going to do a screen test for. Mary said I should have taken the part. And Ms. Patsy says maybe I will be in the movies some day. I guess she knows I'm hoping to be more than a model. Mary says she wants to come with me to Montana next summer. Dad would definitely not like Mary. I am being very good and doing just what I am supposed to be doing. For now! I am learning a lot that should help me in the future.

"Oh, Oscar looks weird now (yes, I know, you always thought Oscar looked weird for a rag doll - ha ha). You'll be delighted to know he looks weirder. The only thread I found to stitch his eye back on when it fell out was red. So Oscar's got a red-rimmed eye now. (Ha ha again).

"It's Saturday night and Mary is out on the town, as I told you she's neat but kind of wild.

"Love, Janice."

Janice did not tell Melissa the whole truth. At times she was very much at sixes and sevens about modeling. She was tired of Ms. Patsy telling her she had to do this and do that as long as she was a model, meaning eating right, getting to bed early, exercising, that it was important to take extraordinary care of her body in order to look and feel her best at all times.

I've been doing all right so far, thought Janice. I don't think I should have to follow the rigid schedule Ms. Patsy says I should. If I were an actress I wouldn't be bound by such an exacting schedule. I could have fun and go places to be seen as well as do my work. Not like a model who has to go to bed early every night and be up at dawn the next day to pose for pictures! Right now I can think of nothing more boring. Dad and Ms. Patsy both told me I have to be here for three to six months. Then I can go out on my own. So I'll put up with it and learn all I can. I can use all the modeling tips in movies too, if maybe that is what I want to do.

I am a little afraid of Ms. Patsy. She's strict in a matter-of-fact cunning way. I'm never sure of what she is thinking. And she glares at Mary when we have lunch or dinner together. It is very unsettling. I'm really not as happy as I pretend to be.

Janice did not always enjoy the company of her moody roommate. That was one reason she steadily declined Mary's offer to go out with her on Saturday nights with a 'blind date,' even though it was boring staying behind. She felt like a flower with two sets of petals. She loved the attention she received each day, at night she hated the restrictiveness. Anyway, Mary was unsettling. She would be up in the clouds, absolutely joyful for ten minutes and then suddenly become inexplicably depressed. When she was in one of those morosely, withdrawn moods she was difficult to talk to. If you asked her a question, she spit back at you. In another few minutes, usually after going into the bathroom, she would rush back and beg forgiveness for her outbursts. Thank goodness, these episodes were few and far between.

"Why do we have to have chaperones," Janice timidly complained of Ms. Patsy at dinner after Dracula had taken her and Mary on a chaperoned shopping tour.

'Did you see the stares you received?" Ms. Patsy answered. "As long as you reside under my roof, you will be protected," Ms. Patsy answered severely.

On the first of their once-weekly shopping tours, Janice and Mary, accompanied by Mitzi and a male employee (plus the driver) were taken in Patsy's limo to the corner of 57th and Fifth Avenue. There the four left the limo and strolled down the Avenue. Mary halted frequently, recklessly buying shoes (they were her current passion), along with several dresses. The others had to patiently wait. When Mary's arms were full of packages, Janice said, "Now it's my turn. I want to buy some books."

"That's stupid," said Mary. "Ms. Patsy has a whole library filled with books."

"Well, I want something to read that I want to read. There is a Barnes and Noble book store on our way back to the limo." Janice purchased a dozen romance novels the first trip and several each succeeding trip. She filled most of her free time reading, yearning for a love like those in the stories she read.

Saturday nights after Mary had gone out, she would walk down the escalator steps to the second floor library, pull out world history books from the shelves (she loved Greek and Roman history), plunk herself down in one of the comfortable armchairs and read. After a bit her eyes would leave the page and closing them, she would think about being in the arms of her history teacher. She missed him, she missed Rob, the ranch hand. Then she would open her eyes and laugh to herself. She realized she just wanted to be loved by someone. That's probably why on the weekly shopping trips, she would stare at each man they passed on the Avenue, searching for handsome ones, then wondering how he would be in bed. She excused herself for thinking as she did, I'm almost twenty-one, I'm grown up, she told herself.

Several times she slammed the history books shut, pulled herself up into a ball in the armchair and bemoaned her time at Ms. Patsy's, wishing for something exciting to happen, featuring a man, of course. Back upstairs in bed, she waxed thankful the heroines in the romance novels she favored never acted as Mary did. She knew if Mary wasn't so unpredictable she would go out with her on Saturday nights.

But Mary habitually returned to their room late, invariably past Ms. Patsy's explicit midnight curfew and usually slightly tipsy.

Once, when Janice helped Mary undress, she whispered, "You are over an hour past our curfew. It's after one o'clock." Mary answered haughtily, "What is she going to do, ring a bell like they did at the factories during the middle ages? And everybody fall down and sleep till it's time to go to work again?" She giggled. Janice pulled back from Mary's whiskey breath. "Janice, this is the 21st century. I have a wad of money at my disposal . . . so does Ms. Patsy for my room and board. I can do what I damn please. I don't care if I am living in her grand house. She's lucky to have me as a budding Models Plus model."

"Ssssh," whispered Janice, who did not want one thing to go wrong while she lived there. "Somebody might hear."

"So what!" Mary retorted, slurring her words. "Stop the whispering. Ms. Patsy saw me come in. Her stupid rules are not going to stop me from having fun. She knows what side of the bread hers is buttered on. She'd be nothing without her models. Say," she added, slurring over the words, "I met Mr. Good Looking again tonight. He's not my type but he could be yours. Tall, dark with black eyes that go right through you; he undresses you every time he looks at you. He's a yum-yum man." She giggled louder. "He told my boy friend he'd like to meet you."

"Mary, lift your left foot. I want to take off your shoe."

"Oh, you are sooooo sweet, Janice." With that, Mary fell back on the bed and in a moment was sound asleep.

Chapter Twenty-Three

W ill asked Janice and Mary one afternoon if the two of them would like to go to a symphony with him that night.

Mary, sitting cross-legged on an exercise pad on his bare loft floor, gazing out the ceiling to floor window, bending and straightening her arms in a lackadaisical pretence of exercising, practically shouted in answer, "God damn, as my father would say, symphonies! Ugh. I had enough of them as a child."

"I'd love to go," interspersed Janice. "I used to go with my Dad to the symphonies in Great Falls. We have a fabulous symphony director, Gordon Johnson. He has conducted all over the world, but he likes living in Great Falls. We're lucky."

"Good," answered Will. "Yo Yo Ma is performing tonight in New Jersey. You would appreciate him. He is a master at the cello and the consummate showman. I'll pick you up at Patsy's after dinner, it's only a forty-five-minute drive. The concert begins at 7:30, so finish your dessert by six. Oh, and a skirt and sweater under your winter coat will be appropriate."

Janice had been standing in front of the loft windows, her head in shadows and Will did not see the flash of anger cross her face as he was putting covers on his equipment.

"You sound like my father," she suddenly blurted, her voice bristling. "How come no matter where I go in my life,

I'm being bossed. My father, then Ms. Patsy, now you. Why can't you be my friend and not tell me what to do or what to wear every minute of every day. I'm trying to do everything right so I learn. I never say no to what anybody asks. I say, yes, yes, yes. Yes, Ms. Patsy; yes, Miss Clarice; yes, Will. Yes sir! Yes ma'am. I yes everyone all day long. I'm tired of it. I just want to be me for a change." She burst into tears.

Mary had fallen backwards on the exercise pad and was listening to Janice with a big grin on her face. "Atta girl," she said, "you tell him. I feel the same way."

Will's lips formed a whistle as Janice started crying. He went over to her, took her in his arms and said delicately, "Yes, you've been worked hard, Janice. You've done well and are a superb pupil, but you haven't had any time off. That's the problem. I'm going to see you get some."

"Me too?" asked Mary derisively. She had risen and was taking her coat off the coat rack.

"Mary, you do relax. Janice is wound up tight."

"I don't see how a stupid concert is going to relax her. Take her and me to a dance club. A couple of cocktails and a whirl around the floor will be a God damn hell of a lot more relaxing."

"She's coming to my apartment after the concert for a late dinner."

"Ho ho ho. A late dinner or a rape." Mary smirked at Will. "But you don't rape, do you Will." It was a statement, not a question.

Will swung away from Janice who had stopped crying. He faced Mary squarely, his slate eyes glinting. "Mind your manners, Miss Mary."

Mary, ignoring him, stretched gracefully and then leered at Will, saying meanly, "Yes, Mr. Will. I'll mind my manners." She put on her jacket. "Will, take us back to Patsy's." She turned to Janice. "Come on, honey, you need to have time to choose the right sweater and skirt for your ugh! concert date with Mr. Will."

Janice chose a long, slim black skirt, a black turtleneck sweater topped with a white cashmere sweater. Pearl earrings dangled from her ears, half hidden under her long, flowing hair. She had allowed it to fall free and her slightest movement swept strands that lay back of her shoulders forward until they covered her ears. Only when she gently lifted the hair away with her fingers were the pearls her father sent her, exposed.

She began shivering repeatedly as soon as the heavy front door on Patsy's brownstone closed. She realized the black wool cape she wore was too flimsy for the cold night. Will, who was holding her arm protectively on the icy sidewalk, guiding her to his car, asked, "Do you want to get something warmer?"

"No," she answered quickly. "Your car will be warm. Let's get into it."

The car was warm. The symphony hall, packed with people, was warm.

"What a funny world this is," Janice said to Will as they climbed the stairs to the loge. "I see jeans, long shimmering gowns, tee shirts, ties, even a few tuxedos. Anything goes as far as dress, doesn't it, Will?"

He nodded. They had arrived twenty minutes before curtain time. Will had secured seats on the front row of the loge and Janice could lean over the gleaming copper railing watching patrons take their seats in the orchestra section below.

"You will notice," explained Will, his voice rising above the din made by the chatter of arriving concert goers and instruments being tuned by musicians, "that Mr. Ma is celebrated not only for his brilliant mastery of the cello and the emotion with which he plays, but also because as he plays, he communicates with the orchestra he is working with and with the audience. Yo Yo Ma is a great team player as well as a great musician.

"This is what you as a future model must be. You want to work as a team with the photographer, the client, the makeup artist, the designer, the manicurist; everyone involved in one ad. Teamwork will establish connection and spill out to the reading audience who sees you in the ad. Don't frown, Janice. Mary, for instance, is not a team player, so she'll soon fade away. She cannot give of herself and it will show up in her work. You have the capacity for stimulating the awareness needed to sell products. Even though your charisma will most often be on the printed page, it will inspire. It will sell. Now sit back and enjoy the artistry of Yo Yo Ma. Note how he inspires."

When the concert was over, the two moved slowly with the noisy and lunging crowd towards the exit and Janice remarked, her eyes glistening, "He was magnificent. And Will, you were right. He was at one with everyone. I see what you mean. Thank you for taking me and thank you for explaining what my goal as a model should be. I certainly saw the perfect example watching and listening to Yo Yo. He was inspiring. He was truly magnificent," she repeated.

Will pressed her hand. "Come now. We'll have a late dinner at my apartment. Then I'll take you back to Patsy's."

They were both silent on the trip back to Manhattan. Janice's first thoughts dwelled on Yo Yo's compelling performance. Her second one plunged her into wondering if Will was going to tempt her into going to bed with him. She sat stiffly in her seat, closing her eyes against the traffic lights heading into the city, musing. Although Will was years her elder, she had from her first meeting found him attractive. Goodness knows she longed for someone to hold her close. She was getting so tired of the workday, the training, the book reading, the diet! How she wanted to go out on a date. But would it be good for Ms. Patsy's lead photographer to romance an aspiring model? On the other hand, he was, if always a little distant, ever protective. She sighed. That he had asked her out to the symphony knowing Mary would not accept, and the way he held her arm, she was positive these were signs he liked her. She glanced at him repeatedly as he drove, receiving a warm smile from him each time her head turned towards his. She sighed again.

"What is it?" Will asked. "Did you want to ask me something? That was a big sigh."

"No. It's been a wonderful evening, Will."

"And it's not over yet."

She smiled demurely. "No."

She looked at him again. Oh dear, I like him as a friend, she thought, someone I can talk to as a father. I don't think I want him to kiss me when we get to his apartment. I really want him just to be my friend, not a lover. And I wouldn't be able to say no to him. Oh dear. She closed her eyes. Let him stay just my friend, she pleaded to herself.

"Perhaps you had better just take me to Patsy's," she ventured, gaining courage as the lights of Broadway appeared.

"I would," said Will, grinning, although he kept his eyes on the traffic ahead of him, "but my roommate would be offended. You see, he has cooked a very special dinner for lovely Janice."

"Your roommate?" She gasped. "You never told me you had a roommate."

Will chuckled. "You never asked."

Will lived on the mideast side, his apartment on a street containing 40-year-old, look-alike, elderly apartment buildings. He parked on the street in the only parking space available, a space marked 'reserved.'

"How do you rate a parking spot on the street?"

"My spare," he grinned, before he moved to the curb to open her door. "It's prearranged with the garage attendant. The parking space is filled until just minutes before I arrive. I'm a prompt individual, as you know."

"Yes." She laughed.

"Come, we are taking the steps to the second floor. Our elevator has had an accident."

Old though the apartment building was, it appeared well preserved. The stairwell was clean, freshly painted a calm tan, its banisters a gleaming dark brown gloss. It opened onto a rich and newly deep tan, carpeted hallway. There were two doors on each side of the corridor. Will led her to the left door. It opened before they reached it.

A man in faded blue jeans, a red and white striped shirt, his shirt and jeans partially hidden by a long grey apron, faced them. The heavy delicious odors of a roast accompanied him into the hallway.

"That was a long concert," the man said as he reached out to Will kissing him squarely on the lips.

Janice's mouth fell open. Her face reddened. She was totally unprepared for the spectacle of one man kissing another.

Both men grinned at her. Will said, matter of factly, without any embarrassment, "She had no idea."

"Ah," exclaimed his roommate, removing his hands from Will's shoulders and pulling all of Janice's beauty into his eyes. "She is truly beautiful. No wonder you are smitten with her.

"I am Dwight, Will's partner," he said softly to her, putting his arm around her and leading her into the apartment.

Janice pulled away from him, not able to speak. She was humiliated. She stared first at the man, Dwight, who was moving her forward and then at Will. She lowered her eyes, blushed and breathing slowly, said in a strained voice, "I see. How do you do."

These are gay men, she said to herself, stunned. She had never come across gay men before. She and her friends had talked about them in school, and they had whispered and nudged each other when they came across a boy who walked with a lighter, more delicate step than his classmates or spoke with a lisp, but no one was ever sure the boy who gestured like a dancer was gay. Neither of these two men acted effeminate. That was how gay men were supposed to act, wasn't it? The man now standing dead in front of her put his feet down squarely as he moved. He appeared well over forty, and the round shape of a heavy belly bulged under his long, enfolding apron. His hair was dead white, very long, and pulled smoothly back from his temple into a neat ponytail, accentuating his high forehead (high because his hair had disappeared). His face didn't appear to need a shave ever. It was red and cherub like, its skin smooth and unblemished. Neither his face nor his body was attractive, even the lines of laughter wrinkles that clung to the edges of his large blue eyes were deeply grooved. Lines and lines of tiny wrinkles inhabited the corners of his mouth.

He beckoned her to enter the small and delicious smelling kitchenette as he patiently waited for her to recover from her shock. She stood in its doorway watching him as he stirred mushrooms, onions, parsley and oil in a skillet. Removing the pan from the fire, he turned.

"Smells good in here, doesn't it," he said easily as Will took her cape from her.

"Delicious," wanly, not as yet able to face up to the situation.

"We wanted you to enjoy an escape from Patsy's grim fare so I went all out to please you."

"Thank you." She studied this man Dwight again closely. He did possess a pleasing and warm demeanor, and he smiled at her again as he opened the oven door bending low to check what was baking there. All of a sudden she relaxed. Effortlessly, he had put her at ease with his open air of comfort.

With regained composure, she turned around and studied the dining area and living room.

"What a gorgeous apartment," she said. "I want a tour. It feels comfortable, like you are."

Dwight's wrinkles merged. He took her arm and led her through the apartment. She inspected the two bedrooms, the office, a studio, a long living room and its adjoining tiny kitchenette with a round glass table sitting near its edge. The furnishings were exquisite. What she could not take her eyes away from were the color photographs lining the pale bedroom walls in magnificent glass and wood frames. Each room she examined looked like what she had envisioned a fashionable New York apartment should look like, elegant, decorative, fastidious, and yet comfortable.

As they entered the studio, she gasped delightedly, "Which one of you is the artist who paints these watercolors?" All sorts of birds graced the delicately tinted leaves and boughs, held in tight, identical frames.

"We work as a team," Dwight told her, his wrinkles crinkling with pleasure. "Will takes pictures of beautiful people and I paint the fauna. But come, our dinner is ready. I do not like to serve leftovers. In my book leftovers are tasteless warmed-up main courses."

Janice did not believe she would ever forget the dinner. Each course was served in husky, handsome ceramic bowls with scenes of New York City decorating each plate edge. First, a clear soup, and until she asked, she could not tell what ingredients made it so serene. Each spoonful slid down her throat gladly. A mixed green salad decorated with small slices of avocado and slivers of purple onions was next. Third was a rack of lamb, fresh mint leaves scattered down its pyramid sides, served with mashed potatoes, mushrooms, onions and the parsley she had watched him sautéing. Butter glazed asparagus was the vegetable. Lastly, when she thought she could eat no more, Dwight carried in raspberry sherbet, topped with fresh raspberries. It was one of her favorite desserts.

"Where did you get these in the wintertime?" she asked, her spoon capturing a raspberry.

Dwight grinned again, shrugging his shoulders. "I have good connections."

"How could you guess I love raspberries?"

"Will listens. He made up the menu."

"Oh, it was a fabulous dinner."

"Our pleasure for a beautiful young lady."

"What do you do, Dwight?" she asked as they relaxed at the table with cups of delicate green tea.

"As you have surmised from my pictures, I am an artist. I make my livelihood with watercolors of birds, leaves, flowers, the gentle things ladies adore. I have a ready market and a backlog of orders from specialty stores all across the country. As you can tell, both of us are artistic. I can't match Will's genius for his remarkable photographic portraits but place a brush in his hand, and birds don't look like birds." Dwight's open smile was infectious.

"Thank you both," said Janice. "I've just had a most fabulous evening with two such warm and wonderful people. I think it's now time I go back to Ms. Patsy's. This is the first time I've been away for an evening. It feels so good to be here I hate to leave."

"You must visit us often," said Dwight. "I would have thought you have many friends here."

"No. I have none."

"None?"

"No. And Ms. Patsy keeps a close eye on me."

"You are then quite lonely, I take it."

"Yes, Dwight."

"Well now, we've got to do something about that. This modeling business is going to be a huge success for you. Will has exclaimed often how much he thinks of your talents and beauty and how hard you are working to do well. But success doesn't mean a thing without friends. You will consider us your friends, won't you?"

"Yes." She beamed.

Dwight reached out and folded a large, chubby hand over hers. "And when you feel lost and lonely - all New Yorkers do at times - remember, we are your friends and want you to come to us for solace."

"I will remember that," answered Janice gratefully.

Will said, "Yes, and it's time for Patsy to give you some assignments."

"Oh Will, please. I think I'm ready." Her eyes lit up in eagerness.

"You certainly are," remarked Will. "I'll speak to her tomorrow. Now, let's get you back to reality."

Reality was encountering a weeping Mary, who flung her arms around Janice the moment she entered their bedroom. "Patsy's throwing me out next week," she wailed. "The spiteful old bitch. She doesn't like the hours I'm keeping. Says I'm touchy. Says I imbibe too much liquor and . ." If she finished the sentence it was lost in sobs as she flung herself dramatically down on her bed.

"Oh, Mary."

"She told my mother. Between them, they found a stupid apartment for me. She says I have two modeling jobs set up, but," she added resentfully, "...but I have to do my own portfolio. That what I do is all up to me." Anger cloaked her voice. "That's all right by me, I don't need her. Oh, Janice, I don't want to leave." She began wailing again.

Janice sat down beside her, bending low to hug her. "I don't want you to leave either. And neither of us are ready for big-time modeling."

"Well, I am," defiantly.

" Mary, I wish you had someone who could help you."

"I do. My boyfriend," and she giggled through her sobs, "but he's not after just modeling jobs for me. He's after me too."

"Men!"

"Course I can get him to help me."

"I haven't met him, Mary, but I think when you go out with him you drink too much. What does your boyfriend do?"

"Well, he's a good friend of a producer. And he told me he could get me a great movie job. But there's a catch."

"What is that?"

"He wants me to bring you to the dance club."

"Why?"

"He wants you to meet his boss - this producer."

"What producer?"

"I don't know his name. He's the one who wants to meet

you."

"The tall man with dark hair and black eyes?"

"Yes."

"Is his name Territoni?"

"That rings a bell."

Something hit Janice's stomach. "He's not supposed to be any good," she finally said.

"Well, Ann Gaynor likes him. And she just auditioned for a leading role in a movie he's producing."

"Who's Ann Gaynor?"

"She's a model. She works for the January Agency."

"Oh."

Janice rose and began pacing up and down the bedroom.

"What's the matter?" asked Mary, wiping her eyes with a Kleenex.

"I'm just thinking." She was quiet for another moment, her mind dwelling on Andrew and George Culbertson. Then she asked quietly, "Where is your apartment?"

"I don't know. I'm packing my bags next Monday morning and am supposed to exit Ms. Patsy's in the afternoon. My Mother is coming to take me there."

"Can I go with you to see it?"

"If Ms. Patsy lets you get away."

"After you move, will you be going to the dance club that this producer frequents on Saturday nights?"

"Yes, of course." Mary jumped up. "Oh goodie. You'll go with me."

"Yes. I'll meet that producer."

"Yipee. God damn. Maybe moving won't be so bad after all if you're going to be my friend."

Chapter Twenty-Four

J anice looked ahead to her Saturday night dance club outing with Mary carefully, if wistfully. She kept thinking of her sister Melissa. She wished Melissa was in New York with her and they could go after the producer Territoni together, that is, if he was the producer Mary was talking about who wanted to meet her. She had never been very close to her younger sister until Andrew's sickness. Awful that it took Andrew's illness to bring them together, as sisters should be. Even now, far away from home, she felt closer to Melissa than she ever had when they lived together in the same house. She looked forward to Melissa's weekly letters full of local gossip. And she enjoyed writing the letters she wrote in which she could pour out her thoughts as they came to her. Melissa always answered as if she understood exactly the lonely moments Janice experienced and her doubts about becoming a model. As she had written once to Melissa, "I loved it when Will showed us a DVD with some of Models Plus models selling products with their voices, not just their faces and bodies. It makes me feel as if modeling is like being an actress, only of course, one doesn't fall in love with a bar of soap."

She told Mary she would go with her the next, not this coming, Saturday night.

"But I'll have already moved," pouted Mary. "That means my boyfriend and I will have to come back here to pick you up."

"I can meet you at your apartment."

"And who will drive you there?"

"I'll take a cab."

"Ms. Patsy is so protective of you she probably won't let you go without a chaperone. But, you know, I can teach you how to duck anyone they send to check on you while you are at the dance club." Mary giggled. "I don't know why you can't go with me this Saturday night." Mary was raucous now. Her voice had become more strident the past two weeks. She was sometimes so deliriously happy, other times so morose, Janice was almost glad she was leaving Ms. Patsy's. She seldom knew what to expect from Mary's irascible moods. "Dear Mary," she answered gently, "Ms. Patsy will be out of town next weekend."

"Oh ho! You are afraid of Patsy."

"I'm not. I need to get a new dress on our next shopping trip."

"You can wear one of mine."

"Thank you, Mary. You have beautiful clothes. It's just I want something to wear that looks like me."

Their conversation was interrupted by the noise of the escalator motor.

"Geez," said Mary, jumping up from the bed and moving towards the bathroom, "I haven't heard that in a long time. Patsy is the only one who uses the escalator. I bet she is coming up here. If she is," she said to Janice, pushing the door to the bathroom wide open, "tell her I'm taking a shower." She shut the door behind her.

It was Ms. Patsy. Janice recognized the click of her high heels as she stepped off the escalator and moved down the hallway to their room. Janice greeted her at the door.

"Ms. Patsy," she said, an uneasy smile crossing her lips, "it's nice to see you visiting Mary and me."

"I wish to explain several things to both of you," Ms. Patsy said, as she came into the room. "Where is Mary?"

"Taking a shower."

"Get her out of there. I wish to speak to both of you. No, never mind calling her," she interrupted herself, waving her heavily-ringed fingers. "I'll speak to you privately first."

She sat down on Janice's small blue armchair, photographing in her mind every article that lay upon Janice's desk as Janice sat on her bed facing Ms. Patsy.

"I have spoken with Will. I agree with him that you need to gain friends. You can't do that unless you mix with people. I want you to have two nights out a week, under supervision, of course," and her elegant and well-manicured fingers went up into the air. "Will shall escort you to select dinners and events where you can meet young people of your age. Good young people," she emphasized, frowning, as she turned her black-haired head towards the bathroom. "I do not want you mixed up with the wrong crowd. I promised your father I would take care of you, and for those reasons you'll stay here another three months. Do you realize the first three month period is almost over?"

Janice nodded. She was sitting n the edge of her bed, both hands closed in tight fists, she was so nervous.

"You will have two modeling jobs next week also," added Ms. Patsy, smiling solemnly at Janice, yet giving her the news in a matter-of-fact voice. "One will be for a camera client, the other will be for a famous dress designer, modeling clothes. Who knows, you might end up with a year's contract with one or both clients."

Janice felt her heart flutter. She sat taller and a gleam of pleasure filled her eyes. Thank you," she said demurely. She never felt confident when with Ms. Patsy.

"I also want you to know why Mary's stay here is forfeited as of next week. Perhaps you know why already." Ms. Patsy's black eyes were directed at Janice and held a thin edge of hostility.

She blushed. "No, I don't," she answered defensively.

Ms. Patsy moved her head towards the closed bathroom door.

"Mary takes drugs."

"She what?" Janice's body stiffened in shock.

"You did not know?"

"No." Mary's bizarre actions swept through her mind. But that was her personality, she insisted to herself defensively. Mary had had such a rotten childhood, that's why her manner was usually odd.

"I don't believe it. Mary's not a drug addict."

Ms. Patsy sat silent, staring grimly at Janice, studying her face.

Janice shook her head. "I don't believe you," she repeated, looking dead square at Ms. Patsy.

"I see you care for her."

"Of course I do. She's my friend. I know she drinks too much, but. . ."

"We have empty packets."

"From where?"

"Under her mattress, in her clothes."

"You came in here spying?" Janice's voice rose.

"Not spying, my dear." Ms. Patsy reached out and patted her hand. "Our housekeeper found them. We had to make an examination."

"You are certain they were Mary's?" Janice was almost antagonistic.

"They are yours?"

"No." Her face fell. "I don't want to believe this."

"Of course you don't."

"She's my friend."

At that moment, the ugly sound of a distressed water pipe came clanging into the room.

"What in the world is that noise?" asked Ms. Patsy sharply.

"That's the pipe in the second shower. It always makes that noise when we turn the hot water faucet off."

"How long has that been going on?"

"As long as I've been here."

"Why isn't it fixed? Haven't you told anyone about this defective pipe?"

"No."

"How are my maintenance people able to fix it if you don't speak up?"

Janice did not answer because she was no longer thinking about the pipe, she was thinking about Mary and drugs . . . about Andrew's being a drug carrier, even if only once.

"Come," said Ms. Patsy soberly, rising and moving towards the door, fully cognizant of Janice's distress. "I don't want to talk to Mary after all. Nor do I want her to hear what I am going to say to you. Come with me. We will finish our conversation in the library."

As they entered the library, one flight below, Ms. Patsy flicked on three switches and the warm maple shelves with their lighted displays of books, most encased in colorful jackets, seemed to welcome them to the comfortable, deep armchairs, each with a reading lamp standing at its side.

"Here, sit in this chair," directed Ms. Patsy, pointing to a chair nearest the door, which she then closed. She chose a chair several feet away from Janice, moved it so that it faced Janice fully, a small library table between them.

"Mary has been in two drug rehabilitation programs," Ms. Patsy said.

Janice's mouth dropped. "She couldn't have," she exclaimed, disbelieving.

"The first time," Ms. Patsy continued, her mouth forming a grim line as she spoke, "was after she was given drugs by her father."

"Her father?" Janice was visibly agitated.

"What in the world has Mary been telling you?"

"Well," began Janice hesitantly, "after her father and mother divorced, and her mother kept marrying, she was abused by both stepfathers."

"Both stepfathers?"

"Yes."

"Mary is a habitual liar," said Ms. Patsy, sighing. "Mary has not had two stepfathers; her mother has only been married twice - once to Mary's father and now to a fine man. Mary's mother, Martha, is a friend of mine," she explained. "She almost did not remarry because of the problems she was having with Mary. Ssssh, allow me to finish." She raised her hand to stop Janice from interrupting. Janice's expression left no doubt she could not believe what Ms. Patsy was telling her.

"Mary's father abused her. He started her on drugs when she was eleven years old to ward off any complaints about what he had her do. But Mary, in a state of euphoria, which occurs in drug highs, told her mother how wonderful her father was in bed. Her mother immediately took Mary to a psychiatrist. Because of the resulting stories she told both her mother and the psychiatrist, Martha divorced Mary's father, and she hired counselors for herself as well as for Mary. Mary rebelled. She hated her mother for sending her father away and being denied drugs. After a hellish year, Martha had to place Mary in a rehabilitation home. She hoped they could cure her of both her drug addiction and her rebellion against her. Mary had continued to obtain drugs, selling her mother's clothes, jewels and whatever to support her habit. She was only fifteen! While she was in the rehabilitation clinic, Martha and a psychiatrist at the clinic fell in love. She refused to marry him until Mary was cured. It was only after Mary was back with her mother for a whole year that Martha agreed to marry Grant. First though, she took Mary on a three month trip to Europe. Martha hoped the closeness and the adventures they had together would help heal her daughter and strengthen their bond. Mary acted as if everything was all right. She convinced her mother she had overcome her cocaine addiction - and through therapy was overcoming the overwhelming hate and rebellion caused by the trauma she had been through. Her mother didn't reckon with Mary's ability to con. As soon as she returned home, Mary told anybody who would listen she was abused by her mother throughout the trip. Martha did not discover this until after she and Grant were married. Within six months Mary was again on drugs. Again she was placed in rehab, this time for nine months, undergoing intense psychiatric care.

"When she was released, I offered to take her under my wing and train her to be a model so she could learn how to take care of herself. That is the reason she has been here. She has been under the care of a psychiatrist the two afternoons a week you are apart and I have kept a close watch on her, hoping for progress. There hasn't been any. She remains out of control. God knows what stories she has told you."

Janice sat profoundly stunned as Ms. Patsy talked, her face becoming whiter and whiter. When Ms. Patsy stopped speaking, the only sound in the library was the tick-tick-tick of the small ornamental antique looking but battery-operated clock that sat on a shelf of a bookcase devoted to mementoes.

Ms. Patsy's eyes remained on Janice's bowed head during the long drawn-out silence that followed.

"Isn't there something we can do to help her?" Janice finally lamented, her lovely face a study in misery.

"It's been attempted by experts," answered Ms. Patsy quietly.

"Why didn't you tell me? Maybe I could have helped her."

"If I had forewarned you, it would have led to one of two outcomes. She could have drawn you in or turned against you. My hope was that some of your qualities would rub off on her. Monkey see, monkey do. Hah, we are fighting a losing battle. I have been through this twice before with models; I do not wish to waste my time on another."

Janice sat numbed. She had scrunched her body in a fetal-like position in the deep-cushioned chair, her yellow hair hanging down over her chest, her face strained, her expression forlorn.

Ms. Patsy rose from her chair, moved away the small table that sat between them, perched her body on the arm of Janice's chair and placed her arm around her.

"My dear child," she said tenderly, "Mary must want to take control of her life. Without her desire to do so, we are at a loss in being able to help her. No matter how concerned, how anxious, how - in fact - desperate her mother is to help her - ah, you don't know how many steps have been taken to return her to a wholesome life."

"She was abused by her father!" Janice exclaimed defensively.

"Many children have been abused by close relatives. Many youngsters have had terrible traumas inflicted upon them. There is no doubt dreadful experiences produce neurosis. But many have pulled themselves up and away. Both my father and an uncle abused me. I recovered. I moved up to a better life, and I worked hard at erasing those memories. I was pretty so I went into modeling to prove I could stand tall by myself and not be held unworthy. The experiences spurred me to help other girls achieve stature through their wholesome beauty. I do not like to see women allow themselves to be pushed down by a still belittling, sometimes barbarous male society.

"As far as Mary, there is no easy solution in ridding her of this dependency. She fulfills herself with drugs. Each of us stands alone in life, Janice. And Mary is bent on ignoring all the good around her; cocaine is her mother, her father, her lover.

"Enough," concluded Ms. Patsy emphatically. "I am going upstairs to speak to Mary. I wish to speak to her alone. You can follow me in about five minutes."

"I don't want to go up there at all. I can't face Mary until I can make sense of what you have told me. Please. I want to sit here for awhile."

Ms. Patsy fell silent. Then she rose, nodding agreement.

"Do you have any books on drugs?" asked Janice quickly before Ms. Patsy had a chance to open the door.

"Yes."

"May I read them?"

"Yes, of course, my dear. They are over here." She motioned her to follow her, pointing them out on one of the bookshelves.

"Thank you. Oh, may I tell Mary I know?"

"I see no harm in that now. Just be careful you are not pulled in by her lies."

Ms. Patsy closed the door sharply behind her.

Janice pulled out three books from the shelves and then returned to the chair. Before opening one, she sat huddled for a long while, her legs pulled up in a fold, trying to reconcile what Ms. Patsy had told her with what she had believed of Mary and her actions. Finally, her face still damp from tears, she began reading. It was late when she wearily put the books away and headed up the escalator steps. Mary, she felt sure, would be asleep. She wanted to get into bed and ponder on steps to take, to help Mary.

Chapter Twenty-Five

I t was after midnight when Janice opened the bedroom door. She moved through the darkened room - long and heavy but spring-patterned drapes pulled tight to protect against winter-cold drafts. A night-light dimly pointed the way to the bathroom. She moved as quietly as she could. She looked at Mary's sprawled form as she passed her bed thankful Mary was asleep.

She hurried to undress, then sank gratefully into bed, pulling the covers up around her chin, hugging Oscar, not wanting to think about anything, just wanting to go to sleep. She was dreadfully weary; wretched was the word, particularly in her mind. There were so many question marks scouring around in her brain.

Sleep escaped her. Mary had completely fooled her. The information she had discovered in the books downstairs told her it was possible relatives often did not suspect a close relative was an addict, well, up to a certain point, when a myriad of surprising behaviors turned up in the afflicted.

Teenagers usually got started in drugs as part of a game, a fun challenge or because one was rebellious or despondent or abused, as the case of Mary. Mary's father had put her on drugs and naturally Mary continued to crave them because she was in continual mental turmoil over the awful experiences of her childhood.

Thoughts relentlessly boiled about in her mind; another was that she was very excited about finally realizing several modeling jobs. Two of them! She also wanted to find the producer, Territoni; if it turned out he was not the one that Mary wanted her to meet, she had to seek him out. As far as she knew, nothing was happening in Montana about George Culbertson's murder and here she was in Manhattan where the possible murderer lived. It was providence she was here if Territoni had anything to do with the murder. Well, she should be able to find out.

She tossed one way and another begging of herself, I want to go to sleep. Yet she was still awake at 3 a.m. when Mary woke up with a groan, rose unsteadily and went into the bathroom, not bothering to close the door. She heard Mary turn on the faucet, splash cold water on her face, take a plastic glass out of the cupboard and fill it with water. Then there was silence. It was at least five minutes before she heard the toilet flush, then a damn and a moan. She finally heard the toilet flush again. Constipation, she suddenly remembered from what she read, was one of the pronounced side effects of drug use. Mary reentered the bedroom. Janice kept her eyes shielded by Oscar's rag head and watched as Mary bent over the small chest she kept beside her bed, opened it and took out a small bottle. Mary went back to the bathroom and she heard the faucet in the sink turn on and off. Mary reappeared and moved again towards her chest. Janice could not resist speaking. She should have been quiet and pretended to be asleep but since she had to foolishly open her mouth she should have asked if Mary had a headache, no! Instead, because she was so upset and at the same time wanted to help, she blurted, "What kind of pill did you take, Mary?"

Mary swung about, surprised. Obviously wide-awake, she snarled, "What in the hell business is it of yours?"

"I love you, Mary. You are my friend." Janice bolted into a sit. Oscar fell off her narrow bed. She bent down and picked him up.

"I just took a sleeping pill, for God's sake. What are you doing awake?"

"I've had to deal with something I didn't want to deal with so I couldn't sleep."

"Yeah," angrily. "I noticed you were downstairs a long time. What did you and Patsy talk about? Me?"

"Yes. You."

"Damn bitch. I suppose she told you a bunch of lies about me."

"No. No lies. She's concerned about you."

"Yeah? How'"

"She told me you took drugs."

"Well, fuck her."

"Mary!"

"Oh, don't Mary me. I take them once in a while to have fun. It doesn't hurt anything."

"Drugs are addictive, Mary."

"Well, I'm not addicted to them. My God damn mother wishes I was though." Mary was now sitting on her bed, glaring at Janice.

"I understand your Mother is also very concerned about you."

"Bullshit. She's never liked me. I keep interfering with her love affairs."

"Mary, you are lying."

"Oh, so you're on their side now. Go fuck yourself." Mary slammed the lid of her small trunk shut.

Silence.

"Mary, please. You are my dear friend."

"Then let me alone. I know how people get addicted and I'm not denying I take drugs occasionally. I can take something when I feel badly. That's what medicines are for."

"Drugs are not medicines."

"Well, huh, think of this. Back in the early 1900s, heroin, cocaine and morphine were heralded to be good for your health. They were sold over the counter in all the drugstores. It's because of politics that they are forbidden now. Anyway, if you have had such an awful life as I have had, you'd take drugs too."

"Number one, Mary, we are far more educated now than we were back in the early 1900s. Medical technology has taken us a long way forward. Number two, your life is looking up, you're going to begin a beautiful career as a model. You need to get a positive outlook."

"Bullshit."

"Please let me help you."

"Go fuck yourself."

It was senseless to continue to try to talk to Mary.

Janice lay back down on her bed and turned over, her back to Mary.

"You can always have one of my sleeping pills if you can't sleep," chided Mary, insolently, giggling, "and I can give you a pill to wake you up too."

"Mary!" Miranda sat bolt upright again.

Mary laughed. "Want one?"

"Where do you get them, Mary?"

"I have friends," she taunted. "Goodnight, Janice." Mary slid into bed. "I'll tell you in the morning. That blessed pill is right now putting me to sleep."

Chapter Twenty-Six

Neither Janice nor Mary mentioned their conversation when morning came. They both awakened at about the same time - habit - rose and silently pulled on their exercise suits. They grabbed towels and without speaking made their way down the escalator steps, one behind the other, to the exercise room. They entered the endless pool. "Dracula" looked at them curiously.

"My, you girls are quiet this morning," she remarked, as she moved to the switch.

They did not answer. Neither did they speak or look at each other as they swam, each endeavoring to swim faster than the other.

Janice broke the silence as they climbed out of the pool.

"Tomorrow is Saturday. I would like to go with you to meet that producer."

Mary swung a foot backwards, deliberately splashing Janice's face. "Yeah. And to spy on me."

"No, Mary."

"Well, I don't want you to go with me. I don't want to have anything to do with you ever. You are hateful."

"Oh, Mary! Mary, please. I really want to meet that producer. I'm tired of just being here all the time."

"How will you get away from your dear Ms. Patsy?"

"I figure you can arrange that. You always seem to be able to leave unnoticed."

"You told me the other day," and she turned to Janice,

giving her a chilly smile, "you wanted to go next week because you had to buy a dress. You don't like mine." They were climbing the escalator steps to go back to their rooms to dress.

"I do too, Mary. I know which dress I'd like to borrow."

"Yeah? Which one?"

"The grey one with the spaghetti straps."

"That thing? Well, okay." Mary's mood changed. Now she gave Janice a warm smile. "Just don't berate me anymore."

"No, I won't."

"Treat me nice."

"Most of the time I will," said Janice lovingly. Then she laughed softly. "As long as you are on good behavior."

Mary laughed back. "Oh, I'm glad we are friends again."

"So am I."

"And we'll have fun, fun, fun on Saturday night."

Saturday morning, when Janice tried on the grey dress, it hugged her body so closely Mary whistled in awe.

"It didn't fit me like that," she cried out.

"It isn't your type of dress. That's what I thought when you bought it; you saw it, told the salesperson you wanted it and to wrap it up. You didn't even try it on. And I didn't realize it would fit me like this."

"Like a glove. You can't wear a bra with that, you know, Janice, just panty hose. Not even a panty."

She was right. The thin spaghetti straps led the way over Janice's shoulders down to the rise of her high young breasts where they held up a close fitting, elegantly designed silk sheath. Her body pressed softly against the silk, accentuating her youthful curves with every move she made.

"I don't know what I'll wear to match that," sighed Mary. "The grey and your golden hair - oh, Janice, Patsy is right. You will be a top model one of these days."

"How kind of you, my dear, beautiful friend, Mary."

"Wait until the producer sees you. Bet he'll want to steal you away from Patsy and make a movie star out of you."

Janice sighed wistfully. "I might like that." Then she thought of the producer, Territoni. Her stomach tightened. She had liked him when she had met him in Montana, but if he was involved with killing their neighbor and hired Andrew to be a drug carrier as Melissa had told her sister to sister (but don't tell anyone that), why wasn't he in jail? She certainly wanted nothing to do with him. Her stomach tightened; she didn't want to meet him again.

The plan was for Ann, the model from the January agency, to come to Ms. Patsy's in a taxi and pick up Janice and Mary. Presumably, they were going to a movie. Mary showed Janice how she could hold up her dress so it would not show under her winter coat. She would wear sturdy pumps and carry her evening shoes in her purse.

"You can place a bandana over your head so Patsy can't see your earrings. Wear a heavy muffler around your neck to hide your necklace," Mary pointed out.

"I don't want to wear any jewelry," Janice answered. "I'm going to wear my hair in a low bun. I want the dress to express me. Nothing else."

Their careful plans were unnecessary. At Saturday lunch, Ms. Patsy told the girls over delicious warm pea soup, she was headed out of New York on a plane at 3 p.m.

"I have to fly to Miami to meet a prospective client who

wants me to supply models for a big chain's dress catalog. If I bag it, it will mean several weeks work for a number of models. I shall include both of you - if you behave." She peered over her bifocals at Mary. (Ms. Patsy wore glasses only on weekends.) Contacts served her during the workweek.

"What are you doing tonight?" she asked Janice.

"We're going to a movie."

"We?"

"Mary, Ann and I."

"Ann?"

"From the January agency."

"Oh yes. She's been a dependable model."

Mary almost smirked. If Patsy only knew.

The two girls smiled broadly climbing back to their room.

Mary had been in a gracious mood since morning but once they entered their room and Janice lay down on her bed to spend an hour reading, Mary disappeared into the bathroom. She had not opened her chest, but she was in the bathroom a long time. When reappearing she began rambling on and on about going to Paris for a modeling job with her boyfriend, and making up a portfolio, about how awful to model clothes, about what kind of money she would make when she left Patsy's, and about visiting Janice in Montana the coming summer.

"You do want me to come with you, please," she pleaded over and over. "Say yes, yes!"

"Yes," answered Janice at least a dozen times. Suddenly Mary became so distraught, she burst out crying.

"Please don't tell me I can't come to Montana with you on

our summer vacation. I have to get away from here and all these nasty people."

Janice comforted her. She finally excused herself, went into the bathroom, looked in the wastebasket and found a small empty packet. Where had Mary stashed that, she wondered. When she came out of the bathroom, Mary had dozed off. Thank goodness, thought Janice, I don't think I could have stood her ramblings and angry incongruous chatter another minute.

She went downstairs to the library. She wanted to check two drugs she had read about the evening before. Their layman descriptions were found in *Buzzed* (2003). The other two books on drugs in Ms. Patsy's library were dull and tedious treatises most of which she did not understand.

The first drug was known as Ecstasy (MDMA). She could not pronounce or even remember its clinical name. She knew MDMA was popular at dance halls and was tasteless in a drink. *Buzzed* gave its effects as 'good feelings' and 'you feel loving.' That means goodbye to inhibitions, thought Janice. The second one was called "buzundunga," which makes those who ingest it develop an amnesia like state. It too could be disguised in drinks. This drug, or one similar, was used in a South American country on unsuspecting tourists.

She also glanced through several recent newspapers that were lying on one of the desks. Circled in black pencil, by Ms. Patsy no doubt, was a report from the United Nations Committee on drugs. The writer mentioned that at least 75 million men in Asia regularly buy sex from sex workers while another 20 million men inject drugs into drug users. Presumably most of those were sex workers. And she thought about Ann, the model that was going to Asia with Territoni. If what they were saying about him were true, would he with drugs force her to become a sex worker in the illicit human sex trade? If he was a part of a criminal organization that did those things, he could make a lot of money with just one girl working for him. She shivered, remembering the audition in Territoni's studio. That might have happened to her. She sat in the library for a long time, thinking.

Chapter Twenty-Seven

Merry answered the phone while the family was eating dinner. "It's Janice," she called from the kichen where she was cutting pieces of chocolate pie for dessert.

Marv, Melissa and Andrew each ran to their land phones since Janice was not allowed to have a cell phone in Patsy's house. Marv and Annabelle shared the one in the living room while both Melissa and Andrew dashed upstairs to their bedrooms. Melissa helped Andrew climb the stairs because even after a month at home he could not race up them as he used to do.

Janice told them she was fine but would not be coming home for either the Christmas or the New Year holidays. We are in training, she said, "and I love every minute of it. Ms. Patsy will be away for the New Year, but Mary and I (that's my roommate, remember) will be going out on the town. We only have three days to play and then it is back to training. Oh, I have to tell you, I did a hair commercial last week but you hardly see my face. The photographer has my hair blowing in the wind. It's a wonderful commercial though and it will probably air in February, I'll let you know when and on what network." Each then chatted with her separately and she told them all how much she loved them, particularly Andrew. She kept saying, "I love you, Andrew, and can't wait till I see you again" over and over. "Take care. Call me on Christmas," and she hung up.

When the four came together in the living room, they

looked at each other, laughing joyfully. "Well, she's happy," said Marv. "Doing what she wants."

"I agree," echoed Melissa. "And please Dad, let us have a quiet Christmas. I don't feel like doing much of anything."

"Neither do I," said Andrew, "but you two know that."

Andrew now went outside daily to walk. It was exercise Dr. Witt insisted he do. After Marv made a measured mile path around the valley, with white lettering on little brown signs on posts driven into the ground every quarter of a mile, Andrew walked the path twice a day with either Marv or Melissa (and Lincoln) accompanying him. He also went with Marv and Annabelle (Marv wanted Annabelle by his side every place he went) or Lamedeer on trips to either Mission or Great Falls, waiting in the car while they accomplished errands. Afternoons Andrew sat in front of his computer, his main interest learning about human trafficking all over the world. One afternoon when Marv was walking the path with him, Marv asked him if he wanted to go back to school.

"No," Andrew said. "I want to become a government agent and help destroy the human trafficking industry."

"What?" exclaimed Marv, stopping dead in the path.

"Dad," said Andrew, "Human trafficking is the fastest growing industry in the world. More than ten billions annually go to the criminals who run these illicit organizations."

"Where did you hear that, son?" asked Marv, his eyebrows just about reaching up to the top of his forehead, so surprised he was at his son's remark.

"Come with me upstairs to my computer," Andrew said, "and you'll find out some of it. It's a terrible story of the awful things humans do. There's more slavery in the world now than ever before in the history of the world. Not only prostitution, Dad, but kids, little kids, both girls and boys, kidnapped, coerced, drugged and then forced to do all manner of horrible things. Parents sell their children for practically nothing, just so they can buy food for themselves and the rest of the family. A lot of these innocent kids end up sold to work in the fields or factories where they work seven days a week, others are sold and trained to become soldiers or kept in a gang, and of course, they are often kidnapped like Betty was (at age thirteen).

. That's what Betty was, Dad, a slave. She didn't want to do what she did. I want to become a government or private agent and help get rid of these criminals, protect kids and tell people what is going on under their faces. There just aren't enough families that realize how dangerous it is for kids to go out alone or be left alone. And I wish I knew what they did with poor Betty." Andrew sat down on the path and began crying. And his dad, Marv, sat down beside him and held him while he cried.

That night Marv told Annabelle he wanted to ask forgiveness of his son because of the way he used to think about him. "There doesn't seem to be anything I can do to mitigate the guilt I have for the way I often ignored him."

He added that it was almost eerie when he and Andrew were walking together and encountered deer close to the path. The animal appeared to know who Andrew was; it didn't run from him. "He seems to understand why each creature moves like it does and behaves like it does. He'll greet them and they stand and look at him as if he was God."

"But I am at a loss when I talk to him. It's like I don't know how to converse. Help me, Annabelle."

"My dearest, just be yourself and love him. He is coming around. I see evidence of that each day. He shares such a bright smile with me when I talk about you – and I do, Marv – I let him know how much you love him. Right now, love him. He'll find his way out of what he has been through. I think he is doing very well learning how to leave those happenings behind. He even told me he has changed his mind about the computer world. He now wants to go to Missoula, to the University, and take majors that will get him into law enforcement. That tells both of us he has been strongly affected by what he went through. And you know, Marv, it's a fact of life that the more traumatic experiences we go through, if we've been brought up with common sense, the better person we become. Andrew was endowed with your strength; he knows you love him and that there is no forgiveness necessary."

Peter called the next week asking them to be together that afternoon for an interview with an FBI agent.

"This is an official visit," the agent told them after Peter introduced him. He was a short, grim faced man by the name of Claude Bannin, dressed casually in a blue sport shirt and jeans, his gun in a holster under his black jacket, and his hands holding a tape recorder which he placed on the library table and put into movement. He questioned Melissa first.

"Do you remember the little blond waitress in the restaurant, Shingles and Eaves?"

"No. I never saw her," Melissa answered. "The waitress I saw was a brunette."

"She may have dyed her hair." He took a photograph out from an envelope, asking her if she recognized the girl in it.

"No, I do not." Melissa answered as Andrew came up beside her.

"Let me see the photograph."

Claude Bannin asked Andrew, "Would you like to sit down as you look at the photograph?"

"Oh, I'm okay," said Andrew, pushing at his hair that hung down over his forehead.

"Is this Betty?"

Andrew could not answer directly, his eyes squeezing together, his face blanching. He stared at the photograph. He looked at his father, at Peter, and then with his voice quavering, his eyes filling with tears, he nodded and asked, "How was she killed?"

"Her body was found in the Spokane River several days after you were found. She was not identified until yesterday. Can you vouch for her identity?" asked Claude.

"I can," Andrew answered, sitting down on the couch, Marv quickly coming to his side. "She waited on me, we became friends, I drove to Canada with her and she went with me to the shed with the drugs, and I loved her." He buried his face in his father's chest.

"Peter, show him the other photo." Peter took it out of its plastic cover. It was a photo of John Territoni.

"Is this the man you delivered the drugs to?"

"It was very dark that night and I could not see his features. I don't know," Andrew replied, after studying it. "I would know his voice though. I don't think I could ever forget his voice."

Melissa asked to see the photo. "This is that awful man who stared at me in Shingles and Eaves," she said.

Handing the photo to her father, Marv's only comment was, "This is Territoni?"

"Yes," Claude and Peter both answered.

"Can't you arrest the bastard before he kills any more? Before he does any more damage to young girls?" asked Marv.

"We need more than circumstantial evidence. We presently have Territoni under heavy surveillance," answered Claude. "Do your part, Mr. Alicorn, by making sure your daughters are safe. We have talked to Ms. Stanton of the Models Plus agency in New York and alerted her. We presently don't see any problem for your daughter there, but you, young lady, must be careful. Do not leave this ranch without a guardian. You saw him and he knows who you are."

Chapter Twenty-Eight

The two girls, at 7 p.m., resplendent in their evening clothes, Janice in the grey sheath and Mary in a short, shoulder-less multi-layered froth of fragile black net, emerged from the staid brownstone on their way to the dance hall.

Both, of course, wore evening coats. Janice's was black and hung no longer than her waist. Mary's was black and short too, its wool hem edged with sparkling rhinestones. Neither coat had been stitched for warmth, so both shivered as they closed the heavy door behind them. It had rained earlier and the blustery, raw, wet wind attacked them head on as they moved down the steps.

Janice's stomach was doing somersaults, so many that she thought of fleeing back into the brownstone, dashing upstairs, settling in her bed, and reading. Good grief, she mused, don't get reclusive like Dad and Andrew tend to be. Being alone and secluded in Ms. Patsy's home these months was almost turning her that way. She flung away those thoughts, forcing a smile and an eager greeting to Ann, the January model, as she lifted her long skirt to get into the taxi.

They arrived at the dance club in minutes. An iron-barred gate exposed two steps leading down into a narrow, squat patio and she could see by the low light coming from the ornate glass door ahead of them that it contained several wrought-iron tables and chairs, evidently used in the summertime.

They entered the dance hall. A former warehouse, it had been refurbished with a long curvaceous bar, a dance floor and a small stage. At its far end were rest rooms and a door guarded by an attendant, which evidently led into a back room. Even at this early hour of the evening, the bar was crowded. On the floor, dancers were bumping into each other. Acoustics were excellent because Janice had heard no noise outside. Inside, cigarette smoke hung down from the low ceiling like a dark cloud swallowing most of the air. The smell of liquor was pervasive and the loud music along with the noise of people chatting, yelling, laughing, was deafening. Dancers were bobbing up and down, seemingly in a frantic mode, their bodies keeping the beat of a quirky song she had never heard before.

Janice opened her eyes wide in distress. She thought everything was awful. I'm also too well dressed for this horrid dance hall, she thought, as Mary pushed and squeezed their way through the crowd to the long bar.

"Oh, good," Mary exclaimed, pointing to an empty bar stool, "You sit here, Janice. I saw my boyfriend as we came in, so the producer who wants to meet you can't be far behind. I'll send him over and we'll see you later, about midnight. Come on, Ann, we're late." She swung around after moving several steps away and said, with Janice staring askance at her, "Don't dance with just anyone, cause some of these guys are quite unorthodox to say the least. Wait for that good-looking producer. I'm going to send him right over." She shot a farewell feigned smile which left Janice, who had sat down on the barstool, confused and aggrieved at Mary's hurried and impolite departure.

She wanted to get right up and head out the door. How dare Mary leave her alone like this! Then she thought of what would face her outside - a scary darkness in a strange part of the city she had yet to know. She had no cell phone so how would she get a taxi?

She was aware more than a few men hunched around the bar were staring at her. Why didn't Mary tell her she would be conspicuous in the lovely grey spaghetti dress? It was too elegant for the crowd in this dance hall that was for sure.

As she glanced around her, she remembered the comment she had made to Will at the YoYo symphony about the prevalent "anything goes" dress code. What a awful group of people, she thought, as she looked around her trying to ascertain the types who frequented this place. Most certainly they did not appear to be of the caliber with whom she wanted to associate. She turned timidly back to the bar, uncomfortable from the stares of those near her. In Montana, she loved being stared at. Here in New York she felt intimidated.

"What'll you have, Ms. Gorgeous?" A bartender stood in front of her.

The dark eyed, greasy-haired man sitting to the left of her reached over, put a hard hand on her naked shoulder and said, "I'm buying."

"I am waiting for someone. I will buy my own," she answered icily, vehemently separating his hand from her shoulder.

"Oh ho," said the man, "you're a handful, huh, baby." His hand again covered her shoulder.

Another man who pushed himself next to Janice, flung it

off.

"It's nice to see you again," the stranger said, his body protecting her from the usurper.

She looked at him in surprise and gratitude, but did not answer him.

"Your drink, Miss Gorgeous?" repeated the bartender.

"A coke. In a can," she replied, thinking a canned drink could not be tampered with.

"No cans here," the bartender answered. "Straight out of the spicket."

"You can watch him pour it," said her rescuer, who had successfully edged the greasy interloper away.

Janice turned to look at him. Blond headed like herself, he stood several inches above her, possessed straight and wide shoulders on a slim build. He was dressed fastidiously in a brown shirt and brown sweater, a tie of the same tone peeking out from the neck of the sweater. His eyes were a piercing deep green. So intense was his gaze they almost blotted out the rest of his narrow, handsome face. She was reminded of her Dad's eyes as she stared at him, and he looked as clean as his clean-shaven face.

"I am waiting for someone," she said, relieved she was talking to someone she thought was like herself, even though her voice held a tinge of aloofness. Her words were meant to discourage another come on.

"I assumed so," he answered quietly. "However, it looked like you needed temporary rescuing. Hope I helped."

Moved by his words, she answered, "Yes, you did. Thank you." She turned away surveying the crush of moving bodies dancing to a wild tune.

Then she saw him, John Territoni. He was walking towards her down the narrow aisle between the bar and the dance floor dressed in a dark wheaten colored suit that accentuated his handsome boyish face. He walked towards her in a smooth, confident, arrogant stride, his black eyes fixed on her and as he closed in, he broke into a sensual smile, his eyes devouring her.

She trembled violently. She was afraid of him she knew that. Yet he affected her here as he had in Montana in the Mission motel restaurant. She could not help admiring him even though she remembered what her sister had said when she saw him in the Spokane restaurant. "He had evil black eyes."

"My dear Miss Janice Alicorn," he said huskily, reaching her, opening his arms as if to embrace her. "I have been looking everywhere for you and here you sit, the most beautiful girl in the world, awaiting me."

His arms fell to his sides. They stared at one another.

"You are extraordinarily beautiful."

She blushed.

"Ah, and how sweet you are."

She sat immobilized.

"Come dance with me," said John Territoni. "I want to put my arms around you and never let you get away again."

She turned to excuse herself from the blond stranger but he had disappeared.

She rose as in a stupor. She felt his eyes go over her whole body, lingering on her breasts and the area between her thighs. She stood taller, strangely upset, because she liked him looking at her that way.

He took her hand and led her down the long crowded aisle to where the band was playing on the small stage. He excused himself, still probing her with his eyes, holding her completely under his sensuous spell, saying, "Don't you dare move." He backed away as if regretfully, spoke to the band's leader and returned to her.

"I can't lose you," he whispered to her easily, taking in her rapt expression. Again he looked hungrily at her as she stood in front of him trembling because she knew what he was thinking.

His hands moved and captured her waist pressing her to him as they moved onto the floor. A slow, insistent drum roll introduced the number and despite some calls of "Hey, we want fast music," it played the slow, slow drum beating number John Territoni had asked them to play. He gathered every bit of her body against his as they moved in rhyme to the music not allowing her to move away. She could feel his chest bones, his stomach, and his thighs hard against her body.

Her heart beat wildly.

"You will be mine tonight," he whispered huskily, lifting her face to his with one hand.

She took a deep breath knowing she must compose herself. She did not want to act this way with him, but she was.

"I have a question to which I need an answer," she said hesitatingly, looking up into his eyes.

"What is it, my lovely Janice? Don't be hesitant."

In one way she did not want to ask the question because she liked him but she had to. It was a stupid question to ask a man like him. Nevertheless, she had to know, so she had to ask so it could be done with.

He pulled her closer; she could feel his heart beating. Was it pounding as hard as hers? Endeavoring to be practical and remember what everyone she knew said about him, she tried to pull away from him but he pulled her even closer.

She looked up into his eyes, his searing black eyes while he caressed her back with his hands, going up and down.

She had to ask. Then it would be done with.

So she asked, yet afraid to, her voice just above a whisper, "Did you kill George Culbertson?"

His reaction was almost imperceptible, but she felt it, saw it. His eyes grew blacker as if he pulled a film over them, impenetrable to a normal onlooker, but not to her. She, who so wanted to believe this man could not mistake the instant chill, the pull away, the tightening of all his muscles as they strained abruptly away from her. It was the most disquieting moment in her life. Her emotions had been so strong, his so strong; now she felt as if she was in the arms of an iceberg, that was how quickly, how devastatingly, he had changed.

He looked down at her stricken face saying coldly, "No." Then abruptly, "Come, let us have a drink." Although he let go of her body he grasped her arm so tightly it hurt and she had to follow him off the dance floor. She trembled, her emotion now pure fear. His reaction had been overpoweringly explicit. She knew he had killed George Culbertson.

 He grabbed hold of her arm possessively, too tightly for her to escape leading her to an end section of the bar, close to the door at the back. A baldheaded man who had watched them approach stood up.

"John, here's a seat for the lady."

John did not reply as he pulled her to the bar stool and said tersely, "Sit here, my dear Janice. You must excuse me a moment. Rick," and he was speaking to the baldheaded man, "Keep her safe, she is precious commodity. You are, you know," he continued smoothly, pointedly but vacantly staring at her. She saw his eyes and turned away from them quickly. She remembered again what her sister had said when she saw the man peer out at her from a door at the bar in Spokane. "They were venomous black, cold, malignant eyes." The eyes of the man she was looking at were cold, black, and malignant, he could not hide their expression.

He said to the bartender who was waiting for an order (not the one who had served her earlier), she assumed there were four or five along the busy bar serving drinks, "Make this young lady my favorite drink. One for me too." With that he moved away.

'"I don't feel well," Miranda said to the baldheaded man. "I think it would be best for me to leave," and she started to rise.

The baldheaded man had his arm around her shoulders instantly.

"You'll have to wait for John. He'll take you home." He pushed her until she was again sitting.

"Here's your drink, Miss," the bartender said, placing what looked like a tall "Shirley Temple" in front of her.

She shook with fright. "I'll sit this one out because if I drink it, I'll be sick to my stomach."

The bartender and the baldheaded man exchanged glances.

The baldheaded man said, "Too bad you don't feel well,

young lady. Fred and I," and he nodded towards the man sitting to the right of Janice, "will do our best to make you feel better while you wait for John."

At that moment a young man came up to Janice.

"Dance, Miss?"

"She's with me. No, she doesn't care to dance."

Janice's face blanched, she was trapped. Oh God, how did this happen? Oh, Daddy, please come get me, she cried to herself. She straightened herself on the bar stool. She turned to the man on her right who didn't appear as menacing as the baldheaded man.

"Are you a New Yorker?" she asked.

"Born and raised. You?" He was civil, just!

"I'm from Montana."

"Way up there? That's a remote place."

"No, not really."

"Oh?" He went back to his drink.

"Drink your drink, Miss," said the baldheaded man.

"No." She moved her hand towards the glass, lifted it, and then forced it to turn and spill. Liquid went coursing along the bar.

"Hey, Joe," called the baldheaded man, "she knocked over the drink."

The bartender came rushing back, picked up a cloth from under the bar and began wiping up the liquid.

There was a heavy silence.

Meanwhile, John Territoni had the guard, who had been nonchalantly leaning against the back wall, unlock the door he guarded. John went in and the guard closed and locked the door behind him.

There were six couches in the room. On each lay a girl - Mary and Ann were two of them - in different stages of undress. Several men were gathered around each while two other men took pictures.

John passed through the room disgustingly. "God damn fucking fools," he commented as he unlocked a door, entered a small office, slammed and locked the door behind him, turned on the lights and leaning against a small desk pulled out his cell phone and dialed. He heard it ring three times.

"Hello," a voice said.

"Mike, I want you to go to the office."

"John, I'm watching a movie."

"Fuck the movie."

"Why? Is this that important?"

"I wouldn't call if it wasn't."

"Can't it wait until tomorrow?"

"I want you to take pictures."

"Of whom?"

"A goddamn spy."

"Spy?"

"That's what I said."

Mike's voice was conciliatory. "What is she spying on, John?"

"Me, you goddamn fool."

"Why do you have to do this tonight? Why won't it hold?"

"It won't."

"Where did you meet her, John?"

"She's the Montana cunt."

"You mean that redhead's sister?"

"Yeah."

"John, she's poison. Leave her alone."

"Shut up. Go to the office and set it up. You can even have a piece when I get through with her."

"John, you are asking for trouble."

"I know what the hell I'm doing."

"All right, John. I'll be there. But I'll want to talk to you as soon as you get there."

"Hurry up. I'm leaving here now."

"She's with you?"

"Yeah."

"At the dance hall?"

"Yeah."

"She wants to be with you?"

"She's a spying cunt, Mike. I got to fix her up right. Hurry up."

John slammed shut the cell phone case, turned off the light, unlocked the door, left the office, locked the door, spat on one of the girls and tapped twice on the door leading back to the dance hall.

When it opened, he went straight to the bar.

The bartender had just slicked the bar dry from the spilled drink.

"She tossed the drink, John," said the baldheaded man.

"That ain't all she's tossing," John muttered, turning to her. "Come on, lovely creature," he crooned in a suavely smooth but cold voice. "I want to show you the letter the FBI sent me absolving me of any connection with that man's death."

"You have a letter from the FBI?" She was astonished.

"Yes. I want to convince you I am an honorable producer

who is going to make you the biggest sex symbol in the movie world." He opened his mouth in a boyish, pleasing smile.

She saw his eyes and stammered, "We don't need to do this tonight. I do not feel well. I need to go home."

"We do need to do this tonight." He was quite exact. "It won't take a few minutes. I want everything on the up with you, my dear Janice."

She struggled to answer with thoughts on how to possibly escape him racing through her mind. "I have to wait for Mary."

"Mary?" he sneered a laugh. "She's busy. She'll get home later.

"Come." He took out the cell phone again, dialed, and spoke into it, "Have my car ready, I am leaving."

Putting the phone back in to his suit pocket, he took hold of her arm.

"Come along," he said, pulling her along.

Chapter Twenty-Nine

T he driver of his limousine opened the door and John held her arm so tightly she knew she could not escape him.

How did she get herself in this terrible predicament? How was she going to get out of it? She knew where the limo was headed, to his studio. She remembered it was on 8th Avenue on the west side in an old, decrepit building. She also remembered unsavory bystanders had been lounging around the entry doors the day she and Merry had gone there for her audition. Obviously, she would not be able to escape from him there. But where could she make a break? It would have to be in his studio - somehow there would have to be a right moment.

That is what her father had drilled into her. "When you are in a tight situation in life," he told her, "and you will encounter those times," he continued, as she nestled her head against his chest, looking up at his grand face, "be calm. As calm as you can be. Size up the situation you have found yourself in. Do it calmly."

"What does size mean, Daddy?"

"Size in this instance, my dear sweet girl, means to look at everything around you very carefully. Study the situation closely in your mind. Think about what is going on in the minds of the people around you. Memorize the physical environment. There always a remedy, a break, a right moment, when you can set yourself free. Don 't be impatient, impetuous, but seize only that special moment as we did with the grizzly bear." Her mind immediately placed her in the forest as clearly as if what had happened then was happening now.

Her father had taken the three of them - Andrew, Melissa and herself - on a picnic in Glacier National Park. As they were heading back to their car parked against the path on an off-shoot Park road, she had passed a wild flower so beautiful she ran back to take a second look at it. She knew she could not tear it off its stem and take it home - her father had told his children that Park regulations forbade picking flowers - but she could implant the color and shape of it in her mind's 'picture memory bank' - that's what her Dad called it. As she stood in the silent forest gazing rapturously at the flower, she heard a step behind her. Dad! She spun around. She was staring at the stomach of a grizzly bear and she could smell every soiled, rancid, smelly hair on its body. It was a huge, dark brown grizzly standing on two of its four feet, towering above her with it's huge teeth exposed, its long claws right above her eyes, as if it was hungrily contemplating its first bite of her. She froze. The grizzly froze too. It had presumably never seen a human being before, and this was a quavering nine-year-old child in a bright red shirt and blue jeans staring up at it. Seconds passed. Then she heard a voice, an even toned voice - low, smooth, cautious, belonging to her father.

"Keep still, child. Remain just as you are until I say move. When I do, run to the car quickly, the door is open. Jump in and close the door. Don't move yet."

Her heart was tearing out of her chest. She stood still, her eyes staring up into the eyes of this giant animal, almost gagging from its foul odor. She heard its every breath. He was that close. Suddenly, she heard a loud crash in front of her. At the same instant, an urgent voice, "MOVE!"

She ran. She ran as fast as her legs could carry her to the car, jumped inside and slammed the door behind her. She heard the driver's door open and close. She knew her father was shouting something. She didn't know what it was because she was crying and gasping for breath as she reached out her arms to her sister and brother. The car started rushing down the road, her father reassuring his three screaming children as he drove. She looked through scalding tears behind her out of the rear window. The grizzly was not on the road. It was nowhere to be seen.

"How did you do that, Daddy?" she finally asked, her voice weary from sobbing.

"I chose the right moment to fling a rock that would land on another with a resounding crash. The bear turned defensively to the sound. It was a rare break, but at the right moment."

The right moment! Would there be a right moment tonight in this horrible, real life nightmare? She felt in the bottom of her heart that this man, whom just an hour ago she thought she could reason with, now meant to do her harm. She was terribly afraid.

She felt her heart pounding as the limousine carried them to the studio. Could the man sitting next to her with his arms tight over her shoulders - he did not pause at the coat rack to get her winter jacket - feel her terror? He was silent except for what he said to her soothingly, charmingly, as they entered the car. "The letter will explain their mistake," his voice carrying ice.

"I'm glad." She tried to be pleasant, but her voice sounded false. Would he detect it?

Oh dear God, she cried to herself, if I get out of this alive, I'll be different. I've always only thought of myself, of what I wanted to do. I've not been a good sister to poor Andrew, nor to Melissa. I've used my Dad to get what I wanted. I've been mean to Merry and I haven't even been fair to Ms. Patsy. Oh, please God, help me get away from this.

I'm going to look at everything around me. I'm going to memorize everything I see. Wait for the right moment. I can do it. Her heart gradually slipped back into its normal rhythm. She looked up at John and smiled.

He said smugly, "You want to be with me, don't you, dear Janice!" It was a statement, not a question.

"Yes." Would he believe her? Would he now be nice to her?

"You'll be with me." He smiled with a polished, affected chuckle, a chuckle that held a sharp knife edge to it.

The limousine stopped.

"We're here," said John Territoni.

Janice got out of the car. Immediately he took her arm in a vise grip.

"That hurts," she said, trying to pull away.

"Sorry." He loosened his grip for a moment, then grasped it tightly again. She glared at him while he looked down at her with his false smile.

She tried to ignore the grip and the smile. Instead, she concentrated on sizing up the entrance, silently counting the steps they took from the curb to the revolving door, the steps from the door to the elevator. Her eyes took in the door at the back of the small, square lobby. She checked the buttons in the elevator and counted the seconds it took in its ascent to the eighth floor - the button John Territoni had punched.

They were now in the front office. She remembered sitting on the couch to the left at her audition. The silent office was dimly lit; there were no windows, but there was a door next to the sole elevator with its embedded 'stairway' sign.

"Is the letter in this desk?" she asked brightly, tentatively forming a small smile at John and hoping.

"No." He was short-voiced. "It's in my office."

He led her through a door - not the one to the auditorium she had gone through several months earlier, but through a side door leading into a scantly furnished, smallish room. What a room! Her eyes flew over it. It contained a pink, silken clothed bar with two matching pink clothed stools, a side rack with a pink curtain half hiding a bench seat, foremost in the room were a series of long pink, satin drapes, covering something. It was an ugly room. She tried to keep her heart from racing in fright thinking of what could take place here - and to her. "There are no files here."

"I will get the letter. First, I shall fix a drink for both of us. Then when I go to get the letter," he relaxed his grip on her arm but pulled her to him, crushing her against his body, "you can take your clothes off. Our bed is behind those drapes. We will make love." He thrust his mouth against hers, his tongue searching between her teeth. She pulled back as his hands ripped one spaghetti strap off her dress and pushed down the silk exposing one breast. He laughed as she struggled, pushing her away so he could look at her breast.

"That is what you wanted when we danced together, isn't it, sweet Janice?" He smiled, his eyes knife edged.

"No. I don't feel well. I need to go home."

"By the way you moved when we were dancing, you told me this is what you desired."

She could not answer.

"No one teases John Territoni," he said roughly, pulling her again to him with one hand squeezing her exposed breast. "We'll have one drink. It will relax you. I can admire you while we drink to our lovemaking. Stand still," he commanded, as she tried to draw away from him choking on her sobs. "Oh God, what am I going to do?" She almost screamed the words aloud.

"Sit here." He roughly pushed her down on one of the bar stools and went behind the bar. As he moved away from her she looked around for escape. She saw the door they had entered and which he had locked with a key as they had come into the room. Her eyes widened because he had left the key in the lock. She turned away from it quickly, hoping he had forgotten about it. Glancing about she saw another door at the end of the drapes.

She held her breath as she watched him fill the glasses, first with liquor - she knew not what kind, then with sparkling soda - then something else. She could not tell from his hidden hands behind the bar what he had added in either one or both glasses. She shivered. "Be calm; watch for a break," she heard her father say in her mind.

John placed both glasses on the bar. She noted only one of them held a straw in it and that was the glass he placed in front of her. The other held no straw. As he moved around the side of the bar, his back to her, he saw the key in the door lock and went to retrieve it.

It was her first break. She seized it. She deftly lifted out the straw, placed it in his glass and switched glasses. If he had put drugs in her drink, he would now drink them. He had turned away to get the key and had not noticed.

He came back looking at her exposed breast, even though she swiftly moved her arm to cover it. "Oh, what a lovely thing," he said. He caressed her breast and said, "Drink, my lovely. As soon as I return with the letter, I shall make love to you."

Her heart was in her throat. She didn't dare fight him, he was much too powerful. She had to pretend. She was in his studio in a horrible room set up for lovemaking. Perhaps he would be easier to get away from when he was ready to take her to bed. Until then she had to pretend and somehow retrieve the key. She lifted her glass and sipped while he watched her drink. Satisfied, he drank from his. She drank again, smiling at him.

"That's my Janice," he said heavily. "Did I tell you I'm going to make you a big star?"

"Oh!"

"We're going to fly to the Philippines next week."

"The Philippines. Why?"

"That is where you will train for your stardom."

"Oh?" Her heart crashed. She knew from what she had been reading that the Philippines was one of the places they sent girls from the U.S. to work in brothels.

"When I get the letter for you to see you can also sign a

paper to your modeling agency that Ms. Patsy owns, canceling your contract there."

"I do not want to do that." She shook violently.

"You will," smugly. He took her face in his hand and kissed her, his tongue moving deeply inside her mouth.

She almost threw up. Oh God, save me, she cried inside.

"You are not relaxed yet." Suddenly he winced, raising his hand to his temple.

"What is it?" she asked.

He did not answer.

"Drink," he said gruffly.

"If you do."

Both raised their glasses and drank.

He rose. "Remain just as you are," he slurred. "I will be right back."

He moved unsteadily to the door beside the drapes. There he stopped, drew a handkerchief from his pocket - the same pocket he had shoved the key in, and wiped his mouth. The key fell to the floor; he did not see it drop but kept on moving and went out through the door, closing it behind him.

She was ready. She sprang up from the bar stool, grabbed the key and started towards the door he had locked. She stopped because could not resist - she had to look behind the drapes. A bed was there. A mural covered the wall.

She ran to the door, unlocked it, ran through the front office, pushed the elevator button, and then decided the stairs would be safer. He could probably halt the elevator in motion. She didn't care that the door made noise as it slammed behind her. She started down the stairs.

Chapter Thirty

M ike had heard what was said from the amplifier in the next room. The large mural behind the bed was a one-way window for capturing with a camera what went on in the bed. He had been sitting behind a camera in front of his chair that would document pictorially everything that occurred.

He was not pleased. He was getting too old for these dangerous shenanigans of John's, which sometimes ended in a girl's death before they could get her on a jet to an Asian or European brothel. Not that they weren't ready for a brothel when it was their time to go. They were too drugged up to care plus John's abuse took the spunk out of the best of them. Then, of course, there was John's father. He was no longer reliable on the fetishes he used on the girls. He was in his seventies, and Mike was certain he suffered dementia. All he wanted to do was to put the girls in handcuffs, tie their feet and mutilate them with objects since he could no longer perform.

Mike needed to persuade John to leave Janice alone. Although he did not suspect FBI surveillance (it had been too quiet), he could not prove they were not watching John, hoping for a slip. John was becoming increasingly careless. The murder of the rancher might have gone unsolved, but the Montana film game was a mistake. Still, Mike had had no choice but to help. He thought back to the long-ago burglary job John had bungled, and he had to take the heat. If he hadn't, John's father told him, his body would be floating in the Hudson. Sitting in jail, he had spent most of the time thinking of ways to get away from the Territoni gang when he was let out. Then the unthinkable happened. His fraternal twin, his sister, Annie, was badly hurt in a car accident. Her left leg had to be amputated and the accident left her paralyzed from the waist down. Worse still, she became partially brain dead. John's father came to him in prison and said tersely, "I'll take care of your sister if you take care of John." John's father proved true to his word placing Annie in a nursing home, paying all her bills.

He still heard John's father saying to him, "I'll take care of her as long as you take care of John. I can't trust him but I love him. You've always been smarter than John and after this stint in jail, you can outwit him when he gets out of control."

So, when he got out of jail that was his life. Some of it had been okay, but these last few years he had tired of always trying to placate John, to foresee what John was thinking of doing and to dissuade him from following through. Here again he had to stop John from touching this Montana girl, it didn't make sense to attack her. But how to do it? John's behavior was turning so violent even he no longer felt safe from John's irrational anger.

Annie, his sister, he felt could now be taken care of by Medicaid; probably as good as she was now. He intended to make inquiries because he knew John's father was failing. When the gang's leadership changed, Annie's care money would disappear. So would his job of guarding John. It was almost a guarantee the new boss would have John weighed down with cement and dumped. And good riddance, Mike thought. The man was absolutely crazy. Someone had called him a psychopathic nut – he liked to kill, he never showed remorse, he treated the girls like commodities, not humans. Mike remembered one beautiful fifteen-year-old that John sold to a corporation in France for over $100,000 dollars. She was so popular he made his money back in a year, but of course, the girl was dead then too, of an overdose.

John entered the room where Mike sat. He looked strangely unlike himself. His eyes were glaring but vacantly, his body shook and he staggered.

"What is it, John?"

`"I don't know. Give me something quick. I couldn't have . . . she couldn't have . . . but I feel as if I had been drugged."

"Oh, my God." Mike got up quickly; in a way, he was glad. If she had been smart enough to accomplish that!

"Sit down, John. I've got to take a look to see what she is doing."

He helped John sit. John's eyes rolled, and he murmured, "I'm sick. What in the hell did that cunt do to me?"

Mike felt like laughing aloud, "Just what you have done to all of them." Instead he said kindly, "I'll be right back."

He went to the door, opened it cautiously; the room was empty. "Stay here," he said, turning to John, who was sitting on the chair, head down, mouth open, a sign of coming nausea on his lips.

"Yep," exclaimed Mike to himself. "She did it. She drugged him." He went into the room, pulled back the drapes to ensure that the bed was empty. Damn it, where did she go? He would have to find her, take her back to the dance hall and drop her off. Get her away from John for her sake.

He returned to John, who had now slumped in the chair and was vomiting. Repulsed but satisfied John could be left alone Mike ran out of the room, into the office, glanced at the elevator door but decided on the stairs.

Janice had only descended to the seventh floor landing when a shadow approached. She screamed. It reached out and grabbed her, and put its hands over her mouth before she could scream again.

"You are safe. I'm FBI." The shadow, a man, half led and half pulled her into the office across from the stairway.

"Get under the desk. Don't say a word no matter what happens. Be absolutely still, Janice."

She wanted to ask the man, whose face she could not see, how he knew her name. She crawled under the desk. She felt papers being thrown down on top of her.

On the desk above, music flared. It stopped. She heard the man who grabbed her, say, "Okay folks, that's it for tonight," then all she heard was static. An eternity of static. Suddenly, she heard banging on the office door.

The man sitting at the desk, shouted, "Go away, we're closed."

The banging continued. The man got up, went to the door and unlocked it. Although she could not hear what was said, she did hear several sets of footsteps. They became louder. They were right above her at the desk. Then the voice.

"How many are there, did you say?"

"Two of us."

"What's the other one do?"

"He's my partner."

"You are sure you didn't hear anything?"

"Hey man, no one comes through my locked door."

"Doesn't look like it. What in the hell do you guys do?"

"We're . . . a . . . computer experts."

"Yeah?"

"Yeah, man."

'"You don't look like the good kind."

The FBI man laughed. "Yeah, man, you got it. Hey, man, if I hear some girls I'll let you know."

"It's one girl. Here's my number."

"Okay, man. I'll watch out for her."

Both sets of footsteps faded. The door closed and a bolt secured the lock. The footsteps came back to the desk. She listened to more static.

She was cold. Her head and shoulders were aching from bending scrunched up. But she was safe, at least she thought she was. She moved to change position of a shoulder.

"Sssssssh."

She stopped moving.

Several more minutes passed. She heard the man get up and go back to the door. Because of lack of sound, she assumed he must have been standing there, listening. She heard him come back to the desk. In a moment his legs were in front of her. He was bending down lifting her to her feet. He put his finger against his mouth.

He whispered, "My partner is on his way here. He's bringing a change of clothes for you. Until he gets here, we'll listen to static. Be as quiet as you can."

He looked familiar. She knew she had seen him before. Suddenly she recognized him. She whispered, "You're the one at the bar, the one who rescued me."

He nodded.

"Were you following me?"

"We knew Territoni was meeting someone. When we saw you we knew he was meeting you."

"You are FBI?"

"Yes."

"Have you been following Mr. Territoni, the producer?"

He shook his head affirmatively, motioned her again to be quiet, moved softly to the door and listened, his head almost touching the frame. Satisfied, he returned to her where she sat on his desk chair, holding her left arm tight across her chest, hiding her bare breast.

He leaned close to her and whispered, "You are going to be okay now."

Her eyes clouded. "Thank you." She could feel his breath against her cheek as he spoke; it was a nice breath. He was nice too. She looked up into his deep, green eyes so close to her face. She knew he had sensed her fear. Her lips trembled.

He reassured her again. "You are safe. Keep your chin up," he whispered. "You can cry later. Right now, we have work to do. We need to get out of here unnoticed. And we will very soon, I promise." He moved away again, standing close to the door, periodically looking at his watch. Ten minutes passed. A light tap on the door alerted him and he unlocked it. The man who accompanied him into the room, nodded to Janice as he handed her a bulging paper bag, smiling as he did exposing buckteeth. Other than that he was nice looking, about thirty, dark haired and heavily built. Wearing a black wool jacket and jeans, his feet in black tennis shoes., he said in a low voice to the FBI man, "All clear but we better hurry."

The FBI man instructed Janice, "Change in there," he said, nodding towards a door, presumably a bathroom. "Put everything you take off in the paper bag. We'll not leave anything of yours behind. Hurry."

In less than four minutes, Janice reappeared. She wore old jeans that were too big but secured around her waist with a belt, a heavy wool shirt and tennis shoes, the latter a size too large. A felt cap was in her hands.

The FBI man came over to her and told her to gather her hair inside the cap.

"As much of it as you can," he said. "My name is Bill Smith. This is Ernest Argentine. We're going to get you out of here. Be very quiet as we move and don't ask questions. Stay right with me. Ernest will lead the way."

He took the paper bag with Janice's dress and shoes in one hand and with the other took hold of hers, leading her out the door after Ernest. Ernest locked it.

Ernest was a dozen steps ahead as they descended. Four flights down, Ernest opened the stairway door and with a hand motion, bade them wait. An instant later he reappeared, motioning them forward. He had unlocked an office door which he relocked after they entered and led them down a dark corridor. At the end of the corridor he unlatched a window.

"We are going to cross four rooftops," whispered Bill. "You have to take a big step down right here. Ernest will grab you if you fall." She almost did. After that, the three made their way silently across the rooftops, night darkened yet with enough light to see from the stars above and the city lights below. They passed several groups of people, busy in their own recreations on the rooftops. Nobody paid any attention to them.

Ernest opened a tenement stairwell roof door and they went uneventfully down several flights of stairs. Again, Ernest bade them wait at the entrance, returning several moments later, and rushing them out into a street and into a car.

"Get down as low as you can," cautioned Bill, as Ernest started the car. They began moving.

"Cruise," said Bill sharply.

Ernest began a series of maneuvers, turning corners, moving quickly through traffic for several blocks, turning corners sharply, and finally parking. After a wait of about 30 seconds, he moved into traffic again, repeating evasive tactics.

"We're okay," Bill said. He motioned to Janice who was crouched on the seat to sit beside him. "I need to ask you a few questions about tonight, and then I'll take you back to Ms. Patsy's."

"Oh no, please don't. She is away all weekend. Only Norma the cook and Ben the maintenance man will be there. Territoni knows where I live. He could come after me there."

"A friend you would like to stay with?"

"I don't have any. Well, yes, Will and Dwight, but I'm not sure where they live."

"We know where Will lives."

"I couldn't wake them up now."

"We'll set you up in a motel."

"No." Her voice was frantic. "He'll find me."

"Ernest, Riverside Drive." Bill took her hand. "I can keep you at my apartment until the morning, Janice. Then we need to get you to friends. You should not be alone."

"Thank you. I promise I won't be any trouble."

Chapter Thirty-One

Bill Smith's apartment was on the ground floor of a fashionable building on Riverside Drive. In the kitchenette living room, while Bill turned on lights and Ernest busied himself making a cup of instant coffee, Janice slid wearily onto a low couch, taking off her cap, her hair cascading over her shoulders. Bill and Ernest both stared at her; she was very beautiful.

"We are going to ask you a few questions," said Bill, reaching for a notepad that lay on a cluttered cocktail table in front of the couch. "We know you are tired, however, the events are fresh in your mind. Then you can sleep in my bedroom. I'll bunk here and Ernest will go on home. Would you like a cup of coffee or a soda?"

She shook her head, dreading the questions, but she answered them holding her head high, pretending not to care what they thought of her when she told them about her initial feelings for Territoni. It was when she told them that she asked Territoni if he killed George Culbertson that she broke down.

"The way he responded," she said between sobs, "I knew he had killed him. I don't know how I could have ever thought of liking him."

"What did he say that made you so sure he killed Mr. Culbertson?"

"It was the way he reacted. As we were dancing, I looked up at him and asked, 'Did you kill George Culbertson, the rancher?' and when he looked back at me he wasn't the same man he had been the moment before. His whole body stiffened. I don't know how to explain it, but something awful was taking place inside him. A shudder went through me because I remembered what my sister had said when he looked at her in Spokane - his eyes were evil. I looked in his eyes when I asked him that question and I saw evil; there was no doubt in my mind he killed George Christianson."

"Why didn't you leave him on the dance floor?"

"He wouldn't let me. He held onto my arm so tightly I thought my arm would break. Yet he sweet-talked me. I was very frightened."

"And at the bar?"

"He put me between two men who wouldn't allow me to leave. The bartender tried to drug me with a drink Territoni told him to give me. I spilled it deliberately. I knew I couldn't get away from him. If I had screamed, I don't know what those men would have done to me. I felt my only chance was to get away from him in the studio."

"You were a very brave girl."

Her eyes thanked him silently.

"Now I am going to send you off to bed. The bathroom is right off the bedroom. I'll use it first. Ernest will sit with you until I get back."

Ernest, with a dark shadow of a day's growing stubble, a mustache hiding his undershot bite, sat down beside her on the couch. They were silent. He drank his coffee. "You did well," he said. "You were in an extremely dangerous situation."

"How did you two know what was going on in the studio?"

Bill had returned. He carried a blanket and pillow and placed them on the floor beside the couch. "We were able to get out devices there a week ago, on the stage and in the pink room."

"Oh."

"We were ready to rescue you."

"You were?"

He nodded. But he did not explain. He said, "You are safe now. And we will make sure you remain safe until we get you back to Montana."

"Back to Montana?"

"New York is dangerous for you until we get Territoni behind bars."

"I have modeling contracts this week."

"They can wait. You need to go home."

"I need to go home right now, too," said Ernest, rising and going to the door. "I'm bushed."

"See you at nine," said Bill.

"If you think I should go back to our office, Bill," he began.

"It will be on tape, Ernest."

"Yeah. Right. Night, Miss Janice. Night, Bill. Take care." He left.

Janice slowly rose from the couch. "Can I cry now?" she asked, half laughing, half crying, her expression that of a lost little girl.

"You go right ahead." Bill took her in his arms. "Hold on tight," he said, "go ahead and explode."

She allowed him to cradle her while she cried. At last her breath ceased laboring and she lifted her eyes to him.

"I don't want to go to sleep yet."

"Are you still frightened?"

"No. . no. Somehow, I feel secure right now. You make me feel secure."

"Part of my job."

"Oh." She was disappointed in his answer.

"Well now," he said gently, aware he had offended her, "it is also my pleasure."

Raising her hand, she grabbed the stray strands of hair that had gathered on her cheeks and swept them back of her ears. "You don't have to flatter me. Please let me talk. It's been so long since I had someone to talk to. I'm bursting with things I've been holding inside. I do have a roommate and we talk, but I don't think she ever listens." She laughed softly. "She is always busy thinking of something she should or should not do. And do you know what is funny? I believe my roommate, Mary, is mixed up. Right now, I'm mixed up." She laughed.

"Tell me about Montana. It's a state I've always wanted to visit."

She began talking. She told him first about Lamedeer, Merry and Swallow. Then she told him how she grew up with the shadow of her mother's image and her grave always upon her. About her father. And how he always compared her to her mother. "At first I liked it, but then I resented the comparison and likeness. So, I was always a bit resentful. She was dead, and I wanted the memories to go away. My brother was as bothered about it as I was.

Not my sister, Melissa, though. She takes everything in stride. She likes everything in life. I didn't like much of anything until I fell in love with my history teacher at high school."

"And how did that go?"

"Merry found out. Everyone squashed it so my father would not know. After that, I was watched closely. I seldom had any fun." She shook her head. She began to be embarrassed by what she had admitted to Bill. She wanted him to think well of her. She rose and moved to one of the two kitchenette stools. There was a brief silence. Bill did not take his eyes off of her. Then slowly she went on. "I know I am pretty, Bill, and I could have had a lot of boyfriends, but every time I went out with one, I wanted to fall in love."

"Of course you did," said Bill, flashing her a comforting smile, his eyes lingering on this girl who had come into his life. "You are a very romantic young lady."

"And I am ashamed to say this, Bill, but I really thought Mr. Territoni was something special." She hung her head. "I was attracted to him."

"That was natural, Janice," Bill said, rising from the couch and crossing over to her, putting his hands against his chin and leaning against the kitchenette bar. "Territoni has had great practice in making beautiful girls fall for him."

Janice was taken aback. She had never thought of that.

"Many much more sophisticated than you have fallen deeply for him. To their sorrow," he added. "Don't feel guilty. Territoni has great magnetism. His charm can be very charismatic." He straightened up. "Now you can forget this episode. You can go ahead with the good things that are going to happen to you. You have everything ahead of you, Janice." He moved to the sink where he poured himself a glass of water. Turning around to face her, he said stoically, "Your father supplied pictures of you when we took over Territoni's case. I particularly liked your high school graduation picture. However, the faces in the pictures around you in the album were all smiling. Your face was sad. Why? Why were you so sad?"

"I was always a little angry, Bill. I hated living on a ranch. I hated forever going out to Mother's grave like we were on a picnic outing. I always wanted to be someplace else. Tonight, when I was so afraid, I prayed to God and told him if he saved me, I would change."

"Don't change too much. I like you just the way you are."

She stared at him steadily for a long moment, scrutinizing his lean and intelligent face, with those wonderful, steady, blue eyes smiling at her. Suddenly she felt an uncontrollable shiver taking control of her body. Suddenly she knew she wanted to be in his arms. Along with his fabulous form, he was comfortable. She felt exquisite warmth in her throat, a tingling sensation traveling swiftly down her arms, legs, inside her stomach; sensations she had never felt before. Yes, she had sexual desire for the three men she had been with. Nothing like this. She felt enveloped in a warm, happy, comfortable aura along with the extraordinary, unsettling arousement that coursed through her whole body. It was heavenly.

She moved close to his side. "Would you hold me for a minute?"

Bill shook his head. "No, young lady. I think you ought to go off to bed. You could get into trouble."

She blushed, but said boldly, "I suppose you want to go to bed with me."

He laughed in astonishment.

He answered, "You are amazing, Janice." He shook his head. "I'll be quite honest with you. I can't take my eyes off of you. Yes, I want to go to bed with you, but no, I don't want a one-night-stand with you."

"Oh?"

"I'll level with you, my dear beautiful girl. I fell in love with your graduation picture. Tonight, I am falling head over heels in love with the person you are. But you are going back to Montana. I might not ever see you again. Going to bed with you tonight is not the kind of memory I wish to keep of you."

I'm not going to stay in Montana."

He laughed again, staring at her speculatively. "You mean there is hope?"

She evaded his question. "I want to come back to New York. Even though I have not seen much of it, I love this city. It's a big, exciting city. And this is always where I have wanted to live."

Bill moved in front of her and took her hand. In a split second he thought of the disparity between them, she was twenty, he was twenty-nine. He knew this girl was special, his gut told him that. He had never felt such a strong pull towards any woman he had ever been with. She was invading his whole system, all his senses. As he looked at her and felt an extraordinary rush of desire, he knew he had to resist temptation. So he shrugged, a trace of a wistful smile on his lips, not revealing the real reason for holding her hand. "It's time for you to go to bed. Good night, my beautiful Janice. Tomorrow will be a full day for both of us." He led her to the bedroom door, closed it behind her and with a huge sigh arranged the bedding he had carried to the couch. But he could not sleep. His desire for her had taken him over and he could not push it aside. He got up, went to the kitchenette, opened a cabinet and brought down a bottle of bourbon. He filled a double-shot glass, drank it and went back to the couch. He was not good at holding liquor, it affected him quickly, and he was soon fast asleep. Not for long. Janice awakened him. She sat beside him, wanting to lie down.

"Please comfort me," she whispered. "I don't want to be alone."

So he held her in his arms the remainder of the night, not daring to move - afraid to move - for if he did, he knew he would begin running his hands over her, thrilling to the touch of her body, and make love to her. Here he was, holding this beautiful young woman on a sofa that was barely wide enough to support two at extremely close quarters. One arm clasped about her waist, the other tucked under the pillow under his head, he longed to touch her skin under the flannel pajamas she was wearing. She was certainly pliable enough, he thought, else she wouldn't have asked to be held. He thought back to her presence in the dance hall when he watched her move innocently, naively, to the bar. He had marveled at her bold sensual walk; her demeanor that stated she was absolutely convinced she could take care of herself. She had been completely unaware of the evil that lay beneath the contrived laugher and platitudes of the tough dance hall sophisticates. How vulnerable she was. As he held her he knew this was a girl he could marry. He knew also this was not the time to make love to her. He sidled over her sleeping body and went into the bathroom. God damn nature, he said to himself. Nature insisted on propagation from the lowest to the highest forms of life because without new life there would be no world. So not making love when such an opportunity arose gave him excruciating pain. He took a long cold shower attempting to settle his hormones. When he returned and very quietly turned on the stove light so he could see to make coffee, he heard her stir. When he looked around in the dim light, she was sitting up, her blond hair falling over her shoulders. He knew that when she stood up, her hands would disappear under the pajama sleeve cuffs and the pajama pants would come tumbling down unless she held onto them. He also knew, looking at her, her eyes still full of sleep, her lips unfolding into a smile, he desired her desperately.

"Welcome to the morning," he said, pushing the coffee decanter under the cold water faucet. "The shower is waiting for you."

She rose. "I have nothing to wear."

"You'll have clothes here shortly. Ernest is bringing some. Wear my robe until then."

"Is he getting mine from Ms. Patsy's?"

"No. We're steering clear of there until we have you safe. I've been on the phone to Ernest and also to Will. We know your size."

"What time is it?"

"About five."

"You woke them up this early?"

"Ernest and I are early risers. If Will wasn't, he is now. And he and Dwight are delighted to have you as their guest." Bill finished with his coffee making and flicked a switch. The coffee began percolating.

She came over to him. "I shall delight in a cup of coffee," she said. "Coffee is a no-no at Ms. Patsy's, bad for our skin." She ran her hand across one of her lovely cheekbones.

"What frightened you last night?" he asked, wanting to know why she came to him.

"Nothing." She smiled seductively.

"You wanted me to make love to you?"

She did not answer.

"You wanted comfort?"

"Yes. Anyway, I always sleep with Oscar."

He couldn't help himself. "Who in the hell is Oscar?" he demanded.

She laughed merrily, remembering how he had held her, how he was right now looking at her with those wonderful green eyes. "Oscar is my rag doll."

"Your what?"

"My ragdoll Oscar has slept with me since I was a baby."

"And obviously you are still acting like a little girl." He shook his head. He was silent for a moment, thinking. Then he came to her, took her hand, and sat her on the couch. He sat down next to her.

"I would suggest, my girl, you throw Oscar off your bed."

"Why?"

"Because you are now grown up. Your rag doll can't comfort you even though you think it can. What it does is rob you of your strengths. I saw a great deal of strength and maturity in you tonight with Territoni. Chuck Oscar. A rag doll sleeping mate has no place in your present life."

She did not know what to say or think, except to cry out, "Oh Bill, I am still scared."

"What are you frightened of?"

"Of that horrible man."

"He's not going to hurt you."

"He has already hurt me. He killed Mr. Culbertson. And he's out there, free."

"He won't be free long. Come." He led her to a kitchenette stool. "Your coffee. Black? Cream? Sugar?"

"Cream and sugar." Her voice was tremulous. "When am I going to have to go home?"

"As soon as your father gets here. First, we need to get you to Will's. Second, I have a meeting to attend. Thirdly, I want to confer with Ms. Patsy. We'll formulate our plans after we talk with her."

Ms. Patsy had her own plan.

Chapter Thirty-Two

J anice sat cross-legged on the floor in Dwight's studio watching him draw the outline of a bird.

"That's a yellow tail, just like what you see on a brand of wine."

"Long tail."

"Beautiful tail."

"Yes," replied Janice, admiring the design.

"What is your hobby, Janice?"

"I don't have one."

"Nothing you like to do for fun when you are not doing something you have to do?"

"Well, my favorite thing in Montana was to go shopping for clothes. Not that I could wear all the clothes I bought, but I got tired of riding our horses and being out in awful weather. Where I live in Montana, it is very windy and I hate the wind."

"That was your hobby? Going shopping?"

"I know that sounds pretty stupid, Dwight. But I could travel all over Montana and shop at different stores. Dad let me do that. Of course, Merry, Lamedeer's wife, always chaperoned me. I could never go alone."

"Merry? Lamedeer?"

Janice leaned back, stretched her arms wide, and laughed. "Dwight, do I have to tell you all about Montana?"

"Please do. It sounds fascinating."

So she spent the next hour telling Dwight about her life in

Montana. "It wasn't very much fun going out to my mother's grave every weekend," she concluded. "And the sadness Annabelle always felt when she visited us hurt. But it's okay now. Dad and Annabelle finally got married. I love her and I know he is truly happy. Except, of course, we're all unhappy about Andrew and what happened to him."

"Well, your father allowed you to come to New York and start your own life."

"Yes," she said, "and my three months at Ms. Patsy's has been almost as confining as when I was home. I haven't been allowed to do anything but train. I have tried very hard to do everything I am told to do, but now I realize it hasn't been easy doing it. I don't know anyone but Mary - and Mary is rather odd at times." She did not wish to tell Dwight she suspected Mary was on drugs. "Although I love her. Because of my isolation while being schooled, I just feel I have left one prison for another."

"Will tells me you are beginning to have modeling assignments."

"Yes, but now I have to go home. Bill tells me I have to stay there until Territoni is put in jail."

"You have a boyfriend there?"

"As I told you, Dad didn't like me to have boy friends."

"But you had them just the same."

"Yes," she admitted.

"Did you love any of them?"

She laughed merrily. "I loved all of them. That's why I am confused now." Her face became thoughtful. "And I don't know if I want to be a model. I don't want to be so circumspect and watch what I eat and when I go to bed so I look okay the next day. I want to go out and have fun."

Dwight guffawed. "You can still do all that. Give yourself a chance."

"Well, I do want to live here. I truly do. I love New York - the buildings, the people, the sophisticated climate with theatres, museums - oh, so many, many avenues of things to see and do. To me a big city is exciting. But people here can make you feel lonely. At home, strangers smile at you and you smile back at them. Here they walk by you with a grumpy face. I guess when it all comes down to it, Dwight, I don't like being alone."

"The best part of life, dear Janice, is when you fall in love with the right person. You can have all the money, the careers, the accolades of fame, but the essence of living a good life is loving someone and having that someone as your partner for life. Love between two people is based in part on sexual attraction, yes, but it is much more than that. Loving is to delight in each other's companionship, your partner is a friend and you share affection without censure."

"I'll remember that. That's how you and Will are."

"Yes." Dwight smiled. "Until you do find that someone, working is the best therapy. It leads you to fulfillment. You are a very beautiful young girl and you have a fabulous opportunity to show off your beauty and make people happy looking at you and want what you wear, what you eat, and what you do. So go home, do what you have to do and think about how lucky you are to have the family you have, the education you have and the health and beauty you have. Stop thinking about what you think your Dad made you do or about the things you couldn't do. Think about the things that made you who you are and the wonderful life you have in front of you. Then come back here. You can enjoy a fabulous modeling career until you find that special someone. Will and I will be glad to help keep you from being lonely. Consider us your friends."

"Thank you, Dwight," said Janice, uncrossing her legs and rising. She thought about Bill. "You can fall in love with someone right away too, can't you, Dwight? The first time you meet him?"

He guffawed again. "Yes. But if you don't have something to go with that physical attraction you're in deep trouble. Physical attraction can fall apart, and if you don't like the same things and aren't friends, you're in big trouble."

She thought about that for a minute. Then she asked, "Do you mind if I take a nap? I am still undone about last night."

"Of course not." Dwight led her down the hall and into a bedroom, getting a blanket from the closet. "You may rest here. When it is time to start dinner, I'll wake you. And you can help by setting the table."

"I'd love to."

Ms. Patsy and Bill arrived with Will in the early evening. They entered the apartment as if a whoosh of cold wind had blown them in. It was obvious something of importance had been discussed and that Ms. Patsy was victorious.

Ms. Patsy was, as usual, fashionably dressed. Tonight she wore a tan velvet slack suit with a cowl neck. Three large copper buttons decorated the jacket on the right side, and a stunning diamond pin shimmered in the light on the left. The monotone of color and startling jewel appeared to be the correct background to point out her elegance along with her straight hair coiffure and tanned vibrant face.

As Ms. Patsy took off her tan gloves, she immediately let everyone know Janice was not returning to Montana.

"She has contracts to fulfill beginning this coming week. This girl is about to embark on an exciting career and I'm not going to have her leave on a wild goose chase and that is what it is," she exclaimed decisively, tossing her head vehemently, her hair flying about with each sprayed hair remaining in its groomed place. "Afraid for her safety? Bosh! She'll be safe with me. I'll have young men guard her if need be. So she made a mistake and tried to capture that neighbor's killer all by herself. I shall keep a close eye on her. She can talk to her dear father and family on the phone every night if she wishes and they can come here to visit her. She will remain here." As if for emphasis, she flung her gloves down on a side table and crossed to where aproned Dwight was standing.

"Now let's enjoy one of Dwight's fabulous dinners." She opened her arms so he could hug her. "Your deliciously smelling dinner is awaiting us, is it not?" she asked, beaming.

"You bet," Dwight's eyes crinkled a wide smile on his face, "and Janice set the table."

She had been standing at the entrance to the kitchen as Ms. Patsy, Will and Bill entered. She remained there, watching them shed their wraps, her eyes gravitating to Bill as he came forward. Ms. Patsy observed the look they exchanged and the look of sweet pleasure both faces bore. Her eyebrows rose as she unnecessarily but deliberately spoke, looking for a further reaction, "Janice, my dear, you have become acquainted with Bill Smith, have you not? He was one of your rescuers, wasn't he?"

"Yes," answered Janice demurely, lowering her eyes, turning quickly back to the kitchen and asking Dwight how she could help further.

"Come, sit here, Patsy," Will said immediately to Patsy, sizing up Ms. Patsy's intention.

Each sat down in a designated chair. Bill sat opposite Janice who gave him a lovely smile. Bill smiled back, his eyes holding hers. Then he turned and began conversing with Patsy, remaining aloof to Janice, chatting with Ms. Patsy most of the time.

A Greek salad stacked with sliced avocados, tomatoes, slivers of onions, chopped celery and olives, was followed by roasted duck nestled in a mound of wild rice, with squash as a side dish. Coffee and cheesecake completed the meal.

When each had folded their napkins and retreated to the living room, Bill conversed with Will, leaving Janice perplexed.

Ms. Patsy said, "Please keep Janice here until tomorrow afternoon. I'll bring clothes for you," she told her, still dressed in the ill-fitting tee shirt and jeans. "There are a few things I must clean up in the house before you return." Ms. Patsy wanted Mary out of the house. She did not want the two girls to see each other again. "We must be on our way now. I'm grateful to Bill Smith for picking me up. Shall we leave?" she asked, turning to him.

He nodded, secured their wraps, said goodnight to Will and Dwight and then turned to Janice.

His head nodded as if in a slight bow as he murmured politely, "We shall do all we can to bring Territoni to justice." With those words, he turned and went out the door.

Janice's mouth flew open. She was sure he was as interested in her as she was in him; she knew he was. How could he say goodnight to her like that? Her eyes clouded over. When she turned, she saw both Will and Dwight watching her.

Will said quietly, "Patsy can throw a hook at times. I would take no offense, Janice. It's obvious to us Bill Smith is taken with you. He could not keep his eyes off you. Come," and Will put his arm around her, "you need a good night's sleep. Tomorrow your new life begins."

On the ride back to Ms. Patsy's brownstone in her limousine the next afternoon, Ms. Patsy told Janice, "I had a long talk with your father this morning. He will call you this evening. Before you speak to him, I want you to know your trial period is over. I do ask you to remain in my home until that monster, Territoni, is put away. However, you will be free to come and go as you please, with this exception. I must know where you are going and with whom you will be. We must be circumspect. No one wants anything bad to happen to you. I also had a talk with Bill Smith. While you will not be under direct surveillance, he has promised to look out for you. He told me Territoni is on his way to the Philippines. We don't know how long he will be gone. Bill said he will know when he returns and if they have solid evidence he will be arrested or if they still don't, he will be kept under close surveillance until they do. Tomorrow, you need to be up bright and early. Your first assignment is a catalog assignment. I assure you, it's going to give you lots of fun. You also have a new room at my home. You will like it."

Janice's bedroom was now on the second floor, right next to Ms. Patsy's. It was charmingly decorated; pale green curtains with a matching comforter bedspread imparted a mellow look. Janice was delighted that she would now sleep in a double bed. Its bedposts, the bedside table, desk and dressing table were warm oak, and a large overstuffed armchair hugging a two shelved bookcase completed the furnishings. On the desk sat a computer, a small printer and a telephone. The connecting bathroom was small, containing a shower, toilet and washbasin with only a small mirror above the washbasin. "That is why you have a dressing table," explained Ms. Patsy, flicking a switch on the off-white wall beside the dressing table. Twenty bulbs surrounding its large mirror burst into light.

"Oh, I love it," Janice thanked Ms. Patsy enthusiastically. "And I am glad you are protecting me."

"You'll find a phone card next to the phone," Ms. Patsy smiled warmly. "This one has 800 minutes on it. It's on me. You'll have to purchase your own after this. And please, always use the phone card. Its use saves a great deal of work for my accountant. Your clothes are hung up in the closet. I had some of your things placed in boxes that are either on the shelf or floor of the closet. You'll have to sort through them for missing items." She strode to the door, pleased with her offerings. "And the library is right next door. I noted you enjoy history as well as romance. I ordered several books you will find interesting. Dinner is at six tonight. We leave for the office tomorrow at 7:30; breakfast will be at 6:30. I know you must be looking forward to your first modeling assignment."

"I am. I am very excited." Then as Ms. Patsy was leaving,

she called after her, wistfully, "Is Mary upstairs?"

"No." Ms. Patsy frowned, tightening her lips. They formed a thin line of displeasure that Janice had even asked the question. "She is gone." She closed the door firmly behind her.

"Oh Mary," Janice muttered to herself, the happiness she had been feeling, falling away, "I want to know where you are. You are my friend. I know you need me." She silently pondered their closeness in the past months and hoped she would see her the next day. She sat down on the bed, dejected. Then, her eyes staring at the bed but seeing nothing, she sighed, rose and re-examined everything in the room, but not in the cheerful state she had been in earlier. After a long sigh, she went to the telephone and called home. The call lifted her spirits. She spoke with her father, Melissa, Annabelle and Andrew. She told them everything that had happened to her the past weekend but omitted Bill Smith. Thinking about him, like thinking about Mary, made her pensive. The phone card of 800 minutes went down to 650 minutes before she hung up.

She opened the closet door, looked over her clothes, unpacked boxes and arranged the items to her satisfaction. She started to open the last box which assumed would contain Oscar, but stopped after remembering what Bill had said, "A rag doll sleeping mate has no place in your present life." She pushed the box back against the closet wall.

She went to bed, sitting quietly on its edge, excited about the next day's work and looking forward to seeing Mary. She could not know that the next time she would see her friend, Mary's life would end in unimaginable horror.

Chapter Thirty-Three

The following days sped by like a whirlwind! Miranda had little time to think about anything but what she was doing and the adulations she was receiving from photographers, company executives, hairdressers and stagehands. Her first assignment, the catalog job, was initially frightening. But by the time she had taken three steps down the stage runway she was aglow with confidence. She knew she had been taught well.

She and another model, Sarah by name, first met in the models' dressing room. They donned short evening dresses which were then pinned and basted to their bodies appropriately by two middle-aged dressmakers. They were then taken out to a large staging area and directed to walk down a runway, a sky-blue backdrop behind them. In the small auditorium, the photographers were waiting with their cameras.

"No smiles," they were told. "Keep the expression on your faces bland and walk showing off the outfit you are wearing. Show us with your eyes and your walk exactly how much you like the beautiful dress you are wearing. Nothing more."

They moved. The cameras flashed. After two sets of dresses, the other model, Sarah, was excused.

"I only want the blond," Janice heard a man say to Ms. Patsy. "She isn't acting like a hanger. She embodies the dresses with personality. Look at the way she walks. She promotes what she is wearing. That's the look I want."

For eight hours for three days, garments were basted on her with hairdressers arranging her hair in different styles. It was piled on top of her head with single golden strands hanging down enticingly over her eyes, fashioned in a low bun, or gathered behind her ears and allowed to fall in a cascade of curls over her shoulders; it was parted in the middle of her crown, in a side part, in no part at all. Her face was only lightly powdered with a trace of mascara on her lashes and a touch of eyeliner on her eye lids, a soft rose lipstick decorating her mouth.

"She is gorgeous. Look at that walk. Come on honey, walk to your lover, let's see the desire in your eyes. No, not a wide smile, just a smooth flicker."

She modeled twenty-four outfits for the catalog, six short evening dresses (two she did not like - funky!), eight shirts or tops with skirts, two coats and skirts, three jackets and pants, three bathing suits, and finally, two long evening dresses. She was exhausted each night, joyfully excited. She adored the adulation, the looks she received, and the check Ms. Patsy presented her with on the evening of the third day.

"They absolutely adore you," Ms. Patsy told Janice. "And you are their choice for their fall catalog. Come, we're going to look at the slides of your pictures."

Her next assignment placed her on the ferry boat going to the Statue of Liberty. For the beginning of the commercial she stood with her back against the rail, her blond hair blowing out behind her, the smile on her face given to an imaginary man (she pretended it was Bill). The next segment for a perfume ad was taken with a male model approaching her for a kiss, as between lovers. Another assignment placed her in front of a bathroom backdrop. She had to smile at a shampoo bottle, her hair gently spinning around her shoulders (tossed about by an off-stage fan). She also did a nylon-stocking ad, an engagement ring ad and she stood in a beautiful, black-silk sheath holding a purse in front of a skyscraper backdrop. She sat waiting for several hours while clients discussed a scene. Every movement she made had to be explicit, nothing careless. She realized how lucky she was to have been trained and ready for each demand.

She went out on dinner dates three times; the first with a male model (he was boring), the second with a shampoo manufacturer (he was much too pushy, although incredibly rich, rather handsome and single), and the last with a photographer (who wanted her to go to bed with him and told her so continually during their dinner). While they were waiting for dessert, she excused herself to go to the bathroom and left by a side exit, sending a note by a waiter stating she had taken ill. He assaulted her verbally the next day.

When she wasn't thinking about her assignments, she daydreamed about Bill Smith. His handsome face with those bright green eyes and comforting smiles! She ached to see him again.

Then on a Tuesday in early April, the day everything unraveled and became absolutely, insanely, unbelievably horrible, she did see him.

She and Sarah and Trish, fellow models and new friends, went to lunch together. As they entered the restaurant of choice, Janice saw Bill at a table with a brunette. The brunette was pretty and they were in a serious conversation with his hand stretched across an empty plate. He was patting her hand, obviously consoling her.

Janice pursed her lovely lips into an angry line, then deliberately dropped her purse as she passed. She wanted to glare at him scornfully if he chose to retrieve it.

He did.

"Janice," he exclaimed happily, picking up her purse, his piercing eyes traveling lovingly over her face as if he owned it. "I am so glad to see you."

She glared at him.

"I've been about to call you," he continued, handing her the purse. "I'd like to take you to dinner tonight. What time shall I pick you up?"

Her mouth opened to say "No." What came out was, "Six o'clock."

"Six o'clock it will be." His green eyes intensely scanned her face again. She looked back at him, frozen in motion, a blush slowly spreading over her face.

The brunette at the table stared at her. Sarah and Trish stared at her.

Bill spoke again. "I'll see you at six," he said quietly, nodding pleasantly to Trish and Sarah. Janice turned and moved swiftly down the table aisle with her friends, the two models burning with curiosity.

"Oh, he is a hunk!" exclaimed Trish. "What a smile. And the way he looked at you. What in the world does he want with that brunette? Of course, she looked at him the way he looked at you." Sarah muttered something but Janice wasn't listening. All she could see was the brunette's face as she had looked at Bill.

"He's someone I met several weeks ago," she answered

dismissively, deliberately taking a seat at the table with her back to the table where Bill and the brunette were sitting.

Scarcely were they seated when the waiter appeared with menus and after they had placed their orders Janice changed the subject. Soon the three were chatting that warm, friendly way compatible co-workers have with one another. Janice sighed silently. She did not want to explain Bill Smith to anyone. She could hardly explain him to herself!

She soon regretted her chair choice for Trish kept looking Bill's way, but she held both her tongue and her head from turning. Trish whooped suddenly, looking at her watch.

"I'm due to have my toenails done at two for the Clartoni ad. You two ready?"

Both Sarah and Janice had just finished their chicken salads. They nodded and rose. Janice quickly turned to see if Bill and the brunette were still there. The table was empty.

As they waited for the cashier to take their monies, anxiety traveled through Janice's body thinking ahead to dinner with Bill. She would find out then who that girl was. She realized she had been daydreaming about a man she knew nothing about. She only knew she didn't want him to want anyone else but her. Hopefully the girl was his sister.

"Let's rush," said Sarah as they left the restaurant and each quickly dashed down the entrance steps to the sidewalk. "I have to be back before two. And it is almost that now."

The three started down the street together, Janice glancing across the street. Her mouth fell open. She stopped. She stopped so abruptly the person walking in back of her bumped into her. She did not notice. Directly across the street from her she saw through the fronts and backs of the automobiles as they slowly followed one another down the car swollen Sixth Avenue, horns honking (drivers were not supposed to honk), a far-away siren entering the already noisy air and becoming louder and louder - Mary! She was headed in the other direction, walking towards Seventh Avenue. Janice knew it was Mary even though it didn't look like her. But it was she. The walk was Mary's. The tall, willowy girl in the very short dress almost up to her hips (a prostitute's tell-tale outfit), was moving erratically, dejectedly against the squalliest April wind, high heels on exquisitely long legs, scraping, not gliding, on the sidewalk. It was Mary's reddish brown hair wind-swirling around her exquisite, thin, delicate face. It was surely, sadly, Mary.

"I'll be with you later," she called out to Trish and Sarah, as she hurried out into the street, scurrying to cross between the slow-moving cars.

"Watch out, Janice," yelled Trish, as she watched a taxi lurch so as not to hit her. Janice did not look back. She dashed across the Avenue in short, sharp bursts, dodging cars, ignoring shouts. She made it across but lost sight of Mary. She pushed past a group of slow-moving pedestrians. She closed her eyes briefly in despair as she edged her way through the normal New York noonday mid-town Avenue crowd. She had lost sight of Mary. There were two buildings she could have disappeared into. Which one? The first was an office building, the second an old tenement. "You can't be in that one," she gasped, swallowing hard, yet logically it had to be.

The narrow hallway smelled. It was an old, moldy, urine tainted smell. There was no one in the hallway. Then she heard the sound of high-heeled shoes on steps going up and she rushed to the dimly lighted stairwell, racing up the steps breathlessly, calling "Mary, Mary. Stop. Wait. It's me, Janice." As she reached the top of the stairs - the second floor - she saw her. Mary had swung about when she heard Janice's voice and stood, her whole face slack, her eyes glowing.

"Janice, Janice. Oh God damn you, you finally decided to come see me." With obvious effort she pushed her arms out from her sides welcoming her. As she did so she stumbled against the wall for support. She immediately began laughing.

"Look at you," she giggled in a scornful voice, "just as I am leaving, you come to see me."

"I didn't know where you were," Janice cried out, reaching Mary and grasping her body, crushing it against hers. "No one would tell me." She backed off. Mary smelled.

"Yeah, I know. I don't believe you, God damn you. Well, I'm here. You found me. And I'm busy. Go away."

"Do you live here?" Janice didn't want to believe Mary did. It was a squalid, miserable hallway they were standing in.

Mary giggled again. "Of course I live here. I moved out of the apartment my mother had found for me. She spied on me. Come on in just for a minute. My boy friend will be here soon. And we're leaving."

"Where are you going?" Mary did not look in any condition to go anywhere.

"We're on our way to Paris for a shoot." Mary fumbled in the large and dirty purse she was carrying, took out two keys and inserted one in a door at the end of the long, dark and dank hallway.

"A shoot? In Paris?"

"Yeah, what's wrong with that? And we got to hurry. Plane time is only three hours away. We got to drive to the airport. God damn knows what traffic will be like at this horrendous time of day." Mary stumbled over her words as she led Janice into her rooms.

The rooms were miserable. The walls had once been painted white. They were stained now, with goodness knows what. A dilapidated couch sat against the wall, its three cushions piled with dirty paper plates and odds and ends of clothes. In front of the couch a well-stained coffee table was crowded with more dirty paper plates, cups and bottles. On the other side of the room was a kitchenette bar, cluttered also. Behind the bar was an old stove (Janice knew if she looked at it it would be filthy) and a sink clogged with dishes and bits of old food floating on dirty sink water. Nothing was free of cockroaches that scattered at Mary's footsteps. Oh God, how awful!

"I'm nervous. I don't want you here," said Mary. "I'll call you at Ms. Patsy's next week from the photo shoot. I know I got that number in one of my suitcases. Go away now. I don't want you here when my boy friend comes, he might like you more than me."

Janice stood in the middle of the room, her face blanched, her eyes wide and disbelieving.

"Mary, you don't know what you are saying. Please let me take you out of here."

"Get away, friend that you aren't. Did you know I have

Oscar, that stupid rag doll you always sleep with?"

"My rag doll Oscar?"

"Yeah, Miss somebody. Well, I took him when I left Patsy's. But I don't have him now. And don't you dare tell anyone about Oscar or that I sent him to you in Montana."

"What do you mean you took Oscar and sent him to Montana?"

Mary giggled. "Well, I did. You promised me I could go there with you next summer, so I am. As soon as we return from the Paris shoot I will. He's got new stuffing inside him," she giggled again, smirking at Miranda, "just for me when I get there. Wow, what stuffing! And you didn't even miss him! Ha ha! I put one over on you."

"Mary, I don't believe you know what you are saying."

"Oh, I know what I am saying all right," Mary snapped, staggering towards Janice. "Now get out of my way. I have to go to the bathroom."

Mary pushed Janice aside and opened the door to another room, a bedroom. The floor on the side of the bed facing the door was stacked with more discarded clothes.   Janice followed Mary into the room to the bathroom; she backed away after glancing at the clogged toilet.

Mary watched her, giggling. Then she ran out of the bedroom, slamming the door behind her, crying out, "You stay in here while I get ready to leave." She pushed against the door as Janice tried to reopen it.

At that very moment the front door of the apartment flew open. Janice turned around, startled, and then hid frightened behind the door after she saw what was entering the apartment.

Two men were dragging a man through the door, one on each side of him. The dragged man didn't appear to be hurt, but he was walking with great difficulty. His hair fell over his forehead, his face was colored red and blue as if he had been hit repeatedly, his mouth was awry and there was a glazed look in his eyes. He didn't appear to see Mary who ran forward to him when the men had forced their way in.

Janice stood shaking, hearing everything that was said. She couldn't see unless she peered between the doorframe and the wall. She was too frightened to move.

Mary's voice was first. "What's the matter? How did Larry get hurt?" She looked at each of the two men in turn, as she rushed to put her arms around Larry.

'He's not hurt," laughed the man on the left of Larry pushing Mary away roughly. He was tall, lanky, straggly haired, with a pockmarked face and a perpetual sneer on his lips. "He was reluctant to give us the information we wanted so we taught him how to answer." He laughed again.

Janice winced. Something went blank in the pit of her stomach and she felt sick. Could they see her, she wondered, her face turning white again.

"We brought him here," said the short, unbearably ugly man on the other side of Larry, "because he told us you knew where the money and the drugs are."

"What money?" Mary asked, shaking from the tips of her toes to the top of her head. How stupid she was to have told Larry about the money.

"Look, you're asking for it," replied the short guy, his bloated lips remaining open in a snarl. "Your boy friend would be in better shape if it hadn't taken so long to pry the information loose from him."

"Level with us right now," said the tall, lanky man. "You'll look worse than he does if you don't."

Mary flashed her eyes at Larry, hanging between the two men, his arms flopping. It was obvious that at the moment he didn't know who he was or where he was.

"My God, you doped him," she screamed.

"Lady, you look like you're doped up yourself," laughed the tall man.

Mary decided to fake it. "I don't know what money you're talking about."

"The money you stole from our boss, John Territoni, last week." The words came out of the tall man's mouth like a whip.

"I didn't steal any money from that bastard."

"Lady, pretty lady," and the tall, lanky one took time out from speaking to leer at her, "we know you did. John's father told us you did. We're not here for pleasure. We don't wait around while you ply us with pleasant conversation. So tell us where it is now."

Mary stuck to her guns. "No."

"Okay," said the stocky one, whose name was Joe. "We'll help you open your mouth." He nodded to his friend. "Okay, Matt."

They dropped Larry. With nothing to hold on to, he crumbled to the floor. Mary stared at him with wide eyes, her heart racing wildly. Matt shoved Larry aside with a swift kick and reached for Mary.

Janice almost screamed.

Mary gasped.

While she was gasping, Matt grabbed her by the arm and twisted it completely around. It appeared he pulled it out of its socket. Her screams where thwarted by a wad of cloth shoved into her mouth by Joe at the instant of pulling.

The pain was so terrible Mary fainted.

"Hey, Matt, you overdid it," said Joe.

"I'll bring her back," was his answer.

Matt lifted Mary up from the floor and hit her under the chin, knocking her flat on the floor again. He heard teeth crack. Then he leaned down and shook her. She opened her eyes slowly.

"Where is the money?"

"Oscar . . ." That was all Mary could say. She fainted again.

"Damn it. Bring her back again."

"One more time, lady," said Matt. He was holding her half upright. Then he flung her onto a chair. "Wake up, you fuckin' bitch, wake up."

Mary, blood gushing out of her mouth, her left arm dangling, half opened glazed eyes.

"Where is Oscar? I want to know right now. You'll die if you don't tell me."

"Montana." The one word came out in a long, slow drawn-out mumble. Mary began vomiting.

"Ah, you bitch. Where in Montana?"

But Mary couldn't answer. She was vomiting blood.

Matt shook her again. Mary fell out of the chair splattering him with her blood.

"Jeez, what's the matter with her? I hardly touched her." Matt shook her again. Mary's body jiggled. Her head dropped and her bladder erupted.

"Ugh," said Joe. "I really wanted to have her piece of ass. But I don't like blood or pee. I don't think we're going to get anything else."

"She's finished." Matt stood up, his mouth hanging open. "I don't know why. I hadn't begun to work on her."

"What about him?" Joe looked at Larry, still crumbled on the floor.

"He's not with it," laughed Matt.

"Well, knock them together. I don't care how you do it."

"Not so much blood with a pillow."

"Okay, a pillow. Hurry. We gotta' go."

"One minute."

Matt grabbed a pillow off the couch. He bent over the young man, yanked on him until his face lay facing the ceiling, shoved the pillow in front of his nose and mouth and held it there until the young man's body went limp. He threw the pillow away.

"Hey, it'll even be sweeter this way." And he took a silencer from his inner suit pocket, opened Larry's mouth with its muzzle and pulled the trigger.

"John will be angry we didn't get more than Oscar and Montana. That's a big state," said Joe, kicking Larry to be sure he was dead. "Let's get out of here."

"She's got an address book over there on the kitchen counter," Matt said, heading that way. "They won't be able to trace her so quickly."

"Let's not be leaving finger traces anywhere," said Joe.

"I'll clean the doorknobs. It's the only thing we touched."

In less than a minute they were gone. Janice stood behind

the bedroom door, stupefied. She stood there a long time, not moving, not doing anything, her breath going in and out faster and faster. Suddenly she slumped to the floor, the door closing in front of her. A cockroach skittered over her chest. Before she fell unconscious she heard someone scream in her voice. The voice screamed and screamed and screamed.

That was where the NYPD found her.

Chapter Thirty-Four

J anice woke up. She was groggy. She opened her eyes and saw her father and Annabelle standing in front of her bed, smiling. Bill Smith was standing behind them. He was smiling. Beside him, close to her bed was a man she had never seen before. He was smiling too.

She looked down at her hands as she lifted them up and pressed them across her eyes so she could see clearly. Something was stuck on her left wrist. It was an IV connected to a tube. Then she knew she was lying on a hospital bed in a hospital room and her father and Annabelle had flown to New York to be with her. She must be in New York City because the man she had fallen madly in love with was in the room with her father and Annabelle. The man standing beside her bed staring compassionately at her must be a doctor, even though he was dressed in a dark suit with a red spotted tie, the spots dizzily jumping at her from his tie.

She stared at each in turn. Each kept smiling so she said their names so they would change their expression. There was nothing to smile about. Each moved their head forward when she spoke their name and broke into a wider smile.

She remembered. "Oh, my God, Mary?" she cried out. "Mary."

A picture of Mary jumped into her mind. She saw Mary's arm being pulled out of its shoulder socket. "Oh, Daddy, Annabelle, come here, I need you." And she burst out sobbing as they put their arms around her.

When she awoke again, it was night. The man who had worn the red tie was beside her. He was now wearing a different suit coat and a different tie. She could see it because the top button of his jacket was unbuttoned. This was a yellow tie. It had figures on it. Her eyes were clouded, and she couldn't tell what kind of figures they were. Anyway, the room was dark, not totally dark, but dark enough so that she could not make out who or how many people were looking at her. Perhaps that was the reason she couldn't see the tiny figures on the yellow tie or the face of the doctor holding her hand. Or was his hand on her wrist because he was checking her pulse?

"Please turn on the light," she heard herself saying. She didn't know why she said that because she didn't want a light turned on. If it was on, she might see Mary and her arm being pulled out of her shoulder socket and the blood running out of her mouth.

"Oh, God," she moaned. She pushed herself into a sitting position.

She felt an arm go right around her shoulder - no, two arms. She knew without looking that one of them belonged to the doctor and the other one belonged to Bill - the man she didn't know very well, but with whom she was in love. His was a strong, comforting arm, much more so than the doctor's arm.

That was one of the reasons she was in love with him. He exuded comfort.

"Oh, Bill, you are here. Hold me close."

The light above the head of the bed came on just as Bill put his arm around her. That was when she saw her father and Annabelle. They were sitting just beyond the end of the bed. She could see their heads above the bed railing. They did not get up and come over to her.

"I'm alive," she said aloud to the room. "How long have I been here? "

"You were brought here two nights ago," said the doctor. "You were in pretty bad shape. The reason you are groggy now is because we gave you sedatives." After a while the doctor asked, "Are you aware of what happened?"

She did not answer.

There was another silence. The doctor began again, "Can you answer yes or no?"

She did not want to remember what happened and at this moment she wasn't really sure of what had happened. It was something so terrible that her mind did not want to recall it. She clenched her teeth. It is important that I talk about what happened so the horrible pictures will stop flooding my memory. So she sat very straight and very rigid, believing this posture would protect her. She closed her eyes and allowed the horrible pictures to once again take over. She did so deliberately;. she had to recall them to lose them.

No one in the room spoke.

She asked in a very low, pitiful voice, "Is Mary really dead?"

"Yes, she is."

"Mary was my friend."

"Yes."

"I loved Mary."

"Yes."

"Did she die the way I saw her die?"

"How did you see her die?" A strange voice asked that question. It wasn't the doctor who kept saying 'yes' to her. She didn't know who it was. She closed her eyes even tighter. She wanted to tell what happened without being asked questions so the awful pictures would disappear.

She felt Annabelle's arms around her shoulder.

"Thank goodness you are here, Annabelle."

"Both Marv and I are here."

"I know. I am so glad."

After a while she said, "It is difficult to talk about what happened."

"You don't have to now," interjected Bill gently.

"Can I get up and leave? I want to go home. I want to be in my own bed. I want Oscar." As soon as she said 'Oscar,' she remembered something. She turned to Bill accusingly, opening her eyes, "If you hadn't told me I didn't need Oscar, he'd be with me now. Mary wouldn't have been able to take him away. He wouldn't be stuffed full of money and drugs and sent to Montana and Mary wouldn't have been killed." She said all of that in one big breath and then stopped, thought deeply for a moment, her brow creasing. She opened her eyes wider. She saw Bill's face very close to hers and she began sobbing. The tears streamed down her face and onto her hands, which she held clutched tightly together at her waist.

Bill was beginning to speak. She pushed her free hand against his mouth so he would close it again.

"Bill, do you know Territoni killed Mary?" She began crying very hard again.

Her father came over to her and knelt beside the bed,

taking one of her hands. "Rest now."

"No." She looked at the doctor who was checking her pulse again.

"Do you know that Mary mailed Oscar to us in Montana? He is full of a whole bunch of bad stuff. Territoni is going there to kill us. God help us."

She grabbed the doctor's arm. "You must let me out of here." She turned to Bill. "Please." She held out her arms to her father and Annabelle.

"And you must get us back to Montana - right now." Then she went limp. "I'm sorry." She closed her eyes again and lay down. She raised the hand that did not contain the IV. She raised it in the air to silence the commotion that had erupted.

She had heard a voice say, "When you get back to Montana, you need to get her to a psychotherapist who can help her deal with this tragedy."

"Wait," she interrupted. "Let me speak. I didn't bury anything in my memory. I recall everything that happened in Mary's awful place. I have to tell you about it so it will go away. It will be catharsis, so what happened will leave my soul. That's the reason you are here, isn't it, Bill, to hear what I have to say? To see if I am in my right mind?" She was crying softly now, her head lowered and the wetness covering everything in front of her. "Daddy and Annabelle, you came because I needed you; you know I don't need a psychiatrist. I have to be well to go after Mary's killer and I know who he is - Territoni. First though I need to know exactly where I am." She saw the people in the room, the IV stand, the silent TV set that sat on a wall bench almost as high as the ceiling, and the venetian blind covered window that presumably looked out on city streets.

"Where am I?"

"You are in the Mt. Sinai Hospital in New York City. You have been here two days," said Bill.

"Annabelle and I flew in yesterday," said her father.

"I am with the NYPD," said the strange voice. She looked past her Daddy and saw a pleasant-faced, fiftyish, grey-headed man. "We have many unanswered questions about what happened," he continued. "We are hoping you can answer some of these questions - when you are able to do so."

"I can answer them now," Janice told him, jutting out her chin. "I need to. Then we have to get back to Montana before Territoni gets there."

"He is still out of the country," Bill said soothingly.

"But his goons aren't. They are the ones who killed Mary and her boyfriend. I know they are his goons. They told Mary he told them what to do."

As she spoke, her tears dried up, her eyes grew larger and rounder and her voice became steadier.

"You are my very wonderful brave girl," Marv said, reaching out to touch her hand.

She pulled at his shirt to get him closer. "Please hug me, Daddy. I love you."

Marv sat on the edge of the bed beside Bill and embraced her. Then he took hold of her hand and squeezed it lovingly.

She turned to the doctor. "I know what the books say. That when something terrible happens one can get amnesia so the memory can be buried. Well, I remember. If I tell you what I remember, please, will that memory go away? I don't want it inside me."

"We are going to help you get it out of your system. In fact, I am surprised you can function as you are. You are a very strong girl."

"I don't know how strong I am going to be in telling you what I witnessed and could not defend, but I know I have to. We have to get Territoni for all the girls he has drugged and ruined."

Her voice became muffled because she was again hugging Marv so tightly her face was pressed against his chest.

"I can only tell you this once," she said, after she raised her head. "Please don't interrupt me or ask me questions because I don't think I can go over anything twice. Bill, it all began to unravel after I saw you in the restaurant with that girl,"

"My foster sister," he said quietly.

She stopped for a moment, thinking. "Oh good. That's who it was." Unbelievably, a little smile erupted. Then she spoke as if she was making an important decision.

"Please raise my bed and put another pillow in back of me. I have to sit up straight to tell the story."

It was done.

She told them everything that had happened the afternoon Mary was killed. She struggled with words at times as if they became stuck in her throat - no, stuck in her soul - her eyes teared again and again. Several times she closed them, hoping to shut out the world as she spoke; her face furrowed over with tiny lines. She battled through the story with a stark, white face.

The silence in the hospital room was profound. Everyone

listening kept their reactions to themselves even though their faces contorted at times. When she grew quiet for long moments, they were afraid she could not continue. Yet she broke all her silences. When she had finished she hid her face in her hands and cried out, "Daddy, Daddy, I'm so glad you are here."

Marv held her close again.

"My dear young girl. It's going to be all right now. You brave, brave girl."

"Thank you, Daddy," she managed to say. "Can we go home now?"

"Very soon, my dear."

She turned to the doctor. "May I have a sleeping pill, please? I don't want to think about anything for awhile."

"I have an intravenous sedative for you. I'll be back with it in a moment."

She lay back and took a kiss and hug from Annabelle.

Shortly after the doctor returned with the sedative, she was fast asleep.

"We need her to describe those two men," said the grey-haired NYPD detective, "before she can go home."

"That's going to be tough on her," said Marv.

"It's got to be done."

"And Mary's mother wants to see her."

"She will tomorrow," said Annabelle. "I'm staying with her tonight. Marv, you have many things to get done before we can go home. You also need some rest. You and Bill both."

Chapter Thirty-Five

"The flight from Denver to Great Falls takes just about an hour, sweetie," Marv said to his daughter whose hand he was holding. "So we should land in Great Falls at about noon if this 777 gets to Denver on time. By the map here," Marv took his hand away and gestured to the small screen on the back of the seat in front of him, "it appears we will be on time."

Janice, looking fragile, her face pale, her cheekbones sunken, her eyes appearing larger by the deep circles beneath them, felt a slight surge of excitement. It was going to be wonderful to be home again with her sister and brother, particularly with Merry and Lamedeer. Her heart had ached for them. She could always unburden herself with Merry. She could rant and rave and scream and Merry would always condone. Maybe Merry could help erase the awful pictures that lay just below the surface of her mind. Right now, she felt ravaged by them.

She stared out the window of the plane, momentarily comforted with the thought of loosening her emotions with Merry. She saw by the map on the small screen in front of her that the plane was cruising at 40 thousand feet. Tiny icicles were clawing at the window pane, delicate little spheres clinging on for dear life as though they were aware the bright sun surrounding them would erase them (and it would) even while they were forming their myriad sparkles to the travelers inside.

She shut her eyes. It was good to be flying home with her father, Annabelle, Bill and the other FBI agent. She glanced back and smiled at Bill who had his wonderful eyes focused on her. Hers was a wan smile yet full of emotion. Bill and the other agent were seated several rows behind Marv, Annabelle and herself.

And her father liked Bill. "Looks like you found yourself a fine man," he told Janice before they left New York. "We've had a long talk. I like him. So does Annabelle."

Bill had nursed her through the difficult recalled descriptions of the two men who had murdered Mary and her boyfriend. The descriptions had been, of course, measured by the fact she could only see the killers through the door jamb when she had dared put her eyes that way. She had been frightened to death since she knew if the two goons had heard her breathe or move, she would now be as dead as Mary and her boyfriend. She shuddered anew!

After two sessions of recall, the NYPD had shown her two pictures of one small man - a known killer. She had scrutinized it over and over convinced it was the same. "I would have to hear his voice," she ended up saying. "I could not allow myself to judge him unless I did."

The tall man was not known to either the NYPD or the FBI. "He is not a given at this point in time," and she knew she would have to come forward at some future date to identify a suspect. She dreaded the prolonging of this real life nightmare. She grabbed hold of Marv's hand again, looked at him pleadingly, and without a word between them, swallowed the small pill he extracted from a bottle he kept in his pocket, sighed, looked back at Bill for comfort, then leaned against the head rest and fell into a troubled nap.

Bill watched anxiously. He and Marv exchanged consoling glances before each settled back in their seats awash in their own thoughts. Bill thought back to his initial meeting with Marv and Annabelle when he and Ms. Patsy met them at the airport.

"I am in love with your daughter," he had told Marv after they had been indoctrinated on her condition and were on the way to the hospital. "She's the girl I want to marry. Right now she thinks she is in love with me. We do have powerful chemistry working between us. But since I rescued her from a terrible situation I have to be sure she's in love with me, not in love with love."

At another meeting he explained himself.

"I was an orphan at six," he related. "My mother, father and an older brother were killed in an auto accident. The fourth set of foster parents helped me put my feet back on the ground. I was a lost kid before that. I've a law degree now thanks to their backing and at present, the FBI is giving me valuable lessons in life."

When Ms. Patsy saw Janice she cried over her as if she was her daughter. "As soon as you are ready to return to New York my dear child," she told her, "our clothing client — you remember the one you did the complete catalog for?" Janice nodded. "He demands to pay your expenses to get you back here. He wanted me to give you this dress as a token of appreciation for the spectacular one-model catalog you helped this company produce. Every one in the business is raving about it."

When Janice saw the dress, one of her lovely smiles

almost came into view. It was one of the funky dresses, the one she disliked most. She asked Ms. Patsy to thank the client in a voice that carried the traces of her once-upon-a-time happy laugh.

"You are in demand," said Ms. Patsy, hugging her. "And when you choose to return you can live with me, or if you are settling some place else," and she winked at Bill, "we can adjust your assignments to suit you."

Mary's mother and stepfather visited her in the hospital. Mary's mother and Janice both tried to keep the conversation on the good times they had had with Mary; still the tears fell and they hugged and cried together before they said goodbye.

The plane landed in Denver a few minutes early.

Marv was immediately on his cell phone calling Lamedeer. He kept calling as the five moved quickly along the walk-ways to the B terminal.

"Damn," Marv said to Annabelle, who was holding hands with Janice.

. "Lamedeer has a habit of forgetting to recharge his cell phone. I can't convince him that he always needs to make sure it is charged. Well, sweetie," he said, turning to Janice, "Melissa, Merry and Swallow will be at the airport with Lamedeer to welcome you. You'll like that, won't you, dear?"

"Yes, Daddy. I'll be so happy to see them again. But please stop treating me as if I were sick. I am capable of dealing with what I saw."

Annabelle pressed her hand. "You need some clean Montana air, good food and lots of hugs from your family. And you are going to have all that, my dear."

A man approached Bill and his companion when they reached terminal B, where the plane headed for Great Falls was on the tarmac.

The man said to Bill, flashing a badge, "I'd like to speak to you for a moment. You are Bill Smith."

"Yes."

Everyone stopped.

"Can we talk as we walk?" asked Bill.

"It is in confidence."

"Then hold it until we get to the flight counter," Bill said briskly. "Unless we are in immediate danger."

"You are okay," was his answer as the agent lowered his voice. "It's not okay in Great Falls."

Bill looked quickly at Marv who had not heard what was being said but was disturbed by this meeting of agents. "Wait until they get on the plane." Bill smiled at Marv. They moved on in silence.

"You four get on board," Bill motioned to Marv, giving Janice a wide smile. "We need to confer for a moment. We'll follow you shortly."

"Is everything all right?" asked Marv, with a sense of foreboding.

"Everything is under control. We'll follow you on board in a minute. Our seats are right behind yours."

The agents watched as the Alicorns disappeared down the ramp to the plane.

"All hell's broken loose at the Alicorn ranch."

"Tell us."

"Territoni landed in Seattle last night. We lost him."

"Damn. God damn."

"He must have gotten to the ranch. All I know is someone there is dead, the foreman, Lamedeer, and a woman are on the way to the hospital and Territoni is presumed loose."

"Damn. Why didn't they have protection?"

"Territoni was out of the country. I'm getting on the plane with you now."

"Keep your mouth shut. I won't have the Alicorns on pins and needles until we land. We'll have an escort when we get there, right?"

"You bet."

"This law against the use of cell phones on planes stymies us."

"You ought to be glad. They won't know what has happened until we land."

Chapter Thirty-Six

Melissa sang to herself as she drew open the curtains in her bedroom and looked out at the dawning sky. There were just enough clouds to capture the rays of the awakening sun and transform their fluffy white masses into dazzling moving kaleidoscopes of springtime violets and pinks.

It was April and the Great Falls weather station had forecast summer-like temperatures for the next three days running. These first days at home, smiled Melissa, would be exhilarating for Janice. No wind, no clouds, no rain. Springtime days of glorious, glowing sun. They could go riding together if Janice remembered how (she laughed) - of course she did. They could share at a gallop the wild beauty of their ranch.

Janice could tell her all about New York. She could explain just how she modeled those ads, particularly two she had done and sent copies of to Melissa. Melissa had had the copies blown up at a print shop in Great Falls, framed and hung in her sister's bedroom. She and Annabelle had also spent hours shopping for just the right print for the new bedspread and curtains. Yellow roses (Janice's favorite) highlighted the cheery pattern designed to lift the spirits of her sister who had just been through hell.

She tore her eyes away from the exquisitely colored sunrise and hurried to dress. A quick shower and toweling. She lingered over drying her hair. It was still chilly at six and she wanted her hair completely dry before she ventured downstairs. She also wanted to be the one to get the living room warm this morning and add logs to the banked fire in the huge stone fireplace. When Swallow and Merry arrived, she said to herself, they would have enough to do to prepare breakfast and then bake those apple and cherry pies Janice loved. They had to leave for the airport at 11 a.m. And Swallow and Merry commonly found just one more thing to do before leaving for anyplace! Today Melissa wanted to be on time.

She put on her town clothes even though her chores would take her out in the open. A fresh white blouse, new jeans and her best boots. Brrrrr. I have to put a sweater on. It's still chilly. Which one? The green cardigan. That's the one Peter liked best on her. "Makes your short hair look like wind-tossed cornflowers above your beautiful freckled face," he teased her. Too bad he was on assignment today. She really had wanted Peter to go to the airport with them.

No matter! His day off was tomorrow. Anyway, if he was here today, she simply couldn't be as attentive to her sister as she should be. When Peter was around she always thought only of him and what he wanted to do. Annabelle had even commented, "Ah, Melissa, I don't think you'll get anything accomplished once you are married. You will be on a perpetual honeymoon. You are absolutely giddy in the presence of your betrothed."

Marv already had an architect draw the design for a two-bedroom house. It was going to be built just a half mile from this one right on the top of a small hill overlooking the long first valley of the ranch. "The wind will hit it on all sides,"

Marv had warned when Melissa had told him of the site she wanted for the house. "I love the wind," Melissa countered. "I'll be able to see just everywhere. Don't you agree, Peter?" Of course he did. And she would still work on the ranch while her husband to be (she drew a deep breath in joy at the thought of him) would work in Great Falls and commute.

She stopped at Andrew's room and woke her red haired brother (oh, how she wished she had red hair). She knew he was going with Lamedeer into the field this morning to do something with fences, and then she flew down the stairs, Lincoln trailing behind her. She looked back at him and noted he was still limping. Somehow or other (and it had to be 'other'), he had either pulled a muscle or tendon in his right front leg yesterday. She had not seen him stumble or trip over a gopher hole (the large rodents had recently awakened from the winter's hibernation and were busy enlarging their underground apartments so the babies could get out; holes were everywhere), but he had injured it somehow. She was going to make certain he remained in the house while she did her barn chores.

Downstairs the fire was already blazing, the living room toasty warm. Just the way she liked it when the springtime early morning temperatures were still below freezing. Who beat her to the laying on of logs? She hurried into the kitchen to find out.

Swallow was sweeping up flour, which covered quite a bit of the floor. On one of the counters lay three beautiful, deep-dish piecrusts.

Melissa burst out laughing.

"What in the world happened?" Melissa asked, reaching

for the dustpan and kneeling down with it so Swallow could push flour onto it.

"I dropped the bag of flour," Swallow giggled. "Don't ask me how. It just sort of fell out of my hands. Look at this counter." Melissa and Swallow laughed together hilariously.

Melissa sniffed the air. "You are making pies before you put on coffee?"

"I forgot," answered Swallow sheepishly. "I want to make four pies and since this oven only holds two at once, I thought I had better get started. Anyway, Merry was supposed to be here before this."

"Lincoln, you are traipsing flour all over the place. Go into the living room." Melissa shooed him away with the broom. "Oh, Swallow, before I forget, you and Merry have to keep Lincoln in the house this morning. He's limping. I don't know what he did to his right front leg. He didn't flinch when I tested it earlier, but it is obviously very tender."

"Something under his pads?"

"No, I checked them."

"He'll start whining if you go out without him."

"Put him down in the cellar. Shut the door on him."

Just then they heard the front door closing. Merry had arrived.

She was not amused at the flour strewn haphazardly across the counters and floor. "I just scrubbed yesterday," she chided, frowning. "How could you be so clumsy? And that was our last bag of flour. Anyway, Swallow, I told you to wait for me."

"I wanted to be able to tell Janice these were my pie crusts," Swallow retorted. "I guess I won't bother helping after this."

"Good."

Sensing the tightness in the air, Melissa changed the subject quickly. "Where is Lamedeer?"

"He had to go out to the far pasture, one of the fences needs mending. Andrew is going to take over for him when he comes in for breakfast."

"Oh. Please put on some oatmeal, Merry, while I finish helping Swallow clean up. And Merry, don't you think Swallow's pie crusts look great?"

"Yes, they do," answered Merry in a conciliatory voice. "I taught her well, didn't I?" Merry never held anger for long.

"Yes, Merry." Swallow put aside the broom and gave Merry a hug as Merry reached for the oatmeal.

"And if you make me spill the oatmeal, we'll have none of that left."

Andrew hurried into the kitchen, ate breakfast with Melissa and then hurriedly left. "I'm late," he said.

Melissa fed Lincoln, and reminded Merry to keep him inside the house. "I'm just going to walk him outside so he can do his chores, then I'll put him in your hands. I've got to get to the barn."

"Whee," she said, as she returned with Lincoln, "it's quiet around here this morning. With Gustav away in Arizona visiting his sister and Lamedeer and Andrew out in the field and Dad and Annabelle gone - it's eerie. Don't you feel it?" She looked at Merry and Swallow.

They looked at each other and shrugged their shoulders. "No," said Merry. "It's peaceful! Lamedeer ought to be back shortly. You are just anxious."

"I guess so. Well, I'm off to do my barn chores."

Merry took Lincoln with her into the food cellar, the door of which opened into the kitchen. The steps led down into a thickly cemented area where the household's wine, potatoes, apples and other fruit and vegetables from the last year's harvest were stored.

Atlas was neighing so loudly with horse pleasure as his mistress pushed the brush across his back that she did not hear the car drive up to the house. Inside the black limousine sat John Territoni with his bodyguard, Mike, as driver. Territoni had purchased the car the afternoon before in Seattle and headed directly for this ranch. He was after the man Oscar who evidently lived here and where the boy, Andrew, the drug courier who tricked him, lived.

Mike, after driving twelve straight hours while John slept most of the time in the luxurious and commodious back section, fitted with curtains, a small serving galley and seats, was weary. Territoni was freshly awake as the two exited the car in front of the ranch house. Mike tested Marv's front door, which was seldom locked and it opened immediately. He drew his gun as the two entered silently. They heard a sound in the kitchen. They found Swallow there, sitting on a stool peeling apples. She turned, startled, when she saw the menacing faces, and cried to herself, "Oh, my God."

Her mouth flew open. "Who are you?" Her heart began shaking.

"We are looking for Oscar," said Mike.

"Oscar? Oscar who?" She was petrified.

"We know he lives here," snarled John Territoni.

Swallow tried to hide her panic while she thought. She

knew who the tall dark man with the large, black, evil bloated eyes was. Marv had warned them. If she sent them upstairs to Janice's room after the rag doll, Oscar (it was surely with Janice on the plane), she could run outside and get someone if anyone was around. Oh God, please, let someone be in sight or hearing distance!

"He's upstairs," she blundered, after a slight, uneasy pause.

Mike grabbed her immediately. "Lead the way."

The two men pushed her in front of them. Out of the kitchen, through the living room to the stairs and up the stairs, they went.

"Maybe he isn't here," she finally uttered, her voice shaking as terribly as her body.

"Then there will be hell to pay," warned Territoni.

They moved down the hall to Janice's room.

Swallow could not go on with the charade. "He's not here. He's in New York." She swung her elbow as hard as she could against Territoni's chest and began to race back down the hallway to the stairs.

"Get her," yelled Territoni.

"If I do, it'll bring somebody else here," Mike shouted back at him.

"Well, I'll get her." Territoni lunged after Swallow, grabbed her at the top of the steps and tackled her. She lost her balance and began tumbling down the stairs, yelping like a puppy until the bottom step, then lay silent. Territoni sped down the steps, kicked her, and satisfied she remained motionless; he called to Mike, who stood at the top landing watchful with narrowed, disturbed eyes, "Check each of those rooms. Don't forget the closets." Mike quickly and systematically entered each room, opened closet doors and looked under beds, coming out empty handed.

Territoni stood at the bottom of the steps waiting. Before Mike reached the landing, while he was out of sight examining the last room, the front door opened. Territoni, who had kept his eyes on Mike, did not see it open. It was Lamedeer with a gun in hand. He was very quiet. Silently he moved to the kitchen where he had an advantage of sight in case there was more than one man in the house. He heard the voice of Merry who was coming up from the cellar with Lincoln. He ran quickly to the cellar door, shut it noiselessly, turned the key to lock it and placed the key in his pocket. He moved to the doorway of the living room.

Mike had appeared on the landing.

Lamedeer saw the scene, including his wife Swallow unconscious at the foot of the stairs. His face turned savage as he glared at both Territoni and Mike.

"Get down here or I'll empty this gun on both of you." Lamedeer's voice emphasized each word forcefully, quietly.

"Are you Oscar?" Territoni had turned instantly to face him, his voice contemptuous. Before Lamedeer could answer, Mike had leveled his gun at him.

"Shoot him," screamed Territoni.

Mike aimed.

Without a moment's hesitation, Lamedeer pulled the trigger on his. Two shots rang out at once. Lamedeer fell. Mike fell.

"Mike, get up!" yelled Territoni, alarmed.

Lamedeer had shot Mike through the heart. With gasps

and a horrible cry, Mike lay dead. Lamedeer watched with satisfaction from where he lay, his left side where the bullet had struck, beginning to bleed and bend him over with great pain.

Territoni struck him hard in the head with his foot. "Get up, you fucking Indian and tell me where Oscar is."

But Lamedeer had lost consciousness.

The front door opened again. Melissa had heard the two shots and came running from the barn.

She and Territoni faced each other.

"You bitch," he yelled, as he ran to her and grabbed her arm. "Where is Oscar?"

"What have you done?" Her eyes burst with horror at the sight in front of her. "Oh my God, Lamedeer, Swallow!" She tried to pull out of Territoni's grasp. She could not.

"Let's go find Oscar. Right now," he told her grimly. "You know where he is, don't you."

She winced. "Yes," she answered in a petrified voice.

"Then let's hurry." He pushed her out the front door, grasping her arm in a vise grip. For a long moment he had a kind of irrational hypnotic control over her. She moved towards the barn as if she were moving forward in a robot body, her mind having no life of its own. Halfway to the barn, she suppressed her fear and felt the blood once more run through her veins. Her whole being was pulsing in anger and grim determination to fight this monster who had taken her neighbor's life and would take hers the moment she gave him the rag doll, Oscar.

It was only yesterday that the package had arrived via the postman in a badly wrapped box. She had carried it to the barn where she was readying Atlas for a ride. She had left her cell phone lay on a shelf in Atlas' stall and before she even took the package into the house she wanted to call her father. He had forewarned her. "Be sure to let me know if and when - and at the very moment - you get a package from New York. It may or may not have Janice's return address on it. Her rag doll, Oscar, will be in it. I want you to hide it. It contains dangerous stuff. Call me immediately. Write down my number."

Her cell phone battery was still alive, so she had called Marv at his hotel. He asked her where she was. "In the barn," she had replied. "Good," he answered. "Leave it there. Cover it up but keep it away from the horses. We don't want them sampling anything inside." So she had left it in front of Atlas' stall, a mound of straw covering it completely.

Would Atlas kick Territoni as she hoped if she brought Territoni into the stall? No, she could not count on it. And she could not escape his grip. His hold was monstrous. Her arms and back were in pain because he had wrenched her arms behind her back and held them so tightly, it was difficult to walk straight. She knew he would kill her the moment he saw what Oscar was. She could not take him into the barn.

But where?

They were almost at the door.

Suddenly, she veered away towards the south end of the barn. She knew what to do. *Oh God, Almighty, I know what to do,* she screamed inside herself in gladness. *It was a heaven-sent idea. The den!*

Looking up into the cloudless blue sky, feeling the gradual

sweet warmth of the April sun upon her, she knew the snakes would be moving out from their winter den near the end of the south pasture, close to the old line shack - just as they had been doing every spring for as long as she was alive. They would be squirming and twisting and turning their triangular shaped heads and straight-on eyes and their unique flexible, slinking skeletal bodies, scouring the weeds nearby for spaces in the vegetation or seeking warm rocks on which to sun themselves after long months of hibernation. If she could steer Territoni in that direction and then break free while she guided him to step on the emptying den - he would be bitten, she was sure of that. The snakes never hissed at her or slithered towards her in their instinctive and determined bluffs to scare her off. She respected them. She refrained from interfering with their haunts. Most ranchers and farmers welcomed a few snakes on lands infested with rabbits, gophers and other rodents. The rattlers, which only hunted prey they could swallow whole, while never denuding the area of all rodents, kept them in check. They acted as nature's rodent balance.

Territoni would hopefully fall apart in fright if he landed where she planned to have him place his feet. The snakes would then feel threatened. Some, not all, would commence to hiss horribly, their rattles sizzling; they would coil up and strike in defense. And that would be the end of Territoni, or at least the beginning of his end.

The den was a far safer bet than Atlas and his hoofs. The problem was she had to get him there. The den lay a good quarter of a mile to the south in tall weeds, close to the old-line shack (discarded primarily because of its proximity to the den).

"I forgot," she said, taking a deep breath, "Oscar told me he was going back to his shack. It is this way." She spoke calmly, not betraying her almost overpowering fear.

"He better be there. If not, it will be your end."

It will be mine anyway if I lead you to the package containing Oscar, she said to herself.

He will be," she answered, her voice holding back her desire to explode in a scream. Oh, Andrew, somebody, please come here and find us, she cried inside to herself, but help did not seem possible. Three of the ranch hands were up in the hills, and Andrew was on the other side of the valley mending a fence.

Then she remembered the law. If she deliberately took him to the den, if she deliberately placed him in harm's way, she might be prosecuted if he died, even if he was hurt badly.

They walked through the short wintertime stubble of straw and withered weeds, a few new, green shoots lifting themselves out of the ground, spurred into life by the April warming of the soil.

"Oh dear," she cried aloud, as they began moving through the tall weeds that would prove there was no pathway.

"You don't dare fool me," he said threateningly.

"No. Oscar is (and she enunciated 'is') at the line shack. Just five more minutes and we'll be there."

They walked on. Thank God, she said to herself, I have my boots on. His feet are in slick dress shoes. She began trying to whack the weeds and brush in the meadow doing so with her legs moving in and out. As they neared the den she stopped. I can't do this, she cried to herself. I can't deliberately take him into harm's way. Oh yes, I can! I know he shot Lamedeer and probably shot Swallow too. And he intends to kill me! Come on, snakes. Wake up. Bite him!

"What are you mumbling?" he yelled at her. Turning to her, he tripped over a gopher's fresh hole. He let go of her arm to steady himself.

She was free! It was her break! She couldn't help herself. She had to shout it gleefully. "Watch out, there's a rattlesnake!" She yelled the words at the top of her voice, placing all the feigned fear she could muster into those words.

That did it! Territoni freaked. He screamed. He flung out his hands and railed his arms. His face went grey. He lost his balance and his legs looked as if they were flying through the air. He fell face down in the weeds.

She had to laugh as she began to run. Laughing did not stop her from running. Fear plummeted her forward. She ran as fast as her legs could carry her — away from him — to the house.

She looked back once. She saw him attempt to get up and then fall back again, screaming at the top of his lungs. She did not know if a rattler had frightened him or bit him; she only knew she had to keep running.

Then she saw Andrew. She saw him rushing towards her as fast as he could and knew it was he because his red hair was flopping up and down in the wind. She met him breathlessly and told him where Territoni had fallen.

"But you better come with me. He is dangerous."

She ran on breathlessly, crying aloud, "Thank you, God, thank you, God," and when she turned to make sure Andrew was with her, she saw him running the other way, after Territoni. Then she heard two screams, one from Andrew and the other had to be from Territoni. She started to turn back, but heard Andrew yelling as loud as he could, "I'm okay. Hurry, get help."

So she rushed forward and into the house. Once inside she grabbed the phone from the table in the living room as she crossed the floor as fast as she could. She first kneeled in front of Lamedeer, then Swallow.

"911," she said breathlessly, gasping into the phone to the dispatcher. "Come to Alicorn's. Send two ambulances. Lamedeer has been shot. He is not dead but bleeding badly. He's unconscious. And Swallow, something has happened to her. Her leg doesn't appear to be in the place it should be. She's unconscious too. And get the Sheriff out here right away. With men. That killer, Territoni, from New York, is here and I'm afraid he has Andrew. Oh, send someone from Fish and Game. Someone who deals with rattlers. This is Melissa Alicorn. Hurry."

Chapter Thirty-Seven

It was early August. Janice was relaxing in the exquisitely comfortable armchair. A plate of crackers, a small bucket of cheese, and a glass of wine sat on the small table beside her chair. She had just returned to the apartment after posing for a wine commercial and she was weary. She was leaning back in the chair recalling the events that followed the evenful day in April when she had returned to the ranch.

When the plane had landed at the Great Falls airport that fateful day, a cordon of police cars had greeted them, isolating them from the other travelers. They were rushed in two siren blasting cars to the Great Falls hospital where both Lamedeer and Swallow were undergoing surgery and Andrew treated for a rattler bite. Lamedeer had a big hole in his belly. Thank God the bullet was partially deflected by his heavy belt or he would have died of the wound. Swallow had a broken pelvis and left leg and most of her body was black and blue. Both remained in serious condition for several days.

Swallow came home first. She was so pampered by the constant attentions she received, Merry began complaining that she would probably have to do every bit of work herself - "forever and ever!" Since that was the way she liked it (Merry enjoyed control of all household duties), no one paid much attention to her complaints. Instead, they laughed affectionately with her.

When Lamedeer returned home, he overdid the second day

after his arrival and landed back in the hospital. He took it easy the second time around and became almost as pampered as Swallow.

The Alicorns' faces were smug whenever Territoni's fate came up. Territoni was in jail awaiting trial. He had been bitten by a rattler and had suffered greatly. Andrew had been bitten also, but did not become seriously ill as Territoni. Anyway, while Andrew was in the hospital the girls from neighboring ranches visited him constantly and kept visiting the ranch to see him even after he was on his feet again. He was enjoying the attention immensely and would until he left in the fall to study at the University of Montana in Missoula. Andrew had to complete one hundred hours of county service for his assistance to Betty delivering drugs to Territoni. Part of his sentence was to accompany Peter and he did, becoming a nuisance plying Peter with every question about human trafficking he thought of.

Melissa was not charged with wrongdoing; she was feted for her bravery in handling the situation and both she and Andrew were credited with capturing Territoni.

Janice had firmly dismissed the counsel of a psychiatrist. "I'm okay now. I am with my family." Her eyes had included Bill as family in her vehement denial of help. Instead, she and Melissa shared the myriad patient and household chores with Annabelle and Merry until Marv complained he was not getting any attention. They ignored his complaints and continued their nursing and household chores tirelessly until Marv hired two nurses and two housekeepers plus one cook. (The cook lasted two days.) Merry took back her job with no complaints.

The FBI had immediately descended on Joseph and John Territoni's Spokane and New York operations. They found enough proof of the Culbertson murders, plus that of the waitress (Betty) along with several others. The FBI was still uncovering and closing down dozens of the elder Territoni's prostitute houses. Bill Smith had left for New York almost immediately, but not before he asked Marv for permission and then proposed to Janice.

He returned in July with Ms. Patsy for Melissa's wedding. That was when Janice and Ms. Patsy decided to set up a safe house in New York City to shelter girls abused by sexual violence and forced or lured into slavery. Some of the monies from Janice's now flourishing modeling career were pledged for this safe house, named "Mary's Inn." Each girl they harbored was given a mentor to help them develop both social and educational skills, which would aid them through expected very tough emotional relapses. Once those hurdles were passed (and not all of them made it, their brainwashing had left them untreatably crippled), other mentors became loving support systems for the girls.

"Mentors have to continually encourage the girls. The sufferings these girls have experienced have implanted such negativity that the girls think everything they do is wrong. We must bolster their egos before they can be secure in their new world."

In Montana, Marv set up a perpetual "Betty Scholarship" with the Great Falls Technology College.

Mary's boyfriend, it was learned, had been an "undercover goon" of a rival sex slave organization. John's dementia-ridden father had easily been taken in by the con from this goon, supposedly a highly rated accountant. He even gave her boyfriend access to his money, drugs and notebooks detailing his organization. Miranda's rag doll Oscar had been sent to Montana containing not only money and drugs but the revealing notebooks.

Tears suddenly welled in her eyes and flooded her cheeks. Mary's beautiful face grinned at her from her mental picture memory. She liked to think her friend - her dear, wild, sweet, irascible, tormented, dear, dear friend Mary - in one of her lucid moments, had sent Oscar back with the revealing notebook to rescue girls, not to hoard drugs and money.

She swallowed, brushing her hand across her wet cheeks, rising and going to the living room window to look out. The afternoon sun was beating against the panes and the brightness of its rays obscured her vision of the Hudson River. Bill and she were living on the top floor of a brand new apartment building on Riverside Drive. He now was a prosecutor with the NYPD.

She fled from the window and the Hudson River view as she heard him place his key in the door.

"Oh Bill, you are here," she cried out, happily.

"Yes, my beloved."

"I have a glass of wine ready for you. Some cheese and crackers too."

He tossed his briefcase and jacket on a chair.

She looked at him with her incomparable smile. "I have been waiting for you. I want you."

He grinned and came to her, lifting her face to his, kissing her and sending thrills up and down her whole body as his tongue sought hers and pressed it together with his. Then he picked her up and carried her into their bedroom and placed her on the bed.

"My love, you are a vixen," he told her as he began to unbutton her blouse.

"Your vixen," she answered in a breathless voice, as she pushed his sweater up over his head.

"You want to try right now for a baby?"

"Yes."

"Then kiss me, my dearest. If we don't succeed this loving, we will the next."

ADDENDUM

Although this is a work of fiction as stated on the Title Page, bear in mind that human trafficking, in all its vile forms, has never been so extensive in the history of the world as right now. In many countries children five and six years of age are sold by their parents for as little as $100 to live out their lives as slaves working in factories, as soldiers, as suicide bombers, as agricultural slaves, as sex slaves. Yes, and the kidnapping of young girls and boys and sold as sex slaves happens here in the United States.

A recent 2009 report by the United Nations Office on Drugs and Crime (UNODC) tells us that in Asia alone, over 75 million men buy sex from sex workers.

The majority of sex workers (of both sexes) are 'sex slaves,' forced to service men or women by threat, abuse, deception, false affection, clothes, drugs or abduction. The criminal organizations that head up these operations profit in the multi-billions each year off of the girls and boys and men and women they treat as commodities, not human beings.

Did you know that the Department of State (by law) must submit a report to the U.S. Congress each year explaining what foreign governments are doing to eliminate "severe forms" of human trafficking?

The Trafficking Victims Protection Act of 2000 (TVPA) ensures punishment of traffickers as well as endeavoring to prevent and protect victims. The United States also has the Protect Act of 2003 (Prosecutorial Remedies and Other Tools to end the Exploitation of Children Today), a law signed by President George W. Bush on April 30, 2003. The Amber Alert is another helpmate the United States has given law enforcement agencies. But heavy enforcement of many laws is difficult when personnel and money are not available.

Clamping down on the failure of foreign governments to enforce laws on human trafficking, President George W. Bush, on January 16, 2009, signed a Proclamation that suspends "Entry as Immigrants and Nonimmigrants of Foreign Government Officials Responsible For Failing to Combat Trafficking in Persons." Section 5 of this Proclamation gives the Secretary of State power to implement this Proclamation "as the Secretary, in consultation with the Secretary of Homeland Security, may establish."

Many Americans have read about or listened to some of the horrifying stories told by a few escaping "slaves," but as yet we, because of lack of public outcry, do not take these stories to heart. We do not believe anything like that could happen to a member of our family.

It can and does.

"The noblest motive is the public good."

Sir Richard Steele, 1744

ABOUT THE AUTHOR

Kathryn Braund grew up in San Francisco, leaving at age 18 to play summer and winter stock in the east. Her stage work included working with movie actress, Zazu Pitts, on a U.S. and Canadian tour, a year with the USO in Europe (landing in Italy on World War Two's VJ day), working in vaudeville, and as leading lady in stock and off-Broadway shows.

After ten years of stage work, she married, returned to the west coast and bore two sons. Divorced, she married the late Cyril J Braund (Buzz), a former Air Force Captain. They had forty wonderful years together. He enjoyed her writing, so Kitty began writing dog stories (she owned dogs as pets most of her life), winning over thirty Best awards from her dog world peers. For sixteen years she was Newsletter Editor for the Dog Writers Association of America, for ten years Obedience Editor for *The Spotter* (Dalmatian Club of America) and Editor for *The Courier* (Portuguese Water Dog Club of America), At present she is Editor/Publisher of the Havanese magazine, *Our Havanese.*

Shattered Innocence is Kitty's second novel. She says, "I had to give up seven of my nine wonderful dogs, Portuguese Water Dogs and Havanese, when I became ill last winter. In good health again, I have time to write since I moved to and enjoy living in an excellent retirement community. Two of my Havanese live with me, and I keep busy researching and writing. I hope God allows me to stay here a good while longer. At eighty nine, one wonders how much time one has left on this wonderful earth.